"GOLD FROM THE PULPS"

"There is no more powerful name in popular science today than Asimov's. However, it was as a science fiction reader and fan, then as a teenage science fiction writer that he first became known. He wrote during the so-called 'Golden Age' of science fiction, the late 30's and early 40's . . .

"Asimov and Greenberg have gone back to those times to bring us the finest stories of those years from the pulps—*Astounding, Unknown, Amazing, Fantastic, Startling Stories, Thrilling Wonder,* and others—written by SF's finest . . .

"These great science fiction books are produced by DAW, shorthand for Donald A. Wollheim, one of the founders of the science fiction fan movement, and, for the past four decades, one of the most distinguished editors and publishers in science fiction. DAW's anthology by Asimov is recommended without reservation."

—Richard Heller
Gannett Westchester Newspapers

Anthologies from DAW

ISAAC ASIMOV

Presents

THE GREAT SCIENCE FICTION STORIES

Volume 6, 1944

Edited by

Isaac Asimov and
Martin H. Greenberg

DAW BOOKS, INC.
DONALD A. WOLLHEIM, PUBLISHER
1633 Broadway, New York, NY 10019

Cover design by One Plus One Studios.
Cover art by Oliviero Berni.

FIRST PRINTING, DECEMBER 1981

1 2 3 4 5 6 7 8 9

 DAW TRADEMARK REGISTERED
U.S. PAT. OFF. MARCA
REGISTRADA. HECHO EN U.S.A.

PRINTED IN U.S.A.

ACKNOWLEDGMENTS

TABLE OF CONTENTS

Introduction

In the world outside reality, things continued to improve on the war fronts. On January 22 Allied forces landed on the beach at Anzio in Italy, inaugurating a long and bloody campaign, while on January 27 the gallant residents of Leningrad were finally liberated from the German siege of that war-torn city. On March 4 Soviet armies swept back into the Ukraine, and by the 19th the Russians had crossed the Dniester River in force. Meanwhile, on the Ides of March, American forces launched a heavy attack on the monastery on top of Monte Cassino, destined to become one of the most famous battlefields of the war. Monte Cassino finally fell on May 18.

By April 2 Soviet troops were in the Crimea, and on May 21 the Allies finally broke through the "Hitler Line" in Italy, the U.S. Fifth Army entering Rome on June 4. Two days later, on "The Longest Day," a giant Allied invasion force began to come ashore on the beaches of Normandy—the long-awaited invasion of Europe had begun. By June 27 the Allies had taken Cherbourg, complete with its umbrellas. But the Germans still had a few unpleasant tricks left, as Britishers found out on June 13, the day the first V-1 "buzz bomb" fell on London, to be followed by the first V-2 rocket on September 8.

On July 20 members of the German General Staff attempted to kill Hitler with a bomb but failed. The conspirators (and many others) paid for failure with their lives. Three days later Soviet troops began to cross into Poland. Back in Italy, Florence was liberated on August 19, while Brest-Litovsk fell to the relentlessly advancing Russians on July 28. On August 1st the Polish resistance rose against the German occupiers in Warsaw, only to be ruthlessly crushed long before Soviet forces reached the city. In the West, Paris was

9

liberated on August 25, and on September 4 the Allies captured Antwerp, giving them a major deep-water port for the landing of supplies. A week later the first American troops crossed into Germany in the vicinity of Trier, while the Soviets entered Yugoslavia on September 29 and Hungary on October 23.

In November, President Roosevelt was reelected, defeating Thomas Dewey by 3,500,000 votes, and Edward Stettinius replaced Cordell Hull as Secretary of State. The year ended with Allied and Soviet armies closing in on Germany, which tried one last major gambit—an offensive in the Ardennes that became known as "The Battle of the Bulge."

In the Pacific, U.S. forces took the last island in the Solomons group from the Japanese on February 15, while the British launched a major offensive in upper Burma on the 28th. Saipan fell to American troops on June 19—on July 18 General Tojo resigned as the head of the Japanese war machine. On October 19 the first U.S. troops, led by General MacArthur, landed in the Phillipines. By the end of the year American forces were advancing steadily through the Philippine Archipelago, while northern Burma had been cleared of Japanese troops.

During 1944 Ingrid Bergman won an Academy Award for her performance in *Gaslight*, while Sumner Welles published *The Time for Decision*. The United States Military Academy was the number one ranked college football team. Tennessee Williams's *The Glass Menagerie* was produced on Broadway. Clinton, Tennessee was the site of the world's second uranium pile. Pensive was the surprise winner of the Kentucky Derby. Carl Jung published his influential *Psychology and Religion*, while the hit films of the year included *Zola, Henry V* (starring the great Laurence Olivier), *The White Cliffs of Dover*, and Hitchcock's *Lifeboat*.

The United States Open Golf Championship was again called because of war. Quinine was successfully synthesized for the first time. Alberto Moravia published *Agostino*. The Green Bay Packers were National Football League Champions. Lewis Mumford's *The Condition of Man* was widely hailed, as was Somerset Maugham's *The Razor's Edge*. Sargent Frank Parker won the United States Tennis Championship, while Pauline Betz repeated as women's champ. Sutherland painted "Christ on the Cross."

T. S. Eliot published *Four Quartets* and Joe Louis was still the Heavyweight Champion of the World. Bela Bartok's Violin Concerto was performed, as was Dmitri Shostakovich's Eighth Symphony. Marty Marion of the St. Louis Cardinals and Hal Newhouser of the Detroit Tigers were Most Valuable Players in the National and American Leagues respectively. Bing Crosby won the Academy Award for his performance in *Going My Way,* which walked away with the Best Film Oscar. St. Louis went crazy as the Cardinals defeated the crosstown Browns four games to two to take the World Series. Paul Hindemith's opera *Herodias* was performed. The semi-official world record for the mile run was 4:02.6 by Arne Andersson of Sweden, but he had a 4:01.6 in 1944—the international certifying committee still could not meet because of World War II.

Death took Wendell Willkie and Lucien Pissarro.

Mel Brooks was still Melvin Kaminsky.

In the real world it was another good year, despite the preoccupations of the war and the death of *Captain Future* in the Spring.

Wondrous things were happening: Olaf Stapledon published *Sirius. Renaissance* by Raymond F. Jones and *The Riddle of the Tower* by J. D. Beresford and Esme Wynne-Tyson appeared as did *World's Beginning* by Robert Ardrey, who would later achieve fame in another field. *The Lady and the Monster,* one of several film versions of Curt Siodmak's *Donovan's Brain,* was released. And an Australian sailor named A. Bertram Chandler made his maiden voyage into reality in May with "This Means War."

And distant wings were beating as P. J. Plauger, James Sallis, Bruce Pennington, Stanley Schmidt, George Lucas, Katherine Kurtz, Vernor Vinge, Jack Chalker, David Gerrold, Peter Weston, and Vance Aandahl were born.

Let us travel back to that honored year of 1944 and enjoy the best stories that the real world bequeathed to us.

FAR CENTAURUS

Astounding,
January

by A. E. van Vogt (1912-   )

1943 was a productive year for A. E. van Vogt, a year which saw him publish a half dozen or more excellent stories as well as The Weapons Makers *(serialized in* Astounding*). 1944 was not as productive for him, but the year began with what many feel is his best story of the war years, "Far Centaurus." The theme of extended space voyages lasting for centuries had been pioneered by Robert A. Heinlein (and perhaps others before him), but van Vogt's treatment of and variation on the theme were superb.*

As Sam Moskowitz has pointed out, 1944 was also personally important for van Vogt, for that was the year that saw him move to California and acquire interests that would eventually take him away from sf for years.

(The "interests" Marty speaks of, included, among other things, "dianetics," which was still half a dozen years in the future, but which was to have some effects on science fiction that were devastating. (There will be more to say on the subject in future volumes, I'm sure.) The saddest loss we might trace to dianetics was A. E. van Vogt. Next to Robert Heinlein, he was the brightest luminary of the Golden Age, but whereas Heinlein and many others continued to shine to the present day, van Vogt took up dianetics, clung to it even after John Campbell himself abandoned it, and as a direct result, van Vogt gave up writing science fiction and went into eclipse for many years. What a shame.—I.A.)

I wakened with a start, and thought: How was Renfrew taking it?

I must have moved physically, for blackness edged with pain closed over me. How long I lay in that agonized faint, I have no means of knowing. My next awareness was of the thrusting of the engines that drove the spaceship.

Slowly this time, consciousness returned. I lay very quiet, feeling the weight of my years of sleep, determined to follow the routine prescribed so long ago by Pelham.

I didn't want to faint again.

I lay there, and I thought: It was silly to have worried about Jim Renfrew. He wasn't due to come out of his state of suspended animation for another fifty years.

I began to watch the illuminated face of the clock in the ceiling. It had registered 23:12; now it was 23:22. The ten minutes Pelham had suggested for a time lapse between passivity and initial action were up.

Slowly, I pushed my hand toward the edge of the bed. *Click!* My fingers pressed the button that was there. There was a faint hum. The automatic massager began to fumble gently over my naked form.

First, it rubbed my arms; then it moved to my legs, and so on over my body. As it progressed, I could feel the fine slick of oil that oozed from it working into my dry skin.

A dozen times I could have screamed from the pain of life returning. But in an hour I was able to sit up and turn on the lights.

The small, sparsely furnished, familiar room couldn't hold my attention for more than an instant. I stood up.

The movement must have been too abrupt. I swayed, caught on to the metal column of the bed, and retched discolored stomach juices.

The nausea passed. But it required an effort of will for me to walk to the door, open it, and head along the narrow corridor that led to the control room.

I wasn't supposed to so much as pause there, but a spasm of absolutely dreadful fascination seized me; and I couldn't help it. I leaned over the control chair, and glanced at the chronometer.

It said: 53 years, 7 months, 2 weeks, 0 days, 0 hours and 27 minutes.

Fifty-three years! A little blindly, almost blankly, I thought: Back on Earth, the people we had known, the young men we'd gone to college with, that girl who had kissed me at the party given us the night we left—they were all dead. Or dying of old age.

I remembered the girl very vividly. She was pretty, vivacious, a complete stranger. She had laughed as she offered her red lips, and she had said "A kiss for the ugly one, too."

She'd be a grandmother now, or in her grave.

Tears came to my eyes. I brushed them away, and began to heat the can of concentrated liquid that was to be my first food. Slowly, my mind calmed.

Fifty-three years and seven and one half months, I thought drably. Nearly four years over my allotted time. I'd have to do some figuring before I took another dose of Eternity drug. Twenty grains had been calculated to preserve my flesh and my life for exactly fifty years.

The stuff was evidently more potent than Pelham had been able to estimate from his short-period advance tests.

I sat tense, narrow-eyed, thinking about that. Abruptly, I grew conscious of what I was doing. Laughter spat from my lips. The sound split the silence like a series of pistol shots, startling me.

But it also relieved me. Was I sitting here actually being critical?

A miss of only four years was a bull's-eye across that span of years.

Why, I was alive and still young. Time and space had been conquered. The universe belonged to man.

I ate my "soup," sipping each spoonful deliberately. I made the bowl last every second of thirty minutes. Then, greatly refreshed, I made my way back to the control room.

This time I paused for a long look through the plates. It took only a few moments to locate Sol, a very brightly glowing star in the approximate center of the rear-view plate.

Alpha Centauri required longer to locate. But it shone finally, a glow point in a light sprinkled darkness.

I wasted no time trying to estimate their distances. They

looked right. In fifty-four years we had covered approximately one tenth of the four and one-third light-years to the famous nearest star system.

Satisfied, I threaded my way back to the living quarters. Take them in a row, I thought. Pelham first.

As I opened the air-tight door of Pelham's room, a sickening odor of decayed flesh tingled in my nostrils. With a gasp I slammed the door, stood there in the narrow hallway, shuddering.

After a minute, there was still nothing but the reality.

Pelham was dead.

I cannot clearly remember what I did then. I ran; I know that. I flung open Renfrew's door, then Blake's. The clean, sweet smell of their rooms, the sight of their silent bodies on their beds brought back a measure of my sanity.

A great sadness came to me. Poor, brave Pelham. Inventor of the Eternity drug that had made the great plunge into interstellar space possible, he lay dead now from his own invention.

What was it he had said: "The chances are greatly against any of us dying. But there is what I am calling a death factor of about ten percent, a by-product of the first dose. If our bodies survive the initial shock, they will survive additional doses."

The death factor must be greater than ten percent. That extra four years the drug had keep me asleep—

Gloomily, I went to the storeroom, and procured my personal spacesuit and a tarpaulin. But even with their help, it was a horrible business. The drug had preserved the body to some extent, but pieces kept falling off as I lifted it.

At last, I carried the tarpaulin and its contents to the air lock, and shoved it into space.

I felt pressed now for time. These waking periods were to be brief affairs, in which what we called the "current" oxygen was to be used up, but the main reserves were not to be touched. Chemicals in each room slowly refreshed the "current" air over the years, readying it for the next to awaken.

In some curious defensive fashion, we had neglected to allow for an emergency such as the death of one of our members; even as I climbed out of the spacesuit, I could feel the difference in the air I was breathing.

I went first to the radio. It had been calculated that half a light-year was the limit of radio reception, and we were approaching that limit now.

Hurriedly, though carefully, I wrote my report out, then read it into a transcription record, and started sending. I set the record to repeat a hundred times.

In a little more than five months hence, headlines would be flaring on Earth.

I clamped my written report into the ship log book, and added a note for Renfrew at the bottom. It was a brief tribute to Pelham. My praise was heartfelt, but there was another reason behind my note. They had been pals, Renfrew, the engineering genius who built the ship, and Pelham, the great chemist-doctor, whose Eternity drug had made it possible for men to take this fantastic journey into vastness.

It seemed to me that Renfrew, walking up into the great silence of the hurtling ship, would need my tribute to his friend and colleague. It was little enough for me to do, who loved them both.

The note written, I hastily examined the glowing engines, made notations of several instrument readings, and then counted out fifty-five grains of Eternity drug. That was as close as I could get to the amount I felt would be required for one hundred and fifty years.

For a long moment before sleep came, I thought of Renfrew and the terrible shock that was coming to him on top of all the natural reactions to his situations, that would strike deep into his peculiar sensitive nature—

I stirred uneasily at the picture.

The worry was still in my mind when darkness came.

Almost instantly, I opened my eyes. I lay thinking. The drug! It hadn't worked.

The draggy feel of my body warned me of the truth. I lay very still watching the clock overhead. This time it was easier to follow the routine except that, once more, I could not refrain from examining the chronometer as I passed through the galley.

It read: 201 years, 1 month, 3 weeks, 5 days, 7 hours, 8 minutes.

I sipped my bowl of that super soup, then went eagerly to the big log book.

It is utterly impossible for me to describe the thrill that

coursed through me, as I saw the familiar handwriting of Blake, and then, as I turned back the pages, of Renfrew.

My excitement drained slowly, as I read what Renfrew had written. It was a report; nothing more; gravitometric readings, a careful calculation of the distance covered, a detailed report on the performance of the engines, and finally, an estimate of our speed variations, based on the seven consistent factors.

It was a splendid mathematical job, a first-rate scientific analysis. But that was all there was. No mention of Pelham, not a word of comment on what I had written or on what had happened.

Renfrew had wakened; and, if his report was any criterion, he might as well have been a robot.

I knew better than that.

So—I saw as I began to read Blake's report—did Blake.

Bill:

TEAR THIS SHEET OUT WHEN YOU'VE READ IT!

Well, the worst has happened. We couldn't have asked fate to give us an unkindlier kick in the pants. I hate to think of Pelham being dead. What a man he was, what a friend! But we all knew the risk we were taking, he more than any of us. So all we can say is, 'Sleep well, good friend. We'll never forget you.'

But Renfrew's case is now serious. After all, we were worried, wondering how he'd take his first awakening, let alone a bang between the eyes like Pelham's death. And I think that the first anxiety was justified.

As you and I have always known, Renfrew was one of Earth's fair-haired boys. Just imagine any one human being born with his combination of looks, money and intelligence. His great fault was that he never let the future trouble him. With that dazzling personality of his, and the crew of worshipping women and yes-men around him, he didn't have much time for anything but the present.

Realities always struck him like a thunderbolt. He could leave those three ex-wives of his—and they weren't so ex, if you ask me—without grasping that it was forever.

That good-by party was enough to put anyone into a sort of mental haze when it came to realities. To wake up a hundred years later, and realize that those he loved had withered, died, and been eaten by worms—well-l-l!

(I deliberately put it as baldly as that, because the human mind thinks of awfully strange angles, no matter how it censures speech.)

I personally counted on Pelham acting as a sort of psychological support to Renfrew; and we both knew that Pelham recognized the extent of his influence over Renfrew. That influence must be replaced. Try to think of something, Bill, while you're charging around doing the routine work. We've got to live with that guy after we all wake up at the end of five hundred years.

Tear out this sheet. What follows is routine.

Ned

I burned the letter in the incinerator, examined the two sleeping bodies—how deadly quiet they lay!—and then returned to the control room.

In the plate, the sun was a very bright star, a jewel set in black velvet, a gorgeous, shining brilliant.

Alpha Centauri was brighter. It was a radiant light in that panoply of black and glitter. It was still impossible to make out the separate suns of Alpha A, B, C, and Proxima, but their combined light brought a sense of awe and majesty.

Excitement blazed inside me; and consciousness came of the glory of this trip we were making, the first men to head for far Centaurus, the first men to dare aspire to the stars.

Even the thought of Earth failed to dim that surging tide of wonder; the thought that seven, possibly eight generations, had been born since our departure; the thought that the girl who had given me the sweet remembrance of her red lips, was now known to her descendants as their great-great-great-great grandmother—if she was remembered at all.

The immense time involved, the whole idea, was too meaningless for emotion.

I did my work, took my third dose of the drug, and went to bed. The sleep found me still without a plan about Renfrew.

When I woke up, alarm bells were ringing.

I lay still. There was nothing else to do. If I had moved, consciousness would have slid from me. Though it was mental torture even to think it, I realized that, no matter what the danger, the quickest way was to follow my routine to the second and in every detail.

Somehow I did it. The bells changed and *brrred*, but I lay there until it was time to get up. The clamor was hideous, as I passed through the control room. But I *passed* through and sat for half an hour sipping my soup.

The conviction came to me that if that sound continued much longer, Blake and Renfew would surely waken from their sleep.

At last, I felt free to cope with the emergency. Breathing hard, I eased myself into the control chair, cut off the mind-wrecking alarms, and switched on the plates.

A fire glowed at me from the rear-view plate. It was a colossal *white* fire, longer than it was wide, and filling nearly a quarter of the whole sky. The hideous thought came to me that we must be within a few million miles of some monstrous sun that had recently roared into this part of space.

Frantically, I manipulated the distance estimators—and then for a moment stared in blank disbelief at the answers that clicked metallically onto the product plate.

Seven miles! *Only* seven miles! Curious is the human mind. A moment before, when I had thought of it as an abnormally shaped sun, it hadn't resembled anything but an incandescent mass. Abruptly, now, I saw that it had a solid outline, an umistakable material shape.

Stunned, I leaped to my feet because—

It was a spaceship! An enormous, mile-long ship. Rather—I sank back into my seat, subdued by the catastrophe I was witnessing, and consciously adjusting my mind— the flaming hell of what had been a spaceship. Nothing that had been alive could possibly still be conscious in that horror of ravenous fire. The only possibility was that the crew had succeeded in launching lifeboats.

Like a madman, I searched the heavens for a light, a glint of metal that would show the presence of survivors.

There was nothing but the night and the stars and the hell of burning ship.

After a long time, I noticed that it was farther away, and

seemed to be receding. Whatever drive forces had matched its velocity to ours must be yielding to the fury of the energies that were consuming the ship.

I began to take pictures, and I felt justified in turning on the oxygen reserves. As it withdrew into distance, the miniature nova that had been a torpedo-shaped space liner began to change color, to lose its white intensity. It became a red fire silhouetted against darkness. My last glimpse showed it as a long, dull glow that looked like nothing else than a cherry colored nebula seen edge on, like a blaze reflecting from the night beyond a far horizon.

I had already, in between observations, done everything else required of me; and now I re-connected the alarm system and, very reluctantly, my mind seething with speculation, returned to bed.

As I lay waiting for my final dosage of the trip to take effect, I thought: the great star system of Alpha Centauri must have inhabited planets. If my calculations were correct, we were only one point six light-years from the main Alpha group of suns, slightly nearer than that to red Proxima.

Here was proof that the universe had at least one other supremely intelligent race. Wonders beyond our wildest expectations were in store for us. Thrill on thrill of anticipation raced through me.

It was only at the last instant, as sleep was already grasping at my brain that the realizations struck that I had completely forgotten about the problem of Renfrew.

I felt no alarm. Surely, even Renfrew would come alive in that great fashion of his when confronted by a complex alien civilization.

Our troubles were over.

Excitement must have bridged that final one hundred fifty years of time. Because, when I wakened, I thought:

"We're here! It's over, the long night, the incredible journey. We'll all be waking, seeing each other, as well as the civilization out there. Seeing, too, the great Centauri suns."

The strange thing, it struck me as I lay there exulting, was that the time seemed long. And yet . . . yet I had been awake only three times, and only once for the equivalent of a full day.

In the truest sense of meaning, I had seen Blake and Renfrew—and Pelham—not more than a day and a half ago. I had had only thirty-six hours of consciousness since a pair of soft lips had set themselves against mine, and clung in the sweetest kiss of my life.

Then why this feeling that millenniums had ticked by, second on slow second? Why this eerie, empty awareness of a journey through fathomless, unending night?

Was the human mind so easily fooled?

It seemed to me, finally, that the answer was that *I* had been alive for those five hundred years, all my cells and my organs had existed, and it was not even impossible that some part of my brain had been horrendously aware throughout the entire unthinkable period.

And there was, of course, the additional psychological fact that I knew now that five hundred years had gone by, and that—

I saw with a mental start, that my ten minutes were up. Cautiously, I turned on the massager.

The gentle, padded hands had been working on me for about fifteen minutes when my door opened; the light clicked on, and there stood Blake.

The too-sharp movement of turning my head to look at him made me dizzy. I closed my eyes, and heard him walk across the room toward me.

After a minute, I was able to look at him again without seeing blurs. I saw then that he was carrying a bowl of the soup. He stood staring down at me with a strangely grim expression on his face.

At last, his long, thin countenance relaxed into a wan grin.

" 'Lo, Bill," he said. *"Ssshh!"* he hissed immediately. "Now, don't try to speak. I'm going to start feeding you this soup while you're still lying down. The sooner you're up, the better I'll like it."

He was grim again, as he finished almost as if it were an afterthought: "I've been up for two weeks."

He sat down on the edge of the bed, and ladled out a spoonful of soup. There was silence, then, except for the rustling sound of the massager. Slowly, the strength flowed through my body; and with each passing second, I became more aware of the grimness of Blake.

"What about Renfrew?" I managed finally, hoarsely. "He awake?"

Blake hesitated, then nodded. His expression darkened with frown; he said simply:

"He's mad, Bill, stark, staring mad. I had to tie him up. I've got him now in his room. He's quieter now, but at the beginning he was a gibbering maniac."

"Are you crazy?" I whispered at last. "Renfrew was never so sensitive as that. Depressed and sick, yes; but the mere passage of time, abrupt awareness that all his friends are dead, couldn't make him insane."

Blake was shaking his head. "It isn't only that. Bill—"

He paused, then: "Bill, I want you to prepare your mind for the greatest shock it's ever had."

I stared up at him with an empty feeling inside me. "What do you mean?"

He went on grimacing: "I know you'll be able to take it. So don't get scared. You and I, Bill, are just a couple of lugs. We're along because we went to U with Renfrew and Pelham. Basically, it wouldn't matter to insensitives like us whether we landed in 1,000,000 B.C. or A. D. We'd just look around and say: 'Fancy seeing you here, mug.' or 'Who was that pterodactyl I saw you with last night? That wasn't no pterodoctyl; that was Unthahorsten's bulbous brained wife.' "

I whispered, "Get to the point, Bill. What's up?"

Blake rose to his feet. "Bill, after I'd read your reports about, and seen the photographs of, that burning ship, I got an idea. The Alpha suns were pretty close two weeks ago, only about six months away at our average speed of five hundred miles a second. I thought to myself: 'I'll see if I can tune in some of their radio stations.'

"Well," he smiled wryly, "I got hundreds in a few minutes. They came in all over the seven dial waves, with bell-like clarity."

He paused; he stared down at me, and his smile was a sickly thing. "Bill," he groaned, "we're the prize fools in creation. When I told Renfrew the truth, he folded up like ice melting into water."

Once more, he paused; the silence was too much for my straining nerves.

"For heavens sake, man—" I began. And stopped. And lay there, very still. Just like that the lightning of understanding flashed on me. My blood seemed to thunder through my veins. At last, weakly, I said: "You mean—"

Blake nodded. "Yeah," he said. "That's the way it is. And they've already spotted us with their spy rays and energy screens. A ship's coming out to meet us."

"I only hope," he finished gloomily, "they can do something for Jim."

I was sitting in the control chair an hour later when I saw the glint in the darkness. There was a flash of bright silver, that exploded into size. The next instant an enormous spaceship had matched our velocity less than a mile away.

Blake and I looked at each other. "Did they say," I said shakily, "that that ship left its hangar ten minutes ago?"

Blake nodded. "They can make the trip from Earth to Centauri in three hours," he said.

I hadn't heard that before. Something happened inside my brain. "What!" I shouted. "Why, it's taken us five hund—"

I stopped; I sat there. "Three hours!" I whispered. "How *could* we have forgotten human progress?"

In the silence that fell then, we watched a dark hole open in the clifflike wall that faced us. Into this cavern, I directed our ship.

The rear-view plate showed that the cave entrance was closing. Ahead of us lights flashed on, and focused on a door. As I eased our craft to the metal floor, a face flickered onto our radio plate.

"Cassellahat!" Blake whispered in my ear. "The only chap who's talked direct to me so far."

It was a distinguished, a scholarly looking head and face that peered at us. Cassellahat smiled, and said:

"You may leave your ship, and go through the door you see."

I had a sense of empty spaces around us, as we climbed gingerly out into the vast receptor chamber. Interplanetary spaceship hangars were like that, I reminded myself. Only this one had an alien quality that—

"Nerves!" I thought sharply.

But I could see that Blake felt it, too. A silent duo, we filed through the doorway into a hallway, that opened into a very large, luxurious room.

It was such a room as a king or a movie actress on set might have walked into without blinking. It was all hung with gorgeous tapestries—that is, for a moment, I thought they were tapestries; then I saw they weren't. They were—I couldn't decide.

I had seen expensive furniture in some of the apartments Renfrew maintained. But these settees, chairs, and tables glittered at us, as if they were made of a matching design of differently colored fires. No, that was wrong; they didn't glitter at all. They—

Once more I couldn't decide.

I had no time for more detailed examination. For a man arrayed very much as we were, was rising from one of the chairs. I recognized Cassellahat.

He came forward, smiling. Then he slowed, his nose wrinkling. A moment later, he hastily shook our hands, then swiftly retreated to a chair ten feet away, and sat down rather primly.

It was an astoundingly ungracious performance. But I was glad that he had drawn back that way. Because, as he shook my hand so briefly, I had caught a faint whiff of perfume from him. It was a vaguely unpleasant odor; and, besides—a man using perfume in quantities!

I shuddered. What kind of foppish nonsense had the human race gone in for?

He was motioning us to sit down. I did so, wondering: Was this our reception? The erstwhile radio operator began:

"About your friend, I must caution you. He is a schizoid type, and our psychologists will be able to effect a temporary recovery only for the moment. A permanent cure will require a longer period, and your fullest cooperation. Fall in readily with all Mr. Renfrew's plans, unless, of course, he takes a dangerous turn.

"But now"—he squirted us a smile—"permit me to welcome you to the four planets of Centauri. It is a great moment for me, personally. From early childhood, I have been trained for the sole purpose of being your mentor and guide; and naturally I am overjoyed that the time has come when my exhaustive studies of the middle-period American language and customs can be put to the practical use for which they were intended."

He didn't look overjoyed. He was wrinkling his nose in that funny way I had already noticed, and there was a generally pained expression on his face. But it was his words that shocked me.

"What do you mean," I asked, "studies in American? Don't people speak the universal language any more?"

"Of course"—he smiled—"but the language has developed to a point where—I might as well be frank—you would have difficulty understanding such a simple word as 'yeih.' "

"Yeih?" Blake echoed.

"Meaning 'yes.' "

"Oh!"

We sat silent. Blake chewing his lower lip. It was Blake who finally said:

"What kind of places are the Centauri planets? You said something on the radio about the population centers having reverted to the city structure again."

"I shall be happy," said Cassellahat, "to show you as many of our great cities as you care to see. You are our guests, and several million credits have been placed to your separate accounts for you to use as you see fit."

"Gee!" said Blake.

"I must, however," Cassellahat went on, "give you a warning. It is important that you do not disillusion our peoples about yourselves. Therefore, you must never wander around the streets, or mingle with the crowds in anyway. Always, your contact should be via newsreels, radio, or from the *inside* of a closed machine. If you have any plan to marry, you must now finally give up the idea."

"I don't get it!" Blake said wonderingly; and he spoke for us both.

Cassellahat finished firmly: "It is important that no one becomes aware that you have an offensive physical odor. It might damage your financial prospects considerably.

"And now"—he stood up—"for the time being, I shall leave you. I hope you don't mind if I wear a mask in the future in your presence. I wish you well, gentlemen, and—"

He pushed, glanced past us, said: "Ah, here is your friend."

I whirled, and I could see Blake twisting, staring—

"Hi, there, fellows," Renfrew said cheerfully from the door, then wryly: "Have we ever been a bunch of suckers?"

I felt choked. I raced up to him, caught his hand, hugged him. Blake was trying to do the same.

When we finally released Renfrew, and looked around, Cassellahat was gone.

Which was just as well. I had been wanting to punch him in the nose for his final remarks.

"Well, here goes!" Renfrew said.

He looked at Blake and me, grinned, rubbed his hands together gleefully, and added:

"For a week I've been watching, thinking up questions to ask this cluck and—"

He faced Cassellahat. "What," he began, "makes the speed of light constant?"

Cassellahat did not even blink. "Velocity equals the cube of the cube root of *gd*," he said, "*d* being the depth of the space time continuum, *g* the total tolerance or gravity, as you would say, of all the matter in that continuum."

"How are planets formed?"

"A sun must balance itself in the space that it is in. It throws out matter as a sea vessel does anchors. That's a very rough description. I could give it to you in mathematical formula, but I'd have to write it down. After all, I'm not a scientist. These are merely facts that I've known from childhood, or so it seems."

"Just a minute," said Renfrew, puzzled. "A sun throws this matter out without any pressure other than its—desire—to balance itself?"

Cassellahat stared at him. "Of course not. The reason, the pressure involved, is very potent, I assure you. Without such a balance, the sun would fall out of this space. Only a few bachelor suns have learned how to maintain stability without planets."

"A few what?" echoed Renfrew.

I could see that he had been jarred into forgetting the questions he had been intending to ask one by swift one. Cassellahat's words cut across my thought; he said:

"A bachelor sun is a very old, cooled class M star. The hottest one known has a temperature of one hundred ninety degrees F., the coldest forty-eight. Literally, a bachelor is a rogue, crotchety with age. Its main feature is that it permits no matter, no planets, not even gases in its vicinity."

Renfrew sat silent, frowning, thoughtful. I seized the opportunity to carry on a train of ideas.

"This business," I said, "of knowing all this stuff without being a scientist, interests me. For instance, back home every kid understood the atomic-rocket principle practically from the day he was born. Boys of eight and ten rode around in specially made toys, took them apart and put them together again. They *thought* rocket-atomic, and any new development in the field was just pie for them to absorb.

"Now, here's what I'd like to know: what is the parallel here to that particular angle?"

"The adeledicnander force," said Cassellahat. "I've already tried to explain it to Mr. Renfrew, but his mind seems to balk at some of the most simple aspects."

Renfrew roused himself, grimaced. "He's been trying to tell me that electrons think; and I won't swallow it."

Cassellahat shook his head. "Not think; they don't think. But they have a psychology!"

"Electronic psychology!" I said.

"Simply adeledicnander," Cassellahat replied. "Any child—"

Renfrew groaned: "I know. Any child of six could tell me."

He turned to us. "That's why I lined up a lot of questions. I figured that if we got a good intermediate grounding, we might be able to slip into this adeledicnander stuff the way their kids do."

He faced Cassellahat. "Next question," he said. "What—"

Cassellahat had been looking at his watch. "I'm afraid, Mr. Renfrew," he interrupted, "that if you and I are going to be on the ferry to the Pelham planet, we'd better leave now. You can ask your questions on the way."

"What's all this?" I chimed in.

Renfew explained: "He's taking me to the great engineering laboratories in the European mountains of Pelham. Want to come along?"

"Not me," I said.

Blake shrugged. "I don't fancy getting into one of those suits Cassellahat has provided for us, designed to keep our odor in, but not theirs out."

He finished: "Bill and I will stay here and play poker for some of that five million credits worth of dough we've got in the State bank."

Cassellahat turned at the door; there was a distinct frown

on the flesh mask he wore. "You treat our government gift very lightly."

"Yeih!" said Blake.

"So we stink," said Blake.

It was nine days since Cassellahat had taken Renfrew to the planet Pelham; and our only contact had been a radio telephone call from Renfrew on the third day, telling us not to worry.

Blake was standing at the window of our penthouse apartment in the city of Newmerica; and I was on my back on a couch, in my mind a mixture of thoughts involving Renfrew's potential insanity and all the things I had heard and seen about the history of the past five hundred years.

I roused myself. "Quit it," I said. "We're faced with a change in the metabolism of the human body, probably due to the many different foods from remote stars that they eat. They must be able to smell better, too, because just being near us is agony to Cassellahat, whereas we only notice an unpleasantness from him. It's a case of three of us against billions of them. Frankly, I don't see an early victory over the problem, so let's just take it quietly."

There was no answer; so I returned to my reverie. My first radio message to Earth had been picked up; and so, when the interstellar drive was invented in 2320 A. D., less than one hundred forty years after our departure, it was realized what would eventually happen.

In our honor, the four habitable planets of the Alpha A and B suns were called Renfrew, Pelham, Blake, and Endicott. Since 2320, the populations of the four planets had become so dense that a total of nineteen billion people now dwelt on their narrowing land spaces. This in spite of migrations to the planets of more distant stars.

The space liner I had seen burning in 2511 A. D. was the only ship ever lost on the Earth-Centauri lane. Traveling at full speed, its screens must have reacted against our spaceship. All the automatics would instantly have flashed on; and, as those defenses were not able at that time to stop a ship that had gone Minus Infinity, every recoil engine aboard had probably blown up.

Such a thing could not happen again. So enormous had been the progress in the adeledicnander field of power, that the greatest liners could stop dead in the full fury of midflight.

We had been told not to feel any sense of blame for that one disaster, as many of the most important advances in adeledicnander electronic psychology had been made as the result of theoretical analyses of that great catastrophe.

I grew aware that Blake had flung himself disgustedly into a nearby chair.

"Boy, oh, boy," he said, "this is going to be some life for us. We can all anticipate about fifty more years of being pariahs in a civilization where we can't even understand how the simplest machines work."

I stirred uneasily. I had had similar thoughts. But I said nothing. Blake went on:

"I must admit, after I first discovered the Centauri planets had been colonized, I had pictures of myself bowling over some dame, and marrying her."

Involuntarily my mind leaped to the memory of a pair of lips lifting up to mine. I shook myself. I said:

"I wonder how Renfrew is taking all this. He—"

A familiar voice from the door cut off my words. "Renfrew," it said, "is taking things beautifully now that the first shock has yielded to resignation, and resignation to purpose."

We had turned to face him by the time he finished. Renfrew walked slowly toward us, grinning. Watching him, I felt uncertain as to just how to take his built-up sanity.

He was at his best. His dark, wavy hair was perfectly combed. His startlingly blue eyes made his whole face come alive. He was a natural physical wonder; and at his normal weight he had all the shine and swagger of an actor in a carefully tailored picture.

He wore that shine and swagger now. He said:

"I've bought a spaceship, fellows. Took all my money and part of yours, too. But I knew you'd back me up. Am I right?"

"Why, sure," Blake and I echoed.

Blake went on alone: "What's the idea."

"I get it," I chimed in. "We'll cruise all over the universe, live our life span exploring new worlds. Jim, you've got something there. Blake and I were just going to enter a suicide pact."

Renfrew was smiling, "We'll cruise for a while anyway."

Two days later, Cassellahat having offered no objection and no advice about Renfrew, we were in space.

It was a curious three months that followed. For a while I felt a sense of awe at the vastness of the cosmos. Silent planets swung into our viewing plates, and faded into remoteness behind us, leaving nostalgic memory of uninhabited, windlashed forests and plains, deserted, swollen seas and nameless suns.

The sight and the remembrance brought loneliness like an ache, and the knowledge, the slow knowledge, that this journeying was not lifting the weight of strangeness that had settled upon us ever since our arrival at Alpha Centauri.

There was nothing here for our souls to feed on, nothing that would satisfactorily fill one year of our life, let alone fifty.

I watched the realization grow on Blake, and I waited for a sign from Renfrew that he felt it, too. The sign didn't come. That of itself worried me; then I grew aware of something else. Renfrew was watching us. Watching us with a hint in his manner of secret knowledge, a suggestion of secret purpose.

My alarm grew; and Renfrew's perpetual cheerfulness didn't help any. I was lying on my bunk at the end of the third month, thinking uneasily about the whole unsatisfactory situation, when my door opened and Renfrew came in.

He carried a paralyzer gun and a rope. He pointed the gun at me and said:

"Sorry, Bill. Cassellahat told me to take no chances, so just lie quiet while I tie you up."

"Blake!" I bellowed.

Renfrew shook his head gently. "No use," he said. "I was in his room first."

The gun was steady in his fingers, his blue eyes were steely. All I could do was tense my muscles against the ropes as he tied me, and trust to the fact that I was twice as strong, at least, as he was.

I thought in dismay: Surely I could prevent him from tying me too tightly.

He stepped back finally, said again, "Sorry, Bill." He added: "I hate to tell you this, but both of you went off the deep end mentally when we arrived at Centauri; and this is the cure prescribed by the psychologists whom Cassellahat consulted. You're supposed to get a shock as big as the one that knocked you for a loop."

The first time I'd paid no attention to his mention of Cassellahat's name. Now my mind flared with understanding.

Incredibly, Renfrew had been told that Blake and I were mad. All these months he had been held steady by a sense of responsibility toward us. It was a beautiful psychological scheme. The only thing was: *what* shock was going to be administered?

Renfrew's voice cut off my thought. He said:

"It won't be long now. We're already entering the field of the bachelor sun."

"Bachelor sun!" I yelled.

He made no reply. The instant the door closed behind him, I began to work on my bonds; all the time I was thinking:

What was it Cassellahat had said? Bachelor suns maintained themselves in this space by a precarious balancing.

In *this* space! The sweat poured down my face, as I pictured ourselves being precipitated into another plane of the space-time continuum—I could feel the ship falling when I finally worked my hands free of the rope.

I hadn't been tied long enough for the cords to interfere with my circulation. I headed for Blake's room. In two minutes we were on our way to the control cabin.

Renfrew didn't see us till we had him. Blake grabbed his gun; I hauled him out of the control chair with one mighty heave and dumped him onto the floor.

He lay there, unresisting, grinning up at us. "Too late," he taunted. "We're approaching the first point of intolerance, and there's nothing you can do except prepare for the shock."

I scarcely heard him. I plumped myself into the chair, and glared into the viewing plates. Nothing showed. That stumped me for a second. Then I saw the recorder instruments. They were trembling furiously, registering a body of INFINITE size.

For a long moment I stared crazily at those incredible figures. Then I plunged the decelerator far over. Before that pressure of full-driven adeledicnander, the machine grew rigid; I had a sudden fantastic picture of two irresistible forces in full collision. Gasping, I jerked the power out of gear.

We were still falling.

"An orbit," Blake was saying. "Get us into an orbit."

With shaking fingers, I pounded one out on the keyboard basing my figures on a sun of Sol-ish size, gravity, and mass.

The bachelor wouldn't let us have it.

I tried another orbit, and a third, and more—finally one that would have given us an orbit around mighty Antares itself. But the deadly reality remained. The ship plunged on, down and down.

And there was nothing visible on the plates, not a real shadow of substance. It seemed to me once that I could make out a vague blur of greater darkness against the black reaches of space. But the stars were few in every direction and it was impossible to be sure.

Finally, in despair, I whirled out of the seat, and knelt beside Renfrew, who was still making no effort to get up.

"Listen, Jim," I pleaded, "what did you do this for? What's going to happen?"

He was smiling easily. "Think," he said, "of an old, crusty, human bachelor. He maintains a relationship with his fellows, but the association is as remote as that which exists between a bachelor sun and the stars in the galaxy of which it is a part."

He added: "Any second now we'll strike the first period of intolerance. It works in jumps like quantum, each period being four hundred ninety-eight years, seven months and eight days plus a few hours."

It sounded like gibberish. "But what's going to happen?" I urged. "For Heaven's sake, man!"

He gazed up at me blandly; and, looking up at him, I had the sudden, wondering realization that he was sane, the old completely rational Jim Renfrew, made better somehow, stronger. He said quietly:

"Why, it'll just knock us out of its toleration area; and in doing so will put us back—"

JERK!

The lurch was immensely violent. With a bang, I struck the floor, skidded, and then a hand—Renfrew's—caught me. And it was all over.

I stood up, conscious that we were no longer falling. I looked at the instrument board. All the lights were dim, untroubled, the needles firmly at zero. I turned and stared at Renfrew, and at Blake, who was ruefully picking himself from the floor.

Renfrew said persuasively: "Let me at the control board, Bill. I want to set our course for Earth."

For a long minute, I gazed at him; and then, slowly, I stepped aside. I stood by as he set the controls and pulled the accelerator over. Renfrew looked up.

"We'll reach Earth in about eight hours," he said, "and it'll be about a year and a half after we left five hundred years ago."

Something began to tug at the roof of my cranium. It took several seconds before I decided that it was probably my brain jumping with the tremendous understanding that suddenly flowed in upon me.

The bachelor sun, I thought dazedly. In easing us out of its field of toleration, it had simply precipitated us into a period of time beyond its field. Renfrew had said . . . had said it worked in jumps of . . . four hundred ninety-eight years and some seven months and—

But what about the ship? Wouldn't twenty-seventh century adeledicnander brought to the twenty-second century, before it was invented, change the course of history? I mumbled the question.

Renfrew shook his head. "Do *we* understand it? Do we even dare monkey with the raw power inside those engines? I'll say not. As for the ship, we'll keep it for our own private use."

"B-but—" I began.

He cut me off. "Look, Bill," he said, "here's the situation: that girl who kissed you—don't think I didn't see you falling like a ton of bricks—is going to be sitting beside you fifty years from now, when *your* voice from space reports to Earth that you had wakened on your first lap of the first trip to Centaurus."

That's exactly what happened.

DEADLINE

Astounding,

March

by Cleve Cartmill (1908-1964)

"Deadline" proved to be the most controversial story of the year, although not within the science fiction community. The author's speculations on some of the fine points of nuclear fission attracted the attention of the U.S. Government, who wanted to know who had been leaking secrets from the Manhattan Project, then in the process of developing the first nuclear weapon. There has been some controversy about exactly what happened, but U.S. intelligence personnel did visit the offices of John W. Campbell, Jr., editor of Astounding *(and also visited the author, who lived in Manhattan Beach). Various sources say it was the FBI, others military intelligence—once convinced that all concerned were clean and working from public knowledge, they apparently requested that no more similar stories be published—to which Campbell (depending on the version repeated) either told them to buzz off, or convinced them that to stop publishing stories about atomic energy would tip off the enemy concerning the direction of American research and development.*

The story is obviously Cartmill's most famous, although his "Space Salvage" stories in Thrilling Wonder *were popular.*

(For years, I included the tale of Cartmill's story and the visit of intelligence agents to Campbell's office in my talks. The tale was always successful, especially at colleges. I would describe how Campbell pulled out news items on the discovery of uranium fission (freely discussed, until scientists

imposed self-censorship for obvious reasons) and explained that a nuclear bomb was an inevitable inference. The agents, thinking deeply, finally saw that, but ordered him to stop publishing such stories and Campbell explained that that would be a dead giveaway (at least that's how I heard it). At this, I went on to say, "the intelligence agents underwent an ordeal of enormous magnitude for Campbell was asking them to think a second time on the same day" and that invariably brought the house down.—I.A.)

DETONATION AND ASSEMBLY

12.16. As stated in Chapter II, it is impossible to prevent a chain reaction from occurring when the size exceeds the critical size. For there are always enough neutrons (from cosmic rays, from spontaneous fission reactions, or from alpha-particle-induced reactions in impurities) to initiate the chain. Thus until detonation is desired, the bomb must consist of a number of separate pieces, each one of which is below the critical size either by reason of small size or unfavorable shape. To produce detonation, the parts of the bomb must be brought together rapidly. In the course of this assembly process the chain reaction is likely to start—because of the presence of stray neutrons—before the bomb has reached its most compact (most reactive) form. Thereupon the explosion tends to prevent the bomb from reaching that most compact form. Thus it may turn out that the explosion is so inefficient as to be relatively useless. The problem, therefore, is twofold: (1) to reduce the time of assembly to a minimum; and (2) to reduce the number of stray (predetonation) neutrons to a minimum.

Official Report: *Atomic Energy for Military Purposes*

Henry D. Smyth

Heavy flak burst above and below the flight of bombers as they flashed across the night sky of the planet Cathor. Ybor

Sebrof grinned as he nosed his glider at a steep angle away from the fireworks. The bombers had accomplished their mission: they had dropped him near Nilreq, had simulated a raid.

He had cut loose before searchlights slatted the sky with lean, white arms. They hadn't touched the glider, marked with their own insignia. Their own glider, in fact, captured when Seilla advanced columns had caught the Namo garrison asleep. He would leave it where he landed, and let Sixa intelligence try to figure out how it got there.

Provided, of course, that he landed unseen.

Sixa intelligence officers would have another job, too. That was to explain the apparent bombing raid that dropped no bombs. None of the Seilla planes had been hit, and the Sixa crowd couldn't know that the bombers were empty: no bombs, no crews, just speed.

He could see tomorrow's papers, hear tomorrow's newscasts. "Raiders driven off. Craven Democracy pilots cringe from Nilreq ack-ack." But the big bugs would worry. The Seilla planes *could* have dropped bombs, if they'd had any bombs. They had flitted across the great industrial city with impunity. They could have laid their eggs. The big bugs would wonder about that. Why? they would ask each other profoundly. What was the reason?

Ybor grinned. He was the reason. He'd make them wish there *had* been bombs instead of him. Possibility of failure never entered his mind. All he had to do was to penetrate into the stronghold of the enemy, find Dr. Sitruc, kill him, and destroy the most devastating weapon of history. That was all.

He caught a sharp breath as a farmhouse loomed some distance ahead, and veered over against the dark edge of a wood. The green-gray plane would be invisible against the background, unless keen eyes caught its shadow under a fugitive moon.

He glided silently now, on a little wind that gossiped with tree-tops. Only the wind and the trees remarked on his passing. They could keep the secret.

He landed in a field of grain that whispered fierce protest as the glider whished through its heavy-laden plumes. These waved above the level of the motorless ship, and Ybor decided that it would not be seen before harvesting machines gathered the grain.

The air was another problem. He did not want the glider discovered just yet, particularly if he should be intercepted on his journey into the enemy capital. Elementary intelligence would connect him with this abandoned ship if he were stopped in this vicinity for any reason, and if the ship should be discovered on the morrow.

He took a long knife from its built-in sheath in the glider and laid about him with it until he had cut several armloads of grain. He scattered these haphazardly—not in any pattern—over parts of the ship. It wouldn't look like a glider now, even from the air.

He pushed through the shoulder-high growth to the edge of the wood.

He moved stealthily here. It was almost a certainty that big guns were hidden here, and he must avoid discovery. He slipped along the soft carpet of vegetation like a nocturnal cat, running on all fours under low branches, erect when possible.

A sharp scent of danger assailed his nostrils, and he crouched motionless while he sifted this odor. It made a picture in his head: men, and oil, and the acrid smoke of exploded gases. A gun crew was directly ahead.

Ybor took to the trees. He moved from one to the other, with no more sound than soft-winged night birds, and approached the source of the odor. He paused now and then, listening for a sentry's footsteps. He heard them presently, a soft *pad-pad* which mingled, in different rhythm, with snores which became audible on the light wind.

The better part of valor, Ybor knew, was to circle this place, to leave the sentry unaware of his passage through the wood. But habit was too strong. He must destroy, for they were the enemy.

He moved closer to the sound of footsteps. Presently, he crouched above the line of the sentry's march, searching the darkness with eye and ear. The guard passed below, and Ybor let him go. His ears strained through snores from nearby tents until he heard another guard. Two were on sentry duty.

He pulled the knife from his belt and waited. When the

sentry shuffled below him, Ybor dropped soundlessly onto the man's shoulders, stabbing as he fell.

There was a little noise. Not much, but a little. Enough to bring a low-voiced hail from the other guard.

"Namreh?" called the guard. "What happened?"

Ybor grunted, took the dead man's gun and helmet and took over his beat. He marched with the same rhythm the enemy feet had maintained until he met the second guard. Ybor silenced questions with a swift slash of the knife, and then turned his attention to the tents.

Presently, it was done. He clamped the fingers of the first guard around the knife hilt and went away. Let them think that one of their men had gone mad and killed the others before suiciding. Let the psychologists get a little workout on this.

When he had penetrated to the far edge of the wood, dawn had splashed pale color beyond Nilreq, pulling jumbled buildings into dark silhouette. There lay his area of operations. There, perhaps, lay his destiny, and the destiny of the whole race.

This latter thought was not born of rhetorical hyperbole. It was cold, hard fact. It had nothing to do with patriotism, nor was it concerned with politico-economic philosophy. It was concerned with a specific fact only: if the weapon, which was somewhere in the enemy capital, were used, the entire race might very well perish down to the last man.

Now began the difficult part of Ybor's task. He started to step out of the wood. A slight sound from behind froze him for the fraction of a second while he identified it. Then, in one incredibly swift motion, he whirled and flung himself at its source.

He knew he was fighting a woman after the first instant of contact. He was startled to some small extent, but not enough to impair his efficiency. A chopping blow, and she lay unconscious at his feet. He stood over her with narrowed eyes, unable to see what she looked like in the leafy gloom.

Then dawn burst like a salvo in the east, and he saw that she was young. Not immature, by any means, but young. When a spear of sunlight stabbed into the shadow, he saw that she was lovely.

Ybor pulled out his combat knife. She was an enemy, and

must be destroyed. He raised his arm for the *coup de grace*, and held it there. He could not drive the blade into her. She seemed only to sleep, in her unconsciousness, with parted ripe lips and limp hands. You could kill a man while he slept, but Nature had planted a deep aversion in your instincts to killing a helpless female.

She began to moan softly. Presently she opened her wide brown eyes, soft as a captive fawn's.

"You hit me." She whispered the accusation.

Ybor said nothing.

"You hit me," she repeated.

"What did you expect?" he asked harshly. "Candy and flowers? What are you doing here?"

"Following you," she answered. "May I get up?"

"Yes. Why were you following?"

"When I saw you land in our field, I wondered why. I ran out to see you cover your ship and slip into the woods. I followed."

Ybor was incredulous. "You followed me through those woods?"

"I could have touched you," she said. "Any time."

"You lie!"

"Don't feel chagrined," she said. She flowed to her feet in a liquid movement. Her eyes were almost on a level with his. Her smile showed small, white teeth. "I'm very good at that sort of thing," she said. "Better than almost anybody, though I admit you're no slouch."

"Thanks," he said shortly. "All right, let's hear the story. Most likely it'll be the last you'll ever tell. What's your game?"

"You speak Ynamren like a native," the girl said.

Ybor's eyes glinted. "I am a native."

She smiled her disbelief. "And you kill your own soldiers? I think not. I saw you wipe out that gun crew. There was too much objectivity about you. One of us would do it with hatred. For you, it was a tactical maneuver."

"You're cutting your own throat," Ybor warned. "I can't let you go. You're too observing."

She repeated, "I think not." After a pause, she said, "You'll need help, whatever your mission. I can offer it."

He was contemptuous. "You offer my head a lion's mouth. I can hide it there? I need no help. Especially from anybody clumsy enough to be caught. And I've caught you, my pretty."

She flushed. "You were about to storm a rampart. I saw it in your odd face as you stared toward Nilreq. I caught my breath with hope that you could. That's what you heard. If I'd thought you were my enemy, you'd have heard nothing. Except, maybe, the song of my knife blade as it reached your heart."

"What's odd about my face?" he demanded. "It'd pass in a crowd without notice."

"Women would notice it," she said. "It's lopsided."

He shrugged aside the personal issue. He took her throat in his hands. "I have to do this," he said. "It's highly important that nobody knows of my presence here. This is war. I can't afford to be humane."

She offered no resistance. Quietly, she looked up at him and asked, "Have you heard of Ylas?"

His fingers did not close on the soft flesh. "Who has not?"

"I am Ylas," she said.

"A trick."

"No trick. Let me show you." As his eyes narrowed—"No, I have no papers, of course. Listen. You know Mulb, Sworb, and Nomos? I got them away."

Ybor hesitated. She could be Ylas, but it would be a fantastic stroke of luck to run into the fabulous director of Ynamre's underground so soon. It was almost beyond belief. Yet, there was a chance she was telling the truth. He couldn't overlook that chance.

"Names," he said. "You could have heard them anywhere."

"Nomos has a new-moon scar on his wrist," she said. "Sworb is tall, almost as tall as you, and his shoulders droop slightly. He talks so fast you can hardly follow. Mulb is a dope. He gets by on his pontifical manner."

These, Ybor reflected, were crisp thumbnail sketches.

She pressed her advantage. "Would I have stood by while you killed that gun crew if I were a loyal member of the Sixa Alliance? Wouldn't I have cried a warning when you killed the first guard and took his helmet and gun?"

There was logic in this, Ybor thought.

"Wasn't it obvious to me," she went on, "that you were a

Seilla agent from the moment that you landed in my grain field? I could have telephoned the authorities."

Ybor took his hands from her throat. "I want to see Dr. Si-truc," he said.

She frowned off toward Nilreq, at towers golden in morning sunlight. Ybor noted indifferently that she made a colorful picture with her face to the sun. A dark flower, opening toward the dawn. Not that it mattered. He had no time for her. He had little time for anything.

"That will take some doing," she said.

He turned away. "Then I'll do it myself. Time is short."

"Wait!" Her voice had a quality which caused him to turn. He smiled sourly at the gun in her hand.

Self-contempt blackened Ybor's thoughts. He had had her helpless, but he had thought of her as a woman, not as an armed enemy. He hadn't searched her because of callow sentimentality. He had scaled the heights of stupidity, and now would plunge to his deserved end. Her gun was steady, and purpose shone darkly in her eyes.

"I'm a pushover for a fairy tale," she said. "I thought for a while that you really were a Seilla agent. How fiendishly clever you are, you and your council! I should have known when those planes went over. They went too fast."

Ybor said nothing. He was trying to absorb this.

"It was a smart idea," she went on in her acid, bitter voice. "They towed you over, and you landed in my field. A coincidence, when you come to think of it. I have been in that farmhouse only three days. Of all places, you pick it. Not by accident, not so. You and the other big minds on the Sixa council knew the planes would bring me to my window, knew my eyes would catch the shadow of your glider, knew I'd investigate. You even killed six of your own men, to dull my suspicions. Oh, I was taken in for a while."

"You talk like a crazy woman," Ybor said. "Put away that gun."

"When you had a chance to kill me and didn't," she said, "my last suspicion died. The more fool I. No, my bucko, you are not going back to report my whereabouts, to have your goons wait until my committee meets and catch us all. Not so. You die here and now."

Thoughts raced through Ybor's head. It would be a waste of energy to appeal to her on the ground that if she killed

him she would in effect destroy her species. That smacked of
oratory. He needed a simple appeal, crisp and startling. But
what? His time was running short; he could see it in her dark
eyes.

"Your last address," he said, remembering Sworb's tale of
escape, "was 40 Curk Way. You sold pastries, and Sworb got
sick on little cakes. He was sick in your truck, as it carted
him away at eleven minutes past midnight."

"Bull's-eye." Determination to kill went out of her eyes as
she remembered. She was thoughtful for a moment.

Then her eyes glinted. "I've not heard that he reached
Acireb safely. You could have caught him across the Enarta
border and beaten the truth out of him. Still," she reflected,
"you may be telling the truth . . ."

"I am," Ybor said quietly. "I am a Seilla agent, here on a
highly important mission. If you can't aid me directly, you
must let me go. At once."

"You might be lying, too, though. I can't take the chance.
You will march ahead of me around the wood. If you make
one overt move, or even a move that I don't understand, I'll
kill you."

"Where are you taking me?"

"To my house. Where else? Then we'll talk."

"Now listen to me," he said passionately, "there is no time
for—"

"March!"

He marched.

Ybor's plan to take her unawares when they were inside
the farmhouse dissolved when he saw the great hulk who admitted them. This was a lumpish brute with the most powerful body Ybor had ever seen, towering over his own more
than average height. The man's arms were as thick as Ybor's
thighs, and the yellow eyes were small and vicious. Yet,
apelike though he was, the giant moved like a mountain cat,
without sound, with deceptive swiftness.

"Guard him," the girl commanded, and Ybor knew the yellow eyes would not leave him.

He sank into a chair, an old chair with a primitive tail slot,
and watched the girl as she busied herself at the mountainous
cooking range. This kitchen could accommodate a score of
farmhands, and that multiple-burner stove could turn out hot
meals for all.

"We'd better eat," she said. "If you're not lying, you'll need strength. If you are, you can withstand torture long enough to tell us the truth."

"You're making a mistake," Ybor began hotly, but stopped when the guard made a menacing gesture.

She had a meal on the table soon. It was a good meal, and he ate it heartily. "The condemned man," he said, and smiled.

For a camaraderie had sprung up between them. He was male, not too long past his youth, with clear, dark eyes, and he was put together with an eye to efficiency; and she was a female, at the ripening stage. The homely task of preparing a meal, of sharing it, lessened the tension between them. She gave him a fleeting, occasional smile as he tore into his food.

"You're a good cook," he said, when they had finished.

Warmth went out of her. She eyed him steadily. "Now," she said crisply. "Proof."

Ybor shrugged angrily. "Do you think I carry papers identifying me as a Seilla agent? 'To whom it may concern, bearer is high in Seilla councils. Any aid you may give him will be appreciated.' I have papers showing that I'm a newspaper man from Eeras. The newspaper offices and building have been destroyed by now, and there is no means of checking."

She thought this over. "I'm going to give you a chance," she said. "If you're a top-flight Seilla agent, one of your Nilreq men can identify you. Name one, and we'll get him here."

"None of them know me by sight. My face was altered before I came on this assignment, so that nobody could give me away, even accidentally."

"You know all the answers, don't you?" she scoffed. "Well, we will now take you into the cellar and get the truth from you. And you won't die until we do. We'll keep you alive, one way or another."

"Wait a moment," Ybor said. "There is one man who will know me. He may not have arrived. Solraq."

"He came yesterday," she said. "Very well. If he identifies you, that will be good enough. Sleyg," she said to the huge guard, "fetch Solraq."

Sleyg rumbled deep in his throat, and she made an impatient gesture. "I can take care of myself. Go!" She reached inside her blouse, took her gun from its shoulder holster and pointed it across the table at Ybor. "You will sit still."

Sleyg went out. Ybor heard a car start, and the sound of its motor faded rapidly.

"May I smoke?" Ybor asked.

"Certainly." With her free hand she tossed a pack of cigarettes across the table. He lighted one, careful to keep his hand in sight, handed it to her, and applied flame to his own. "So you're Ylas," he said conversationally.

She didn't bother to reply.

"You've done a good job," he went on. "Right under their noses. You must have had some close calls."

She smiled tolerantly. "Don't be devious, chum. On the off chance that you might escape, I'll give you no data to use later."

"There won't be any later if I don't get out of here. For you, or anybody."

"Now you're melodramatic. There'll always be a later, as long as there's time."

"Time exists only in consciousness," he said. "There won't be any time, unless dust and rocks are aware of it."

"That's quite a picture of destruction you paint."

"It will be quite a destruction. And you're bringing it nearer every minute. You're cutting down the time margin in which it can be averted."

She grinned. "Ain't I nasty?"

"Even if you let me go this moment—" he began.

"Which I won't."

"—the catastrophe might not be averted. Our minds can't conceive the unimaginable violence which might very well destroy all animate life. It's a queer picture," he mused, "even to think about. Imagine space travelers of the future sighting this planet empty of life, overgrown with jungles. It wouldn't even have a name. Oh, they'd find the name. All traces of civilization wouldn't be completely destroyed. They'd poke in the crumbled ruins and find bits of history. Then they'd go back to their home planet with the mystery of Cathor. Why did all life disappear from Cathor? They'd find skeletons enough to show our size and shape, and they'd decipher such records as were found. But nowhere would they find even a hint of the reason our civilization was destroyed. Nowhere would they find the name of Ylas, the reason."

She merely grinned.

"That's how serious it is," Ybor concluded. "Not a bird in the sky, not a pig in a sty. Perhaps no insects, even. I wonder," he said thoughtfully, "if such explosions destroyed life in other planets in our system. Lara, for example. It *had* life, once. Did civilization rise to a peak there, and end in a war that involved every single person on one side or another? Did one side, in desperation, try to use an explosive available to both but uncontrollable, and so lose the world?"

"*Shh!*" she commanded. She was stiff, listening.

He heard it then, the rhythmic tramp of feet. He flicked a glance through the window toward the wood. "Ynamre," he said.

A sergeant marched a squad of eight soldiers across the field toward the house. Ybor turned to the girl.

"You've got to hide me! Quick!"

She stared at him coldly. "I have no place."

"You must have. You must take care of refugees. Where is it?"

"Maybe you've caught me," she said grimly, "but you'll learn nothing. The Underground will carry on."

"You little fool! I'm with you."

"That's what you say. I haven't any proof."

Ybor wasted no more time. The squad was almost at the door. He leaped over against the wall and squatted there. He pulled his coat half off, shook his black hair over his eyes, and slacked his face so that it took on the loose, formless expression of an idiot. He began to play with his fingers, and gurgled.

A pounding rifle butt took the girl to the door. Ybor did not look up. He twisted his fingers and gurgled at them.

"Did you hear anything last night?" the sergeant demanded.

"Anything?" she echoed. "Some planes, some guns."

"Did you get up? Did you look out?"

"I was afraid," she answered meekly.

He spat contemptuously. There was a short silence, disturbed only by Ybor's gurgling.

"What's that?" the sergeant snapped. He stamped across the room, jerked Ybor's head up by the lock of hair. Ybor gave him an insane, slobbering grin. The sergeant's eyes were contemptuous. "Dummy!" he snarled. He jerked his hand away. "Why don't you kill it?" he asked the girl. "All the more food for you. Sa-a-a-y," he said, as if he'd seen her for the first time, "not bad, not bad. I'll be up to see you, cookie, one of these nights."

Ybor didn't move until they were out of hearing. He got to his feet then, and looked grimly at Ylas. "I could have been in Nilreq by now. You'll have to get me away. They've discovered that gun crew, and will be on the lookout."

She had the gun in her hand again. She motioned him toward the chair. "Shall we sit down?"

"After that? You're still suspicious? You're a fool."

"Ah? I think not. That could have been a part of the trick, to lull my suspicions. Sit—down!"

He sat. He was through with talking. He thought of the soldiers' visit. That sergeant probably wouldn't recognize him if they should encounter each other. Still, it was something to keep in mind. One more face to remember, to dodge.

If only that big ape would get back with Solraq. His ears, as if on cue, caught the sound of an approaching motor. He was gratified to see that he heard it a full second before Ylas. Her reflexes weren't so fast, after all.

It was Sleyg, and Sleyg alone. He came into the house on his soft, cat feet. "Solraq," he reported, "is dead. Killed last night."

Ylas gave Ybor a smile. There was deadliness in it.

"How very convenient," she said, "for you. Doesn't it seem odd even to you, Mr. Sixa Intelligence Officer, that of all the Seilla agents you pick a man who is dead? I think this has gone far enough. Into the cellar with him, Sleyg. We'll get the truth this time. Even," she added to Ybor, "though it'll kill you."

The chair was made like a strait jacket, with an arrangement of clamps and straps that held him completely motionless. He could move nothing but his eyeballs.

Ylas inspected him. She nodded satisfaction. "Go heat your irons," she said to Sleyg. "First," she explained to Ybor, "we'll burn off your ears, a little at a time. If that doesn't wear you down, we'll get serious."

Ybor said, "I'll tell you the truth now."

She sneered at that. "No wonder the enemy is knocking at your gates. You were driven out of Aissu on the south, and

Ytal on the north. Now you are coming into your home country, because you're cowards."

"I'm convinced that you are Ylas," Ybor went on calmly. "And though my orders were that nobody should know of my mission, I think I can tell you. I must. I have no choice. Then listen. I was sent to Ynamre to—"

She cut him off with a fierce gesture. "The truth!"

"Do you want to hear this or not?"

"I don't want to hear another fairy tale."

"You are going to hear this, whether you like it or not. And you'll hold off your gorilla until I've finished. Or have the end of the race on your head."

Her lip curled. "Go on."

"Have you heard of U-235? It's an isotope of uranium."

"Who hasn't?"

"All right. I'm stating fact, not theory. U-235 has been separated in quantity easily sufficient for preliminary atomic-power research, and the like. They got it out of uranium ores by new atomic isotope separation methods; they now have quantities measured in pounds. By 'they,' I mean Seilla research scientists. But they have *not* brought the whole amount together, or any major portion of it. Because they are not at all sure that, once started, it would stop before all of it had been consumed—in something like one micromicrosecond of time."

Sleyg came into the cellar. In one hand he carried a portable forge. In the other, a bundle of metal rods. Ylas motioned him to put them down in a corner. "Go up and keep watch," she ordered. "I'll call you."

A tiny exultation flickered in Ybor. He had won a concession. "Now the explosion of a pound of U-235," he said, "wouldn't be too unbearably violent, though it releases as much energy as a hundred million pounds of TNT. Set off on an island, it might lay waste the whole island, uprooting trees, killing all animal life, but even that fifty thousand tons of TNT wouldn't seriously disturb the really unimaginable tonnage which even a small island represents."

"I assume," she broke in, "that you're going to make a point? You're not just giving me a lecture on high explosives?"

"Wait. The trouble is, they're afraid that that explosion of energy would be so incomparably violent, its sheer, minute concentration of unbearable energy so great, that surrounding matter would be set off. If you could imagine concentrating half a billion of the most violent lightning strokes you ever saw, compressing all their fury into a space less than half the size of a pack of cigarettes—you'd get some idea of the concentrated essence of hyperviolence that explosion would represent. It's not simply the *amount* of energy; it's the frightful concentration of intensity in a minute volume.

"The surrounding matter, unable to maintain a self-supporting atomic explosion normally, might be hyper-stimulated to atomic explosion under U-235's forces and, in the immediate neighborhood, release its energy, too. That is, the explosion would not involve only one pound of U-235, but also five or fifty or five thousand tons of other matter. The extent of the explosion is a matter of conjecture."

"Get to the point," she said impatiently.

"Wait. Let me give you the main picture. Such an explosion *would* be serious. It would blow an island, or a hunk of continent, right off the planet. It would shake Cathor from pole to pole, cause earthquakes violent enough to do serious damage on the other side of the planet, and utterly destroy everything within at least one thousand miles of the site of the explosion. And I mean everything.

"So they haven't experimented. They could end the war overnight with controlled U-235 bombs. They could end this cycle of civilization with one or two *uncontrolled* bombs. And they don't know which they'd have if they made 'em. So far, they haven't worked out any way to control the explosion of U-235."

"If you're stalling for time," Ylas said, "it won't do you any good, personally. If we have callers, I'll shoot you where you sit."

"Stalling?" Ybor cried. "I'm trying my damnedest to shorten it. I'm not finished yet. Please don't interrupt. I want to give you the rest of the picture. As you pointed out the Sixa armies are being pushed back to their original starting point: Ynamre. They started out to conquer the world, and they came close, at one time. But now they are about to lose it. We, the Seilla, would not dare to set off an experimental atomic bomb. This war is a phase, to us; to the Sixa, it is the whole future. So the Sixa are desperate, and Dr. Sitruc has made a bomb with not one, but *sixteen* pounds of U-235 in it. He may have it finished any day. I must find him and destroy that bomb. If it's used, we are lost either way. Lost the war, if the experiment is a success; the world, if not. You, and you alone stand between extinction of the race and continuance."

She seemed to pounce. "You're lying! Destroy it, you say. How? Take it out in a vacant lot and explode it? In a desert? On a high mountain? You wouldn't dare even to drop it in the ocean, for fear it might explode. Once you had it, you'd have ten million tigers by the tail—you wouldn't dare turn it loose."

"I can destroy it. Our scientists told me how."

"Let that pass for the moment," she said. "You have several points to explain. First, it seems odd that *you* heard of this, and we haven't. We're much closer to developments than you, across three thousand miles of water."

"Sworb," Ybor said, "is a good man, even if he can't eat sweets. He brought back a drawing of it. Listen, Ylas, time is precious! If Dr. Sitruc finishes that bomb before I find him, it may be taken any time and dropped near our headquarters. And even if it doesn't set off the explosion I've described— though it's almost certain that it would—it would wipe out our southern army and equipment, and we'd lose overnight."

"Two more points need explaining," she went on calmly. "Why *my* grain field? There were others to choose from."

"That was pure accident."

"Perhaps. But isn't that string of accidents suspiciously long when you consider the death of Solraq?"

"I don't know anything about that. I didn't know he was dead."

She was silent. She strode back and forth across the cellar, brows furrowed, smoking nervously. Ybor sat quietly. It was all he could do; even his fingers were in stalls.

"I'm half inclined to believe you," she said finally, "but look at my position. We have a powerful organization here. We've risked our lives, and many of us have died, in building it up. I know how we are hated and feared by the authorities. If you are a Sixa agent, and I concluded that you were by the way you spoke the language, you would go to any length, even to carrying out such an elaborate plot as this might be, to discover our methods and membership. I can't risk all that labor and life on nothing but your word."

"Look at my position," Ybor countered. "I might have escaped from you, in the wood and here, after Sleyg left us. But I didn't dare take a chance. You see, it's a matter of time. There is a definite, though unknown, deadline. Dr. Sitruc may finish that bomb any time, and screw the fuse in. The bomb may be taken at any time after that and exploded. If I had tried to escape, and you had shot me—and I'm sure you would—it would take weeks to replace me. We may have only hours to work with."

She was no longer calm and aloof. Her eyes had a tortured look, and her hands clenched as if she were squeezing words from her heart: "I can't afford to take the chance."

"You can't afford not to," Ybor said.

Footsteps suddenly pounded overhead. Ylas went rigid, flung a narrowed glance of speculation and suspicion at Ybor, and went out of the cellar. He twisted a smile; she hadn't shot him, as she had threatened.

He sat still, but each nerve was taut, quivering, and raw. What now? Who had arrived? What could it mean for him? Who belonged to that babble upstairs? Whose feet were heavy? He was soon to know, for the footsteps moved to the cellar door, and Ylas preceded the sergeant who had arrived earlier.

"I've got orders to search every place in this vicinity," the sergeant said, "so shut up."

His eyes widened when they fell on Ybor. "Well, well!" he cried. "If it isn't the dummy. Sa-a-ay, you snapped out of it!"

Ybor caught his breath as an idea hit him.

"I was drugged," Ybor said, leaping at the chance for escape. "It's worn off now."

Ylas frowned, searching, he could see, for the meaning in his words. He went on, giving her her cue: "This girl's servant, that big oaf upstairs—"

"He ran out," the sergeant said. "We'll catch him."

"I see. He attacked me last night in the grain field out there, brought me here and drugged me."

"What were you doing in the grain field?"

"I was on my way to see Dr. Sitruc. I have information of the most vital nature for him."

The sergeant turned to Ylas. "What d'ya say, girlie?"

She shrugged. "A stranger, in the middle of the night, what would you have done?"

"Then why didn't you say something about it when I was here a while ago?"

"If he turned out to be a spy, I wanted the credit for capturing him."

"You civilians," the sergeant said in disgust. "Well, maybe this is the guy we're lookin' for. Why did you kill that gun crew?" he snarled at Ybor.

Ybor blinked. "How did you know? I killed them because they were enemies."

The sergeant made a gesture toward his gun. His face grew stormy. "Why, you dirty spy—"

"Wait a minute!" Ybor said. "What gun crew? You mean the Seilla outpost, of course, in Aissu?"

"I mean our gun crew, you rat, in the woods out there."

Ybor blinked again. "I don't know anything about a gun crew out there. Listen, you've got to take me to Dr. Sitruc at once. Here's the background. I have been in Seilla territory, and I learned something that Dr. Sitruc must know. The outcome of the war depends on it. Take me to him at once, or you'll suffer for it."

The sergeant cogitated. "There's something funny here," he said. "Why have you got him all tied up?"

"For questioning," Ylas answered.

Ybor could see that she had decided to play it his way, but she wasn't convinced. The truth was, as he pointed out, she could not afford to do otherwise.

The sergeant went into an analytical state which seemed to be almost cataleptic. Presently he shook his massive head. "I can't quite put my finger on it," he said in a puzzled tone. "Every time I get close, I hit a blank . . . what am I saying?" He became crisp, menacing. "What's your name, you?" he spat at Ybor.

Ybor couldn't shrug. He raised his eyebrows. "My papers will say that I am Yenraq Ekor, a newspaper man. Don't let them fool you. I'll give my real name to Dr. Sitruc. He knows it well. You're wasting time, man!" he burst out. "Take me to him at once. You're worse than this stupid female!"

The sergeant turned to Ylas. "Did he tell you why he wanted to see Dr. Sitruc?"

She shrugged again, still with speculative eyes on Ybor. "He just said he had to."

"Well, then," the sergeant demanded of Ybor, "why *do* you want to see him?"

Ybor decided to gamble. This goof might keep him here all day with aimless questioning. He told the story of the bomb, much as he had told it to Ylas. He watched the sergeant's face, and saw that his remarks were completely unintelligible. Good! The soldier, like so many people, knew nothing of U-235. Ybor went into the imaginative and gibberish phase of his talk.

"And so, if it's uncontrolled," he said, "it might destroy the planet, blow it instantly into dust. But what I learned was a method of control, and the Seilla have a bomb almost completed. They'll use it to destroy Ynamre. But if we can use ours first, we'll destroy them. You see, it's a neutron shield that I discovered while I was a spy in the Seilla camps. It will stop the neutrons, released by the explosion, from rocketing about space and splitting mountains. Did you know that one free neutron can crack this planet in half? This shield will confine them to a limited area, and the war is ours. So hurry! Our time may be measured in minutes!"

The sergeant took it all in. He didn't dare not believe, for the picture of destruction which Ybor painted was on such a vast scale that sixteen generations of men like the sergeant would be required to comprehend it.

The sergeant made up his mind. "Hey!" he yelled toward the cellar door, and three soldiers came in. "Get him out of that. We'll take him to the captain. Take the girl along, too. Maybe the captain will want to ask her some questions."

"But I haven't done anything," Ylas protested.

"Then you got nothing to be afraid of, beautiful. If they let you go, I'll take personal charge of you."

The sergeant had a wonderful leer.

You might as well be fatalistic, Ybor thought as he waited in Dr. Sitruc's anteroom. Certain death could easily await him here, but even so, it was worth the gamble. If he were to be a pawn in a greater game—the greatest game, in fact—so be it.

So far, he had succeeded. And it came to him as he eyed his two guards that final success would result in his own death. He couldn't hope to destroy that bomb and get out of this fortress alive. Those guarded exists spelled finis, if he could even get far enough from this laboratory to reach one of them.

He hadn't really expected to get out alive, he reflected. It was a suicide mission from the start. That knowledge, he knew now, had given plausibility to his otherwise thin story. The captain, even as the sergeant, had not dared to disbelieve his tale. He had imparted verisimilitude to his story of destruction because of his deep and flaming determination to prevent it.

Not that he had talked wildly about neutron shields to the captain. The captain was intelligent, compared to his sergeant. And so Ybor had talked matter-of-factly about heat control, and had made it convincing enough to be brought here by guards who grew more timid with each turn of the lorry's wheels.

Apparently, the story of the bomb was known here at the government experimental laboratories; for all the guards had a haunted look, as if they knew that they would never hear the explosion if something went wrong. All the better, then. If he could take advantage of that fact, somehow, as he had taken advantage of events to date, he might—might—

He shrugged away speculation. The guards had sprung to attention as the inner door opened, and a man eyed Ybor.

This was a slender man with snapping dark eyes, an odd-shaped face, and a commanding air. He wore a smock, and from its sleeves extended competent-looking hands.

"So you are the end result," he said dryly to Ybor. "Come in."

Ybor followed him into the laboratory. Dr. Sitruc waved him to a straight, uncomfortable chair, using the gun which was suddenly in his hand as an indicator. Ybor sat, and looked steadily at the other.

"What do you mean, end result?" he asked.

"Isn't it rather obvious?" the doctor asked pleasantly. "Those planes which passed over last night were empty; they went too fast, otherwise. I have been speculating all day on their purpose. Now I see. They dropped you."

"I heard something about planes," Ybor said, "but I didn't see 'em."

Dr. Sitruc raised polite eyebrows. "I'm afraid I do not believe you. My interpretation of events is this: those Seilla planes had one objective, to land an agent here who was commissioned to destroy the uranium bomb. I have known for some time that the Seilla command have known of its existence, and I have wondered what steps they would take to destroy it."

Ybor could see no point in remaining on the defensive. "They are making their own bomb," he said. "But they have a control. I'm here to tell you about it, so that you can use it on our bomb. We have time."

Dr. Sitruc said: "I have heard the reports on you this morning. You made some wild and meaningless statements. My personal opinion is that you are a layman, with only scant knowledge of the subject on which you have been so glib. I propose to find out—before I kill you. Oh, yes," he said, smiling, "you will die in any case. In my present position, knowledge is power. If I find that you actually have knowledge which I do not, I propose that I alone will retain it. You see my point?"

"You're like a god here. That's clear enough from the attitude of the guards."

"Exactly. I have control of the greatest explosive force in world history, and my whims are obeyed as iron commands. If I choose, I may give orders to the High Command. They have no choice but to obey. Now, you—your name doesn't matter; it's assumed, no doubt—tell me what you know."

"Why should I? If I'm going to die, anyway, my attitude is to hell with you. I do know something that you don't, and you haven't time to get it from anybody but me. By the time one of your spies could work his way up high enough to learn what I did, the Sixa would be defeated. But I see no reason to give you the information. I'll sell it to you—for my life."

Ybor looked around the small, shining laboratory while he spoke, and he saw it. It wasn't particularly large; its size did not account for the stab of terror that struck his heart. It was the fact that the bomb was finished. It was suspended in a shock-proof cradle. Even a bombing raid would not shake it loose. It would be exploded when and where the doctor chose.

"You may well turn white as a sheet," Dr. Sitruc chuckled. "There it is, the most destructive weapon the world has ever known."

Ybor swallowed convulsively. Yes, there it was. Literally

the means to an end—the end of the world. He thought wryly that those religionists who still contended that this war would be ended miraculously by divine intervention would never live to call the bomb a miracle. What a shot in the doctrine the explosion would give them if only they could come through it unscathed!

"I turned white," he answered Dr. Sitruc, "because I see it as a blind, uncontrolled force. I see it as the end of a cycle, when all life dies. It will be millennia before another civilization can reach our present stage."

"It is true that the element of chance is involved. If the bomb sets off surrounding matter for any considerable radius, it is quite possible that all animate life will be destroyed in the twinkling of an eye. However, if it does not set off surrounding matter, we shall have won the world. I alone—and now you—know this. The High Command sees only victory in that weapon. But enough of chitchat. You would bargain your life for information on how to control the explosion. If you convince me that you have such knowledge, I'll set you free. What is it?"

"That throws us into a deadlock," Ybor objected. "I won't tell you until I'm free, and you won't free me until I tell."

Dr. Sitruc pursed thin lips. "True," he said. "Well, then, how's this? I shall give the guards outside a note ordering that you be allowed to leave unmolested after you come through the laboratory door."

"And what's to prevent your killing me in here, once I have told you?"

"I give you my word."

"It isn't enough."

"What other choice have you?"

Ybor thought this over, and conceded the point. Somewhere along the line, either he or Dr. Sitruc would have to trust the other. Since this was the doctor's domain, and since he held Ybor prisoner, it was easy to see who would take the other on trust. Well, it would give him a breathing spell. Time was what he wanted now.

"Write the note," he said.

Dr. Sitruc went to his desk and began to write. He shot glances at Ybor which excluded the possibility of successful attack. Even the quickest spring would be fatal, for the doctor was far enough away to have time to raise his gun and fire. Ybor had a hunch that Dr. Sitruc was an excellent shot. He waited.

Dr. Sitruc summoned a guard, gave him the note, and directed that Ybor be allowed to read it. Ybor did, nodded. The guard went out.

"Now," Dr. Sitruc began, but broke off to answer his telephone. He listened, nodded, shot a slitted glance at Ybor, and hung up. "Would it interest you to know," he asked, "that the girl who captured you was taken away from guards by members of the Underground?"

"Not particularly," Ybor said. "Except that . . . yes," he cried, "it does interest me. It proves my authenticity. You know how widespread the Underground is, how powerful. It's clear what happened; they knew I was coming, knew my route, and caught me. They were going to torture me in their cellar. I told that sergeant the truth. Now they will try to steal the bomb. If they had it, they could dictate terms."

It sounded a trifle illogical, maybe, but Ybor put all of the earnestness he could into his voice. Dr. Sitruc looked thoughtful.

"Let them try. Now, let's have it."

The tangled web of lies he had woven had caught him now. He knew of no method to control the bomb. Dr. Sitruc was not aware of this fact, and would not shoot until he was. Ybor must stall, and watch for an opportunity to do what he must do. He had gained a point; if he got through that door, he would be free. He must, then, get through the door—with the bomb. And Dr. Sitruc's gun was in his hand.

"Let's trace the reaction," Ybor began.

"The control!" Dr. Sitruc snapped.

Ybor's face hardened. "Don't get tough. My life depends on this. I've got to convince you that I know what I'm talking about, and I can do that by describing the method from the first. If you interrupt, then to hell with you."

Dr. Sitruc's odd face flamed with anger. This subsided after a moment, and he nodded. "Go on."

"Oxygen and nitrogen do not burn—if they did, the first fire would have blown this planet's atmosphere off in one stupendous explosion. Oxygen and nitrogen *will* burn if heated to about three thousand degrees Centigrade, and they'll give off energy in the process. But they don't give off sufficient energy to maintain that temperature—so they rapidly cool, and the fire goes out. If you maintain that temperature artificially—well, you're no doubt familiar with that process of obtaining nitric oxide."

"No doubt," Dr. Sitruc said acidly.

"All right. Now U-235 can raise the temperature of local matter to where it will, uh, 'burn,' and give off energy. So let's say we set off a little pinch of U-235. Surrounding matter also explodes, as it is raised to an almost inconceivable temperature. It cools rapidly; within perhaps one-hundred-millionth of a second, it is down below the point of ignition. Then maybe a full millionth of a second passes before it's down to one million degrees hot, and a minute or so may elapse before it is visible in the normal sense. Now that visible radiation will represent no more than one-hundred-thousandth of the total radiation at one million degrees—but even so, it would be several hundred times more brilliant than the sun. Right?"

Dr. Sitruc nodded. Ybor thought there was a touch of deference in his nod.

"That's pretty much the temperature cycle of a U-235 plus surrounding matter explosion, Dr. Sitruc. I'm oversimplifying, I guess, but we don't need to go into detail. Now that radiation *pressure* is the stuff that's potent. The sheer momentum, physical pressure of light from the stuff at one million degrees, would amount to tons and tons and *tons* of pressure. It would blow down buildings like a titanic wind if it weren't for the fact that absorption of such appalling energy would volatilize the buildings before they could move out of the way. Right?"

Dr. Sitruc nodded again. He almost smiled.

"All right," Ybor went on. He now entered the phase of this contest where he was guessing, and he'd get no second guess. "What we need is a damper, something to hold the temperature of surrounding matter down. In that way, we can limit the effect of the explosion to desired areas, and prevent it from destroying cities on the opposite side of Cathor. The method of applying the damper depends on the exact mechanical structure of the bomb itself."

Ybor got to his feet easily, and walked across the laboratory to the cradle which held the bomb. He didn't even glance at Dr. Sitruc; he didn't dare. Would he be allowed to reach the bomb? Would an unheard, unfelt bullet reach his brain before he took another step?

When he was halfway across the room, he felt as if he had already walked a thousand miles. Each step seemed to be slow motion, leagues in length. And still the bomb was miles away. He held his steady pace, fighting with every atom of will his desire to sprint to his goal, snatch it and flee.

He stopped before the bomb, looked down at it. He nodded, ponderously. "I see," he said, remembering Sworb's drawings and the careful explanations he had received. "Two cast-iron hemispheres, clamped over the orange segments of cadmium alloy. And the fuse—I see it is in—a tiny can of cadmium alloy containing a speck of radium in a beryllium holder and a small explosive powerful enough to shatter the cadmium walls. Then—correct me if I'm wrong, will you?—the powdered uranium oxide runs together in the central cavity. The radium shoots neutrons into this mass—and the U-235 takes over from there, Right?"

Dr. Sitruc had come up behind Ybor, stood at his shoulder. "Just how do you know so much about that bomb?" he asked with overtones of suspicion.

Ybor threw a careless smile over his shoulder. "It's obvious, isn't it? Cadmium stops neutrons, and it's cheap and effective. So you separate the radium and U-235 by thin cadmium walls, brittle so the light explosion will shatter them, yet strong enough to be handled with reasonable care."

The doctor chuckled. "Why, you *are* telling the truth."

Dr. Sitruc relaxed, and Ybor moved. He whipped his short, prehensile tail around the barrel of Dr. Sitruc's gun, yanked the weapon down at the same time his fist cracked the scientist's chin. His free hand wrenched the gun out of Dr. Sitruc's hand.

He didn't give the doctor a chance to fall from the blow of his fist. He chopped down with the gun butt and Dr. Sitruc was instantly unconscious. Ybor stared down at the sprawled figure with narrowed eyes. Dared he risk a shot? No, for the guards would not let him go, despite the doctor's note, without investigation. Well—

He chopped the gun butt down again. Dr. Sitruc would be no menace for some time, anyway. And all Ybor needed was a little time. First, he had to get out of here.

That meant taking the fuse out of the bomb. He went over

to the cradle, examined the fuse. He tried to unscrew it. It was too tight. He looked around for a wrench. He saw none. He stood half panic-stricken. Could he afford a search for the wrench which would remove the fuse? If anyone came in, he was done for. No, he'd have to get out while he could.

And if anybody took a shot at him, and hit the bomb, it was good-bye Cathor and all that's in it. But he didn't dare wait here. And he must stop sweating ice water, stop this trembling.

He picked up the cradle and walked carefully to the door. Outside, in the anteroom, the guards who had brought him there turned white. Blood drained out of their faces like air from a punctured balloon. They stood motionless, except for a slight trembling of their knees, and watched Ybor go out into the corridor.

Unmolested, Dr. Sitruc had said. He was not only unmolested, he was avoided. Word seemed to spread through the building like poison gas on a stiff breeze. Doors popped open, figures hurried out—and ran away from Ybor and his cargo. Guards, scientists, men in uniform, girls with pretty legs, bare-kneed boys—all ran.

To where? Ybor asked with his heart in his mouth. There was no safe place in all the world. Run how they might, as far as they could, and it would catch them if he fell or if the bomb were accidentally exploded.

He wanted a plane. But how to get one, if everybody ran? He could walk to the airport, if he knew where it was. Still, once he was away from these laboratories, any policeman, ignorant of the bomb, could stop him, confiscate the weapon, and perhaps explode it.

He had to retain possession.

The problem was partly solved for him. As he emerged from the building, to see people scattering in all directions, a huge form came out from behind a pillar and took him by the arm. "Sleyg," Ybor almost cried with terror which became relief.

"Come," Sleyg said, "Ylas wants you."

"Get me to a plane!" Ybor said. He thought he'd said it quietly, but Sleyg's yellow eyes flickered curiously at him.

The big man nodded, crooked a finger, and led the way. He didn't seem curious about the bomb. Ybor followed to where a small car was parked at the curb. They climbed in, and Sleyg pulled out into traffic.

So Ylas wanted him, eh? Why? He gave up speculation to watch the road ahead, cradling the bomb in his arms against rough spots.

He heard a plane, and searched for it anxiously. All he needed at this stage was a bombing raid, and a direct hit on this car. They had promised him that no raids would be attempted until they were certain of his success or failure, but brass hats were a funny lot. You never knew what they'd do next, like countermanding orders given only a few minutes before.

Still, no alarm sirens went off, so the plane must be Sixa. Ybor sighed with relief.

They drove on, and Ybor speculated on the huge, silent figure beside him. How had Sleyg known that he would come out of that building? How had he known he was there? Did the Underground have a pipeline even into Dr. Sitruc's office?

These speculations were useless, too, and he shrugged them away as Sleyg drove out of the city through fields of grain. The Sixa, apparently, were going to feed their armies mush, for he saw no other produce.

Sleyg cut off the main road into a bumpy lane, and Ybor clasped the bomb firmly. "Take it easy," he warned.

Sleyg slowed obediently, and Ybor wondered again at the man's attitude. Ybor did not seem to be a prisoner, yet he was not in command here completely. It was a sort of combination of the two, and it was uncomfortable.

They came to a bare, level stretch of land where a plane stood, props turning idly. Sleyg headed toward it. He brought the car to a halt, motioned Ybor out. He then indicated that Ybor should enter the big plane.

"Give me your tool kit," Ybor said, and the big man got it.

The plane bore Sixa insignia, but Ybor was committed now. If he used the bomb as a threat, he could make anybody do what he liked. Still, he felt a niggling worry.

Just before he stepped on the wing ramp, a shot came from the plane. Ybor ducked instinctively, but it was Sleyg who fell—with a neat hole between his eyes. Ybor tensed himself, stood still.

The fuselage door slid back, and a face looked out.

"Solraq!" Ybor cried. "I thought you were dead!"

"You were meant to think it, Ybor. Come on in."

"Wait till I get these tools." Ybor handed the cradle up to the dark man who grinned down at him. "Hold baby," Ybor said. "Don't drop him. If he cries, you'll never hear him."

He picked up the tool kit, climbed into the plane. Solraq waved a command to the pilot, and the plane took off. Ybor went to work gingerly on the fuse while Solraq talked.

"Sleyg was a cutie," he said. "We thought he was an ignorant ape. He was playing a big game, and was about ready to wind it up. But, when you named me for identification, he knew that he'd have to turn in his report, because we could have sent you directly to Dr. Sitruc, and helped you. Sleyg wasn't ready yet, so he reported me dead. Then he had the soldiers come and search the house, knowing you'd be found and arrested. He got into trouble when that skirt-chasing sergeant decided to take Ylas along. He had to report that to others of the Underground, because he had to have one more big meeting held before he could get his final dope.

"You see, he'd never turned in a report," Solraq went on. "He was watched, and afraid to take a chance. When Ylas and I got together, we compared notes, searched his belongings, and found the evidence. Then we arranged this rendezvous—if you got away. She told Sleyg where you were, and to bring you here. I didn't think you'd get away, but she insisted you were too ingenious to get caught. Well, you did it, and that's all to the good. Not that it would have mattered much. If you'd failed, we'd have got hold of the bomb somehow, or exploded it in Dr. Sitruc's laboratory."

Ybor didn't bother to tell him that it didn't matter where the bomb was exploded. He was too busy trying to prevent its exploding here. At last he had the fuse out. He motioned Solraq to open the bomb bay. When the folding doors dropped open, he let the fuse fall between them.

"Got it's teeth pulled," he said, "and we'll soon empty the thing."

He released the clamps and pulled the hemispheres apart. He took a chisel from the tool kit and punched a hole in each of the cadmium cans in succession, letting the powder drift out. It would fall, spread, and never be noticed by those who would now go on living.

They would live because the war would end before Dr.

Sitruc could construct another bomb. Ybor lifted eyes that were moist.

"I guess that's it," he said. "Where are we going?"

"We'll parachute out and let this plane crash when we sight our ship some fifty miles at sea. We'll report for orders now. This mission's accomplished."

THE VEIL OF ASTELLAR

Thrilling Wonder Stories

Spring

by Leigh Brackett (1915-1978)

The vivid stories of Leigh Brackett first reached the science fiction magazines in 1940, and she soon became a regular contributor to the genre, particularly in the pages of Planet Stories *and* Thrilling Wonder Stories. *Many of her best works were novella length and therefore infrequently reprinted, but a collection of her finest short fiction is available as* The Best of Leigh Brackett, *edited by her late husband, Edmond Hamilton.*

"The Veil of Astellar" is a haunting story of love and the price of love, whose protagonist (according to Ed Hamilton) was probably modeled after Humphrey Bogart.

(So much depends upon timing. When the movie actor James Dean died, he got two obscure inches somewhere in the newspaper interior. After his death, a couple of pictures came out posthumously and he became a national craze. Could he have come back to life and died again two years later, he would have gotten the complete Elvis Presley treatment. Similarly, when Leigh Brackett was writing science fiction in the Forties, she was published only in the minor magazines such as Planet *and* Thrilling Wonder. *Her reputation grew, however, and by the time she was a star of acknowledged first magnitude she was writing for Hollywood. Could her stories of the Forties have been written in the Sixties instead, the best magazines in the field would have clawed at each other for the privilege of publishing them.—I.A.)*

Foreword

A little over a year ago, Solar Arbitrary Time, a message rocket dropped into the receiving chute at the Interworld Space Authority headquarters on Mars.

In it was a manuscript, telling a story so strange and terrible that it was difficult to believe that any sane human being could have been guilty of such crimes.

However, through a year of careful investigation, the story has been authenticated beyond doubt, and now the ISA has authorized its release to the public, just exactly as it was taken from the battered rocket.

The Veil—the light that came from nowhere to swallow ships—has disappeared. Spacemen all over the solar system, tramp traders and captains of luxury liners alike, have welcomed this knowledge as only men can who have lived in constant peril. The Veil is gone, and with it some of the crushing terror of the Alien Beyond.

We know its full name now—the Veil of Astellar.

We know the place of its origin: a world outlawed from space and time. We know the reason for its being. Through this story, written in the agony of one man's soul, we know these things—and we know the manner of the Veil's destruction.

1

Corpse at the Canal

There had been a brawl at Madam Kan's, on the Jekkara Low-Canal. Some little Martian glory-holer had got too high on thil, and pretty soon the spiked knuckle-dusters they use around there began to flash, and the little Martian had pulled his last feed-valve.

They threw what was left of him out onto the stones of the embankment almost at my feet. I suppose that was why I stopped—because I had to, or trip over him. And then I stared.

The thin red sunlight came down out of a clear green sky. Red sand whispered in the desert beyond the city walls, and red-brown water ran slow and sullen in the canal. The Martian lay twisted over on his back, with his torn throat spilling the reddest red of all across the dirty stones.

He was dead. He had green eyes, wide open, and he was dead.

I stood by him. I don't know how long. There wasn't any time. No sunlight shimmered now, no sense of people passing, no sound—nothing!

Nothing but his dead face looking up at me; green-eyed, with his lips pulled back off his white teeth.

I didn't know him. Alive, he was just another Martian snipe. Dead, he was just meat.

Dead, the Martian trash!

No time. Just a dead man's face, smiling.

And then something touched me. Thought, a sudden bursting flame of it, hit my mind, drawing it back like a magnet drawing heavy steel. Somebody's thought, directed at me. A raw, sick horror, a fear, and a compassion so deep it shook my heart— One clear, sharp thrust of word-images came to me now.

"He looks like Lucifer crying for Heaven," the message said. "His eyes. Oh, Dark Angel, his eyes!"

I shut those eyes. Sweat broke cold on me, I swayed, and then I made the world come back into focus again. Sunlight, sand, noise and stench and people crowding, the thunder of rockets from the spaceport two Mars miles away. All in focus. I looked up and saw the girl.

She was standing just beyond the dead man, almost touching him. There was a young fellow with her. I saw him vaguely, but he didn't matter then. Nothing mattered but the girl. She was wearing a blue dress, and she was staring at me with a smoke-gray gaze out of a face as white as stripped bone.

The sunlight and the noise and people went away again, leaving me alone with her. I felt the locket burn me under my spaceman's black, and my heart seemed to stop beating.

"Missy," I said. "Missy."

"Like Lucifer, but Lucifer turned saint," her mind was saying.

I laughed of a sudden, short and harsh. The world came back in place and stayed there, and so did I.

Missy. Missy, bosh! Missy's been dead a long, long time.

It was the red hair that fooled me. The same dark red hair, straight and heavy as a horse's tail, coiled on her white neck, and her smoke-gray eyes. Something, too, about her freckles and the way her mouth pulled up on one side as though it couldn't stop smiling.

Otherwise, she didn't look much like Missy. She was taller and bonier. Life had kicked her around some, and she showed it. Missy never had worn that tired, grim look. I don't know whether she had developed a tough, unbreakable character, like the girl before me, either. I couldn't read minds, then.

This girl, looking at me, had a lot in her mind that she wouldn't want known. I didn't like the idea of her catching me in a rare off-moment.

"What do you babies think you're doing here?" I said.

The young man answered me. He was a lot like her—plain, simple, a lot tougher inside than he looked—a kid who had learned how to take punishment and go on fighting. He was sick now, and angry, and a little scared.

"We thought, in broad daylight it would be safe," he answered.

"Day or night, it's all the same to this hole. I'd get out."

Without moving, the girl was still looking at me, not even realizing that she was doing it. "White hair," she was thinking. "But he isn't old. Not much older than Brad, in spite of the lines. Suffering, not age."

"You're off the *Queen of Jupiter*, aren't you?" I asked them.

I knew they were. The *Queen* was the only passenger tub in Jekkara then. I was interested only because she looked like Missy. But Missy had been dead a long time.

The young man she thought of as Brad spoke.

"Yes," he said. "We're going out to Jupiter, to the colonies." He pulled at the girl gently. "Come on, Virgie. We'd better go back to the ship."

I was sweating, and cold. Colder than the corpse at my feet. I laughed, but not loud.

"Yes," I said. "Get back to the ship, where it's safe."

The girl hadn't stirred, hadn't taken her eyes off me.

Still afraid, not so compassionate now, but still with her mind on me.

"His eyes burn," she was thinking. "What color are they? No color, really. Just dark and cold and burning. They've looked into horror—and heaven . . ."

I let her look into them. She flushed after a while, and I smiled. She was angry, but she couldn't look away, and I held her, smiling, until the young man pulled her again, not so gently.

"Come on, Virgie."

She broke free from me then, turning with an angular, coltish grace. My stomach felt like somebody stabbed it, suddenly. The way she held her head . . .

She looked back at me, sullenly, not wanting to.

"You remind me of someone," she said. "Are you from the *Queen of Jupiter*, too?"

Her voice was like Missy's. Deeper, maybe. Throatier. But enough like it.

"Yeah. Spaceman, First Class."

"Then maybe that's where I noticed you." She turned the wedding ring on her finger, not thinking about it, and frowned. "What's your name?"

"Goat," I said. "J. Goat."

"Jay Goat," she repeated. "What an odd name. But it's not unusual. I wonder why it interests me so much."

"Come on, Virgie," Brad said crossly.

I didn't give her any help. I looked at her until she flushed crimson and turned away. I read her thoughts. They were worth reading.

She and Brad went off toward the spaceport, walking close together, back to the *Queen of Jupiter*, and I stumbled over the dead Martian at my feet.

The pinched grayness had crawled in over his face. His green eyes were glazed and already sunken, and his blood was turning dark on the stones. Just another corpse.

I laughed. I put my black boot under the twist of his back and pushed him off into the sullen, red-brown water, and I laughed because my own blood was still hot and beating in me so hard it hurt.

He was dead, so I let him go.

I smiled at the splash and the fading ripples. "She was

wrong," I thought. "It isn't Jay. It's just plain J. Goat. J for Judas."

There were about ten Mars hours to kill before the *Queen* blasted off. I had a good run at the getak tables in Madam Kan's. She found me some special desert-cactus brandy and a Venusian girl with a hide like polished emerald and golden eyes.

She danced for me, and she knew how. It wasn't a bad ten hours, for a Jekkara dive.

Missy, the dead Martian, and the girl named Virgie went down in my subconscious where they belonged, and didn't leave even a ripple. Things like that are like the pain of an old wound when you twist it. They get you for a minute, but they don't last. They aren't important any more.

Things can change. You planet-bound people build your four little walls of thought and roof them in with convention, and you think there's nothing else. But space is big, and there are other worlds, and other ways. You can learn them. Even you. Try it, and see.

I finished the fiery green brandy. I filled the hollow between the Venusian dancer's emerald breasts with Martian silver and kissed her, and went away with a faint taste of fish on my lips, back toward the spaceport.

I walked. It was night, with a thin, cold wind rustling the sand and the low moons spilling silver and wild black shadows across the dunes. I could see my aura glowing, pale gold against the silver.

I felt swell. The only thing I thought about concerning the *Queen of Jupiter* was that pretty soon my job would be finished and I'd be paid.

I stretched with a pleasure you wouldn't know anything about, and it was a wonderful thing to be alive.

It was lonely out there on the moonswept desert a mile from the spaceport, when Gallery stepped out from behind a ruined tower that might have been a lighthouse once, when the desert was a sea.

Gallery was king-snipe of the glory hole. He was Black Irish, and moderately drunk, and his extra-sensory perception was quivering in him like a sensitive diaphragm. I knew he could see my aura. Very faintly, and not with his eyes, but enough. I knew he had seen it the first time he met me, when I signed aboard the *Queen of Jupiter* on Venus.

You meet them like that occasionally. Celts especially, and Romanies, both Earth and Martian, and a couple of tribes of Venusians. Extra-sensory perception is born into them. Mostly it's crude, but it can get in your way.

It was in my way now. Gallery had four inches on me, and about thirty pounds, and the whisky he'd drunk was just enough to make him fast, mean, and dangerous. His fists were large.

"You ain't human," he said softly.

He was smiling. He might have been making love to me, with his smile and his beautiful soft voice. The sweat on his face made it look like polished wood in the moonlight.

"No, Gallery," I said. "Not any more. Not for a long time."

He swayed slightly, over his flexed knees. I could see his eyes. The blueness was washed out of them by the moonlight. There was only fear left, hard and shining.

His voice was still soft, still singing. "What are you, then? And what will you be wantin' with the ship?"

"Nothing with the ship, Gallery. Only with the people on her. And as to what I am, what difference does it make?"

"None," said Gallery. "None. Because I'm going to kill you, now."

I laughed, not making any sound.

He nodded his black head slowly. "Show me your teeth, if you will. You'll be showin' them to the desert sky soon, out of a picked skull."

He opened his hands. The racing moonlight showed me a silver crucifix in each of his palms.

"No, Gallery," I said softly. "Maybe you could call me a vampire, but I'm not that kind."

He closed his hands again over the crosses and started forward, one slow step at a time. I could hear his boots in the blowing sand. I didn't move.

"You can't kill me, Gallery."

He didn't stop. He didn't speak. The sweat was trickling down his skin. He was afraid, but he didn't stop.

"You'll die here, Gallery, without a priest."

He didn't stop.

"Go on to the town, Gallery. Hide there till the *Queen's* gone. You'll be safe. Do you love the others enough to die for them?"

He stopped, then. He frowned, like a puzzled kid. It was a new thought.

I got the answer before he said it.

"What does love have to do with it? They're people."

He came on again, and I opened my eyes, wide.

"Gallery," I said.

He was close. Close enough so I could smell the raw whisky on his breath. I looked up into his face. I caught his eyes and held them, and he stopped, slowly, dragging his feet as though all of a sudden there were weights on them.

I held his eyes. I could hear his thoughts. They were the same. They're always the same.

He raised his fists up, too slowly, as though he might be lifting a man's weight on each of them. His lips drew back. I could see the wet shine of his teeth and hear the labored breath go between them, hoarse and rough.

I smiled at him, and held his eyes with mine.

He went down to his knees. Inch by inch, fighting me, but down. A big man with sweat on his face and blue eyes that couldn't look away. His hands opened. The silver crosses fell out and lay there glittering on the sand.

His head went back. The cords roped out in his neck and jerked, and then suddenly he fell over on his side and lay still.

"My heart," he whispered. "You've stopped it."

That's the only way. What they feel about us is instinct, and even psycho-surgery won't touch that. Besides, there's never time.

He couldn't breathe now. He couldn't speak, but I heard his thoughts. I picked the crucifixes out of the sand and folded his fingers over them.

He managed to turn his head a little and look at me. He tried to speak, but again it was his thought I answered.

"Into the Veil, Gallery," I whispered. "That's where I'm leading the *Queen*."

I saw his eyes widen and fix. The last thought he had was—well, never mind that. I dragged him back into the ruined tower where no one would be likely to find him for a long time, and started on again for the spaceport. And then I stopped.

He'd dropped the crosses again. They were lying in the path with the moonlight on them, and I picked them up, thinking I'd throw them out into the blowing sand where they wouldn't be seen.

I didn't. I stood holding them. They didn't burn my flesh. I laughed.

Yeah. I laughed. But I couldn't look at them.

I went back in the tower and stretched Gallery on his back with his hands crossed on his chest, and closed his eyes. I laid a crucifix on each of his eyelids and went out, this time for good.

Shirina said once that you could never understand a human mind completely no matter how well you knew it. That's where the suffering comes in. You feel fine, everything's beautiful, and then all of a sudden a trapdoor comes open somewhere in your brain, and you remember.

Not often, and you learn to kick them shut, fast. But even so, Flack is the only one of us that still has dark hair, and he never had a soul to begin with.

Well, I kicked the door shut on Gallery and his crosses, and half an hour later the *Queen of Jupiter* blasted off for the Jovian colonies, and a landing she was never going to make.

2

Voyage into Doom

Nothing happened until we hit the outer fringe of the Asteroid Belt. I'd kept watch on the minds of my crewmates, and I knew Gallery hadn't mentioned me to anyone else. You don't go around telling people that the guy in the next bunk gives off a yellow glow and isn't human, unless you want to wind up in a straitjacket. Especially when such things are something you sense but can't see, like electricity.

When we came into the danger zone inside the Belt, they set the precautionary watches at the emergency locks on the passenger decks, and I was assigned to one of them. I went up to take my station.

Just at the top of the companionway I felt the first faint reaction of my skin, and my aura began to pulse and brighten.

I went on to the Number Two lock and sat down.

I hadn't been on the passenger deck before. The *Queen of*

Jupiter was an old tub from the Triangle trade, refitted for deep-space hauling. She held together, and that's all. She was carrying a heavy cargo of food, seed, clothing, and farm supplies, and about five hundred families trying for a fresh start in the Jovian colonies.

I remembered the first time I saw Jupiter. The first time any man from Earth ever saw Jupiter. That was long ago.

Now the deck was jammed. Men, women, kids, mattresses, bags, bundles, and what have you. Martians, Venusians, Terrans, all piled in together, making a howling racket and smelling very high in the combined heat of the sun and the press of bodies.

My skin was tingling and beginning to crawl. My aura was brighter.

I saw the girl. The girl named Virgie with her thick red hair and her colt's way of moving. She and her husband were minding a wiry, green-eyed Martian baby while its mother tried to sleep, and they were both thinking the same thing.

"Maybe, someday when things are better, we'll have one of our own."

I remember thinking that Missy would have looked like that holding our kid, if we'd ever had one.

My aura pulsed and glowed.

I watched the little worlds flash by, still far ahead of the ship, all sizes, from pebbles to habitable planetoids, glittering in the raw sunlight and black as space on their shadow sides. People crowded up around the ports, and I got to looking at one old man standing almost beside me.

He had space stamped all over him, in the way he carried his lean frame and the lines in his leathery face, and the hungry-hound look of his eyes watching the Belt. An old rocket-hustler who had done plenty in his day, and remembered it all.

And then Virgie came up. Of all the women on deck it had to be Virgie. Brad was with her, and she was still holding the baby. She had her back to me, looking out.

"It's wonderful," she said softly. "Oh, Brad, just look at it!"

"Wonderful, and deadly," the old spaceman said to himself. He looked around and smiled at Virgie. "Your first trip out?"

"Yes, for both of us. I suppose we're very starry-eyed about it, but it's strange." She made a little helpless gesture.

"I know. There aren't any words for it." He turned back to the port. His voice and his face were blank, but I could read his mind.

"I used to kick the supply ships through to the first settlement, fifty years ago," he said. "There were ten of us, doing that. I'm the only one left."

"The Belt was dangerous then, before they got the Rosson deflectors," Brad said.

"The Belt," said the old man softly, "only got three of them."

Virgie lifted her red head. "Then what . . ."

The old man didn't hear her. His thoughts were way off.

"Six of the best men in space, and then, eleven years ago, my son," he said, to no one.

A woman standing beside him turned her head. I saw the wide, raw shine of terror in her eyes, and the sudden stiffness of her lips.

"The Veil?" she whispered. "That's what you mean, isn't it? The Veil?"

The old man tried to shut her up, but Virgie broke in.

"What about the Veil?" she asked. "I've heard of it, vaguely. What is it?"

The Martian baby was absorbed in a silver chain she wore around her neck. I remember thinking it looked familiar. Probably she'd had it on the first time I saw her. My aura glowed, a hot bright gold.

The woman's voice, answering, had an eerie quality of distance in it, like an echo. She was staring out of the port now.

"Nobody knows," she said. "It can't be found, or traced, or tested at all. My brother is a spaceman. He saw it once from a great distance, reaching from nowhere to swallow a ship. A veil of light. It faded, and the ship was gone! My brother saw it out here, close to the Belt."

"There's no more reason to expect it here than anywhere," the old spaceman said roughly. "It's taken ships as far in as Earth's orbit. There's no reason to be afraid."

My aura burned around me like a cloud of golden light, and my skin was alive with a subtle current.

The green-eyed Martian baby yanked the silver chain suddenly and crowed, holding its hands high. The thing on the end of the chain, that had been hidden under Virgie's dress, spun slowly round and round, and drew my eyes, and held them.

I must have made some sound, because Virgie looked around and saw me. I don't know what she thought. I didn't know anything for a long time, except that I was cold, as though some of the dead, black space outside had come in through the port somehow and touched me.

The shiny thing spun on the end of the silver chain, and the green-eyed baby watched it, and I watched it.

After that there was darkness, with me standing in the middle of it quite still, and cold, cold, cold!

Virgie's voice came through the darkness, calm, casual, as though none of it mattered at all.

"I've remembered who it is you made me think of, Mr. Goat," she said. "I'm afraid I was rather rude that day on Mars, but the resemblance puzzled me. Look."

A white object came into my shell of ice and blackness. It was a strong white hand, reddened across the knuckles with work, holding something in the palm. Something that burned with a clear, terrible light of its own. Her voice went on, so very quietly.

"This locket, Mr. Goat. It's ancient. Over three hundred years old. It belonged to an ancestor of mine, and the family has kept it ever since. It's rather a lovely story. She married a young spaceman. In those days, of course, space flight was still new and dangerous, and this young man loved it as much as he did his wife. His name was Stephen Vance. That's his picture. That's why I thought I had seen you somewhere before, and why I asked your name. I think the resemblance is quite striking, don't you?"

"Yes," I said. "Yes, it is."

"The girl is his wife, and of course, the original owner of the locket. He called her Missy. It's engraved on the back of the locket. Anyway, he had a chance to make the first flight from Mars to Jupiter, and Missy knew how much it meant to him. She knew that something of him would die if he didn't go, and so she let him. He didn't know how soon the baby they'd both wanted so much would arrive, for she didn't tell him that. Because she knew he wouldn't go if she did.

"So Stephen had two lockets made, this one and another just like it. He told her they'd make a link between them, he and Missy, that nothing could break. Sometime, somehow, he'd come back to her, no matter what happened. Then he went to Jupiter. He died there. His ship was never found.

"But Missy went on wearing the locket and praying. And when she died she gave it to her daughter. It grew into a sort of family tradition. That's why I have it now."

Her voice trailed off, drowsily, with a faint note of surprise. Her hand and the locket went away, and there was a great stillness all around me, a great peace.

I brought my arms up across my face. I stiffened, and I tried to say something, words I used to say a long, long time ago. They wouldn't come. They won't, when you go into the Beyond Place.

I took my hands away, and I could see again. I didn't touch the locket around my neck. I could feel it against my breast, like the cold of space, searing me.

Virgie lay at my feet. She still held the baby in the bend of one arm. Its round brown face was turned to hers, smiling a little. Brad lay beside them, with one arm flung across them both.

The locket lay on the gentle curve of Virgie's breast, face up, still open, rising and falling slowly to the lift of her breathing.

They don't suffer. Remember that. They don't suffer. They don't even know. They sleep, and their dreams are happy. Remember, please! Not one of them has suffered, or been afraid.

I stood alone in that silent ship. There were no stars beyond the port now, no little worlds riding the Belt. There was only a veil of light wrapped close around the ship, a soft web of green and purple and gold and blue spun on a shimmering gray woof that was no color at all, and held there with threads of scarlet.

There was the familiar dimming of the electrics inside the ship. The people slept on the broad deck. I could hear their breathing, soft and slow and peaceful. My aura burned like a golden cloud around me, and inside it my body beat and pulsed with life.

I looked down at the locket, at Missy's face. If you'd told me. Oh Missy, if you'd only told me, I could have saved you!

Virgie's red hair, dark and straight and heavy in her white

neck. Virgie's smoke-gray eyes, half open and dreaming. Missy's hair. Missy's eyes.

Mine. Part of my flesh, part of my bone, part of my blood. Part of the life that still beat and pulsed inside me.

Three hundred years.

"Oh, if I could only pray!" I thought.

I knelt down beside her. I put out my hand. The golden light came out of the flesh and veiled her face. I took my hand away and got up, slowly. More slowly than Gallery fell when he died.

The shimmer of the Veil was all through the ship, now. In the air, in every atom of its wood and metal. I moved in it, a shining golden thing, alive and young, in a silent, sleeping world.

Three hundred years, and Missy was dead, and now the locket had brought her back.

Did Judas feel like this when the rope tore the life out of him?

But Judas died.

I walked in silence, wrapped in my golden cloud, and my heartbeats shook me like the blows of a man's fist. A strong heart. A young, strong heart.

The ship swerved slowly, drawn out of its arc of free fall toward Jupiter. The auxiliaries had not been cut in yet for the Belt. The Veil just closed around the hull and drew it, easily.

It's just an application of will-power. Teleportation, the strength of mind and thought amplified by the X-crystals and directed like a radio beam. The release of energy between the force of thought and the force of gravity causes the light, the visible thing that spacemen call the Veil. The hypnotic sleep-impulse is sent the same way, through the X-crystals on Astellar.

Shirina says it's a simple thing, a child's trick, in its own space-time matrix. All it requires is a focal point to guide it, a special vibration it can follow like a torch in the void, such as the aura around flesh, human or not, that has bathed in the Cloud.

A Judas goat, to lead the sheep to slaughter.

I walked in my golden light. The pleasure of subtle energies pricked and flared across my skin. I was going home.

And Missy was still alive. Three hundred years, and she

was still alive. Her blood and mine, alive together in a girl named Virgie.

And I was taking her to Astellar, the world its own dimension didn't want.

I guess it was the stopping of the current across my skin that roused me, half an eternity later. My aura had paled to its normal faintness. I heard the faint grating ring of metal on stone, and I knew the *Queen of Jupiter* had made her last landing. I was home.

I was sitting on the edge of my own bunk. I didn't know how I got there. I was holding my head on my clenched fists, and when I opened them my own locket fell out. There was blood on my palms.

I got up and walked through the silence, through the hard impersonal glare of the electrics, to the nearest airlock, and went out.

The *Queen of Jupiter* lay in a rounded cradle of rock, worn smooth. Back at the top of the chute the space doors were closed, and the last echo of the air pumps was dying away against the low roof of the cavern. The rock is a pale translucent green, carved and polished into beauty that stabs you breathless, no matter how many times you see it.

Astellar is a little world, only about half the size of Vesta. Outside it's nothing but black slag, without even a trace of mineral to attract a tramp miner. When they want to they can bend the light around it so that the finest spacescope can't find it, and the same thought-force that makes the Veil can move Astellar where they wish it to go.

Since traffic through the Belt has grown fairly heavy, they haven't moved it much. They haven't had to.

I went across the cavern in the pale green light. There's a wide ramp that goes up from the floor like the sweep of an angel's wing. Flack was waiting for me near the foot of it, outlined in the faint gold of his aura.

"Hi, Steve," he said, and looked at the *Queen of Jupiter* with his queer gray eyes. His hair was as black as mine used to be, his skin space-burned dark and leathery. His eyes looked out of the darkness like pale spots of moonlight, faintly luminous and without a soul.

I knew Flack before he became one of us, and I thought then that he was less human than the Astellarians.

"A good haul this time, Steve?" he asked.

"Yeah." I tried to get past him. He caught my arm.

"Hey—what's eating you?" he said.

"Nothing."

I shook him off. He smiled and stepped in front of me. A big man, as big as Gallery and a lot tougher, with a mind that could meet mine on an equal footing.

"Don't give me that, Stevie. Something's—he-ey!" He pushed my chin up suddenly, and his pale eyes glowed and narrowed.

"What's this?" he said. "Tears?"

He stared at me a minute, slack-jawed, and then he began to laugh. I hit him.

3

Wages of Evil

Flack went sprawling backward onto the lucent stone. I went by him up the curve of the ramp. I went fast, but it was already too late.

The airlocks of the *Queen of Jupiter* opened behind me.

I stopped. I stopped the way Gallery did in the blowing Martian sand, slowly, dragging weights on my feet. I didn't want to. I didn't want to turn around, but there was nothing I could do about it. My body turned, by itself.

Flack was on his feet again, leaning up against the carved green wall, looking at me. Blood ran out over his lip and down his chin. He got out a handkerchief and held it over his mouth, and his eyes never left me, pale and still and glowing. The golden aura made a halo round his dark head, like the painting of a saint.

Beyond him the locks of the ship were open, and the people were coming out.

In their niche on the fourth level of Astellar the X-crystals were pulsing from pale gray to a black as endless and alien as the Coal Sack. Behind them was a mind, kindly and gentle, thinking, and the human cargo of the *Queen* heard its thoughts.

They came out of the locks, walking steadily but without haste. They formed into a loose column and came across the green translucent floor of the cavern and up the ramp. Walk-

ing easily, their breathing deep and quiet, their eyes half open
and full of dreams.

Up the long sweeping ribbon of pale green stone, past
Flack, past me, and into the hall beyond. They didn't see
anything but their dreams. They smiled a little. They were
happy, and not afraid.

Virgie still carried the baby, drowsing in her arms, and
Brad was still beside her. The locket had turned with her
movements, hiding the pictures, showing me only its silver
back.

I watched them go. The hall beyond the ramp was gem-cut
from milky crystal and inlaid with metals that came from another dimension, radioactive metals that filled the crystal
walls and the air between them with softened, misty fire.

They went slowly into the veil of mist and fire, and were
gone.

Flack spoke softly. "Steve."

I turned back toward the sound of his voice. There was a
strange blur over everything, but I could see the yellow glow
of his aura, the dark strength of him outlined against the pale
green rock. He hadn't moved. He hadn't taken his cold light
eyes away from me.

I had left my mind naked, unguarded, and I knew before
he spoke that Flack had read it.

He spoke through his bruised lips.

"You're thinking you won't go into the Cloud again, because of that girl," he whispered. "You're thinking there must
be some way to save her. But there isn't, and you wouldn't
save her if you could. And you'll go into the Cloud again,
Stevie. Twelve hours from now, when it's time, you'll walk
into the Cloud with the rest of us. And do you know why?"

His voice grew soft as the touch of a dove, with a sound of
laughter under it.

"Because you're afraid to die, Stevie, just like the rest of
us. Even me, Flack, the guy that never had a soul. I never
believed in any god but myself and I love life. But sometimes
I look at a corpse lying in the street of some human sinkhole
and curse it with all my heart because it didn't have to be
afraid.

"You'll go into the Cloud, because the Cloud is all that
keeps you alive. And you won't care about the red-haired
girl, Stevie. You wouldn't care if it was Missy herself giving

her life to you, because you're afraid. We're not human any longer, Steve. We've gone beyond. We've sinned—sins there aren't even any names for in this dimension. And no matter what we believe in, or deny, we're afraid.

"Afraid to die, Stevie. All of us. Afraid to die!"

His words frightened me. I couldn't forget them. I was remembering them even when I saw Shirina.

"I've found a new dimension, Stevie," Shirina said lazily. "A little one, between the Eighth and Ninth. It's so little we missed it before. We'll explore it, after the Cloud."

She led me in our favorite room. It was cut from a crystal so black and deep that it was like being in outer space, and if you looked long enough you could see strange nebulae, far off, and galaxies that never were except in dreams.

"How long before it's time?" I asked her.

"An hour, perhaps less. Poor Stevie. It'll be over soon, and you'll forget."

Her mind touched mine gently, with an intimate sweetness and comfort far beyond the touch of hands. She'd been doing that for hours, soothing the fever and the pain out of my thoughts. I lay without moving, sprawled on a couch so soft it was like a cloud. I could see the glow and shimmer of Shirina against the darkness without turning my head.

I don't know how to describe Shirina. Physically she was close enough to humanity. The differences in structure were more subtle than mere shape. They were—well, they were right, and exotic, and beautiful in a way there aren't any words for.

She, and her race, had no need of clothing. Their lazy, sinuous bodies had a fleecy covering that wasn't fur or feathers or tendrils but something of all three. They had no true color. They changed according to light, in an endless spectrum of loveliness that went far beyond the range you humans know.

Now, in the dark, Shirina's aura glowed like warm pearl. I could see her face, faintly, the queer peaked triangular bones covered with skin softer than a hummingbird's breast, the dead-black, bottomless eyes, the crest of delicate antennae tipped with tiny balls of light like diamonds burning under gauze.

Her thoughts clung around me gently. "There's no need to worry, Stevie," she was thinking. "The girl will go last. It's all arranged. You will enter the Cloud first of all, and there won't be the smallest vibration of her to touch you."

"But she'll touch somebody, Shirina," I groaned. "And it makes it all different, somehow, even with the others. Time doesn't seem to mean much. She's—she's like my own kid."

Shirina answered aloud, patiently. "But she isn't. Your daughter was born three hundred years ago. Three hundred years, that is, for your body. For you there isn't any reckoning. Time is different in every dimension. We've spent a thousand years in some of them, and more than that."

Yes. I could remember those alien years. Dimensional walls are no barrier to thought. You lie under the X-crystals and watch them pulse from mist-gray to depthless black. Your mind is sucked out of you and projected along a tight beam of carefully planned vibration, and presently you're in another space, another time.

You can take over any body that pleases you, for as long as you want. You can go between planets, between suns, between galaxies, just by thinking about it. You can see things, do things, taste experiences that all the languages of our space-time continuum put together have no words for.

Shirina and I had done a lot of wandering, a lot of seeing, and a lot of tasting. And the interlocking universes are infinite.

"I can't help worrying, Shirina," I told her. "I don't want to feel like this, but I can't help it. Right now I'm human. Just plain Steve Vance of Beverly Hills, California, on the planet Earth. I can't bear my memories."

My throat closed up. I was sick, and covered with cold sweat, and closer to going crazy than ever before in all my Satan-knows-how-many years.

Shirina's voice came through the darkness. It was like a bird-call, a flute, a ripple of water over stones, and like nothing that any of you ever heard or ever will hear.

"Stevie," she said. "Listen to me. You're not human any more. You haven't been human since the first time you walked in the Cloud. You have no more contact with those people than they have with the beasts they raise for slaughter."

"But I can't help remembering."

"All right. Remember, then. Remember how from birth you were different from other men. How you had to go on and out, to see things no man had ever seen before, to fight space itself with your heart and your ship and your two hands."

I could recall it. The first man to dare the Belt, the first man to see Jupiter blazing in his swarm of moons.

"That's why, when we caught you in the Veil and brought you to Astellar, we saved you from the Cloud. You had something rare—a strength, a sweep of vision and desire. You could give us something we wanted, an easier contact with human ships. And in return, we gave you life and freedom."

She paused, and added softly, "And myself, Stevie."

"Shirina!" A lot of things met and mingled in our thoughts. Emotions born of alien bodies we had shared. Memories of battle and beauty, of terror and love, under suns that never burned afterward, even in one's dreams. I can't explain it. There aren't any words.

"Shirina, help me!"

Shirina's mind cradled mine like a mother's arms.

"You weren't to blame in the beginning, Stevie. We did it to you under hypnosis, so that your brain could assimilate the change gradually, without shock. I led you myself into our world, like someone leading a child, and when you were finally freed, much time had passed. You had gone beyond humanity. Far beyond."

"I could have stopped. I could have refused to go into the Cloud again, when I knew what it was. I could have refused to be a Judas goat, leading the sheep to slaughter."

"Then why didn't you?"

"Because I had what I wanted," I said slowly. "What I'd always wanted and never had a name for. Power and freedom such as no man ever had. I liked having it. When I thought about you and the things we could do together, and the things I could do alone, I'd have led the whole solar system into the Veil, and be hanged to it."

I drew a harsh, tight breath and wiped the sweat from my palms.

"And besides, I didn't feel human any longer. I wouldn't hurt them any more than I'd have mistreated a dog when I was still a man. But I didn't belong to them anymore."

"Then why is it different now?"

"I don't know. It just is. When I think of Virgie going under the crystals, and me walking in the Cloud, it's too much."

"You've seen their bodies afterward," Shirina said gently. "Not one atom is touched or changed, and they smile. There's no easier or kinder death in Creation."

"I know," I said. "I know. But Virgie is my own."

She'd walk under the X-crystals, smiling, with her red hair dark and shining and her smoke-gray eyes half open and full of dreams. She'd still have the baby in her arms, and Brad would walk beside her. And the X-crystals would pulse and burn with black strange fires, and she would lie down, still smiling, and that would be all.

All, forever, for Virgie and Brad and the green-eyed Martian baby.

But the life that had been in their bodies, the force that no man has a name for that makes the breath and blood and heat of living flesh, the ultimate vibration of the human soul—that life-force would rise up from the crystals, up into the chamber of the Cloud. And Shirina, and Shirina's people, and the four other men like me that weren't human any longer, would walk in it so that we could live.

It hadn't really hit me before. It doesn't. You think of it at first but it doesn't mean anything. There's no semantic referent for "soul" or "ego" or "life-force." You don't see anything, you don't have any contact with the dead. You don't even think much of death.

All you know is you walk into a radiant Cloud, and you feel like a god, and you don't think of the human side of it because you aren't human any longer.

"No wonder they threw you out of your own dimension!" I cried out.

Shirina sighed. "They called us vampires; parasites—sybaritic monsters who lived only for sensation and pleasure. And they cast us into darkness. Well, perhaps they were right. I don't know. But we never hurt or frightened anyone, and when I think of the things they did to their own people, in blood and fear and hate, I'm terrified."

She rose and came and stood over me, glowing like warm pearl against the space-deep crystal. The tiny tips of diamond fire burned on her antennae, and her eyes were like black stars.

I put out my hands to her. She took them, and her touch

broke down my control. I was crying suddenly, not making any sound.

"Right or wrong, Stevie, you're one of us now," she said gently. "I'm sorry this happened. I would have spared you, if you'd let me put your mind to sleep until it was over. But you've got to understand that. You left them, the humans, behind you, and you can never, never go back."

After a long time I spoke. "I know, I understand."

I felt her sigh and shiver, and then she drew back, still holding my hands.

"It's time now, Stevie."

I got up, slowly, and then I stopped. Shirina caught her breath suddenly.

"Steve, my hands! You're hurting me!"

I let them go. "Flack," I said, not talking to anybody. "He knew my weakness. At root and base, no matter how much I talk, I'm going into the Cloud again because I'm afraid. That's why I'll always go into the Cloud when it's time. Because I've sinned so deeply I'm afraid to die."

"What is sin?" Shirina whispered.

"God knows. God only knows."

I brought her bird-soft body into my arms and kissed her, brushing my lips across the shining down of her cheek to her little crimson mouth. There was the faint, bitter taste of my tears in the kiss, and then I laughed, softly.

I pulled the chain and locket from around my neck and dropped them on the floor, and we went out together, to the Cloud.

4

Curtain of Darkness

We walked through the halls of Astellar, like people in the heart of a many-colored jewel. Halls of amber and amethyst and cinnabar, of dragon-green and gray the color of morning mist, and colors there are no names for in this dimension.

The others joined us, coming from the crystal cells where they spent their time. Shirina's people, velvet-eyed and gentle, with their crowns of fire-tipped antennae. They were like a living rainbow in the jewel-light of the halls.

Flack and myself and the three others—only five men, in

all the time Astellar had been in our dimension, with the kind
of minds Shirina's people wanted—wore our spaceman's
black, walking in our golden auras.

I saw Flack looking at me, but I didn't meet his eyes.

We came finally, to the place of the Cloud, in the center of
Astellar. The plain ebon-colored doors stood open. Beyond
them there was a mist like curdled sunshine, motes of pure,
bright, gilded radiance, coiling and dancing in a cloud of living light.

Shirina took my hand. I knew she wanted to keep me from
thinking about the place below, where still through hypnotic
command the men and women and children from the *Queen
of Jupiter* were walking under the X-crystals to their last long
sleep.

I held her, tightly, and we stepped through into the Cloud.

The light closed us in. We walked on something that was
not rock, nor anything tangible, but a vibration of force from
the X-crystals that held us on a tingling, buoyant web. And
the golden, living light clung to us, caressing, spilling over the
skin in tiny rippling waves of fire.

I was hungry for it. My body stretched, lifting up. I
walked on the vibrant web of power under my feet, my head
up, the breath stopped in my throat, every separate atom of
my flesh rejuvenated, throbbing and blazing and pulsing with
life.

Life!

And then it hit me.

I didn't want it to. I thought I had it down, down for good
where it couldn't bother me any more. I thought I'd made my
peace with whatever soul I'd had, or lost. I didn't want to
think.

But I did. It struck me, suddenly. Like a meteor crashing a
ship in space, like the first naked blaze of the sun when you
clear the Darkside peaks of Mercury. Like death, the ultimate, final thing you can't dodge or get around.

I knew what that life was and where it came from, and
how it had changed me.

It was Virgie. Virgie with her blasted red hair and her
smoke-gray eyes, and Missy's life in her, and mine. Why did
she have to be sent? Why did I have to meet her beside that
dead Martian, on the Jekkara Low-Canal?

But I had met her. And suddenly I knew. I knew!

I don't remember what I did. I must have wrenched loose from Shirina's hand. I felt her startled thought touch my brain, and then it broke away and I was running through the golden Cloud, toward the exit beyond. Running without control, running at top speed.

I think I tried to scream. I don't know. I was clean crazy. But I can remember even then that I sensed somebody running beside me, pacing me through the brilliant blindness of the Cloud.

I plunged out into the hall beyond. It was blue like still deep water, and empty. I ran. I didn't want to run. Some sane corner of my mind cried out to Shirina for help, but she couldn't get through the shrieking chaos of the rest of it. I ran.

And somebody ran behind me. I didn't turn around. I didn't care. I hardly knew it. But somebody ran behind me, on long fleet legs.

Down the blue hall, and into another one that was all flame-color shot with gray, and down that to a curving ramp cut from dark amber that dropped to the level below.

The level where the X-crystals were.

I rushed down the amber path, bounding like a stag with the hounds close behind, through a crystal silence that threw the sound of my breathing back at me, harsh and tearing. There was a circular place at the bottom of the ramp where four hallways met, a place jewel-carved in somber, depthless purple.

I came into it, and from three of the hall mouths men stepped out to meet me. Men with young faces and snow-white hair, and naked bodies burning gold against the purple.

I stopped in the center of the floor. I heard bare feet racing on the ramp behind me, and I knew without looking who it was.

Flack. He circled and fixed me with his cold strange eyes, like moonlight in his dark face. Somewhere he had found a blaster.

He held it on me. Not on my head or heart, but at my middle.

"I thought you might blow your top, Stevie," he said. "So we kind of stood by, in case you'd try something."

I stood still. I didn't have any feelings. I was beyond that. I was crazy—clean, stark crazy, thinking of time and the crystals pulsing just beyond my reach.

"Get out of my way," I warned him.

Flack smiled. There was no humor in it. The three men moved in a little behind him. They looked at Flack and they looked at me, and they didn't like any of it, but they were afraid.

Afraid to die, like all of us. Even Flack, who never had a soul.

Flack acted like someone being patient with a naughty child.

"Will you come back with us, Stevie, or do I blow your insides out, here and now?" he asked me.

I looked at his cold, queer eyes. "You'd like that."

"Yeah." He ran the red tip of his tongue over his swollen lips. "Yeah. But I'm letting you choose."

"All right," I said. "All right, I'll choose."

I was crazy. I jumped him.

I hit him first with my mind. Flack was strong, but I was fifty years older in the Cloud than he was, and Shirina had taught me things. I gathered all the force I had and let him have it, and he had to marshal his own thought-force to fight it off, so that for a second he couldn't manage the blaster with his conscious mind.

Instinctive reflex sent a crimson stream of deadly power smoking past me when I dived in low. It seared my skin, but that was all.

We fell, threshing, on the purple stone. Flack was strong. He was bigger than I, and heavier, and viciously mean. He beat most of the sense out of me, but I had caught his gun wrist and wouldn't let go. The three others took their golden auras back a little toward the hall mouths, afraid the blaster might let off and hit them.

They thought Flack could handle me, and they were afraid. So they drew back and used their minds on me, trying to hammer me down.

I don't know yet why they couldn't. I guess it was because of a lot of things, Shirina's teaching, my greater age, and the fact that I wasn't thinking consciously of anything. I was just a thing that had started some place and was going through.

Sometimes I wish they had broken me. Sometimes I wish Flack had burned me down on the purple stone.

I shook off their thought-blows. I took the pounding of Flack's big fist and the savaging of his feet and knees, and put all my strength into bending his arm. I yanked it away from me, and up and around where I wanted it.

I got it there. He made his last play. He broke his heart on it, and it didn't do him any good. I saw his eyes, stretched wide in his dark face. I can still see them.

I got my finger past his and pressed the firing stud.

I got up and walked across the floor, carrying the blaster. The three others spread out, warily, ringing me. Naked men glowing gold against the purple stone, their eyes hard, animal-bright with fear.

I blasted one through the head just as his muscles tensed for the leap. The others came in, fast. They knocked me down, and time was passing, and the people walking slowly under the crystals with dreams in their eyes.

I kicked one man under the jaw and broke his neck, and the other tried to take the gun away. I had just come from the Cloud, and he hadn't. I was strong with the life that pulsed up from the X-crystals. I forced his arms back and pressed the stud again, trying not to see his eyes.

And these were my friends. Men I drank and laughed with, and went with sometimes to worlds beyond this universe.

I went on, down a hall the color of a Martian dawn. I was empty. I didn't feel or think. There was a pain a long way off, and blood in my mouth, but such things didn't matter.

I came to the place where the crystals were and stopped.

A lot of them had walked under the crystals. Almost half of the five hundred families from the *Queen of Jupiter*. They lay still on the black floor, and there was plenty of room. They didn't crowd the others coming after them, a slow, quiet stream of human beings with dreams in their eyes.

The crystals hung in a wide circle, tilting slightly inward. They pulsed with a blackness that was beyond mere dark, a negative thing as blazing and tangible as sunlight. The angle of tilt and the tuning of the facets against one another made the difference in the result, whether projecting the Veil, or motive power, or hypnosis, or serving as a gateway to another time and space.

Or sucking the power of life from human bodies.

I could see the pale shimmer of force in the center, a sort

of vortex between the limitless, burning, black facets that rose from the quiet bodies to the chamber of the Cloud above.

I could see the faces of the dead. They were still smiling.

The controls were on the other side. I ran. I was dead inside, as dead as the corpses on the floor, but I ran. I remember thinking it was funny to run when you were dead. I kept on the outside of the crystals and ran with all my strength to the controls.

I saw Virgie. She was way back in the procession, and she was just as I knew she'd be, with Brad beside her and the green-eyed baby still in her arms, asleep.

Virgie, with her gleaming red hair and Missy's eyes!

I grabbed the controls and wrenched them over, and the shimmering vortex disappeared. I spun the great hexagonal wheel and notched it for full-power hypnosis, and ran out onto the floor, among the dead.

I told the living what to do. I didn't waken them. They turned and went back the way they came, back toward the *Queen of Jupiter*, running hard and still smiling, still not afraid.

I went back to the wheel and turned it again, to a notch marked in their danger-color, and then I followed the last of the humans into the hall. At the doorway I turned and raised my blaster.

I saw Shirina standing under the radiant blackness of the crystals, halfway around the curving wall.

I felt her mind touch mine, and then drew back, slowly, the way you take your hand away from someone you loved that has just died. I looked at her eyes. I had to.

Why did I do what I did? What did I care about red hair and smoke-gray eyes, and the three-hundred-year diluted blood of a girl named Missy? I wasn't human any longer. What did I care?

We were apart, Shirina and I. We had gone away from each other and we couldn't touch, even to say good-bye. I caught a faint echo of her thought.

"Oh, Stevie, there were still so many things to do!"

Her great luminous black eyes shining with tears, her jewel-tipped antennae dulled and drooping. And yet I knew what she was going to do.

I couldn't see the crystals, suddenly. I couldn't see anything. I knew there was never going to be anything I wanted to see again. I raised the blaster and fired it full power into one of the hanging crystals, and then I ran.

I felt the bolt of Shirina's lethal thought strike my brain, and weaken, and shatter on something in her own mind, at its source. I ran, a dead thing going on leaden feet, in a halo of golden light.

Behind me the X-crystals, upset by the blaster in their fullest sympathy of power, began to split and crack and tear the world of Astellar to bits.

I don't know much about what happened. I ran and ran, on the heels of the humans who still lived, but I was beyond thinking or feeling. I have vague memories of hallways lined with cells of jewel-toned crystal, halls of amber and amethyst and cinnabar, of dragon-green and gray the color of morning mist, and colors there are no names for in this dimension.

Hallways that cracked and split behind me, falling in upon themselves, shards of broken rainbows. And above that the scream of power from the X-crystals, wrenching and tearing at Astellar.

Then something I heard with my mind, and not my ears. Shirina's people, dying in the wreckage.

My mind was stunned, but not stunned enough. I could still hear. I can still hear.

The *Queen of Jupiter* was safe. The outward-moving vibration hadn't reached her yet. We got aboard her, and I opened the space doors and blasted her off myself, because the skipper and the first and second officers were asleep for good on Astellar.

I didn't watch the death of Astellar. Only after a long time I looked back, and it was gone, and there was only a cloud of bright dust shimmering in the raw sunlight.

I set the Iron Mike for Space Authority headquarters on Mars and turned on the automatic AC warning beam. Then I left the *Queen of Jupiter* in the Number 4 lifeboat, B deck.

That's where I am now, writing this, somewhere between Mars and the Belt. I didn't see Virgie before I went. I didn't see any of them, but especially Virgie. They'll be awake now. I hope their lives are worth what they cost.

Astellar is gone. The Veil is gone. You don't have to be afraid any more. I'm going to put this manuscript in a message rocket and send it on, so you'll know you don't have to fear. I don't know why I care.

I don't know why I'm writing this at all, unless—Bosh, I know! Why lie? At this stage of the game, why lie?

I'm alive now. I'm a young man. But the Cloud that kept me that way is gone, and presently I shall grow old, too old, very quickly, and die. And I'm afraid to die.

Somewhere in the solar system there must be somebody willing to pray for me. They used to teach me, when I was a kid, that prayer helped. I want somebody to pray for my soul, because I can't do it for myself.

If I were glad of what I've done, if I had changed, perhaps then I could pray.

But I've gone beyond humanity, and I can't turn back.

Maybe prayer doesn't matter. Maybe there's nothing beyond death but oblivion. I hope so! If I could only stop being, stop thinking, stop remembering.

I hope to all the gods of all the universes that death is the end. But I don't know, and I'm afraid.

Afraid. Judas—Judas—Judas! I betrayed two worlds, and there couldn't be a hell deeper than the one I live in now. And still I'm afraid.

Why? Why should I care what happens to me? I destroyed Astellar. I destroyed Shirina, whom I loved better than anything in Creation. I destroyed my friends, my comrades—and I have destroyed myself.

And you're not worth it. Not all the human cattle that breed in the solar system were worth Astellar, and Shirina, and the things we did beyond space and time, together.

Why did I give Missy that locket?

Why did I have to meet Virgie, with her red hair?

Why did I remember? Why did I care? Why did I do what I did?

Why was I ever born?

SANITY

Astounding,
April

by Fritz Leiber (1910-   )

Although he appeared much more frequently in the fantasy markets (especially Unknown *and* Weird Tales) *during the first half of the 1940's, Fritz Leiber also published an occasional science fiction story. However, his surge to the forefront of the sf world would have to await the 1950's.*

"Sanity" is particularly interesting because of its moral viewpoint. While it is true that many science fiction writers were anti-militarist and bemoaned the destructiveness of war, relatively few of them allowed any strong pacifist viewpoints to emerge in their stories—after all, they were publishing in magazines that still emphasized action and adventure to a considerable extent, with the partial exception of Astounding. *In addition, the Nazi threat was so great and the war against fascism so just, that almost all writers tended to support the Allied war effort.*

However, Fritz Leiber was so appalled by the destruction that he struck out against the horrors of all wars in this strong story, and in others as well.

(I must pick up Marty's phrase, "the Nazi threat was so great and the war against fascism so just." That's true. Marty didn't live through it and just knows what he reads, he being a young squirt. I, however, lived through it, and remembered the despair and terror of the years in which it seemed that vicious tyrannies were advancing each year. And yet in the long run, the worst thing Hitler did was to make war seem a necessary thing. There is enormous honor we must pay, then, to those who

93

*saw, even in the midst of the special exception, the
general truth that war is evil, and who did so before
the coming of the nuclear bomb made the fact apparent to all but the meanest intelligences.—I.A.)*

"Come in, Phy, and make yourself comfortable."

The mellow voice—and the suddenly dilating doorway—
caught the general secretary of the World playing with a blob
of greenish gasoid, squeezing it in his fist and watching it
ooze between his fingers in spatulate tendrils that did not dis-
sipate. Slowly, crookedly, he turned his head. World Manager
Carrsbury became aware of a gaze that was at once oafish,
sly, vacuous. Abruptly the expression was replaced by a nervous smile. The thin man straightened himself, as much as his
habitually drooping shoulders would permit, hastily entered,
and sat down on the extreme edge of a pneumatically form-fit-
ting chair.

He embarrassedly fumbled the blob of gasoid, looking
around for a convenient disposal vent or a crevice in the
upholstery. Finding none, he stuffed it hurriedly into his
pocket. Then he repressed his fidgetings by clasping his hands
resolutely together, and sat with downcast eyes.

"How are you feeling, old man?" Carrsbury asked in a
voice that was warm with a benign friendliness.

The general secretary did not look up.

"Anything bothering you, Phy?" Carrsbury continued solic-
itously. "Do you feel a bit unhappy, or dissatisfied, about
your . . . er . . . transfer, now that the moment has arrived?"

Still the general secretary did not respond. Carrsbury
leaned forward across the dully silver, semicircular desk and,
in his most winning tones, urged, "Come on, old fellow, tell
me all about it."

The general secretary did not lift his head, but he rolled up
his strange, distant eyes until they were fixed directly on
Carrsbury. He shivered a little, his body seemed to contract,
and his bloodless hands tightened their interlocking grip.

"I know," he said in a low, effortful voice. "You think I'm
insane."

Carrsbury sat back, forcing his brows to assume a baffled frown under the mane of silvery hair.

"Oh, you needn't pretend to be puzzled," Phy continued, swiftly now that he had broken the ice. "You know what that word means as well as I do. Better—even though we both had to do historical research to find out."

"Insane," he repeated dreamily, his gaze wavering. "Significant departure from the norm. Inability to conform to basic conventions underlying all human conduct."

"Nonsense!" said Carrsbury, rallying and putting on his warmest and most compelling smile. "I haven't the slightest idea of what you're talking about. That you're a little tired, a little strained, a little distraught—that's quite understandable, considering the burden you've been carrying, and a little rest will be just the thing to fix you up, a nice long vacation away from all this. But as for your being . . . why, ridiculous!"

"No," said Phy, his gaze pinning Carrsbury. "You think I'm insane. You think all my colleagues in the World Management Service are insane. That's why you're having us replaced with those men you've been training for ten years in your Institute of Political Leadership—ever since, with my help and connivance, you became World manager."

Carrsbury retreated before the finality of the statement. For the first time his smile became a bit uncertain. He started to say something, then hesitated and looked at Phy, as if half hoping he would go on.

But that individual was once again staring rigidly at the floor.

Carrsbury leaned back, thinking. When he spoke it was in a more natural voice, much less consciously soothing and fatherly.

"Well, all right, Phy. But look here, tell me something, honestly. Won't you—and the others—be a lot happier when you've been relieved of all your responsibilities?"

Phy nodded somberly. "Yes," he said, "we will . . . but"—his face became strained—"you see—"

"But—?" Carrsbury prompted.

Phy swallowed hard. He seemed unable to go on. He had gradually slumped toward one side of the chair, and the pressure had caused the green gasoid to ooze from his pocket. His long fingers crept over and kneaded it fretfully.

Carrsbury stood up and came around the desk. His sympathetic frown, from which perplexity had ebbed, was not quite genuine.

"I don't see why I shouldn't tell you all about it now, Phy," he said simply. "In a queer sort of way I owe it all to you. And there isn't any point now in keeping it a secret . . . there isn't any danger—"

"Yes," Phy agreed with a quick bitter smile, "you haven't been in any danger of a *coup d'état* for some years now. If ever we should have revolted, there'd have been"—his gaze shifted to a point in the opposite wall where a faint vertical crease indicated the presence of a doorway—"your secret police."

Carrsbury started. He hadn't thought Phy had known. Disturbingly, there loomed in his mind a phrase *The cunning of the insane*. But only for a moment. Friendly complacency flooded back. He went behind Phy's chair and rested his hands on the sloping shoulders.

"You know, I've always had a special feeling toward you, Phy," he said, "and not only because your whims made it a lot easier for me to become World manager. I've always felt that you were different from the others, that there were times when—" He hesitated.

Phy squirmed a little under the friendly hands. "When I had my moments of sanity?" he finished flatly.

"Like now," said Carrsbury softly, after a nod the other could not see. "I've always felt that sometimes, in a kind of twisted, unrealistic way, you *understood*. And that has meant a lot to me. I've been alone, Phy, dreadfully alone, for ten whole years. No companionship anywhere, not even among the men I've been training in the Institute of Political Leadership—for I've had to play a part with them too, keep them in ignorance of certain facts, for fear they would try to seize power over my head before they were sufficiently prepared. No companionship anywhere, except for my hopes—and for occasional moments with you. Now that it's over and a new regime is beginning for us both, I can tell you that. And I'm glad."

There was a silence. Then—Phy did not look around, but one lean hand crept up and touched Carrsbury's. Carrsbury cleared his throat. Strange, he thought, that there could be even a momentary rapport like this between the sane and the insane. But it was so.

He disengaged his hands, strode rapidly back to his desk, turned.

"I'm a throwback, Phy," he began in a new, unused, eager voice. "A throwback to a time when human mentality was far sounder. Whether my case was due chiefly to heredity, or to certain unusual accidents of environment, or to both, is unimportant. The point is that a person had been born who was in a position to criticize the present state of mankind in the light of the past, to diagnose its condition, and to begin its cure. For a long time I refused to face the facts, but finally my researches—especially those in the literature of the twentieth century—left me no alternative. The mentality of mankind had become—aberrant. Only certain technological advances, which had resulted in making the business of living infinitely easier and simpler, and the fact that war had been ended with the creation of the present world state, were staving off the inevitable breakdown of civilization. But only staving it off—delaying it. The great masses of mankind had become what would once have been called hopelessly neurotic. Their leaders had become . . . you said it first, Phy . . . insane. Incidentally, this latter phenomenon—the drift of psychological aberrants toward leadership—has been noted in all ages."

He paused. Was he mistaken, or was Phy following his words with indications of a greater mental clarity than he had ever noted before, even in the relatively nonviolent World secretary? Perhaps—he had often dreamed wistfully of the possibility—there was still a chance of saving Phy. Perhaps, if he just explained to him clearly and calmly—

"In my historical studies," he continued, "I soon came to the conclusion that the crucial period was that of the Final Amnesty, concurrent with the founding of the present world state. We are taught that at that time there were released from confinement millions of political prisoners—and millions of others. Just who were those others? To this question, our present histories gave only vague and platitudinous answers. The semantic difficulties I encountered were exceedingly obstinate. But I kept hammering away. Why, I asked myself, have such words as insanity, lunacy, madness, psychosis, disappeared from our vocabulary—and the concepts behind them from our thought? Why has the subject 'abnormal psychology' disappeared from the curricula of our schools? Of greater significance, why is our modern psychology strikingly similar to the field of abnormal psychology as taught in the twentieth century, and to that field alone? Why are there no longer, as there were in the twentieth century, any institutions for the confinement and care of the psychologically aberrant?"

Phy's head jerked up. He smiled twistedly. "Because," he whispered slyly, "everyone's insane now."

The cunning of the insane. Again that phrase loomed warningly in Carrsbury's mind. But only for a moment. He nodded.

"At first I refused to make that deduction. But gradually I reasoned out the why and wherefore of what had happened. It wasn't only that a highly technological civilization had subjected mankind to a wider and more swiftly tempoed range of stimulations, conflicting suggestions, mental strains, emotional wrenchings. In the literature of twentieth century psychiatry there are observations on a kind of psychosis that results from success. An unbalanced individual keeps going so long as he is fighting something, struggling toward a goal. He reaches his goal—and goes to pieces. His repressed confusions come to the surface, he realizes that he doesn't know what he wants at all, his energies hitherto engaged in combating something outside himself are turned against himself, he is destroyed. Well, when war was finally outlawed, when the whole world became one unified state, when social inequality was abolished . . . you see what I'm driving at?"

Phy nodded slowly. "That," he said in a curious, distant voice, "is a very interesting deduction."

"Having reluctantly accepted my main premise," Carrsbury went on, "everything became clear. The cyclic six-months' fluctuations in world credit—I realized at once that Morganstern of Finance must be a manic-depressive with a six-months' phase, or else a dual personality with one aspect a spendthrift, the other a miser. It turned out to be the former. Why was the Department of Cultural Advancement stagnating? Because Manager Hobart was markedly catatonic. Why the boom in Extraterrestrial Research? Because McElvy was euphoric."

Phy looked at him wonderingly. "But naturally," he said, spreading his lean hands, from one of which the gasoid dropped like a curl of green smoke.

Carrsbury glanced at him sharply. He replied. "Yes, I know that you and several of the others have a certain warped awareness of the differences between your . . . personalities, though none whatsoever of the basic aberration involved in them all. But to get on. As soon as I realized the situation, my course was marked out. As a sane man, capable of entertaining fixed realistic purposes, and surrounded by individuals of whose inconsistencies and delusions it was easy to make use, I was in a position to attain, with time and tact, any goal at which I might aim. I was already in the Managerial Service. In three years I became World manager. Once there, my range of influence was vastly enhanced. Like the man in Archimedes' epigram, I had a place to stand from which I could move the world. I was able, in various guises and on various pretexts, to promulgate regulations the actual purpose of which was to soothe the great neurotic masses by curtailing upsetting stimulations and introducing a more regimented and orderly program of living. I was able, by humoring my fellow executives and making the fullest use of my greater capacity for work, to keep world affairs staggering along fairly safely—at least stave off the worst. At the same time I was able to begin my Ten Years' Plan—the training, in comparative isolation, first in small numbers, then in larger, as those instructed could in turn become instructors, of a group of prospective leaders carefully selected on the basis of their relative freedom from neurotic tendencies."

"But that—" Phy began rather excitedly, starting up.

"But what?" Carrsbury inquired quickly.

"Nothing," muttered Phy dejectedly, sinking back.

"That about covers it," Carrsbury concluded, his voice suddenly grown a little duller. "Except for one secondary matter. I couldn't afford to let myself go ahead without any protection. Too much depended on me. There was always the risk of being wiped out by some ill-co-ordinated but none the less effective spasm of violence, momentarily uncontrollable by tact, on the part of my fellow executives. So, only because I could see no alternative, I took a dangerous step. I created"—his glance strayed toward the faint crease in the side wall—"my secret police. There is a type of insanity known as paranoia, an exaggerated suspiciousness involving delusions of persecution. By means of the late twentieth century Rand technique of hypnotism, I inculcated a number of these unfortunate individuals with the fixed idea that their lives depended on me and that I was threatened from all sides and must be protected at all costs. A distasteful expedient, even though it served its purpose. I shall be glad, very glad to see it discontinued. You can understand, can't you, why I had to take that step?"

He looked questioningly at Phy—and became aware with a shock that that individual was grinning at him vacuously and holding up the gasoid between two fingers.

"I cut a hole in my couch and a lot of this stuff came out," Phy explained in a thick naive voice. "Ropes of it got all over my office. I kept tripping." His fingers patted at it deftly, sculpturing it into the form of a hideous transparent green head, which he proceeded to squeeze out of existence. "Queer stuff," he rambled on. "Rarefied liquid. Gas of fixed volume. And all over my office floor, tangled up with the furniture."

Carrsbury leaned back and shut his eyes. His shoulders slumped. He felt suddenly a little weary, a little eager for his day of triumph to be done. He knew he shouldn't be despondent because he had failed with Phy. After all, the main victory was won. Phy was the merest of side issues. He had always known that, except for flashes, Phy was hopeless as the rest. Still—

"You don't need to worry about your office floor, Phy," he said with a listless kindliness. "Never any more. Your successor will have to see about cleaning it up. Already, you know, to all intents and purposes, you have been replaced."

"That's just it!" Carrsbury started at Phy's explosive loudness. The World secretary jumped up and strode toward him, pointing an excited hand. "That's what I came to see you about! That's what I've been trying to tell you! I can't be replaced like that! None of the others can, either! It won't work! You can't do it!"

With a swiftness born of long practice, Carrsbury slipped behind his desk. He forced his features into that expression of calm, smiling benevolence of which he had grown unutterably weary.

"Now, now, Phy," he said brightly, soothingly, "if I can't

do it, of course I can't do it. But don't you think you ought to tell me why? Don't you think it would be very nice to sit down and talk it all over and you tell me why?"

Phy halted and hung his head, abashed.

"Yes, I guess it would," he said slowly, abruptly falling back into the low, effortful tones. "I guess I'll have to. I guess there just isn't any other way. I had hoped, though, not to have to tell you everything." The last sentence was half question. He looked up wheedlingly at Carrsbury. The latter shook his head, continuing to smile. Phy went back and sat down.

"Well," he finally began, gloomily kneading the gasoid, "it all began when you first wanted to be World manager. You weren't the usual type, but I thought it would be kind of fun—yes, and kind of helpful." He looked up at Carrsbury. "You've really done the world a lot of good in quite a lot of ways, always remember that," he assured him. "Of course," he added, again focusing the tortured gasoid, "they weren't exactly the ways you thought."

"No?" Carrsbury prompted automatically. *Humor him. Humor him.* The worn-out refrain droned in his mind.

Phy sadly shook his head. "Take those regulations you promulgated to soothe people—"

"Yes?"

"—they kind of got changed on the way. For instance, your prohibition, regarding reading tapes, of all exciting literature . . . oh, we tried a little of the soothing stuff you suggested at first. Everyone got a great kick out of it. They laughed and laughed. But afterwards, well, as I said, it kind of got changed—in this case to a prohibition of all *unexciting* literature."

Carrsbury's smile broadened. For a moment the edge of his mind had toyed with a fear, but Phy's last remark had banished it.

"Every day I coast past several reading stands," Carrsbury said gently. "The fiction tapes offered for sale are always in the most chastely and simply colored containers. None of those wild and lurid pictures that one used to see everywhere."

"But did you ever buy one and listen to it? Or project the visual text?" Phy questioned apologetically.

"For ten years I've been a very busy man," Carrsbury answered. "Of course I've read the official reports regarding such matters, and at times glanced through sample resumes of taped fiction."

"Oh, sure, that sort of official stuff," agreed Phy, glancing up at the wall of tape files beyond the desk. "What we did, you see, was to keep the monochrome containers but go back to the old kind of contents. The contrast kind of tickled people. Remember, as I said before, a lot of your regulations have done good. Cut out a lot of unnecessary noise and inefficient foolishness, for one thing."

That sort of official stuff. The phrase lingered unpleasantly in Carrsbury's ears. There was a trace of irrepressible suspicion in his quick over-the-shoulder glance at the tiered tape files.

"Oh, yes," Phy went on, "and that prohibition against yielding to unusual or indecent impulses, with a long listing of specific categories. It went into effect all right, but with a little rider attached: 'unless you really want to.' That seemed absolutely necessary, you know." His fingers worked furiously with the gasoid. "As for the prohibition of various stimulating beverages—well, in this locality they're still served under other names, and an interesting custom has grown up of behaving very soberly while imbibing them. Now when we come to that matter of the eight-hour working day—"

Almost involuntarily, Carrsbury had got up and walked over to the outer wall. With a flip of his hand through an invisible U-shaped beam, he switched on the window. It was as if the outer wall had disappeared. Through its near-perfect transparency, he peered down with fierce curiosity past the sleekly gleaming facades to the terraces and parkways below.

The modest throngs seemed quiet and orderly enough. But then there was a scurry of confusion—a band of people, at this angle all tiny heads with arms and legs, came out from a shop far below and began to pelt another group with what looked like foodstuffs. While, on a side parkway, two small ovoid vehicles, seamless drops of silver because their vision panels were invisible from the outside, butted each other playfully. Someone started to run.

Carrsbury hurriedly switched off the window and turned around. Those were just off-chance occurrences, he told himself angrily. Of no real statistical significance whatever. For ten years mankind had steadily been trending toward sanity despite occasional relapses. He'd seen it with his own eyes, seen the day-by-day program—at least enough to know. He'd been a fool to let Phy's ramblings effect him—only tired nerves had made that possible.

He glanced at his timepiece.

"Excuse me," he said curtly, striding past Phy's chair, "I'd like to continue this conversation, but I have to get along to the first meeting of the new Central Managerial Staff."

"Oh but you can't!" Instantly Phy was up and pulling at his arm. "You just can't do it, you know! It's impossible!"

The pleading voice rose toward a scream. Impatiently Carrsbury tried to shake loose. The seam in the side wall widened, became a doorway. Instantly both of them stopped struggling.

In the doorway stood a cadaverous giant of a man with a stubby dark weapon in his hand. Straggly black beard shaded into gaunt cheeks. His face was a cruel blend of suspicion and fanatical devotion, the first directed along with the weapon at Phy, the second—and the somnambulistic eyes—at Carrsbury.

"He was threatening you?" the bearded man asked in a harsh voice, moving the weapon suggestively.

For a moment an angry, vindictive light glinted in Carrsbury's eyes. Then it flicked out. What could he have been thinking, he asked himself. This poor lunatic World secretary was no one to hate.

"Not at all, Hartman," he remarked calmly. "We were discussing something and we became excited and allowed our voices to rise. Everything is quite all right."

"Very well," said the bearded man doubtfully, after a pause. Reluctantly he returned his weapon to its holster, but he kept his hand on it and remained standing in the doorway.

"And now," said Carrsbury, disengaging himself, "I must go."

He had stepped on to the corridor slidewalk and had coasted halfway to the elevator before he realized that Phy had followed him and was plucking timidly at his sleeve.

"You can't go off like this," Phy pleaded urgently, with an apprehensive backward glance. Carrsbury noted that Hartman had also followed—an ominous pylon two paces to the rear. "You must give me a chance to explain, to tell you why, just like you asked me."

Humor him. Carrsbury's mind was deadly tired of the drone, but mere weariness prompted him to dance to it a little longer. "You can talk to me in the elevator," he conceded, stepping off the slidewalk. His finger flipped through a U-beam and a serpentine movement of light across the wall traced the elevator's obedient rise.

"You see, it wasn't just that matter of prohibitory regulations," Phy launched out hurriedly. "There were lots of other things that never did work out like your official reports indicated. Departmental budgets for instance. The reports showed, I know, that appropriations for Extraterrestrial Research were being regularly slashed. Actually, in your ten years of office, they increased tenfold. Of course, there was no way for you to know that. You couldn't be all over the world at once and see each separate launching of supra-stratospheric rockets."

The moving light became stationary. A seam dilated. Carrsbury stepped into the elevator. He debated sending Hartman back. Poor babbling Phy was no menace. Still—*the cunning of the insane.* He decided against it, reached out and flipped the control beam at the sector which would bring them to the hundredth and top floor. The door snipped softly shut. The cage became a surging darkness in which floor numerals winked softly. Twenty-one. Twenty-two. Twenty-three.

"And then there was the Military Service. You had it sharply curtailed."

"Of course I did." Sheer weariness stung Carrsbury into talk. "There's only one country in the world. Obviously, the only military requirement is an adequate police force. To say nothing of the risks involved in putting weapons into the hands of the present world population."

"I know," Phy's answer came guiltily from the darkness. "Still, what's happened is that, unknown to you, the Military Service has been increased in size, and recently four rocket squadrons have been added."

Fifty-seven. Fifty-eight. *Humor him.* "Why?"

"Well, you see we've found out that Earth is being reconnoitered. Maybe from Mars. Maybe hostile. Have to be prepared. We didn't tell you . . . well, because we were afraid it might excite you."

The voice trailed off. Carrsbury shut his eyes. How long, he asked himself, how long? He realized with dull surprise that in the last hour people like Phy, endured for ten years, had become unutterably weary to him. For the moment even the thought of the conference over which he would soon be presiding, the conference that was to usher in a sane world, failed to stir him. Reaction to success? To the end of a ten years' tension?

"Do you know how many floors there are in this building?"

Carrsbury was not immediately conscious of the new note in Phy's voice, but he reacted to it.

"One hundred," he replied promptly.

"Then," asked Phy, "just where are we?"

Carrsbury opened his eyes to the darkness. One hundred twenty-seven, blinked the floor numeral. One hundred twenty-eight. One hundred twenty-nine.

Something cold dragged at Carrsbury's stomach, pulled at his brain. He felt as if his mind were being slowly and irresistibly twisted. He thought of hidden dimensions, of unsuspected holes in space. Something remembered from elementary physics danced through his thoughts: If it were possible for an elevator to keep moving upward with uniform acceleration, no one inside an elevator could determine whether the effects they were experiencing were due to acceleration or to gravity—whether the elevator was standing motionless on some planet or shooting up at ever increasing velocity through free space.

One hundred forty-one. One hundred forty-two.

"Or as if you were rising through consciousness into an unsuspected realm of mentality lying above," suggested Phy in his new voice, with its hint of gentle laughter.

One hundred forty-six. One hundred forty-seven. It was slowing now. One hundred forty-nine. One hundred fifty. It had stopped.

This was some trick. The thought was like cold water in Carrsbury's face. Some cunning childish trick of Phy's. An easy thing to hocus the numerals. Carrsbury groped about in the darkness, encountered the slick surface of a holster, Hartman's gaunt frame.

"Get ready for a surprise," Phy warned from close at his elbow.

As Carrsbury turned and grabbed, bright sunlight drenched him, followed by a gripping, heart-stopping spasm of vertigo.

He, Hartman, and Phy, along with a few insubstantial bits of furnishings and controls, were standing in the air fifty stories above the hundred-story summit of World Managerial Center.

For a moment he grabbed frantically at nothing. Then he realized they were not falling and his eyes began to trace the hint of walls and ceiling and floor and, immediately below them, the ghost of a shaft.

Phy nodded. "That's all there is to it," he assured Carrsbury casually. "Just another of those charmingly odd modern notions against which you have legislated so persistently—like our incomplete staircases and roads to nowhere. The Buildings and Grounds Committee decided to extend the range of the elevator for sightseeing purposes. The shaft was made air-transparent to avoid spoiling the form of the original building and to improve the view. This was achieved so satisfactorily that an electronic warning system had to be installed for the safety of passing airjets and other craft. Treating the surfaces of the cage like windows was an obvious detail."

He paused and looked quizzically at Carrsbury. "All very simple," he observed, "but don't you find a kind of symbolism in it? For ten years now you've been spending most of your life in that building below. Every day you've used this elevator. But not once have you dreamed of these fifty extra stories. Don't you think that something of the same sort may be true of your observations of other aspects of contemporary social life?"

Carrsbury gaped at him stupidly.

Phy turned to watch the growing speck of an approaching aircraft. "You might look at it too," he remarked to Carrsbury, "for it's going to transport you to a far happier, more restful life."

Carrsbury parted his lips, wet them. "But—" he said, unsteadily. "But—"

Phy smiled. "That's right, I didn't finish my explanation. Well, you might have gone on being World manager all your life, in the isolation of your office and your miles of taped official reports and your occasional confabs with me and the others. Except for your Institute of Political Leadership and your Ten-Year-Plan. That upset things. Of course, we were as much interested in it as we were in you. It had definite possibilities. We hoped it would work out. We would have been glad to retire from office if it had. But, most fortunately, it didn't. And that sort of ended the whole experiment."

He caught the downward direction of Carrsbury's gaze.

"No," he said, "I'm afraid your pupils aren't waiting for you in the conference chamber on the hundredth story. I'm afraid they're still in the Institute." His voice became gently sympathetic. "And I'm afraid that it's become . . . well . . . a somewhat different sort of institute."

Carrsbury stood very still, swaying a little. Gradually his thoughts and his will power were emerging from the waking nightmare that had paralyzed them. *The cunning of the insane*—he had neglected that trenchant warning. In the very moment of victory—

No! He had forgotten Hartman! This was the very emergency for which that counterstroke had been prepared.

He glanced sideways at the chief member of his secret police. The black giant, unconcerned by their strange position, was glaring fixedly at Phy as if at some evil magician from whom any malign impossibility could be expected.

Now Hartman became aware of Carrsbury's gaze. He divined his thought.

He drew his dark weapon from its holster, pointed it unwaveringly at Phy.

His black-bearded lips curled. From them came a hissing sound. Then, in a loud voice, he cried, "You're dead, Phy! I disintegrated you."

Phy reached over and took the weapon from his hand.

"That's another respect in which you completely miscalculated the modern temperament," he remarked to Carrsbury, a shade argumentatively. "All of us have certain subjects on which we're a trifle unrealistic. That's only human nature. Hartman's was his suspiciousness—a weakness for ideas involving plots and persecutions. You gave him the worst sort of job—one that catered to and encouraged his weaknesses. In a very short time he became hopelessly unrealistic. Why for years he's never realized that he's been carrying a dummy pistol."

He passed it to Carrsbury for inspection.

"But," he added, "give him the proper job and he'd function well enough—say, something in creation or exploration. Fitting the man to the job is an art with infinite possibilities. That's why we had Morgenstern in Finance—to keep credit fluctuating in a safe, predictable rhythm. That's why a euphoric is made manager of Extraterrestial Research—to keep it booming. Why a catatonic is given Cultural Advancement—to keep it from tripping on its face in its haste to get ahead."

He turned away. Dully, Carrsbury observed that the aircraft was hovering close to the cage and sidling slowly in.

"But in that case why—" he began stupidly.

"Why were you made World manager?" Phy finished easily. "Isn't that fairly obvious? Haven't I told you several times that you did a lot of good, indirectly? You interested us, don't you see? In fact, you were practically unique. As you know, it's our cardinal principle to let every individual express himself as he wants to. In your case, that involved letting you become World manager. Taken all in all it worked out very well. Everyone had a good time, a number of constructive regulations were promulgated, we learned a lot—oh, we didn't get everything we hoped for, but one never does. Unfortunately, in the end, we were forced to discontinue the experiment."

The aircraft had made contact.

"You understand, of course, why that was necessary?" Phy continued hurriedly, as he urged Carrsbury toward the opening port. "I'm sure you must. It all comes down to a question of sanity. What is sanity—now, in the twentieth century, any time? Adherence to a norm. Conformity to certain basic conventions underlying all human conduct. In our age, departure from the norm has become the norm. Inability to conform has become the standard of conformity. That's quite clear, isn't it? And it enables you to understand, doesn't it, your own case and that of your protégés? Over a long period of years you persisted in adhering to a norm, in conforming to certain basic conventions. You were completely unable to adapt yourself to the society around you. You could only pretend—and your protégés wouldn't have been able to do even that. Despite your many engaging personal characteristics, there was obviously only one course of action open to us."

In the port Carrsbury turned. He had found his voice at last. It was hoarse, ragged. "You mean that all these years you've just been *humoring* me?"

The port was closing. Phy did not answer the question.

As the aircraft edged out, he waved farewell with the blob of green gasoid.

"It'll be very pleasant where you're going," he shouted, encouragingly. "Comfortable quarters, adequate facilities for exercise, and a complete library of twentieth century literature to while away your time."

He watched Carrsbury's rigid face, white, staring from the vision port, until the aircraft had diminished to a speck.

Then he turned away, looked at his hands, noticed the gasoid, tossed it out the open door of the cage, studied its flight for a few moments, then flicked the downbeam.

"I'm glad to see the last of that fellow," he muttered, more to himself than to Hartman, as they plummeted toward the roof. "He was beginning to have a very disturbing influence on me. In fact, I was beginning to fear for my"—his expression became suddenly vacuous—"sanity."

INVARIANT

Astounding,
April

by John R. Pierce (1910-   )

Now a Professor of Engineering at Cal Tech, Dr. John R. Pierce was for many years the director of the Bell Telephone Laboratories. Although he first appeared in the sf magazines in 1930 he published very little science fiction, some under the name of J. J. Coupling (which he also used for non-fiction articles in Astounding). He is the father of J. J. Pierce, a former editor of Galaxy.

"Invariant" is a charming and profound little tale, the author's most important contribution to the literature of science fiction.

(The way these books are put together is that Marty and I begin by discussing possible stories. Marty then gets about twice as many as we can include and sends me the Xeroxes. I read them all and mark them OK, ?, or X. The first group are in, the third group are out, and the middle group are worth further discussion. Sometimes—I can't help it—other things slip in. For "Invariant" my comment was "Wow!" Incidentally, John R. Pierce is one of those science fiction writers who is a real scientist. He was deeply involved with the launching of the first communications satellites (surely a dream job for any science fiction writer) and he invented the word "transistor."—I.A.)

You know the general facts concerning Homer Green, so I don't need to describe him or his surroundings. I knew as much and more, yet it was an odd sensation, which you don't get through reading, actually to dress in that primitive fashion, to go among strange surroundings, and to see him.

The house is no more odd than the pictures. Hemmed in by other twentieth-century buildings, it must be indistinguishable from the original structure and its surroundings. To enter it, to tread on rugs, to see chairs covered in cloth with a nap, to see instruments for smoking, to see and hear a primitive radio, even though operating really from a variety of authentic transcriptions, and above all to see an open fire; all this gave me a sense of unreality, prepared though I was. Green sat by the fire in a chair, as we almost invariably find him, with a dog at his feet. He is perhaps the most valuable man in the world, I thought. But I could not shake off the sense of unreality concerning the substantial surroundings. He, too, seemed unreal, and I pitied him.

The sense of unreality continued through the form of self-introduction. How many have there been? I could, of course, examine the records.

"I'm Carew, from the Institute," I said. "We haven't met before, but they told me you'd be glad to see me."

Green rose and extended his hand. I took it obediently, making the unfamiliar gesture.

"Glad to see you," he said. "I've been dozing here. It's a little of a shock, the treatment, and I thought I'd rest a few days. I hope it's really permanent.

"Won't you sit down?" he added.

We seated ourselves before the fire. The dog, which had risen, lay down, pressed against his master's feet.

"I suppose you want to test my reactions?" Green asked.

"Later," I replied. "There's no hurry. And it's so very comfortable here."

Green was easily distracted. He relaxed, staring at the fire. This was an opportunity, and I spoke in a somewhat purposeful voice.

"It seems more a time for politics, here," I said. "What the Swede intends, and what the French—"

"Drench our thoughts in mirth—" Green replied.

I had thought from the records the quotation would have some effect.

"But one doesn't leave politics to drench his thoughts in mirth," he continued. "One studies them—"

I won't go into the conversation. You've seen it in Appendix A of my thesis, "An Aspect of Twentieth Century Politics and Speech." It was brief, as you know. I had been very lucky to get to see Green. I was more lucky to hit on the right thread directly. Somehow, it had never occurred to me before that twentieth century politicians had meant, or had thought that they meant, what they said; that indeed, they had in their own minds attached a sense of meaning or relevancy to what seem to us meaningless or irrelevant phrases. It's hard to explain so foreign an idea; perhaps an example would help.

For instance, would you believe that a man accused of making a certain statement would seriously reply, "I'm not in the habit of making such statements?" Would you believe that this might even mean that he had not made the statement? Or would you further believe that even if he had made the statement, this would seem to him to classify it as some sort of special instance, and his reply as not truly evasive? I think these conjectures plausible, that is, when I struggle to immerse myself in the twentieth century. But I would never have dreamed them before talking with Green. How truly invaluable the man is!

I have said that the conversation recorded in Appendix A is very short. There was no need to continue along political lines after I had grasped the basic idea. Twentieth-century records are much more complete than Green's memory, and that itself has been thoroughly catalogued. It is not the dry bones of information, but the personal contact, the infinite variation in combinations, the stimulation of the warm human touch, that are helpful and suggestive.

So I was with Green, and most of a morning was still before me. You know that he is given meal times free, and only one appointment between meals, so that there will be no overlapping. I was grateful to the man, and sympathetic, and I was somewhat upset in his presence. I wanted to talk to him of the thing nearest his heart. There was no reason I shouldn't. I've recorded the rest of the conversation, but not published it. It's not new. Perhaps it is trivial, but it means a great deal to me. Maybe it's only my very personal memory of it. But I thought you might like to know.

"What led to your discovery?" I asked him.

"Salamanders," he replied without hesitation. "Salamanders."

The account I got of his perfect regeneration experiments was, of course, the published story. How many thousands of times has it been told? Yet, I swear I detected variations from the records. How nearly infinite the possible combinations are! But the chief points came in the usual order. How the regeneration of limbs in salamanders led to the idea of perfect regeneration of human parts. How, say, a cut heals, leaving not a scar, but a perfect replica of the damaged tissue. How in normal metabolism tissue can be replaced not imperfectly, as in an aging organism, but perfectly, indefinitely. You've seen it in animals, in compulsory biology. The chick whose metabolism replaces its tissues, but always in an exact, invariant form, never changing. It's disturbing to think of it in a man. Green looked so young, as young as I. Since the twentieth century—

When Green had concluded his description, including that of his own inoculation in the evening, he ventured to prophesy.

"I feel confident," he said, "that it will work, indefinitely."

"It does work, Dr. Green," I assured him. "Indefinitely."

"We mustn't be premature," he said. "After all, a short time—"

"Do you recall the date, Dr. Green?" I asked.

"September 11th," he said. "1943, if you want that, too."

"Dr. Green, today is August 4, 2170," I told him earnestly.

"Look here," Green said. "If it were, I wouldn't be here dressed this way, and you wouldn't be there dressed that way."

The impasse could have continued indefinitely. I took my communicator from my pocket and showed it to him. He watched with growing wonder and delight as I demonstrated, finally with projection, binaural and stereo. Not simple, but exactly the sort of electronic development which a man of Green's era associated with the future. Green seemed to have lost all thought of the conversation which had led to my production of the communicator.

"Dr. Green," I said, "the year is 2170. This is the twenty-second century."

He looked at me baffled, but this time not with disbelief. A strange sort of terror was spread over his features.

"An accident?" he asked. "My memory?"

"There has been no accident," I said. "Your memory is intact, as far as it goes. Listen to me. Concentrate."

Then I told him, simply and briefly, so that his thought processes would not lag. As I spoke to him he stared at me apprehensively, his mind apparently racing. This is what I said:

"Your experiment succeeded, beyond anything you had reason to hope. Your tissues took on the ability to reform themselves in exactly the same pattern year after year. Their form became invariant.

"Photographs and careful measurements show this, from year to year, yes, from century to century. You are just as you were over two hundred years ago.

"Your life has not been devoid of accident. Minor, even major, wounds have left no trace in healing. Your tissues are invariant.

"Your brain is invariant, too; that is, as far as the cell patterns are concerned. A brain may be likened to an electrical network. Memory is the network, the coils and condensers, and their interconnections. Conscious thought is the pattern of voltages across them and currents flowing through them. The pattern is complicated, but transitory—transient. Memory is changing the network of the brain, affecting all subsequent thoughts, or patterns in the network. The network of your brain never changes. It is invariant.

"Or thought is like the complicated operation of the relays and switches of a telephone exchange of your century, but memory is the interconnections of elements. The interconnections on other people's brains change in the process of thought, breaking down, building up, giving them new memories. The pattern of connections in your brain never changes. It is invariant.

"Other people can adapt themselves to new surroundings, learning where objects of necessity are, the pattern of rooms, adapting themselves unconsciously, without friction. You cannot; your brain is invariant. Your habits are keyed to a house, your house as it was the day before you treated yourself. It has been preserved, replaced through two hundred years so that you could live without friction. In it, you live, day after day, the day after the treatment which made your brain invariant.

"Do not think you give no return for this care. You are

perhaps the most valuable man in the world. Morning, afternoon, evening; you have three appointments a day, when the lucky few who are judged to merit or need your help are allowed to seek it.

"I am a student of history. I came to see the twentieth century through the eyes of an intelligent man of that century. You are a very intelligent, a brilliant man. Your mind has been analyzed in a detail greater than that of any other. Few brains are better. I came to learn from this powerful observant brain what politics meant to a man of your period. I learned from a fresh new source, your brain, which is not overlaid, not changed by the intervening years, but is just as it was in 1943.

"But I am not very important. Important workers: psychologists, come to see you. They ask you questions, then repeat them a little differently, and observe your reactions. One experiment is not vitiated by your memory of an earlier experiment. When your train of thought is interrupted, it leaves no memory behind. Your brain remains invariant. And these men, who otherwise could draw only general conclusions from simple experiments on multitudes of different, differently constituted and differently prepared individuals, can observe undisputable differences of response due to the slightest changes in stimulus. Some of these men have driven you to a frenzy. You do not go mad. Your brain cannot change; it is invariant.

"You are so valuable it seems that the world could scarcely progress without your invariant brain. And yet, we have not asked another to do as you did. With animals, yes. Your dog is an example. What you did was willingly, and you did not know the consequences. You did the world this greatest service unknowingly. But we know."

Green's head had sunk to his chest. His face was troubled, and he seemed to seek solace in the warmth of the fire. The dog at his feet stirred, and he looked down, a sudden smile on his face. I knew that his train of thought had been interrupted. The transients had died from his brain. Our whole meeting was gone from his processes of thought.

I rose and stole away before he looked up. Perhaps I wasted the remaining hour of the morning.

CITY

Astounding,

May

by Clifford D. Simak (1904-   )

Clifford D. Simak first appeared in the science fiction magazines with "The World of the Red Sun," in Wonder Stories *in 1931, so he was a veteran sf writer with thirteen years experience when "City" was published. Although well-known in the field, he was not considered on a level with Heinlein, the Kuttners, van Vogt, and others. This evaluation began to change with the three stories in this book and more that followed, and Cliff Simak emerged in the 1950s as one of the great talents in all of science fiction.*

"City" was the first of a series that with additional linking material appeared in book form (as City*) in 1952, and walked off with the second International Fantasy Award in 1953, defeating such tough competition as Kurt Vonnegut's* Player Piano*. Written at a time when the impact of urbanization on modern life was not being discussed in either general or scholarly publications, Simak's emphasis on the pastoral life and rural values proved immensely popular. These themes are still central to his work, which is appearing regularly, even though the author is in his mid-seventies.*

(This is the first time a story of Cliff's appears in this series, so I haven't had a chance to mention before what he meant to me. "The World of the Red Sun" was a story that pinned my 11-year-old self to the wall when it first appeared. It was one of the stories I told to my fellow junior-high-school students when they gathered round me for the only kind of science fiction they could afford. It wasn't

*till years afterward, after Cliff had become a good
friend of mine, that I discovered he had written it.
And, as Marty said, it was his first published story.
He was one of the few pre-Campbell writers who
could grow and become a great Campbell
writer.—I.A.)*

Gramp Stevens sat in a lawn chair, watching the mower at
work, feeling the warm, soft sunshine seep into his bones.
The mower reached the edge of the lawn, clucked to itself
like a contented hen, made a neat turn and trundled down
another swath. The bag holding the clippings bulged.

Suddenly the mower stopped and clicked excitedly. A
panel in its side snapped open and a cranelike arm reached
out. Grasping steel fingers fished around in the grass, came
up triumphantly with a stone clutched tightly, dropped the
stone into a small container, disappeared back into the panel
again. The lawn mower gurgled, purred on again, following
its swath.

Gramp grumbled at it with suspicion.

"Some day," he told himself, "that dadburned thing is going to miss a lick and have a nervous breakdown."

He lay back in the chair and stared up at the sun-washed
sky. A helicopter skimmed far overhead. From somewhere inside the house a radio came to life and a torturing clash of
music poured out. Gramp, hearing it, shivered and hunkered
lower in the chair.

Young Charlie was settling down for a twitch session. Dad-
burn the kid.

The lawn mower chuckled past and Gramp squinted at it
maliciously.

"Automatic," he told the sky. "Ever' blasted thing is automatic now. Getting so you just take a machine off in a corner
and whisper in its ear and it scurries off to do the job."

His daughter's voice came to him out the window, pitched
to carry above the music.

"Father!"

Gramp stirred uneasily. "Yes, Betty."

"Now, father, you see you move when that lawn mower

gets to you. Don't try to out-stubborn it. After all, it's only a machine. Last time you just sat there and made it cut around you. I never saw the beat of you."

He didn't answer, letting his head nod a bit, hoping she would think he was asleep and let him be.

"Father," she shrilled, "did you hear me?"

He saw it was no good. "Sure, I heard you," he told her. "I was just fixing to move."

He rose slowly to his feet, leaning heavily on his cane. Might make her feel sorry for the way she treated him when she saw how old and feeble he was getting. He'd have to be careful, though. If she knew he didn't need the cane at all, she'd be finding jobs for him to do and, on the other hand, if he laid it on too thick, she'd be having that fool doctor in to pester him again.

Grumbling, he moved the chair out into that portion of the lawn that had been cut. The mower, rolling past, chortled at him fiendishly.

"Some day," Gramp told it, "I'm going to take a swipe at you and bust a gear or two."

The mower hooted at him and went serenely down the lawn.

From somewhere down the grassy street came a jangling of metal, a stuttered coughing.

Gramp, ready to sit down, straightened up and listened.

The sound came more clearly, the rumbling backfire of a balky engine, the clatter of loose metallic parts.

"An automobile!" yelped Gramp. "An automobile, by cracky!"

He started to gallop for the gate, suddenly remembered that he was feeble and subsided to a rapid hobble.

"Must be that crazy Ole Johnson," he told himself. "He's the only one left that's got a car. Just too dadburned stubborn to give it up."

It was Ole.

Gramp reached the gate in time to see the rusty, dilapidated old machine come bumping around the corner, rocking and chugging along the unused street. Steam hissed from the overheated radiator and a cloud of blue smoke issued from the exhaust, which had lost its muffler five years or more ago.

Ole sat stolidly behind the wheel, squinting, trying to duck the roughest places, although that was hard to do, for weeds and grass had overrun the streets and it was hard to see what might be underneath them.

Gramp waved his cane.

"Hi, Ole," he shouted.

Ole pulled up, setting the emergency brake. The car gasped, shuddered, coughed, died with a horrible sigh.

"What you burning?" asked Gramp.

"Little bit of everything," said Ole. "Kerosene, some old tractor oil I found out in a barrel, some rubbing alcohol."

Gramp regarded the fugitive machine with forthright admiration. "Them was the days," he said. "Had one myself; used to be able to do a hundred miles an hour."

"Still O.K.," said Ole. "If you could only find the stuff to run them or get the parts to fix them. Up to three, four years ago I used to be able to get enough gasoline, but ain't seen none for a long time now. Quit making it, I guess. No use having gasoline, they tell me, when you have atomic power."

"Sure," said Gramp. "Guess maybe that's right, but you can't smell atomic power. Sweetest thing I know, the smell of burning gasoline. These here helicopters and other gadgets they got took all the romance out of traveling, somehow."

He squinted at the barrels and baskets piled in the back seat.

"Got some vegetables?" he asked.

"Yup," said Ole. "Some sweet corn and early potatoes and a few baskets of tomatoes. Thought maybe I could sell them."

Gramp shook his head. "You won't, Ole. They won't buy them. Folks has got the notion that this new hydroponics stuff is the only garden sass that's fit to eat. Sanitary, they say, and better flavored."

"Wouldn't give a hoot in a tin cup for all they grow in them tanks they got," Ole declared, belligerently. "Don't taste right to me, somehow. Like I tell Martha, food's got to be raised in the soil to have any character."

He reached down to turn over the ignition switch.

"Don't know as it's worth trying to get the stuff to town," he said, "the way they keep the roads. Or the way they don't keep them, rather. Twenty years ago the state highway out there was a strip of good concrete and they kept it patched and plowed it every winter. Did anything, spent any amount of money to keep it open. And now they just forgot about it.

The concrete's all broken up and some of it has washed out. Brambles are growing in it. Had to get out and cut away a tree that fell across it one place this morning."

"Ain't it the truth," agreed Gramp.

The car exploded into life, coughing and choking. A cloud of dense blue smoke rolled out from under it. With a jerk it stirred to life and lumbered down the street.

Gramp clumped back to his chair and found it dripping wet. The automatic mower, having finished its cutting job, had rolled out the hose, was sprinkling the lawn.

Muttering venom, Gramp stalked around the corner of the house and sat down on the bench beside the back porch. He didn't like to sit there, but it was the only place he was safe from the hunk of machinery out in front.

For one thing, the view from the bench was slightly depressing, fronting as it did on street after street of vacant, deserted houses and weed-grown, unkempt yards.

It had one advantage, however. From the bench he could pretend he was slightly deaf and not hear the twitch music the radio was blaring out.

A voice called from the front yard.

"Bill! Bill, where be you?"

Gramp twisted around.

"Here I am, Mark. Back of the house. Hiding from that dadburned mower."

Mark Bailey limped around the corner of the house, cigarette threatening to set fire to his bushy whiskers.

"Bit early for the game, ain't you?" asked Gramp.

"Can't play no game today," said Mark.

He hobbled over and sat down beside Gramp on the bench.

"We're leaving," he said.

Gramp whirled on him. "You're leaving!"

"Yeah. Moving out into the country. Lucinda finally talked Herb into it. Never gave him a minute's peace, I guess. Said everyone was moving away to one of them nice country estates and she didn't see no reason why we couldn't."

Gramp gulped. "Where to?"

"Don't rightly know," said Mark. "Ain't been there myself. Up north some place. Up on one of the lakes. Got ten acres of land. Lucinda wanted a hundred, but Herb put down his foot and said ten was enough. After all, one city lot was enough for all these years."

"Betty was pestering Johnny, too," said Gramp, "but he's holding out against her. Says he simply can't do it. Says it wouldn't look right, him the secretary of the Chamber of Commerce and all, if he went moving away from the city."

"Folks are crazy," Mark declared. "Plumb crazy."

"That's a fact," Gramp agreed. "Country crazy, that's what they are. Look across there."

He waved his hand at the streets of vacant houses. "Can remember the time when those places were as pretty a bunch of homes as you ever laid your eyes on. Good neighbors, they were. Women ran across from one back door to another to trade recipes. And the men folks would go out to cut the grass and pretty soon the mowers would all be sitting idle and the men would be ganged up, chewing the fat. Friendly people, Mark. But look at it now."

Mark stirred uneasily. "Got to be getting back, Bill. Just sneaked over to let you know we were lighting out. Lucinda's got me packing. She'd be sore if she knew I'd run out."

Gramp rose stiffly and held out his hand. "I'll be seeing you again? You be over for one last game?"

Mark shook his head. "Afraid not, Bill."

They shook hands awkwardly, abashed. "Sure will miss them games," said Mark.

"Me, too," said Gramp. "I won't have nobody once you're gone."

"So long, Bill," said Mark.

"So long," said Gramp.

He stood and watched his friend hobble around the house, felt the cold claw of loneliness reach out and touch him with icy fingers. A terrible loneliness. The loneliness of age—of age and the outdated. Fiercely, Gramp admitted it. He was outdated. He belonged to another age. He had outstripped his time, lived beyond his years.

Eyes misty, he fumbled for the cane that lay against the bench, slowly made his way toward the sagging gate that opened onto the deserted street back of the house.

The years had moved too fast. Years that had brought the family plane and helicopter, leaving the auto to rust in some forgotten place, the unused roads to fall into disrepair. Years that had virtually wiped out the tilling of the soil with the rise of hydroponics. Years that had brought cheap land with the disappearance of the farm as an economic unit, had sent city people scurrying out into the country where each man, for less than the price of a city lot, might own broad acres. Years that had revolutionized the construction of homes to a point where families simply walked away from their old homes to the new ones that could be bought, custom-made, for less than half the price of a prewar structure and could be changed at small cost, to accommodate need of additional space or just a passing whim.

Gramp sniffed. Houses that could be changed each year, just like one would shift around the furniture. What kind of living was that?

He plodded slowly down the dusty path that was all that remained of what a few years before had been a busy residential street. A street of ghosts, Gramp told himself—of furtive, little ghosts that whispered in the night. Ghosts of playing children, ghosts of upset tricycles and canted coaster wagons. Ghosts of gossiping housewives. Ghosts of shouted greetings. Ghosts of flaming fireplaces and chimneys smoking of a winter night.

Little puffs of dust rose around his feet and whitened the cuffs of his trousers.

There was the old Adams place across the way. Adams had been mighty proud of it, he remembered. Gray field stone front and picture windows. Now the stone was green with creeping moss and the broken windows gaped with ghastly leer. Weeds choked the lawn and blotted out the stoop. An elm tree was pushing its branches against the gable. Gramp could remember the day Adams had planted that elm tree.

For a moment he stood there in the grass-grown street, feet in the dust, both hands clutching the curve of his cane, eyes closed.

Through the fog of years he heard the cry of playing children, the barking of Conrad's yapping pooch from down the street. And there was Adams, stripped to the waist, plying the shovel, scooping out the hole, with the elm tree, roots wrapped in burlap, lying on the lawn.

May, 1946. Forty-four years ago. Just after he and Adams had come home from the war together.

Footsteps padded in the dust and Gramp, startled, opened his eyes.

Before him stood a young man. A man of thirty, perhaps. Maybe a bit less.

"Good morning," said Gramp.

"I hope," said the young man, "that I didn't startle you."

"You saw me standing here," asked Gramp, "like a danged fool, with my eyes shut?"

The young man nodded.

"I was remembering," said Gramp.

"You live around here?"

"Just down the street. The last one in this part of the city."

"Perhaps you can help me then."

"Try me," said Gramp.

The young man stammered. "Well, you see, it's like this. I'm on a sort of . . . well, you might call it a sentimental pilgrimage—"

"I understand," said Gramp. "So am I."

"My name is Adams," said the young man. "My grandfather used to live around here somewhere. I wonder—"

"Right over there," said Gramp.

Together they stood and stared at the house.

"It was a nice place once," Gramp told him. "Your granddaddy planted that tree right after he came home from the war. I was with him all through the war and we came home together. That was a day for you . . ."

"It's a pity," said young Adams. "A pity . . ."

But Gramp didn't seem to hear him. "Your granddaddy?" he asked. "I seem to have lost track of him."

"He's dead," said young Adams. "Quite a number of years ago."

"He was messed up with atomic power," said Gramp.

"That's right," said Adams proudly. "Got into it just as soon as it was released to industry. Right after the Moscow agreement."

"Right after they decided," said Gramp, "they couldn't fight a war."

"That's right," said Adams.

"It's pretty hard to fight a war," said Gramp, "when there's nothing you can aim at."

"You mean the cities," said Adams.

"Sure," said Gramp, "and there's a funny thing about it. Wave all the atom bombs you wanted to and you couldn't scare them out. But give them cheap land and family planes and they scattered just like so many dadburned rabbits."

John J. Webster was striding up the broad stone steps of the city hall when the walking scarecrow carrying a rifle under his arm caught up with him and stopped him.

"Howdy, Mr. Webster," said the scarecrow.

Webster stared, then recognition crinkled his face.

"It's Levi," he said. "How are things going, Levi?"

Levi Lewis grinned with snagged teeth. "Fair to middling. Gardens are coming along and the young rabbits are getting to be good eating."

"You aren't getting mixed up in any of the hell raising that's being laid to the *houses?*" asked Webster.

"No, sir," declared Levi. "Ain't none of us Squatters mixed up in any wrongdoing. We're law-abiding, God-fearing people, we are. Only reason we're there is we can't make a living no place else. And us living in them places other people up and left ain't harming no one. Police are just blaming us for the thievery and other things that's going on, knowing we can't protect ourselves. They're making us the goats."

"I'm glad to hear that," said Webster. "The chief wants to burn the *houses.*"

"If he tries that," said Levi, "he'll run against something he ain't counting on. They run us off our farms with this tank farming of theirs but they ain't going to run us any farther."

He spat across the steps.

"Wouldn't happen you might have some jingling money on you?" he asked. "I'm fresh out of cartridges and with them rabbits coming up—"

Webster thrust his fingers into a vest pocket, pulled out a half dollar.

Levi grinned. "That's obliging of you, Mr. Webster. I'll bring a mess of squirrels, come fall."

The Squatter touched his hat with two fingers and retreated down the steps, sun glinting on the rifle barrel. Webster turned up the steps again.

The city council session already was in full swing when he walked into the chamber.

Police Chief Jim Maxwell was standing by the table and Mayor Paul Carter was talking.

"Don't you think you may be acting a bit hastily, Jim, in urging such a course of action with the *houses?*"

"No, I don't," declared the chief. "Except for a couple of dozen or so, none of those houses are occupied by their rightful owners, or rather, their original owners. Every one of them belongs to the city now through tax forfeiture. And they are nothing but an eyesore and a menace. They have no value. Not even salvage value. Wood? We don't use wood any more. Plastics are better. Stone? We use steel instead of stone. Not a single one of those houses has any material of marketable value.

"And in the meantime they are becoming the haunts of petty criminals and undesirable elements. Grown up with vegetation as the residential sections are, they make a perfect hideout for all types of criminals. A man commits a crime and heads straight for the *houses*—once there he's safe, for I could send a thousand men in there and he could elude them all.

"They aren't worth the expense of tearing down. And yet they are, if not a menace, at least a nuisance. We should get rid of them and fire is the cheapest, quickest way. We'd use all precautions."

"What about the legal angle?" asked the mayor.

"I checked into that. A man has a right to destroy his own property in any way he may see fit so long as it endangers no one else's. The same law, I suppose, would apply to a municipality."

Alderman Thomas Griffin sprang to his feet.

"You'd alienate a lot of people," he declared. "You'd be burning down a lot of old homesteads. People still have some sentimental attachments—"

"If they cared for them," snapped the chief, "why didn't they pay the taxes and take care of them? Why did they go running off to the country, just leaving the houses standing. Ask Webster here. He can tell you what success he had trying to interest the people in their ancestral homes."

"You're talking about that Old Home Week farce," said Griffin. "It failed. Of course, it failed. Webster spread it on so thick that they gagged on it. That's what a Chamber of Commerce mentality always does."

Alderman Forrest King spoke up angrily. "There's nothing wrong with a Chamber of Commerce, Griffin. Simply because you failed in business is no reason . . ."

Griffin ignored him. "The day of high pressure is over, gentlemen. The day of high pressure is gone forever. Ballyhoo is something that is dead and buried.

"The day when you could have tall-corn days or dollar days or dream up some fake celebration and deck the place up with bunting and pull in big crowds that were ready to spend money is past these many years. Only you fellows don't seem to know it.

"The success of such stunts as that was its appeal to mob psychology and civic loyalty. You can't have civic loyalty with a city dying on its feet. You can't appeal to mob psychology when there is no mob—when every man, or nearly every man has the solitude of forty acres."

"Gentlemen," pleaded the mayor. "Gentlemen, this is distinctly out of order."

King sputtered into life, walloped the table.

"No, let's have it out. Webster is over there. Perhaps he can tell us what he thinks."

Webster stirred uncomfortably. "I scarcely believe," he said, "I have anything to say."

"Forget it," snapped Griffin and sat down.

But King still stood, face crimson, his mouth trembling with anger.

"Webster!" he shouted.

Webster shook his head. "You came here with one of your big ideas," shouted King. "You were going to lay it before the council. Step up, man, and speak your piece."

Webster rose slowly, grim-lipped.

"Perhaps you're too thick-skulled," he told King, "to know why I resent the way you have behaved."

King gasped, then exploded. "Thick-skulled! You would say that to me. We've worked together and I've helped you. You've never called me that before . . . you've—"

"I've never called you that before," said Webster, levelly. "Naturally not. I wanted to keep my job."

"Well, you haven't got a job," roared King. "From this minute on, you haven't got a job."

"Shut up," said Webster.

King stared at him, bewildered, as if someone had slapped him across the face.

"And sit down," said Webster, and his voice bit through the room like a sharp-edged knife.

King's knees caved beneath him and he sat down abruptly. The silence was brittle.

"I have something to say," said Webster. "Something that should have been said long ago. Something all of you should hear. That I should be the one who would tell it to you is the one thing that astounds me. And yet, perhaps, as one who has worked in the interests of this city for almost fifteen years, I am the logical one to speak the truth.

"Alderman Griffin said the city is dying on its feet and his statement is correct. There is but one fault I would find with it and that is its understatement. The city . . . this city, any city . . . already is dead.

"The city is an anachronism. It has outlived its usefulness. Hydroponics and the helicopter spelled its downfall. In the first instance the city was a tribal place, an area where the tribe banded together for mutual protection. In later years a wall was thrown around it for additional protection. Then the wall finally disappeared but the city lived on because of the conveniences which it offered trade and commerce. It continued into modern times because people were compelled to live close to their jobs and the jobs were in the city.

"But today that is no longer true. With the family plane, one hundred miles today is a shorter distance than five miles back in 1930. Men can fly several hundred miles to work and fly home when the day is done. There is no longer any need for them to live cooped up in a city.

"The automobile started the trend and the family plane finished it. Even in the first part of the century the trend was noticeable—a movement away from the city with its taxes and its stuffiness, a move toward the suburb and close-in acreages. Lack of adequate transportation, lack of finances held many to the city. But now, with tank farming destroying the value of land, a man can buy a huge acreage in the country for less than he could a city lot forty years ago. With planes powered by atomics there is no longer any transportation problem."

He paused and the silence held. The mayor wore a shocked

look. King's lips moved, but no words came. Griffin was smiling.

"So what have we?" asked Webster. "I'll tell you what we have. Street after street, block after block, of deserted houses, houses that the people just up and walked away from. Why should they have stayed? What could the city offer them? None of the things that it offered the generations before them, for progress had wiped out the need of the city's benefits. They lost something, some monetary consideration, of course, when they left the houses. But the fact that they could buy a house twice as good for half as much, the fact that they could live as they wished to live, that they could develop what amounts to family estates after the best tradition set them by the wealthy of a generation ago—all these things outweighed the leaving of their homes.

"And what have we left? A few blocks of business houses. A few acres of industrial plants. A city government geared to take care of a million people without the million people. A budget that has run the taxes so high that eventually even business houses will move to escape those taxes. Tax forfeitures that have left us loaded with worthless property. That's what we have left.

"If you think any Chamber of Commerce, any ballyhoo, any hare-brained scheme will give you the answers, you're crazy. There is only one answer and that is simple. The city as a human institution is dead. It may struggle on a few more years, but that is all."

"Mr. Webster—" said the mayor.

But Webster paid him no attention.

"But for what happened today," he said, "I would have stayed on and played doll house with you. I would have gone on pretending that the city was a going concern. Would have gone on kidding myself and you. But there is, gentlemen, such a thing as human dignity."

The icy silence broke down in the rustling of papers, the muffled cough of some embarrassed listener.

But Webster was not through.

"The city failed," he said, "and it is well it failed. Instead of sitting here in mourning above its broken body you should rise to your feet and shout your thanks it failed.

"For if this city had not outlived its usefulness, as did every other city—if the cities of the world had not been deserted, they would have been destroyed. There would have been a war, gentlemen, an atomic war. Have you forgotten the 1950's and the 60's? Have you forgotten waking up at night and listening for the bomb to come, knowing that you would not hear it when it came, knowing that you would never hear again, if it did come?

"But the cities were deserted and industry was dispersed and there were no targets and there was no war.

"Some of you gentlemen," he said, "many of you gentlemen, are alive today because the people left your city.

"Now, for God's sake, let it stay dead. Be happy that it's dead. It's the best thing that ever happened in all human history."

John J. Webster turned on his heel and left the room.

Outside on the broad stone steps, he stopped and stared up at the cloudless sky, saw the pigeons wheeling above the turrets and spires of the city hall.

He shook himself mentally, like a dog coming out of a pool.

He had been a fool, of course. Now he'd have to hunt for a job and it might take time to find one. He was getting a bit old to be hunting for a job.

But despite his thoughts, a little tune rose unbidden to his lips. He walked away briskly, lips pursed, whistling soundlessly.

No more hypocrisy. No more lying awake nights wondering what to do—knowing that the city was dead, knowing that what he did was a useless task, feeling like a heel for taking a salary that he knew he wasn't earning. Sensing the strange, nagging frustration of a worker who knows his work is nonproductive.

He strode toward the parking lot, heading for his helicopter.

Now, maybe, he told himself, they could move out into the country the way Betty wanted to. Maybe he could spend his evenings tramping land that belonged to him. A place with a stream. Definitely it had to have a stream he could stock with trout.

He made a mental note to go up into the attic and check his fly equipment.

Martha Johnson was waiting at the barnyard gate when the old car chugged down the lane.

Ole got out stiffly, face rimmed with weariness.

"Sell anything?" asked Martha.

Ole shook his head. "It ain't no use. They won't buy farm-raised stuff. Just laughed at me. Showed me ears of corn twice as big as the ones I had, just as sweet and with more even rows. Showed me melons that had almost no rind at all. Better tasting, too, they said."

He kicked at a clod and it exploded into dust.

"There ain't no getting around it," he declared. "Tank farming has ruined us."

"Maybe we better fix to sell the farm," suggested Martha.

Ole said nothing.

"You could get a job on a tank farm," she said. "Harry did. Likes it real well."

Ole shook his head.

"Or maybe a gardener," said Martha. "You would make a right smart gardener. Ritzy folks that's moved out to big estates like to have gardeners to take care of flowers and things. More classy than doing it with machines."

Ole shook his head again. "Couldn't stand to mess around with flowers," he declared. "Not after raising corn for more than twenty years."

"Maybe," said Martha, "we could have one of them little planes. And running water in the house. And a bathtub instead of taking a bath in the old washtub by the kitchen fire."

"Couldn't run a plane," objected Ole.

"Sure you could," said Martha. "Simple to run, they are. Why, them Anderson kids ain't no more than knee-high to a cricket and they fly one all over. One of them got fooling around and fell out once, but—"

"I got to think about it," said Ole desperately. "I got to think."

He swung away, vaulted a fence, headed for the fields. Martha stood beside the car and watched him go. One lone tear rolled down her dusty cheek.

"Mr. Taylor is waiting for you," said the girl.

John J. Webster stammered. "But I haven't been here before. He didn't know I was coming."

"Mr. Taylor," insisted the girl, "is waiting for you."

She nodded her head toward the door. It read:

Bureau of Human Adjustment

"But I came here to get a job," protested Webster. "I didn't come to be adjusted or anything. This is the World Committee's placement service, isn't it?"

"That is right," the girl declared. "Won't you see Mr. Taylor?"

"Since you insist," said Webster.

The girl clicked over a switch, spoke into the intercommunicator. "Mr. Webster is here, sir."

"Send him in," said a voice.

Hat in hand, Webster walked through the door.

The man behind the desk had white hair but a young man's face. He motioned toward a chair.

"You've been trying to find a job," he said.

"Yes," said Webster, "but—"

"Please sit down," said Taylor. "If you're thinking about that sign on the door, forget it. We'll not try to adjust you."

"I couldn't find a job," said Webster. "I've hunted for weeks and no one would have me. So, finally, I came here."

"You didn't want to come here?"

"No, frankly, I didn't. A placement service. It has, well . . . it has an implication I do not like."

Taylor smiled. "The terminology may be unfortunate. You're thinking of the employment services of the old days. The places where men went when they were desperate for work. The government operated places that tried to find work for men so they wouldn't become public charges."

"I'm desperate enough," confessed Webster. "But I still have a pride that made it hard to come. But, finally, there was nothing else to do. You see, I turned traitor—"

"You mean," said Taylor, "that you told the truth. Even when it cost you your job. The business world, not only here, but all over the world is not ready for that truth. The businessman still clings to the city myth, to the myth of salesmanship. In time to come he will realize he doesn't need the city, that service and honest values will bring him more substantial business than salesmanship ever did.

"I've wondered, Webster, just what made you do what you did?"

"I was sick of it," said Webster. "Sick of watching men blundering along with their eyes tight shut. Sick of seeing an old tradition being kept alive when it should have been laid away. Sick of King's simpering civic enthusiasm when all cause for enthusiasm had vanished."

Taylor nodded. "Webster, do you think you could adjust human beings?"

Webster merely stared.

"I mean it," said Taylor. "The World Committee has been doing it for years, quietly, unobtrusively. Even many of the people who have been adjusted don't know they have been adjusted.

"Changes such as have come since the creation of the World Committee out of the old United Nations has meant much human maladjustment. The advent of workable atomic power took jobs away from hundreds of thousands. They had to be trained and guided into new jobs, some with the new atomics, some into other lines of work. The advent of tank farming swept the farmers off their land. They, perhaps, have supplied us with our greatest problem, for other than the special knowledge needed to grow crops and handle animals, they had no skills. Most of them had no wish for acquiring skills. Most of them were bitterly resentful at having been forced from the livelihood which they inherited from their forebears. And being natural individualists, they offered the toughest psychological problems of any other class."

"Many of them," declared Webster, "still are at loose ends. There's a hundred or more of them squatting out in the *houses,* living from hand to mouth. Shooting a few rabbits and a few squirrels, doing some fishing, raising vegetables and picking wild fruit. Engaging in a little petty thievery now and then and doing occasional begging on the uptown streets."

"You know these people?" asked Taylor.

"I know some of them," said Webster. "One of them brings me squirrels and rabbits on occasions. To make up for it, he bums ammunition money."

"They'd resent being adjusted, wouldn't they?"

"Violently," said Webster.

"You know a farmer by the name of Ole Johnson? Still sticking to his farm, still unreconstructed?"

Webster nodded.

"What if you tried to adjust him?"

"He'd run me off the farm," said Webster.

"Men like Ole and the Squatters," said Taylor, "are our special problems now. Most of the rest of the world is fairly well-adjusted, fairly well settled into the groove of the present. Some of them are doing a lot of moaning about the past, but that's just for effect. You couldn't drive them back to their old ways of life.

"Years ago, with the advent of industrial atomics in fact, the World Committee faced a hard decision. Should changes that spelled progress in the world be brought about gradually to allow the people to adjust themselves naturally, or should they be developed as quickly as possible, with the committee aiding in the necessary human adjustment? It was decided, rightly or wrongly, that progress should come first, regardless of its effect upon the people. The decision in the main has proved a wise one.

"We knew, of course, that in many instances, this readjustment could not be made too openly. In some cases, as in large groups of workers who had been displaced, it was possible, but in most individual cases, such as our friend Ole, it was not. These people must be helped to find themselves in this new world, but they must not know that they're being helped. To let them know would destroy confidence and dignity, and human dignity is the keystone of any civilization."

"I knew, of course, about the readjustments made within industry itself," said Webster, "but I had not heard of the individual cases."

"We could not advertise it," Taylor said. "It's practically undercover."

"But why are you telling me all this now?"

"Because we'd like you to come in with us. Have a hand at adjusting Ole to start with. Maybe see what could be done about the Squatters next."

"I don't know—" said Webster.

"We'd been waiting for you to come in," said Taylor. "We knew you'd finally have to come here. Any chance you might have had at any kind of job would have been queered by King. He passed the word along. You're blackballed by every

Chamber of Commerce and every civic group in the world today."

"Probably I have no choice," said Webster.

"We don't want you to feel that way about it," Taylor said. "Take a while to think it over, then come back. Even if you don't want the job we'll find you another one—in spite of King."

Outside the office, Webster found a scarecrow figure waiting for him. It was Levi Lewis, snaggle-toothed grin wiped off, rifle under his arm.

"Some of the boys said they seen you go in here," he explained. "So I waited for you."

"What's the trouble?" Webster asked, for Levi's face spoke eloquently of trouble.

"It's them police," said Levi. He spat disgustedly.

"The police," said Webster, and his heart sank as he said the words. For he knew what the trouble was.

"Yeah," said Levi. "They're fixing to burn us out."

"So the council finally gave in," said Webster.

"I just came from police headquarters," declared Levi. "I told them they better go easy. I told them there'd be guts strewed all over the place if they tried it. I got the boys posted all around the place with orders not to shoot till they're sure of hitting."

"You can't do that, Levi," said Webster, sharply.

"I can't!" retorted Levi. "I done it already. They drove us off the farms, forced us to sell because we couldn't make a living. And they aren't driving us no farther. We either stay here or we die here. And the only way they'll burn us out is when there's no one left to stop them."

He shucked up his pants and spat again.

"And we ain't the only ones that feel that way," he declared. "Gramp is out there with us."

"Gramp!"

"Sure, Gramp. The old guy that lives with you. He's sort of taken over as our commanding general. Says he remembers tricks from the war them police have never heard of. He sent some of the boys over to one of them Legion halls to swipe a cannon. Says he knows where we can get some shells for it from the museum. Says we'll get it all set up and then send word that if the police make a move we'll shell the loop."

"Look, Levi, will you do something for me?"

"Sure will, Mr. Webster."

"Will you go in and ask for a Mr. Taylor? Insist on seeing him. Tell him I'm already on the job."

"Sure will, but where are you going?"

"I'm going up to the city hall."

"Sure you don't want me along?"

"No," declared Webster. "I'll do better alone. And, Levi—"

"Yes."

"Tell Gramp to hold up his artillery. Don't shoot unless he has to—but if he has, to lay it on the line."

"The mayor is busy," said Raymond Brown, his secretary.

"That's what you think," said Webster, starting for the door.

"You can't go in there, Webster," yelled Brown.

He leaped from his chair, came charging around the desk, reaching for Webster. Webster swung broadside with his arm, caught Brown across the chest, swept him back against the desk. The desk skidded and Brown waved his arms, lost his balance, thudded to the floor.

Webster jerked open the mayor's door.

The mayor's feet thumped off his desk. "I told Brown—" he said.

Webster nodded. "And Brown told me. What's the matter, Carter. Afraid King might find out I was here? Afraid of being corrupted by some good ideas?"

"What do you want?" snapped Carter.

"I understand the police are going to burn the *houses*."

"That's right," declared the mayor, righteously. "They're a menace to the community."

"What community?"

"Look here, Webster—"

"You know there's no community. Just a few of you lousy politicians who stick around so you can claim residence, so you can be sure of being elected every year and drag down your salaries. It's getting to the point where all you have to do is vote for one another. The people who work in the stores and shops, even those who do the meanest jobs in the factories, don't live inside the city limits. The businessmen quit the city long ago. They do business here, but they aren't residents."

"But this is still a city," declared the mayor.

"I didn't come to argue that with you," said Webster. "I came to try to make you see that you're doing wrong by burning those houses. Even if you don't realize it, the *houses* are homes to people who have no other homes. People who have come to this city to seek sanctuary, who have found refuge with us. In a measure, they are our responsibility."

"They're not our responsibility," gritted the mayor. "Whatever happens to them is their own hard luck. We didn't ask them here. We don't want them here. They contribute nothing to the community. You're going to tell me they're misfits. Well, can I help that? You're going to say they can't find jobs. And I'll tell you they could find jobs if they tried to find them. There's work to be done, there's always work to be done. They've been filled up with this new world talk and they figure it's up to someone to find the place that suits them and the job that suits them."

"You sound like a rugged individualist," said Webster.

"You say that like you think it's funny," yapped the mayor.

"I do think it's funny," said Webster. "Funny, and tragic, that anyone should think that way today."

"The world would be a lot better off with some rugged individualism," snapped the mayor. "Look at the men who have gone places—"

"Meaning yourself?" asked Webster.

"You might take me, for example," Carter agreed. "I worked hard. I took advantage of opportunity. I had some foresight. I did—"

"You mean you licked the correct boots and stepped in the proper faces," said Webster. "You're the shining example of the kind of people the world doesn't want today. You positively smell musty, your ideas are so old. You're the last of the politicians, Carter, just as I was the last of the Chamber of Commerce secretaries. Only you don't know it yet. I did. I got out. Even when it cost me something, I got out, because I had to save my self-respect. Your kind of politics is dead. They are dead because any tinhorn with a loud mouth and a brassy front could gain power by appeal to mob psychology. And you haven't got mob psychology any more. You can't have mob psychology when people don't give a damn what happens to a thing that's dead already—a political system that broke down under its own weight."

"Get out of here," screamed Carter. "Get out before I have the cops come and throw you out."

"You forget," said Webster, "that I came in to talk about the *houses*."

"It won't do you any good," snarled Carter. "You can stand and talk till doomsday for all the good it does. Those *houses* burn. That's final."

"How would you like to see the loop a mass of rubble?" asked Webster.

"Your comparison," said Carter, "is grotesque."

"I wasn't talking about comparisons," said Webster.

"You weren't—" The mayor stared at him. "What were you talking about then?"

"Only this," said Webster. "The second the first torch touches the *houses*, the first shell will land on the city hall. And the second one will hit the First National. They'll go down the line, the biggest targets first."

Carter gaped. Then a flush of anger crawled from his throat up into his face.

"It won't work, Webster," he snapped. "You can't bluff me. Any cock-and-bull story like that—"

"It's no cock-and-bull story," declared Webster. "Those men have cannon out there. Pieces from in front of Legion halls, from the museums. And they have men who know how to work them. They wouldn't need them, really. It's practically point-blank range. Like shooting the broadside of a barn."

Carter reached for the radio, but Webster stopped him with an upraised hand.

"Better think a minute, Carter, before you go flying off the handle. You're on a spot. Go ahead with your plan and you have a battle on your hands. The *houses* may burn but the loop is wrecked. The businessmen will have your scalp for that."

Carter's hand retreated from the radio.

From far away came the sharp crack of a rifle.

"Better call them off," warned Webster.

Carter's face twisted with indecision.

Another rifle shot, another and another.

"Pretty soon," said Webster, "it will have gone too far. So far that you can't stop it."

A thudding blast rattled the windows of the room. Carter leaped from his chair.

Webster felt suddenly cold and weak. But he fought to keep his face straight and his voice calm.

Carter was staring out the window, like a man of stone.

"I'm afraid," said Webster, "that it's gone too far already."

The radio on the desk chirped insistently, red light flashing.

Carter reached out a trembling hand and snapped it on.

"Carter," a voice was saying. "Carter. Carter."

Webster recognized that voice—the bull-throated tone of Police Chief Jim Maxwell.

"What is it?" asked Carter.

"They had a big gun," said Maxwell. "It exploded when they tried to fire it. Ammunition no good, I guess."

"One gun?" asked Carter. "Only one gun?"

"I don't see any others."

"I heard rifle fire," said Carter.

"Yeah, they did some shooting at us. Wounded a couple of the boys. But they've pulled back now. Deeper into the brush. No shooting now."

"O.K.," said Carter, "go ahead and start the fires."

Webster started forward. "Ask him, ask him—"

But Carter clicked the switch and the radio went dead.

"What was it you want to ask?"

"Nothing," said Webster. "Nothing that amounted to anything."

He couldn't tell Carter that Gramp had been the one who knew about firing big guns. Couldn't tell him that when the gun exploded Gramp had been there.

He'd have to get out of here, get over to the gun as quickly as possible.

"It was a good bluff, Webster," Carter was saying. "A good bluff, but it petered out."

The mayor turned to the window that faced toward the *houses*.

"No more firing," he said. "They gave up quick."

"You'll be lucky," snapped Webster, "if six of your policemen come back alive. Those men with the rifles are out in the brush and they can pick the eye out of a squirrel at a hundred yards."

Feet pounded in the corridor outside, two pairs of feet racing toward the door.

The mayor whirled from his window and Webster pivoted around.

"Gramp!" he yelled.

"Hi, Johnny," puffed Gramp, skidding to a stop.

The man behind Gramp was a young man and he was waving something in his hand—a sheaf of papers that rustled as he waved them.

"What do you want?" asked the mayor.

"Plenty," said Gramp.

He stood for a moment, catching back his breath, and said between puffs:

"Meet my friend, Henry Adams."

"Adams?" asked the mayor.

"Sure," said Gramp. "His granddaddy used to live here. Out on Twenty-seventh Street."

"Oh," said the mayor and it was as if someone had smacked him with a brick. "Oh, you mean F. J. Adams."

"Bet your boots," said Gramp. "Him and me, we were in the war together. Used to keep me awake nights telling me about his boy back home."

Carter nodded to Henry Adams. "As mayor of the city," he said, trying to regain some of his dignity, "I welcome you to—"

"It's not a particularly fitting welcome," Adams said. "I understand you are burning my property."

"Your property!" The mayor choked and his eyes stared in disbelief at the sheaf of papers Adams waved at him.

"Yeah, his property," shrilled Gramp. "He just bought it. We just come from the treasurer's office. Paid all the back taxes and penalties and all the other things you legal thieves thought up to slap against them houses."

"But, but—" the mayor was grasping for words, gasping for breath. "Not all of it. Perhaps just the old Adams property."

"Lock, stock and barrel," said Gramp, triumphantly.

"And now," said Adams to the mayor, "if you would kindly tell your men to stop destroying my property."

Carter bent over the desk and fumbled at the radio, his hands suddenly all thumbs.

"Maxwell," he shouted. "Maxwell. Maxwell."

"What do you want?" Maxwell yelled back.

"Stop setting those fires," yelled Carter. "Start putting them out. Call the fire department. Do anything. But stop those fires."

"Cripes," said Maxwell, "I wish you'd make up your mind."

"You do what I tell you," screamed the mayor. "You put out those fires."

"All right," said Maxwell. "All right. Keep your shirt on. But the boys won't like it. They won't like getting shot at to do something you change your mind about."

Carter straightened from the radio.

"Let me assure you, Mr. Adams," he said, "that this is all a big mistake."

"It is," Adams declared solemnly. "A very great mistake, mayor. The biggest one you ever made."

For a moment the two of them stood there, looking across the room at one another.

"Tomorrow," said Adams, "I shall file a petition with the courts asking dissolution of the city charter. As owner of the greatest portion of the land included in the corporate limits, both from the standpoint of area and valuation, I understand I have a perfect legal right to do that."

The mayor gulped, finally brought out some words.

"Upon what grounds?" he asked.

"Upon the grounds," said Adams, "that there is no further need of it. I do not believe I shall have too hard a time to prove my case."

"But . . . but . . . that means . . ."

"Yeah," said Gramp, "you know what it means. It means you are out right on your ear."

"A park," said Gramp, waving his arm over the wilderness that once had been the residential section of the city. "A park so that people can remember how their old folks lived."

The three of them stood on Tower Hill, with the rusty old water tower looming above them, its sturdy steel legs planted in a sea of waist-high grass.

"Not a park, exactly," explained Henry Adams. "A

memorial, rather. A memorial to an era of communal life that will be forgotten in another hundred years. A preservation of a number of peculiar types of construction that arose to suit certain conditions and each man's particular tastes. No slavery to any architectural concepts, but an effort made to achieve better living. In another hundred years men will walk through those houses down there with the same feeling of respect and awe they have when they go into a museum today. It will be to them something out of what amounts to a primeval age, a stepping-stone on the way to the better, fuller life. Artists will spend their lives transferring those old houses to their canvasses. Writers of historical novels will come here for the breath of authenticity."

"But you said you meant to restore all the houses, make the lawns and gardens exactly like they were before," said Webster. "That will take a fortune. And, after that, another fortune to keep them in shape."

"I have too much money," said Adams. "Entirely too much money. Remember, my grandfather and father got into atomics on the ground floor."

"Best crap player I ever knew, your granddaddy was," said Gramp. "Used to take me for a cleaning every pay day."

"In the old days," said Adams, "when a man had too much money, there were other things he could do with it. Organized charities, for example. Or medical research or something like that. But there are no organized charities today. Not enough business to keep them going. And since the World Committee has hit its stride, there is ample money for all the research, medical or otherwise, anyone might wish to do.

"I didn't plan this thing when I came back to see my grandfather's old house. Just wanted to see it, that was all. He'd told me so much about it. How he planted the tree in the front lawn. And the rose garden he had out back.

"And then I saw it. And it was a mocking ghost. It was something that had been left behind. Something that had meant a lot to someone and had been left behind. Standing there in front of that house with Gramp that day, it came to me that I could do nothing better than preserve for posterity a cross section of the life their ancestors lived."

A thin blue thread of smoke rose above the trees far below.

Webster pointed to it. "What about them?"

"The Squatters stay," said Adams, "if they want to. There will be plenty of work for them to do. And there'll always be a house or two that they can have to live in.

"There's just one thing that bothers me. I can't be here all the time myself. I'll need someone to manage the project. It'll be a lifelong job."

He looked at Webster.

"Go ahead, Johnny," said Gramp.

Webster shook his head. "Betty's got her heart set on that place out in the country."

"You wouldn't have to stay here," said Adams. "You could fly in every day."

From the foot of the hill came a hail.

"It's Ole," yelled Gramp.

He waved his cane. "Hi, Ole. Come on up."

They watched Ole striding up the hill, waiting for him, silently.

"Wanted to talk to you, Johnny," said Ole. "Got an idea. Waked me out of a sound sleep last night."

"Go ahead," said Webster.

Ole glanced at Adams. "He's all right," said Webster. "He's Henry Adams. Maybe you remember his grandfather, old F. J."

"I remember him," said Ole. "Nuts about atomic power, he was. How did he make out?"

"He made out rather well," said Adams.

"Glad to hear that," Ole said. "Guess I was wrong. Said he never would amount to nothing. Daydreamed all the time."

"How about that idea?" Webster asked.

"You heard about dude ranches, ain't you?" Ole asked.

Webster nodded.

"Place," said Ole, "where people used to go and pretend they were cowboys. Pleased them because they really didn't know all the hard work there was in ranching and figured it was romantic-like to ride horses and—"

"Look," asked Webster, "you aren't figuring on turning your farm into a dude ranch, are you?"

"Nope," said Ole. "Not a dude ranch. Dude farm, maybe. Folks don't know too much about farms any more, since there ain't hardly no farms. And they'll read about the frost being on the pumpkin and how pretty a—"

Webster stared at Ole. "They'd go for it, Ole," he declared. "They'd kill one another in the rush to spend their vacation on a real, honest-to-God, old-time farm."

Out of a clump of bushes down the hillside burst a shining thing that chattered and gurgled and screeched, blades flashing, a cranelike arm waving.

"What the—" asked Adams.

"It's that dadburned lawn mower!" yelped Gramp. "I always knew the day would come when it would strip a gear and go completely off its nut!"

ARENA

Astounding,
June

by Fredric Brown (1906-1972)

Readers of earlier volumes in this series will be familiar with the multi-talented Fredric Brown, whose sharp, witty, and frequently profound stories graced the pages of many science fiction and mystery magazines during his long career. His satirical humor was one of his strongest attributes, and he maintained an amazingly high standard of quality in his work, which ranged from the short-short story to the novel.

"Arena" is perhaps his most famous story and rightly so, an exciting and yet humanistic account of mortal combat between an Earthman and alien with the survival of their respective battle fleets at stake. Written in the midst of World War II, it manages to be respectful to "the other side" at a time of total war in the present of the writer, never as easy task.

(One of the games one can play with science fiction (or with literature in general) is to trace back the treatment of themes. This is not to say Writer A deliberately copies a story written by Writer B a generation before, or is even consciously influenced by him. However, a successful story makes a dent in literary history; one that influences literary thought thereafter. There was an extremely moving story by Barry Longyear called "Enemy Mine" (which will be a certain inclusion when we reach 1979 in this series) that pitted a human against an alien in a particularly subtle way—and I couldn't help but think of "Arena."—I.A.)

144

Carson opened his eyes and found himself looking upward into a flickering blue dimness.

It was hot, and he was lying on sand, and a sharp rock embedded in the sand was hurting his back. He rolled over to his side, off the rock, and then pushed himself up to a sitting position.

"I'm crazy," he thought. "Crazy—or dead—or something." The sand was blue, bright blue. And there wasn't any such thing as bright blue sand on Earth or any of the planets.

Blue sand.

Blue sand under a blue dome that wasn't the sky nor yet a room, but a circumscribed area—somehow he knew it was circumscribed and finite even though he couldn't see to the top of it.

He picked up some of the sand in his hand and let it run through his fingers. It trickled down onto his bare leg. *Bare?*

Naked. He was stark naked, and already his body was dripping perspiration from the enervating heat, coated blue with sand wherever sand had touched it.

But elsewhere his body was white.

He thought: Then this sand is really blue. If it seemed blue only because of the blue light, then I'd be blue also. But I'm white, so the sand *is* blue. *Blue sand.* There isn't any blue sand. There isn't any place like this place I'm in.

Sweat was running down in his eyes.

It was hot, hotter than hell. Only hell—the hell of the ancients—was supposed to be red and not blue.

But if this place wasn't hell, what was it? Only Mercury, among the planets, had heat like this and this wasn't Mercury. And Mercury was some four billion miles from—

It came back to him then, where he'd been. In the little one-man scouter, outside the orbit of Pluto, scouting a scant million miles to one side of the Earth Armada drawn up in battle array there to intercept the Outsiders.

That sudden strident nerve-shattering ringing of the alarm bell when the rival scouter—the Outsider ship—had come within range of his detectors—

No one knew who the Outsiders were, what they looked

like, from what far galaxy they came, other than that it was in the general direction of the Pleiades.

First, sporadic raids on Earth colonies and outposts. Isolated battles between Earth patrols and small groups of Outsider spaceships; battles sometimes won and sometimes lost, but never to date resulting in the capture of an alien vessel. Nor had any member of a raided colony ever survived to describe the Outsiders who had left the ships, if indeed they had left them.

Not a too-serious menace, at first, for the raids had not been too numerous or destructive. And individually, the ships had proved slightly inferior in armament to the best of Earth's fighters, although somewhat superior in speed and maneuverability. A sufficient edge in speed, in fact, to give the Outsiders their choice of running or fighting, unless surrounded.

Nevertheless, Earth had prepared for serious trouble, for a showdown, building the mightiest armada of all time. It had been waiting now, that armada, for a long time. But now the showdown was coming.

Scouts twenty billion miles out had detected the approach of a mighty fleet—a showdown fleet—of the Outsiders. Those scouts had never come back, but their radiotronic messages had. And now Earth's armada, all ten thousand ships and half-million fighting spacemen, was out there, outside Pluto's orbit, waiting to intercept and battle to the death.

And an even battle it was going to be, judging by the advance reports of the men of the far picket line who had given their lives to report—before they had died—on the size and strength of the alien fleet.

Anybody's battle, with the mastery of the solar system hanging in the balance, on an even chance. A last and *only* chance, for Earth and all her colonies lay at the utter mercy of the Outsiders if they ran that gauntlet—

Oh yes. Bob Carson remembered now.

Not that it explained blue sand and flickering blueness. But that strident alarming of the bell and his leap for the control panel. His frenzied fumbling as he strapped himself into the seat. The dot in the visiplate that grew larger.

The dryness of his mouth. The awful knowledge that this was *it*. For him, at least, although the main fleets were still out of range of one another.

This, his first taste of battle. Within three seconds or less he'd be victorious, or a charred cinder. Dead.

Three seconds—that's how long a space-battle lasted. Time enough to count to three slowly, and then you'd won or you were dead. One hit completely took care of a lightly armed and armored little one-man craft like a scouter.

Frantically—as, unconsciously, his dry lips shaped the word "One"—he worked at the controls to keep that growing dot centered on the crossed spiderwebs of the visiplate. His hands doing that, while his right foot hovered over the pedal that would fire the bolt. The single bolt of concentrated hell that would hit—or else. There wouldn't be time for any second shot.

"Two." He didn't know he'd said that, either. The dot in the visiplate wasn't a dot now. Only a few thousand miles away, it showed up in the magnification of the plate as though it were only a few hundred yards off. It was a sleek, fast little scouter, about the size of his.

And an alien ship, all right.

"Thr—" His foot touched the bolt-release pedal—

And then the Outsider had swerved suddenly and was off the crosshairs. Carson punched keys frantically, to follow.

For a tenth of a second, it was out of the visiplate entirely, and then as the nose of his scouter swung after it, he saw it again, diving straight toward the ground.

The ground?

It was an optical illusion of some sort. It *had* to be, that planet—or whatever it was—that now covered the visiplate. Whatever it was, it couldn't be there. Couldn't possibly. There *wasn't* any planet nearer than Neptune three billion miles away—with Pluto around on the opposite side of the distant pinpoint sun.

His *detectors! They* hadn't shown any object of planetary dimensions, even of asteroid dimensions. They still didn't.

So it couldn't be there, that whatever-it-was he was diving into, only a few hundred miles below him.

And in his sudden anxiety to keep from crashing, he forgot even the Outsider ship. He fired the front braking rockets, and even as the sudden change of speed slammed him forward against the seat straps, he fired full right for an emergency turn. Pushed them down and *held* them down, knowing that he needed everything the ship had to keep from crashing and that a turn that sudden would black him out for a moment.

It did black him out.

And that was all. Now he was sitting in hot blue sand, stark naked but otherwise unhurt. No sign of his spaceship and—for that matter—no sign of *space*. That curve overhead wasn't a sky, whatever else it was.

He scrambled to his feet.

Gravity seemed a little more than Earth-normal. Not much more.

Flat sand stretching away, a few scrawny bushes in clumps here and there. The bushes were blue, too, but in varying shades, some lighter than the blue of the sand, some darker.

Out from under the nearest bush ran a little thing that was like a lizard, except that it had more than four legs. It was blue, too. Bright blue. It saw him and ran back again under the bush.

He looked up again, trying to decide what was overhead. It wasn't exactly a roof, but it was dome-shaped. It flickered and was hard to look at. But definitely, it curved down to the ground, to the blue sand, all around him.

He wasn't far from being under the center of the dome. At a guess, it was a hundred yards to the nearest wall, if it was a wall. It was as though a blue hemisphere of *something*, about two hundred and fifty yards in circumference, was inverted over the flat expanse of the sand.

And everything blue, except one object. Over near a far curving wall there was a red object. Roughly spherical, it seemed to be about a yard in diameter. Too far for him to see clearly through the flickering blueness. But, unaccountably, he shuddered.

He wiped sweat from his forehead, or tried to, with the back of his hand.

Was this a dream, a nightmare? This heat, this sand, that vague feeling of horror he felt when he looked toward that red thing?

A dream? No, one didn't go to sleep and dream in the midst of a battle in space.

Death? No, never. If there were immortality, it wouldn't be a senseless thing like this, a thing of blue heat and blue sand and a red horror.

Then he heard the voice—

Inside his head he heard it, not with his ears. It came from nowhere or everywhere.

"*Through spaces and dimensions wandering,*" rang the words in his mind, "*and in this space and this time I find two peoples about to wage a war that would exterminate one and so weaken the other that it would retrogress and never fulfill its destiny, but decay and return to mindless dust whence it came. And I say this must not happen.*"

"Who . . . what are you?" Carson didn't say it aloud, but the question formed itself in his brain.

"*You would not understand completely. I am—*" There was a pause as though the voice sought—in Carson's brain—for a word that wasn't there, a word he didn't know. "*I am the end of evolution of a race so old the time can not be expressed in words that have meaning to your mind. A race fused into a single entity, eternal—*

"*An entity such as your primitive race might become*"—again the groping for a word—"*time from now. So might the race you call, in your mind, the Outsiders. So I intervene in the battle to come, the battle between fleets so evenly matched that destruction of both races will result. One must survive. One must progress and evolve.*"

"One?" thought Carson. "Mine, or—?"

"*It is in my power to stop the war, to send the Outsiders back to their galaxy. But they would return, or your race would sooner or later follow them there. Only by remaining in this space and time to intervene constantly could I prevent them from destroying one another, and I cannot remain.*

"*So I shall intervene now. I shall destroy one fleet completely without loss to the other. One civilization shall thus survive.*"

Nightmare. This had to be nightmare, Carson thought. But he knew it wasn't.

It was too mad, too impossible, to be anything but real.

He didn't dare ask *the* question—*which?* But his thoughts asked it for him.

"*The stronger shall survive,*" said the voice. "*That I can not—and would not—change. I merely intervene to make it a complete victory, not*"—groping again—"*not Pyrrhic victory to a broken race.*

"*From the outskirts of the not-yet battle I plucked two individuals, you and an Outsider. I see from your mind that in your early history of nationalisms battles between champions, to decide issues between races, were not unknown.*

"*You and your opponent are here pitted against one another, naked and unarmed, under conditions equally unfamiliar to you both, equally unpleasant to you both. There is no time limit, for here there is no time. The survivor is the champion of his race. That race survives.*"

"But—" Carson's protest was too inarticulate for expression, but the voice answered it.

"*It is fair. The conditions are such, that the accident of physical strength will not completely decide the issue. There is a barrier. You will understand. Brain-power and courage will be more important than strength. Most especially courage, which is the will to survive.*"

"But while this goes on, the fleets will—"

"*No, you are in another space, another time. For as long as you are here, time stands still in the universe you know. I see you wonder whether this place is real. It is, and it is not. As I—to your limited understanding—am and am not real. My existence is mental and not physical. You saw me as a planet; it could have been as a dustmote or a sun.*

"*But to you this place is now real. What you suffer here will be real. And if you die here, your death will be real. If you die, your failure will be the end of your race. That is enough for you to know.*"

And then the voice was gone.

Again he was alone, but not alone. For as Carson looked up, he saw that the red thing, the red sphere of horror which he now knew was the Outsider, was rolling toward him.

Rolling.

It seemed to have no legs or arms that he could see, no features. It rolled across the blue sand with the fluid quickness of a drop of mercury. And before it, in some manner he could not understand, came a paralyzing wave of nauseating, retching, horrid hatred.

Carson looked about him frantically. A stone, lying in the sand a few feet away, was the nearest thing to a weapon. It wasn't large, but it had sharp edges, like a slab of flint. It looked a bit like blue flint.

He picked it up, and crouched to receive the attack. It was coming fast, faster than he could run.

No time to think out how he was going to fight it, and how

anyway could he plan to battle a creature whose strength, whose characteristics, whose method of fighting he did not know? Rolling so fast, it looked more than ever like a perfect sphere.

Ten yards away. Five. And then it stopped.

Rather, it *was stopped*. Abruptly the near side of it flattened as though it had run up against an invisible wall. It bounced, actually bounced back.

Then it rolled forward again, but more slowly, more cautiously. It stopped again, at the same place. It tried again, a few yards to one side.

There was a barrier there of some sort. It clicked, then, in Carson's mind. That thought projected into his mind by the Entity who had brought them here: "—accident of physical strength will not completely decide the issue. There is a barrier."

A force-field, of course. Not the Netzian Field, known to Earth science, for that glowed and emitted a crackling sound. This one was invisible, silent.

It was a wall that ran from side to side of the inverted hemisphere; Carson didn't have to verify that himself. The Roller was doing that; rolling sideways along the barrier, seeking a break in it that wasn't there.

Carson took half a dozen steps forward, his left hand groping out before him, and then his hand touched the barrier. It felt smooth, yielding, like a sheet of rubber rather than like glass. Warm to his touch, but no warmer than the sand underfoot. And it was completely invisible, even at close range.

He dropped the stone and put both hands against it, pushing. It seemed to yield, just a trifle. But no farther than that trifle, even when he pushed with all his weight. It felt like a sheet of rubber backed up by steel. Limited resiliency, and then firm strength.

He stood on tiptoe and reached as high as he could and the barrier was still there.

He saw the Roller coming back, having reached one side of the arena. That feeling of nausea hit Carson again, and he stepped back from the barrier as it went by. It didn't stop.

But did the barrier stop at ground level? Carson knelt down and burrowed in the sand. It was soft, light, easy to dig in. At two feet down the barrier was still there.

The Roller was coming back again. Obviously, it couldn't find a way through at either side.

There must be a way through, Carson thought. *Some* way we can get at each other, else this duel is meaningless.

But no hurry now, in finding that out. There was something to try first. The Roller was back now, and it stopped just across the barrier, only six feet away. It seemed to be studying him, although for the life of him, Carson couldn't find external evidence of sense organs on the thing. Nothing that looked like eyes or ears, or even a mouth. There was though, he saw now, a series of grooves—perhaps a dozen of them altogether, and he saw two tentacles suddenly push out from two of the grooves and dip into the sand as though testing its consistency. Tentacles about an inch in diameter and perhaps a foot and a half long.

But the tentacles were retractable into the grooves and were kept there except when not in use. They were retracted when the thing rolled and seemed to have nothing to do with its method of locomotion. That, as far as Carson could judge, seemed to be accomplished by some shifting—just *how* he couldn't even imagine—of its center of gravity.

He shuddered as he looked at the thing. It was alien, utterly alien, horribly different from anything on Earth or any of the life forms found on the other solar planets. Instinctively, somehow, he knew its mind was as alien as its body.

But he had to try. If it had no telepathic powers at all, the attempt was foredoomed to failure, yet he thought it had such powers. There had, at any rate, been a projection of something that was not physical at the time a few minutes ago when it had first started for him. An almost tangible wave of hatred.

If it could project that, perhaps it could read his mind as well, sufficiently for his purpose.

Deliberately, Carson picked up the rock that had been his only weapon, then tossed it down again in a gesture of relinquishment and raised his empty hands, palms up, before him.

He spoke aloud, knowing that although the words would be meaningless to the creature before him, speaking them would focus his own thoughts more completely upon the message.

"Can we not have peace between us?" he said, his voice sounding strange in the utter stillness. "The Entity who brought us here has told us what must happen if our races fight—extinction of one and weakening and retrogression of the other. The battle between them, said the Entity, depends upon what we do here. Why can not we agree to an eternal peace—your race to its galaxy, we to ours?"

Carson blanked out his mind to receive a reply.

It came, and it staggered him back physically. He actually recoiled several steps in sheer horror at the depth and intensity of the hatred and lust-to-kill of the red images that had been projected at him. Not as articulate words—as had come to him the thoughts of the Entity—but as wave upon wave of fierce emotion.

For a moment that seemed an eternity he had to struggle against the mental impact of that hatred, fight to clear his mind of it and drive out the alien thoughts to which he had given admittance by blanking his own thoughts. He wanted to retch.

Slowly his mind cleared as, slowly, the mind of a man wakening from nightmare clears away the fear-fabric of which the dream was woven. He was breathing hard and he felt weaker, but he could think.

He stood studying the Roller. It had been motionless during the mental duel it had so nearly won. Now it rolled a few feet to one side, to the nearest of the blue bushes. Three tentacles whipped out of their grooves and began to investigate the bush.

"O.K.," Carson said, "so it's war then." He managed a wry grin. "If I got your answer straight, peace doesn't appeal to you." And, because he was, after all, a quite young man and couldn't resist the impulse to be dramatic, he added, "To the death!"

But his voice, in that utter silence, sounded very silly, even to himself. It came to him, then, that this *was* to the death. Not only his own death or that of the red spherical thing which he now thought of as the Roller, but death to the entire race of one or the other of them. The end of the human race, if he failed.

It made him suddenly very humble and very afraid to think that. More than to think it, to *know* it. Somehow, with a knowledge that was above even faith, he knew that the Entity who had arranged this duel had told the truth about its intentions and its powers. It wasn't kidding.

The future of humanity depended upon *him*. It was an awful thing to realize, and he wrenched his mind away from it. He had to concentrate on the situation at hand.

There had to be some way of getting through the barrier, or of killing through the barrier.

Mentally? He hoped that wasn't all, for the Roller obviously had stronger telepathic powers than the primitive, undeveloped ones of the human race. Or did it?

He had been able to drive the thoughts of the Roller out of his own mind; could it drive out his? If its ability to project was stronger, might not its receptivity mechanism be more vulnerable?

He stared at it and endeavored to concentrate and focus all his thoughts upon it.

"*Die*," he thought. "*You are going to die. You are dying. You are—*"

He tried variations on it, and mental pictures. Sweat stood out on his forehead and he found himself trembling with the intensity of the effort. But the Roller went ahead with its investigation of the bush, as utterly unaffected as though Carson had been reciting the multiplication table.

So *that* was no good.

He felt a bit weak and dizzy from the heat and his strenuous effort at concentration. He sat down on the blue sand to rest and gave his full attention to watching and studying the Roller. By close study, perhaps, he could judge its strength and detect its weaknesses, learn things that would be valuable to know when and if they should come to grips.

It was breaking off twigs. Carson watched carefully, trying to judge just how hard it worked to do that. Later, he thought, he could find a similar bush on his own side, break off twigs of equal thickness himself, and gain a comparison of physical strength between his own arms and hands and those tentacles.

The twigs broke off hard; the Roller was having to struggle with each one, he saw. Each tentacle, he saw, bifurcated at the tip into two fingers, each tipped by a nail or claw. The claws didn't seem to be particularly long or dangerous. No more so than his own fingernails, if they were let to grow a bit.

No, on the whole, it didn't look too tough to handle physically. Unless, of course, that bush was made of pretty tough stuff. Carson looked around him and, yes, right within reach was another bush of identically the same type.

He reached over and snapped off a twig. It was brittle, easy to break. Of course, the Roller might have been faking deliberately but he didn't think so.

On the other hand, where was it vulnerable? Just how would he go about killing it, if he got the chance? He went back to studying it. The outer hide looked pretty tough. He'd need a sharp weapon of some sort. He picked up the piece of rock again. It was about twelve inches long, narrow, and fairly sharp on one end. If it chipped like flint, he could make a serviceable knife out of it.

The Roller was continuing its investigations of the bushes. It rolled again, to the nearest one of another type. A little blue lizard, many-legged like the one Carson had seen on his side of the barrier, darted out from under the bush.

A tentacle of the Roller lashed out and caught it, picked it up. Another tentacle whipped over and began to pull legs off the lizard, as coldly and calmly as it had pulled twigs off the bush. The creature struggled frantically and emitted a shrill squealing sound that was the first sound Carson had heard here other than the sound of his own voice.

Carson shuddered and wanted to turn his eyes away. But he made himself continue to watch; anything he could learn about his opponent might prove valuable. Even this knowledge of its unnecessary cruelty. Particularly, he thought with a sudden vicious surge of emotion, this knowledge of its unnecessary cruelty. It would make it a pleasure to kill the thing, if and when the chance came.

He steeled himself to watch the dismembering of the lizard, for that very reason.

But he felt glad when, with half its legs gone, the lizard quit squealing and struggling and lay limp and dead in the Roller's grasp.

It didn't continue with the rest of the legs. Contemptuously it tossed the dead lizard away from it, in Carson's direction. It arced through the air between them and landed at his feet.

It had come through the barrier! The barrier wasn't there any more!

Carson was on his feet in a flash, the knife gripped tightly in his hand, and leaped forward. He'd settle this thing here and now! With the barrier gone—

But it wasn't gone. He found that out the hard way, running head on into it and nearly knocking himself silly. He bounced back, and fell.

And as he sat up, shaking his head to clear it, he saw something coming through the air toward him, and to duck it, he threw himself flat again on the sand, and to one side. He got his body out of the way, but there was a sudden sharp pain in the calf of his left leg.

He rolled backward, ignoring the pain, and scrambled to his feet. It was a rock, he saw now, that had struck him. And the Roller was picking up another one now, swinging it back gripped between two tentacles, getting ready to throw again.

It sailed through the air toward him, but he was easily able to step out of its way. The Roller, apparently, could throw straight, but not hard nor far. The first rock had struck him only because he had been sitting down and had not seen it coming until it was almost upon him.

Even as he stepped aside from that weak second throw, Carson drew back his right arm and let fly with the rock that was still in his hand. If missiles, he thought with sudden elation, can cross the barrier, then two can play at the game of throwing them. And the good right arm of an Earthman—

He couldn't miss a three-foot sphere at only four-yard range, and he didn't miss. The rock whizzed straight, and with a speed several times that of the missiles the Roller had thrown. It hit dead center, but it hit flat, unfortunately, instead of point first.

But it hit with a resounding thump, and obviously it hurt. The Roller had been reaching for another rock, but it changed its mind and got out of there instead. By the time Carson could pick up and throw another rock, the Roller was forty yards back from the barrier and going strong.

His second throw missed by feet, and his third throw was short. The Roller was back out of range—at least out of range of a missile heavy enough to be damaging.

Carson grinned. That round had been his. Except—

He quit grinning as he bent over to examine the calf of his leg. A jagged edge of the stone had made a pretty deep cut, several inches long. It was bleeding freely, but he didn't think it had gone deep enough to hit an artery. If it stopped bleeding of its own accord, well and good. If not, he was in for trouble.

Finding out one thing, though, took precedence over that cut. The nature of the barrier.

He went forward to it again, this time groping with his hands before him. He found it; then holding one hand against it, he tossed a handful of sand at it with the other hand. The sand went right through. His hand didn't.

Organic matter versus inorganic? No, because the dead lizard had gone through it, and a lizard, alive or dead, was certainly organic. Plant life? He broke off a twig and poked it at the barrier. The twig went through, with no resistance, but when his fingers gripping the twig came to the barrier, they were stopped.

He couldn't get through it, nor could the Roller. But rocks and sand and a dead lizard—

How about a live lizard? He went hunting, under bushes, until he found one, and caught it. He tossed it gently against the barrier and it bounced back and scurried away across the blue sand.

That gave him the answer, in so far as he could determine it now. The screen was a barrier to living things. Dead or inorganic matter could cross it.

That off his mind, Carson looked at his injured leg again. The bleeding was lessening, which meant he wouldn't need to worry about making a tourniquet. But he should find some water, if any was available, to clean the wound.

Water—the thought of it made him realize that he was getting awfully thirsty. He'd *have* to find water, in case this contest turned out to be a protracted one.

Limping slightly now, he started off to make a full circuit of his half of the arena. Guiding himself with one hand along the barrier, he walked to his right until he came to the curving sidewall. It was visible, a dull blue-gray at close range, and the surface of it felt just like the central barrier.

He experimented by tossing a handful of sand at it, and the sand reached the wall and disappeared as it went through. The hemispherical shell was a force-field, too. But an opaque one, instead of transparent like the barrier.

He followed it around until he came back to the barrier, and walked back along the barrier to the point from which he'd started.

No sign of water.

Worried now, he started a series of zigzags back and forth

between the barrier and the wall, covering the intervening space thoroughly.

No water. Blue sand, blue bushes, and intolerable heat. Nothing else.

It must be his imagination, he told himself angrily, that he was suffering *that* much from thirst. How long had he been here? Of course, no time at all, according to his own space-time frame. The Entity had told him time stood still out there, while he was here. But his body processes went on here, just the same. And according to his body's reckoning, how long had he been here? Three or four hours, perhaps. Certainly not long enough to be suffering seriously from thirst.

But he was suffering from it; his throat dry and parched. Probably the intense heat was the cause. It was *hot!* A hundred and thirty Fahrenheit, at a guess. A dry, still heat without the slightest movement of air.

He was limping rather badly, and utterly fagged out when he'd finished the futile exploration of his domain.

He stared across at the motionless Roller and hoped it was as miserable as he was. And quite possibly it wasn't enjoying this, either. The Entity had said the conditions here were equally unfamiliar and equally uncomfortable for both of them. Maybe the Roller came from a planet where two hundred degree heat was the norm. Maybe it was freezing while he was roasting.

Maybe the air was as much too thick for it as it was too thin for him. For the exertion of his explorations had left him panting. The atmosphere here, he realized now, was not much thicker than that on Mars.

No water.

That meant a deadline, for him at any rate. Unless he could find a way to cross that barrier or to kill his enemy from this side of it, thirst would kill him eventually.

It gave him a feeling of desperate urgency. He *must* hurry.

But he made himself sit down a moment to rest, to think.

What was there to do? Nothing, and yet so many things. The several varieties of bushes, for example. They didn't look promising, but he'd have to examine them for possibilities. And his leg—he'd have to do something about that, even without water to clean it. Gather ammunition in the form of rocks. Find a rock that would make a good knife.

His leg hurt rather badly now, and he decided that came first. One type of bush had leaves—or things rather similar to leaves. He pulled off a handful of them and decided, after examination, to take a chance on them. He used them to clean off the sand and dirt and caked blood, then made a pad of fresh leaves and tied it over the wound with tendrils from the same bush.

The tendrils proved unexpectedly tough and strong. They were slender, and soft and pliable, yet he couldn't break them at all. He had to saw them off the bush with the sharp edge of a piece of the blue flint. Some of the thickest ones were over a foot long, and he filed away in his memory, for future reference, the fact that a bunch of the thick ones, tied together, would make a pretty serviceable rope. Maybe he'd be able to think of a use for rope.

Next, he made himself a knife. The blue flint *did* chip. From a foot-long splinter of it, he fashioned himself a crude but lethal weapon. And of tendrils from the bush, he made himself a rope belt through which he could thrust the flint knife, to keep it with him all the time and yet have his hands free.

He went back to studying the bushes. There were three other types. One was leafless, dry, brittle, rather like a dried tumbleweed. Another was of soft, crumbly wood, almost like punk. It looked and felt as though it would make excellent tinder for a fire. The third type was the most nearly wood-like. It had fragile leaves that wilted at a touch, but the stalks, although short, were straight and strong.

It was horribly, unbearably hot.

He limped up to the barrier, felt to make sure that it was still there. It was.

He stood watching the Roller for a while. It was keeping a safe distance back from the barrier, out of effective stone-throwing range. It was moving around back there, doing something. He couldn't tell what it was doing.

Once it stopped moving, came a little closer, and seemed to concentrate its attention on him. Again Carson had to fight off a wave of nausea. He threw a stone at it and the Roller retreated and went back to whatever it had been doing before.

At least he could make it keep its distance.

And, he thought bitterly, a devil of a lot of good *that* did him. Just the same, he spent the next hour or two gathering stones of suitable size for throwing, and making several neat piles of them, near his side of the barrier.

His throat burned now. It was difficult for him to think about anything except water.

But he *had* to think about other things. About getting through that barrier, under or over it, getting *at* that red sphere and killing it before this place of heat and thirst killed him first.

The barrier went to the wall upon either side, but how high and how far under the sand?

For just a moment, Carson's mind was too fuzzy to think out how he could find out either of those things. Idly, sitting there in the hot sand—and he didn't remember sitting down—he watched a blue lizard crawl from the shelter of one bush to the shelter of another.

From under the second bush, it looked out at him.

Carson grinned at it. Maybe he was getting a bit punch-drunk, because he remembered suddenly the old story of the desert-colonists on Mars, taken from an older desert story of Earth— "Pretty soon you get so lonesome you find yourself talking to the lizards, and then not so long after that you find the lizards talking back to you—"

He should have been concentrating, of course, on how to kill the Roller, but instead he grinned at the lizard and said, "Hello, there."

The lizard took a few steps toward him. "Hello," it said.

Carson was stunned for a moment, and then he put back his head and roared with laughter. It didn't hurt his throat to do so, either; he hadn't been *that* thirsty.

Why not? Why should the Entity who thought up this nightmare of a place not have a sense of humor, along with the other powers he has? Talking lizards, equipped to talk back in my own language, if I talk to them— It's a nice touch.

He grinned at the lizard and said, "Come on over." But the lizard turned and ran away, scurrying from bush to bush until it was out of sight.

He was thirsty again.

And he had to *do* something. He couldn't win this contest by sitting here sweating and feeling miserable. He had to *do* something. But what?

Get through the barrier. But he couldn't get through it, or over it. But was he certain he couldn't get under? And come to think of it, didn't one sometimes find water by digging? Two birds with one stone—

Painfully now, Carson limped up to the barrier and started digging, scooping up sand a double handful at a time. It was slow, hard work because the sand ran in at the edges and the deeper he got the bigger in diameter the hole had to be. How many hours it took him, he didn't know, but he hit bedrock four feet down. Dry bedrock; no sign of water.

And the force-field of the barrier went down clear to the bedrock. No dice. No water. Nothing.

He crawled out of the hole and lay there panting, and then raised his head to look across and see what the Roller was doing. It must be doing something back there.

It was. It was making something out of wood from the bushes, tied together with tendrils. A queerly shaped framework about four feet high and roughly square. To see it better, Carson climbed up onto the mound of sand he had excavated from the hole, and stood there staring.

There were two long levers sticking out of the back of it, one with a cup-shaped affair on the end of it. Seemed to be some sort of a catapult, Carson thought.

Sure enough, the Roller was lifting a sizable rock into the cup-shaped outfit. One of his tentacles moved the other lever up and down for a while, and then he turned the machine slightly as though aiming it and the lever with the stone flew up and forward.

The stone arced several yards over Carson's head, so far away that he didn't have to duck, but he judged the distance it had traveled, and whistled softly. He couldn't throw a rock that weight more than half that distance. And even retreating to the rear of his domain wouldn't put him out of range of that machine, if the Roller shoved it forward almost to the barrier.

Another rock whizzed over. Not quite so far away this time.

That thing could be dangerous, he decided. Maybe he'd better do something about it.

Moving from side to side along the barrier, so the catapult couldn't bracket him, he whaled a dozen rocks at it. But that wasn't going to be any good, he saw. They had to be light rocks, or he couldn't throw them that far. If they hit the framework, they bounced off harmlessly. And the Roller had no difficulty, at that distance, in moving aside from those that came near it.

Besides, his arm was tiring badly. He ached all over from sheer weariness. If he could only rest a while without having to duck rocks from that catapult at regular intervals of maybe thirty seconds each—

He stumbled back to the rear of the arena. Then he saw even that wasn't any good. The rocks reached back there, too, only there were longer intervals between them, as though it took longer to wind up the mechanism, whatever it was, of the catapult.

Wearily he dragged himself back to the barrier again. Several times he fell and could barely rise to his feet to go on. He was, he knew, near the limit of his endurance. Yet he didn't dare stop moving now, until and unless he could put that catapult out of action. If he fell asleep, he'd never wake up.

One of the stones from it gave him the first glimmer of an idea. It struck upon one of the piles of stones he'd gathered together near the barrier to use as ammunition, and it struck sparks.

Sparks. Fire. Primitive man had made fire by striking sparks, and with some of those dry crumbly bushes as tinder—

Luckily, a bush of that type was near him. He broke it off, took it over to the pile of stones, then patiently hit one stone against another until a spark touched the punklike wood of the bush. It went up in flames so fast that it singed his eyebrows and was burned to an ash within seconds.

But he had the idea now, and within minutes he had a little fire going in the lee of the mound of sand he'd made digging the hole an hour or two ago. Tinder bushes had started it, and other bushes which burned, but more slowly, kept it a steady flame.

The tough wirelike tendrils didn't burn readily; that made the fire-bombs easy to make and throw. A bundle of faggots tied about a small stone to give it weight and a loop of the tendril to swing it by.

He made half a dozen of them before he lighted and threw the first. It went wide, and the Roller started a quick retreat, pulling the catapult after him. But Carson had the others ready and threw them in rapid succession. The fourth wedged in the catapult's framework, and did the trick. The Roller tried desperately to put out the spreading blaze by throwing sand, but its clawed tentacles would take only a spoonful at a time and his efforts were ineffectual. The catapult burned.

The Roller moved safely away from the fire and seemed to concentrate its attention on Carson and again he felt that wave of hatred and nausea. But more weakly; either the Roller itself was weakening or Carson had learned how to protect himself against the mental attack.

He thumbed his nose at it and then sent it scuttling back to safety by throwing a stone. The Roller went clear to the back of its half of the arena and started pulling up bushes again. Probably it was going to make another catapult.

Carson verified—for the hundredth time—that the barrier was still operating, and then found himself sitting in the sand beside it because he was suddenly too weak to stand up.

His leg throbbed steadily now and the pangs of thirst were severe. But those things paled beside the utter physical exhaustion that gripped his entire body.

And the heat.

Hell must be like this, he thought. The hell that the ancients had believed in. He fought to stay awake, and yet staying awake seemed futile, for there was nothing he could do. Nothing, while the barrier remained impregnable and the Roller stayed back out of range.

But there must be *something*. He tried to remember things he had read in books of archaeology about the methods of fighting used back in the days before metal and plastic. The stone missile, that had come first, he thought. Well, that he already had.

The only improvement on it would be a catapult, such as the Roller had made. But he'd never be able to make one, with the tiny bits of wood available from the bushes—no single piece longer than a foot or so. Certainly he could figure out a mechanism for one, but he didn't have the endurance left for a task that would take days.

Days? But the Roller had made one. Had they been here days already? Then he remembered that the Roller had many tentacles to work with and undoubtedly could do such work faster than he.

And besides, a catapult wouldn't decide the issue. He had to do better than that.

Bow and arrow? No; he'd tried archery once and knew his own ineptness with a bow. Even with a modern sportsman's durasteel weapon, made for accuracy. With such a crude, pieced-together outfit as he could make here, he doubted if he could shoot as far as he could throw a rock, and knew he couldn't shoot as straight.

Spear? Well, he *could* make that. It would be useless as a throwing weapon at any distance, but would be a handy thing at close range, if he ever got to close range.

And making one would give him something to do. Help keep his mind from wandering, as it was beginning to do. Sometimes now, he had to concentrate a while before he could remember why he was here, why he had to kill the Roller.

Luckily he was still beside one of the piles of stones. He sorted through it until he found one shaped roughly like a spearhead. With a smaller stone he began to chip it into shape, fashioning sharp shoulders on the sides so that if it penetrated it would not pull out again.

Like a harpoon? There was something in that idea, he thought. A harpoon was better than a spear, maybe, for this crazy contest. If he could once get it into the Roller, and had a rope on it, he could pull the Roller up against the barrier and the stone blade of his knife would reach through that barrier, even if his hands wouldn't.

The shaft was harder to make than the head. But by splitting and joining the main stems of four of the bushes, and wrapping the joints with the tough but thin tendrils, he got a strong shaft about four feet long, and tied the stone head in a notch cut in the end.

It was crude, but strong.

And the rope. With the thin tough tendrils he made himself twenty feet of line. It was light and didn't look strong, but he knew it would hold his weight and to spare. He tied one end of it to the shaft of the harpoon and the other end about his right wrist. At least, if he threw his harpoon across the barrier, he'd be able to pull it back if he missed.

Then when he had tied the last knot and there was nothing more he could do, the heat and the weariness and the pain in his leg and the dreadful thirst were suddenly a thousand times worse than they had been before.

He tried to stand up, to see what the Roller was doing now, and found he couldn't get to his feet. On the third try, he got as far as his knees and then fell flat again.

"I've got to sleep," he thought. "If a showdown came now, I'd be helpless. He could come up here and kill me, if he knew. I've got to regain some strength."

Slowly, painfully, he crawled back away from the barrier. Ten yards, twenty—

The jar of something thudding against the sand near him waked him from a confused and horrible dream to a more confused and more horrible reality, and he opened his eyes again to blue radiance over blue sand.

How long had he slept? A minute? A day?

Another stone thudded nearer and threw sand on him. He got his arms under him and sat up. He turned around and saw the Roller twenty yards away, at the barrier.

It rolled away hastily as he sat up, not stopping until it was as far away as it could get.

He'd fallen asleep too soon, he realized, while he was still in range of the Roller's throwing ability. Seeing him lying motionless, it had dared come up to the barrier to throw at him. Luckily, it didn't realize how weak he was, or it could have stayed there and kept on throwing stones.

Had he slept long? He didn't think so, because he felt just as he had before. Not rested at all, no thirstier, no different. Probably he'd been there only a few minutes.

He started crawling again, this time forcing himself to keep going until he was as far as he could go, until the colorless, opaque wall of the arena's outer shell was only a yard away.

Then things slipped away again—

When he awoke, nothing about him was changed, but this time he knew that he had slept a long time.

The first thing he became aware of was the inside of his mouth; it was dry, caked. His tongue was swollen.

Something was wrong, he knew, as he returned slowly to full awareness. He felt less tired, the stage of utter exhaustion had passed. The sleep had taken care of that.

But there was pain, agonizing pain. It wasn't until he tried to move that he knew that it came from his leg.

He raised his head and looked down at it. It was swollen

terribly below the knee and the swelling showed even halfway up his thigh. The plant tendrils he had used to tie on the protective pad of leaves now cut deeply into the swollen flesh.

To get his knife under that imbedded lashing would have been impossible. Fortunately, the final knot was over the shin bone, in front, where the vine cut in less deeply than elsewhere. He was able, after an agonizing effort, to untie the knot.

A look under the pad of leaves told him the worst. Infection and blood poisoning, both pretty bad and getting worse.

And without drugs, without cloth, without even *water*, there wasn't a thing he could do about it.

Not a thing, except *die*, when the poison had spread through his system.

He knew it was hopeless, then, and that he'd lost.

And with him, humanity. When he died here, out there in the universe he knew, all his friends, everybody, would die too. And Earth and the colonized planets would be the home of the red, rolling, alien Outsiders. Creatures out of nightmare, things without a human attribute, who picked lizards apart for the fun of it.

It was the thought of that which gave him courage to start crawling, almost blindly in pain, toward the barrier again. Not crawling on hands and knees this time, but pulling himself along only by his arms and hands.

A chance in a million, that maybe he'd have strength left, when he got there, to throw his harpoon-spear just *once*, and with deadly effect, if—on another chance in a million—the Roller would come up to the barrier. Or if the barrier was gone, now.

It took him years, it seemed, to get there.

The barrier wasn't gone. It was as impassable as when he'd first felt it.

And the Roller wasn't at the barrier. By raising up on his elbows, he could see it at the back of its part of the arena, working on a wooden framework that was a half-completed duplicate of the catapult he'd destroyed.

It was moving slowly now. Undoubtedly it had weakened, too.

But Carson doubted that it would ever need that second catapult. He'd be dead, he thought, before it was finished.

If he could attract it to the barrier, now, while he was still alive— He waved an arm and tried to shout, but his parched throat would make no sound.

Or if he could get through the barrier—

His mind must have slipped for a moment, for he found himself beating his fists against the barrier in futile rage, made himself stop.

He closed his eyes, tried to make himself calm.

"Hello," said the voice.

It was a small, thin voice. It sounded like—

He opened his eyes and turned his head. It *was* a lizard.

"Go away," Carson wanted to say. "Go away; you're not really there, or you're there but not really talking. I'm imagining things again."

But he couldn't talk; his throat and tongue were past all speech with the dryness. He closed his eyes again.

"Hurt," said the voice. "Kill. Hurt—kill. Come."

He opened his eyes again. The blue ten-legged lizard was still there. It ran a little way along the barrier, came back, started off again, and came back.

"Hurt," it said. "Kill. Come."

Again it started off, and came back. Obviously it wanted Carson to follow it along the barrier.

He closed his eyes again. The voice kept on. The same three meaningless words. Each time he opened his eyes, it ran off and came back.

"Hurt. Kill. Come."

Carson groaned. There would be no peace unless he followed the blasted thing. As it wanted him to.

He followed it, crawling. Another sound, a high-pitched squealing, came to his ears and grew louder.

There was something lying in the sand, writhing, squealing. Something small, blue, that looked like a lizard and yet didn't—

Then he saw what it was—the lizard whose legs the Roller had pulled off, so long ago. But it wasn't dead; it had come back to life and was wriggling and screaming in agony.

"Hurt," said the other lizard. "Hurt. Kill. Kill."

Carson understood. He took the flint knife from his belt and killed the tortured creature. The live lizard scurried off quickly.

Carson turned back to the barrier. He leaned his hands and head against it and watched the Roller, far back, working on the new catapult.

"I could get that far," he thought, "if I could get through. If I could get through, I might win yet. It looks weak, too. I might—"

And then there was another reaction of black hopelessness, when pain sapped his will and he wished that he were dead. He envied the lizard he'd just killed. It didn't have to live on and suffer. And he did. It would be hours, it might be days, before the blood poisoning killed him.

If only he could use that knife on himself—

But he knew he wouldn't. As long as he was alive, there was the millionth chance—.

He was straining, pushing on the barrier with the flat of his hands, and he noticed his arms, how thin and scrawny they were now. He must really have been here a long time, for days, to get as thin as that.

How much longer now, before he died? How much more heat and thirst and pain could flesh stand?

For a little while he was almost hysterical again, and then came a time of deep calm, and a thought that was startling.

The lizard he had just killed. *It had crossed the barrier, still alive.* It had come from the Roller's side; the Roller had pulled off its legs and then tossed it contemptuously at him and it had come through the barrier. He'd thought, because the lizard was dead.

But it hadn't been dead; it had been unconscious.

A live lizard couldn't go through the barrier, but an unconscious one could. The barrier was not a barrier, then, to living flesh, but to conscious flesh. It was a *mental* projection, a *mental* hazard.

And with that thought, Carson started crawling along the barrier to make his last desperate gamble. A hope so forlorn that only a dying man would have dared try it.

No use weighing the odds of success. Not when, if he didn't try it, those odds were infinitely to zero.

He crawled along the barrier to the dune of sand, about four feet high, which he'd scooped out in trying—how many days ago?—to dig under the barrier or to reach water.

That mound was right at the barrier, its farther slope half on one side of the barrier, half on the other.

Taking with him a rock from the pile nearby, he climbed up to the top of the dune and over the top, and lay there against the barrier, his weight leaning against it so that if the barrier were taken away he'd roll on down the short slope, into the enemy territory.

He checked to be sure that the knife was safely in his rope belt, that the harpoon was in the crook of his left arm and that the twenty-foot rope fastened to it and to his wrist.

Then with his right hand he raised the rock with which he would hit himself on the head. Luck would have to be with him on that blow; it would have to be hard enough to knock him out, but not hard enough to knock him out for long.

He had a hunch that the Roller was watching him, and would see him roll down through the barrier, and come to investigate. It would think he was dead, he hoped—he thought it had probably drawn the same deduction about the nature of the barrier that he had drawn. But it would come cautiously. He would have a little time—

He struck.

Pain brought him back to consciousness. A sudden, sharp pain in his hip that was different from the throbbing pain in his head and the throbbing pain in his leg.

But he had, thinking things out before he had struck himself, anticipated that very pain, even hoped for it, and had steeled himself against awakening with a sudden movement.

He lay still, but opened his eyes just a slit, and saw that he had guessed right. The Roller was coming closer. It was twenty feet away and the pain that had awakened him was the stone it had tossed to see whether he was alive or dead.

He lay still. It came closer, fifteen feet away, and stopped again. Carson scarcely breathed.

As nearly as possible, he was keeping his mind a blank, lest its telepathic ability detect consciousness in him. And with his mind blanked out that way, the impact of its thoughts upon his mind was nearly soul-shattering.

He felt sheer horror at the utter *alienness*, the *differentness* of those thoughts. Things that he felt but could not understand and could never express, because no terrestrial language had words, no terrestrial mind had images to fit them. The mind of a spider, he thought, or the mind of a praying mantis or a Martian sand-serpent, raised to intelligence and put in telepathic rapport with human minds, would be a homely familiar thing, compared to this.

He understood now that the Entity had been right: Man or Roller, and the universe was not a place that could hold them both. Further apart than god and devil, there could never be even a balance between them.

Closer. Carson waited until it was only feet away, until its clawed tentacles reached out—

Oblivious to agony now, he sat up, raised and flung the harpoon with all the strength that remained to him. Or he thought it was all; sudden final strength flooded through him, along with a sudden forgetfulness of pain as definite as a nerve block.

As the Roller, deeply stabbed by the harpoon, rolled away, Carson tried to get to his feet to run after it. He couldn't do that; he fell, but kept crawling.

It reached the end of the rope, and he was jerked forward by the pull on his wrist. It dragged him a few feet and then stopped. Carson kept on going, pulling himself toward it hand over hand along the rope.

It stopped there, writhing tentacles trying in vain to pull out the harpoon. It seemed to shudder and quiver, and then it must have realized that it couldn't get away, for it rolled back toward him, clawed tentacles reaching out.

Stone knife in hand, he met it. He stabbed, again and again, while those horrid claws ripped skin and flesh and muscle from his body.

He stabbed and slashed, and at last it was still.

A bell was ringing, and it took him a while after he'd opened his eyes to tell where he was and what it was. He was strapped into the seat of his scouter, and the visiplate before him showed only empty space. No Outsider ship and no impossible planet.

The bell was the communications plate signal; someone wanted him to switch power into the receiver. Purely reflex action enabled him to reach forward and throw the lever.

The face of Brander, captain of the *Magellan*, mother-ship

of his group of scouters, flashed into the screen. His face was pale and his black eyes glowing with excitement.

"*Magellan* to Carson," he snapped. "Come on in. The flight's over. We've won!"

The screen went blank; Brander would be signaling the other scouters of his command.

Slowly, Carson set the controls for the return. Slowly, unbelievingly, he unstrapped himself from the seat and went back to get a drink at the cold-water tank. For some reason, he was unbelievably thirsty. He drank six glasses.

He leaned there against the wall, trying to think.

Had it happened? He was in good health, sound, uninjured. His thirst had been mental rather than physical; his throat hadn't been dry. His leg—

He pulled up his trouser leg and looked at the calf. There was a long white scar there, but a perfectly healed scar. It hadn't been there before. He zipped open the front of his shirt and saw that his chest and abdomen were criss-crossed with tiny, almost unnoticeable, perfectly healed scars.

It *had* happened.

The scouter, under automatic control, was already entering the hatch of the mother-ship. The grapples pulled it into its individual lock, and a moment later a buzzer indicated that the lock was airfilled. Carson opened the hatch and stepped outside, went through the double door of the lock.

He went right to Brander's office, went in, and saluted.

Brander still looked dizzily dazed. "Hi, Carson," he said. "What you missed! What a show!"

"What happened, sir?"

"Don't know, exactly. We fired one salvo, and their whole fleet went up in dust! Whatever it was jumped from ship to ship in a flash, even the ones we hadn't aimed at and that were out of range! The whole fleet disintegrated before our eyes, and we didn't get the paint of a single ship scratched!

"We can't even claim credit for it. Must have been some unstable component in the metal they used, and our sighting shot just set it off. Man, oh man, too bad you missed all the excitement."

Carson managed to grin. It was a sickly ghost of a grin, for it would be days before he'd be over the mental impact of his experience, but the captain wasn't watching, and didn't notice.

"Yes, sir," he said. Common sense, more than modesty, told him he'd be branded forever as the worst liar in space if he ever said any more than that. "Yes, sir, too bad I missed all the excitement."

HUDDLING PLACE

Astounding,

July

by Clifford D. Simak

The second of the City Series that brought fame and honors to Cliff Simak, "Huddling Place" is a wonderful story about an important problem—that of breaking away, of starting something entirely new, and of leaving the familiar for the unknown. Few writers have brought the emotion and pathos to this experience achieved by Simak in this moving and quite profound story.

(In 1938, Cliff published "Rule 18" (which I would have fought to include had we not started this series in the year 1939) and I slammed it in a letter to the editor. Cliff wrote to me (initiating a life-long correspondence and asked if I could explain what was wrong with it. I reread it and discovered there was nothing wrong with it. I had simply not read it with sufficient attention. I told him this in all humility and then I went further. So much did I admire the story on rereading that I consciously adopted Cliff's style as best I could and clung to it ever since. It is a pleasant memory that at the Nebula Awards Dinner at which Cliff was honored as Grand Master, I served as Toastmaster. (He is the favorite science fiction writer of my wife, Janet Jeppson, and marriage to me didn't shake her allegiance to him in the least.)—I.A.)

The drizzle sifted from the leaden skies, like smoke drifting through the bare-branched trees. It softened the hedges and hazed the outlines of the buildings and blotted out the distance. It glinted on the metallic skins of the silent robots and silvered the shoulders of the three humans listening to the intonations of the black-garbed man, who read from the book cupped between his hands.

"For I am the Resurrection and the Life—"

The moss-mellowed graven figure that reared above the door of the crypt seemed straining upward, every crystal of its yearning body reaching toward something that no one else could see. Straining as it had strained since that day of long ago when men had chipped it from the granite to adorn the family tomb with a symbolism that had pleased the first John J. Webster in the last years he held of life.

"And whosoever liveth and believeth in Me—"

Jerome A. Webster felt his son's fingers tighten on his arm, heard the muffled sobbing of his mother, saw the lines of robots standing rigid, heads bowed in respect to the master they had served. The master who now was going home—to the final home of all.

Numbly, Jerome A. Webster wondered if they understood—if they understood life and death—if they understood what it meant that Nelson F. Webster lay there in the casket, that a man with a book intoned words above him.

Nelson F. Webster, fourth of the line of Websters who had lived on these acres, had lived and died here, scarcely leaving, and now was going to his final rest in that place the first of them had prepared for the rest of them—for that long line of shadowy descendants who would live here and cherish the things and the ways and the life that the first John J. Webster had established.

Jerome A. Webster felt his jaw muscles tighten, felt a little tremor run across his body. For a moment his eyes burned and the casket blurred in his sight and the words the man in black was saying were one with the wind that whispered in the pines standing sentinel for the dead. Within his brain remembrance marched—remembrance of a gray-haired man stalking the hills and fields, sniffing the breeze of an early morning, standing, legs braced, before the flaring fireplace with a glass of brandy in his hand.

Pride—the pride of land and life, and the humility and greatness that quiet living breeds within a man. Contentment of casual leisure and surety of purpose. Independence of assured security, comfort of familiar surroundings, freedom of broad acres.

Thomas Webster was jiggling his elbow. "Father," he was whispering. "Father."

The service was over. The black-garbed man had closed his book. Six robots stepped forward, lifted the casket.

Slowly the three followed the casket into the crypt, stood silently as the robots slid it into its receptacle, closed the tiny door and affixed the plate that read:

NELSON F. WEBSTER
2034-2117

That was all. Just the name and dates. And that, Jerome A. Webster found himself thinking, was enough. There was nothing else that needed to be there. That was all those others had. The ones that called the family roll—starting with William Stevens, 1920-1999. Gramp Stevens, they had called him, Webster remembered. Father of the wife of that first John J. Webster, who was here himself—1951-2020. And after him his son, Charles F. Webster, 1980-2060. And his son, John J. II, 2004-2086. Webster could remember John J. II—a grandfather who had slept beside the fire with his pipe hanging from his mouth, eternally threatening to set his whiskers aflame.

Webster's eyes strayed to another plate. Mary Webster, the mother of the boy here at his side. And yet not a boy. He kept forgetting that Thomas was twenty now, in a week or so would be leaving for Mars, even as in his younger days he, too, had gone to Mars.

All here together, he told himself. The Websters and their wives and children. Here in death together as they had lived together, sleeping in the pride and security of bronze and marble with the pines outside and the symbolic figure above the age-greened door.

The robots were waiting, standing silently, their task fulfilled.

His mother looked at him.

"You're the head of the family now, my son," she told him.

He reached out and hugged her close against his side. Head of the family—what was left of it. Just the three of them now. His mother and his son. And his son would be leaving soon, going out to Mars. But he would come back. Come back with a wife, perhaps, and the family would go on. The family wouldn't stay at three. Most of the big house wouldn't stay closed off, as it now was closed off. There had been a time when it had rung with the life of a dozen units of the family, living in their separate apartments under one big roof. That time, he knew, would come again.

The three of them turned and left the crypt, took the path back to the house, looming like a huge gray shadow in the midst.

A fire blazed in the hearth and the book lay upon his desk. Jerome A. Webster reached out and picked it up, read the title once again:

Martian Physiology, With Especial Reference to the Brain by Jerome A. Webster, M.D.

Thick and authoritative—the work of a lifetime. Standing almost alone in its field. Based upon the data gathered during those five plague years on Mars—years when he had labored almost day and night with his fellow colleagues of the World Committee's medical commission, dispatched on an errand of mercy to the neighboring planet.

A tap sounded on the door.

"Come in," he called.

The door opened and a robot glided in.

"Your whiskey, sir."

"Thank you, Jenkins," Webster said.

"The minister, sir," said Jenkins, "has left."

"Oh, yes. I presume that you took care of him."

"I did, sir. Gave him the usual fee and offered him a drink. He refused the drink."

"That was a social error," Webster told him. "Ministers don't drink."

"I'm sorry, sir. I didn't know. He asked me to ask you to come to church sometime."

"Eh?"

"I told him, sir, that you never went anywhere."

"That was quite right, Jenkins," said Webster. "None of us go anywhere."

Jenkins headed for the door, stopped before he got there, turned around. "If I may say so, sir, that was a touching service at the crypt. Your father was a fine human, the finest ever was. The robots were saying the service was very fitting. Dignified like, sir. He would have liked it had he known."

"My father," said Webster, "would be even more pleased to hear you say that, Jenkins."

"Thank you, sir," said Jenkins, and went out.

Webster sat with the whisky and the book and fire—felt the comfort of the well-known room close in about him, felt the refuge that was in it.

This was home. It had been home for the Websters since that day when the first John J. had come here and built the first unit of the sprawling house. John J. had chosen it because it had a trout stream, or so he always said. But it was something more than that. It must have been, Webster told himself, something more than that.

Or perhaps, at first, it had only been the trout stream. The trout stream and the trees and meadows, the rocky ridge where the mist drifted in each morning from the river. Maybe the rest of it had grown, grown gradually through the years, through years of family association until the very soil was soaked with something that approached, but wasn't quite, tradition. Something that made each tree, each rock, each foot of soil a Webster tree or rock or clod of soil. It all belonged.

John J., the first John J., had come after the breakup of the cities, after men had forsaken, once and for all, the twentieth century huddling places, had broken free of the tribal instinct to stick together in one cave or in one clearing against a common foe or a common fear. An instinct that had become outmoded, for there were no fears or foes. Man revolting against the herd instinct economic and social conditions had impressed upon him in ages past. A new security and a new sufficiency had made it possible to break away.

The trend had started back in the twentieth century, more than two hundred years before, when men moved to country homes to get fresh air and elbow room and a graciousness in life that communal existence, in its strictest sense, never had given them.

And here was the end result. A quiet living. A peace that could only come with good things. The sort of life that men had yearned for years to have. A manorial existence, based on old family homes and leisurely acres, with atomics supplying power and robots in place of serfs.

Webster smiled at the fireplace with its blazing wood. That was an anachronism, but a good one—something that Man had brought forward from the caves. Useless, because atomic heating was better—but more pleasant. One couldn't sit and watch atomics and dream and build castles in the flames.

Even the crypt out there, where they had put his father that afternoon. That was family, too. All of a piece with the rest of it. The somber pride and leisured life and peace. In the old days the dead were buried in vast plots all together, stranger cheek by jowl with stranger—

He never goes anywhere.

That is what Jenkins had told the minister.

And that was right. For what need was there to go anywhere? It all was here. By simply twirling a dial one could talk face-to-face with anyone one wished, could go, by sense, if not in body, anywhere one wished. Could attend the theater or hear a concert or browse in a library halfway around the world. Could transact any business one might need to transact without rising from one's chair.

Webster drank the whisky, then swung to the dialed machine beside his desk.

He spun dials from memory without resorting to the log. He knew where he was going.

His finger flipped a toggle and the room melted away—or seemed to melt. There was left the chair within which he sat, part of the desk, part of the machine itself and that was all.

The chair was on a hillside swept with golden grass and dotted with scraggly, wind-twisted trees, a hillside that straggled down to a lake nestling in the grip of purple mountain spurs. The spurs, darkened in long streaks with the bluish-green of distant pine, climbed in staggering stairs, melting into the blue-tinged snow-capped peaks that reared beyond and above them in jagged saw-toothed outline.

The wind talked harshly in the crouching trees and ripped the long grass in sudden gusts. The last rays of the sun struck fire from the distant peaks.

Solitude and grandeur, the long sweep of tumbled land, the cuddled lake, the knifelike shadows on the far-off ranges.

Webster sat easily in his chair, eyes squinting at the peaks.

A voice said almost at his shoulder: "May I come in?"

A soft, sibilant voice, wholly unhuman. But one that Webster knew.

He nodded his head. "By all means, Juwain."

He turned slightly and saw the elaborate crouching pedestal, the furry, soft-eyed figure of the Martian squatting on it. Other alien furniture loomed indistinctly beyond the pedestal, half-guessed furniture from that dwelling out on Mars.

The Martian flipped a furry hand toward the mountain range.

"You love this," he said. "You can understand it. And I can understand how you understand it, but to me there is more terror than beauty in it. It is something we could never have on Mars."

Webster reached out a hand, but the Martian stopped him.

"Leave it on," he said. "I know why you came here. I would not have come at a time like this except I thought perhaps an old friend—"

"It is kind of you," said Webster. "I am glad that you have come."

"Your father," said Juwain, "was a great man. I remember how you used to talk to me of him, those years you spent on Mars. You said then you would come back sometime. Why is it you've never come?"

"Why," said Webster, "I just never—"

"Do not tell me," said the Martian. "I already know."

"My son," said Webster, "is going to Mars in a few days. I shall have him call on you."

"That would be a pleasure," said Juwain. "I shall be expecting him."

He stirred uneasily on the crouching pedestal. "Perhaps he carries on tradition."

"No," said Webster. "He is studying engineering. He never cared for surgery."

"He has a right," observed the Martian, "to follow the life that he has chosen. Still, one might be permitted to wish."

"One could," Webster agreed. "But that is over and done with. Perhaps he will be a great engineer. Space structure. Talks of ships out to the stars."

"Perhaps," suggested Juwain, "your family has done enough for medical science. You and your father—"

"And his father," said Webster, "before him."

"Your book," declared Juwain, "has put Mars in debt to you. It may focus more attention on Martian specialization. My people do not make good doctors. They have no background for it. Queer how the minds of races run. Queer that Mars never thought of medicine—literally never thought of it. Supplied the need with a cult of fatalism. While even in your early history, when men still lived in caves—"

"There are many things," said Webster, "that you thought of and we didn't. Things we wonder now how we ever missed. Abilities that you developed and we do not have. Take your own specialty, philosophy. But different than ours. A science, while ours never was more than ordered fumbling. Yours an orderly, logical development of philosophy, workable, practical, applicable, an actual tool."

Juwain started to speak, hesitated, then when ahead. "I am near to something, something that may be new and startling. Something that will be a tool for you humans as well as for the Martians. I've worked on it for years, starting with certain mental concepts that first were suggested to me with arrival of the Earthmen. I have said nothing, for I could not be sure."

"And now," suggested Webster, "you are sure."

"Not quite," said Juwain. "Not positive. But almost."

They sat in silence, watching the mountains and the lake. A bird came and sat in one of the scraggly trees and sang. Dark clouds piled up behind the mountain ranges and the snow-tipped peaks stood out like graven stone. The sun sank in a lake of crimson, hushed finally to the glow of a fire burned low.

A tap sounded from a door and Webster stirred in his chair, suddenly brought back to the reality of the study, of the chair beneath him.

Juwain was gone. The old philosopher had come and sat an hour of contemplation with his friend and then had quietly slipped away.

The rap came again.

Webster leaned forward, snapped the toggle and the mountains vanished; the room became a room again. Dusk filtered through the high windows and the fire was a rosy flicker in the ashes.

"Come in," said Webster.

Jenkins opened the door. "Dinner is served, sir," he said.

"Thank you," said Webster. He rose slowly from the chair.

"Your place, sir," said Jenkins, "is laid at the head of the table."

"Ah, yes," said Webster. "Thank you, Jenkins. Thank you very much, for reminding me."

Webster stood on the broad ramp of the space field and watched the shape that dwindled in the sky with faint flickering points of red lancing through the wintry sunlight.

For long minutes after the shape was gone he stood there, hands gripping the railing in front of him, eyes still staring up into the sky.

His lips moved and they said: "Good-bye, son"; but there was no sound.

Slowly he came alive to his surroundings. Knew that people moved about the ramp, saw that the landing field seemed to stretch interminably to the far horizon, dotted here and there with hump-backed things that were waiting spaceships. Scooting tractors worked near one hangar, clearing away the last of the snowfall of the night before.

Webster shivered and thought that it was queer, for the noonday sun was warm. And shivered again.

Slowly he turned away from the railing and headed for the administration building. And for one brain-wrenching moment he felt a sudden fear—an unreasonable and embarrassing fear of that stretch of concrete that formed the ramp. A fear that left him shaking mentally as he drove his feet toward the waiting door.

A man walked toward him, briefcase swinging in his hand and Webster, eyeing him, wished fervently that the man would not speak to him.

The man did not speak, passed him with scarcely a glance, and Webster felt relief.

If he were back home, Webster told himself, he would have finished lunch, would now be ready to lie down for his midday nap. The fire would be blazing on the hearth and the flicker of the flames would be reflected from the andirons. Jenkins would bring him a liqueur and would say a word or two—inconsequential conversation.

He hurried toward the door, quickening his step, anxious to get away from the bare-cold expanse of the massive ramp.

Funny how he had felt about Thomas. Natural, of course,

that he should have hated to see him go. But entirely unnatural that he should, in those last few minutes, find such horror welling up within him. Horror of the trip through space, horror of the alien land of Mars—although Mars was scarcely alien any longer. For more than a century now Earthmen had known it, had fought it, lived with it; some of them had even grown to love it.

But it had only been utter will power that had prevented him, in those last few seconds before the ship had taken off, from running out into the field, shrieking for Thomas to come back, shrieking for him not to go.

And that, of course, never would have done. It would have been exhibitionism, disgraceful and humiliating—the sort of thing a Webster could not do.

After all, he told himself, a trip to Mars was no great adventure, not any longer. There had been a day when it had been, but that day was gone forever. He, himself, in his earlier days had made a trip to Mars, had stayed there for five long years. That had been—he gasped when he thought of it—that had been almost thirty years ago.

The babble and hum of the lobby hit him in the face as the robot attendant opened the door for him, and in that babble ran a vein of something that was almost terror. For a moment he hesitated, then stepped inside. The door closed softly behind him.

He stayed close to the wall to keep out of people's way, headed for a chair in one corner. He sat down and huddled back, forcing his body deep into the cushions, watching the milling humanity that seethed out in the room.

Shrill people, hurrying people, people with strange, unneighborly faces. Strangers—every one of them. Not a face he knew. People going places. Heading out for the planets. Anxious to be off. Worried about last details. Rushing here and there.

Out of the crowd loomed a familiar face. Webster hunched forward.

"Jenkins!" he shouted, and then was sorry for the shout, although no one seemed to notice.

The robot moved toward him, stood before him.

"Tell Raymond," said Webster, "that I must return immediately. Tell him to bring the 'copter in front at once."

"I am sorry, sir," said Jenkins, "but we cannot leave at

once. The mechanics found a flaw in the atomics chamber. They are installing a new one. It will take several hours."

"Surely," said Webster, impatiently, "that could wait until some other time."

"The mechanic said not, sir," Jenkins told him. "It might go at any minute. The entire charge of power—"

"Yes, yes," agreed Webster. "I suppose so."

He fidgeted with his hat. "I just remembered," he said, "something I must do. Something that must be done at once. I must get home. I can't wait several hours."

He hitched forward to the edge of the chair, eyes staring at the milling crowd.

Faces—faces—

"Perhaps you could televise," suggested Jenkins. "One of the robots might be able to do it. There is a booth—"

"Wait, Jenkins," said Webster. He hesitated a moment. "There is nothing to do back home. Nothing at all. But I must get there. I can't stay here. If I have to, I'll go crazy. I was frightened out there on the ramp. I'm bewildered and confused here. I have a feeling—a strange, terrible feeling. Jenkins, I—"

"I understand, sir," said Jenkins. "Your father had it, too."

Webster gasped. "My father?"

"Yes, sir, that is why he never went anywhere. He was about your age, sir, when he found it out. He tried to make a trip to Europe and he couldn't. He got halfway there and turned back. He had a name for it."

Webster sat in stricken silence.

"A name for it," he finally said. "Of course there's a name for it. My father had it. My grandfather—did he have it, too?"

"I wouldn't know that, sir," said Jenkins. "I wasn't created until after your grandfather was an elderly man. But he may have. He never went anywhere, either."

"You understand, then," said Webster. "You know how it is. I feel like I'm going to be sick—physically ill. See if you can charter a 'copter—anything, just so we get home."

"Yes, sir," said Jenkins.

He started off and Webster called him back.

"Jenkins, does anyone else know about this? Anyone—"

"No, sir," said Jenkins. "Your father never mentioned it and I felt, somehow, that he wouldn't wish me to."

"Thank you, Jenkins," said Webster.

Webster huddled back into his chair again, feeling desolate and alone and misplaced. Alone in a humming lobby that pulsed with life—a loneliness that tore at him, that left him limp and weak.

Homesickness. Downright, shameful homesickness, he told himself. Something that boys are supposed to feel when they first leave home, when they first go out to meet the world.

There was a fancy word for it—agoraphobia, the morbid dread of being in the midst of open spaces—from the Greek root for the fear—literally, of the market place.

If he crossed the room to the television booth, he could put in a call, talk with his mother or one of the robots—or, better yet, just sit and look at the place until Jenkins came for him.

He started to rise, then sank back in the chair again. It was no dice. Just talking to someone or looking in on the place wasn't being there. He couldn't smell the pines in the wintry air, or hear familiar snow crunch on the walk beneath his feet or reach out a hand and touch one of the massive oaks that grew along the path. He couldn't feel the heat of the fire or sense the sure, deft touch of belonging, of being one with a tract of ground and the things upon it.

And yet—perhaps it would help. Not much, maybe, but some. He started to rise from the chair again and froze. The few short steps to the booth held terror, a terrible, overwhelming terror. If he crossed them, he would have to run. Run to escape the watching eyes, the unfamiliar sounds, the agonizing nearness of strange faces.

Abruptly he sat down.

A woman's shrill voice cut across the lobby and he shrank away from it. He felt terrible. He felt like hell. He wished Jenkins would get a hustle on.

The first breath of spring came through the window, filling the study with the promise of melting snows, of coming leaves and flowers, of north-bound wedges of waterfowl streaming through the blue, of trout that lurked in pools waiting for the fly.

Webster lifted his eyes from the sheaf of papers on his desk, sniffed the breeze, felt the cool whisper of it on his cheek. His hand reached out for the brandy glass, found it empty, and put it back.

He bent back above the papers once again, picked up a pencil and crossed out a word.

Critically, he read the final paragraphs:

The fact that of the two hundred fifty men who were invited to visit me, presumably on missions of more than ordinary importance, only three were able to come, does not necessarily prove that all but those three are victims of agoraphobia. Some may have had legitimate reasons for being unable to accept my invitation. But it does indicate a growing unwillingness of men living under the mode of Earth existence set up following the breakup of the cities to move from familiar places, a deepening instinct to stay among the scenes and possessions which in their mind have become associated with contentment and graciousness of life.

What the result of such a trend will be, no one can clearly indicate since it applies to only a small portion of Earth's population. Among the larger families economic pressure forces some of the sons to seek their fortunes either in other parts of the Earth or on one of the other planets. Many others deliberately seek adventure and opportunity in space, while still others become associated with professions or trades which make a sedentary existence impossible.

He flipped the page over, went on to the last one.

It was a good paper, he knew, but it could not be published, not just yet. Perhaps after he had died. No one, so far as he could determine, had ever so much as realized the trend, had taken as matter of course the fact that men seldom left their homes. Why, after all, should they leave their homes?

The televisor muttered at his elbow and he reached out to flip the toggle.

The room faded and he was face-to-face with a man who sat behind a desk, almost as if he sat on the opposite side of Webster's desk. A gray-haired man with sad eyes behind heavy lenses.

For a moment Webster stared, memory tugging at him.

"Could it be—" he asked and the man smiled gravely.

"I have changed," he said. "So have you. My name is Clayborne. Remember? The Martian medical commission—"

"Clayborne! I'd often thought of you. You stayed on Mars."

Clayborne nodded. "I've read your book, doctor. It is a real contribution. I've often thought one should be written, wanted to myself, but I didn't have the time. Just as well I didn't. You did a better job. Especially on the brain."

"The Martian brain," Webster told him "always intrigued me. Certain peculiarities. I'm afraid I spent more of those five years taking notes on it than I should have. There was other work to do."

"A good thing you did," said Clayborne. "That's why I'm calling you now. I have a patient—a brain operation. Only you can handle it."

Webster gasped, his hands trembling. "You'll bring him here?"

Clayborne shook his head. "He cannot be moved. You know him, I believe. Juwain, the philosopher."

"Juwain!" said Webster. "He's one of my best friends. We talked together just a couple of days ago."

"The attack was sudden," said Clayborne. "He's been asking for you."

Webster was silent and cold—cold with a chill that crept upon him from some unguessed place. Cold that sent perspiration out upon his forehead, that knotted his fists.

"If you start immediately," said Clayborne, "you can be here on time. I've already arranged with the World Committee to have a ship at your disposal instantly. The utmost speed is necessary."

"But," said Webster, "but . . . I cannot come."

"You can't come!"

"It's impossible," said Webster. "I doubt in any case that I am needed. Surely, you yourself—"

"I can't," said Clayborne. "No one can but you. No one else has the knowledge. You hold Juwain's life in your hands. If you come, he lives. If you don't, he dies."

"I can't go into space," said Webster.

"Anyone can go into space," snapped Clayborne. "It's not like it used to be. Conditioning of any sort desired is available."

"But you don't understand," pleaded Webster. "You—"

"No, I don't," said Clayborne. "Frankly, I don't. That any-one should refuse to save the life of his friend—"

The two men stared at one another for a long moment, neither speaking.

"I shall tell the committee to send the ship straight to your home," said Clayborne finally. "I hope by that time you will see your way clear to come."

Clayborne faded and the wall came into view again—the wall and books, the fireplace and the paintings, the well-loved furniture, the promise of spring that came through the open window.

Webster sat frozen in his chair, staring at the wall in front of him.

Juwain, the furry, wrinkled face, the sibilant whisper, the friendliness and understanding that were his. Juwain, grasping the stuff that dreams are made of and shaping them into logic, into rules of life and conduct. Juwain, using philosophy as a tool, as a science, as a stepping stone to better living.

Webster dropped his face into his hands and fought the ag-ony that welled up within him.

Clayborne had not understood. One could not expect him to understand since there was no way for him to know. And even knowing, would he understand? Even he, Webster, would not have understood it in someone else until he had discovered it in himself—the terrible fear of leaving his own fire, his own land, his own possessions, the little symbolisms that he had erected. And yet, not he, himself, alone, but those other Websters as well. Starting with the first John J. Men and women who had set up a cult of life, a tradition of be-havior.

He, Jerome A. Webster, had gone to Mars when he was a young man, and had not felt or suspected the psychological poison that ran through his veins. Even as Thomas a few months ago had gone to Mars. But thirty years of quiet life here in the retreat that the Websters called a home had brought it forth, had developed it without his even knowing it. There had, in fact, been no opportunity to know it.

It was clear how it had developed—clear as crystal now. Habit and mental pattern and a happiness association with certain things—things that had no actual value in themselves, but had been assigned a value, a definite, concrete value by one family through five generations.

No wonder other places seemed alien, no wonder other horizons held a hint of horror in their sweep.

And there was nothing one could do about it—nothing, that is, unless one cut down every tree and burned the house and changed the course of waterways. Even that might not do it—even that—

The televisor purred and Webster lifted his head from his hands, reached out and thumbed the tumbler.

The room became a flare of white, but there was no image. A voice said: "Secret call. Secret call."

Webster slid back a panel in the machine, spun a pair of dials, heard the hum of power surge into a screen that blocked out the room.

"Secrecy established," he said.

The white flare snapped out and a man sat across the desk from him. A man he had seen many times before in televised addresses, in his daily paper.

Henderson, president of the World Committee.

"I have had a call from Clayborne," said Henderson.

Webster nodded without speaking.

"He tells me you refuse to go to Mars."

"I have not refused," said Webster. "When Clayborne cut off the question was left open. I had told him it was impossible for me to go, but he had rejected that, did not seem to understand."

"Webster, you must go," said Henderson. "You are the only man with the necessary knowledge of the Martian brain to perform this operation. If it were a simple operation, perhaps someone else could do it. But not one such as this."

"That maybe true," said Webster, "but—"

"It's not just a question of saving a life," said Henderson. "Even a life of so distinguished a personage as Juwain. It involves even more than that. Juwain is a friend of yours. Perhaps he hinted of something he has found."

"Yes," said Webster. "Yes, he did. A new concept of philosophy."

"A concept," declared Henderson, "that we cannot do without. A concept that will remake the solar system, that will put mankind ahead a hundred thousand years in the space of two generations. A new direction of purpose that will aim toward a goal we heretofore had not suspected, had not even known existed. A brand new truth, you see. One that never before had occurred to anyone."

Webster's hand gripped the edge of the desk until his knuckles stood out white.

"If Juwain dies," said Henderson, "that concept dies with him. Maybe lost forever."

"I'll try," said Webster. I'll try—"

Henderson's eyes were hard. "Is that the best you can do?"

"That is the best," said Webster.

"But, man, you must have a reason! Some explanation."

"None," said Webster, "that I would care to give."

Deliberately he reached out and flipped up the switch.

Webster sat at the desk and held his hands in front of him, staring at them. Hands that had skill, held knowledge. Hands that could save a life if he could get them to Mars. Hands that could save for the solar system, for mankind, for the Martians an idea—a new idea—that would advance them a hundred thousand years in the next two generations.

But hands chained by a phobia that grew out of his quiet life. Decadence—a strangely beautiful—and deadly—decadence.

Man had forsaken the teeming cities, the huddling place, two hundred years ago. He had done with the old foes and the ancient fears that kept him around the common campfire, had left behind the hobgoblins that had walked with him from the caves.

And yet—and yet.

Here was another huddling place. Not a huddling place for one's body, but one's mind. A psychological campfire that still held a man within the circle of its light.

Still, Webster knew, he must leave that fire. As the men had done with the cities two centuries before, he must walk off and leave it. And he must not look back.

He had to go to Mars—or at least start for Mars. There was no question there, at all. He had to go.

Whether he would survive the trip, whether he could perform the operation once he had arrived, he did not know. He wondered vaguely whether agoraphobia could be fatal. In its most exaggerated form, he supposed it could.

He reached out a hand to ring, then hesitated. No use having Jenkins pack. He would do it himself—something to keep him busy until the ship arrived.

From the top shelf of the wardrobe in the bedroom, he took down a bag and saw that it was dusty. He blew on it, but the dust still clung. It had been there for too many years.

As he packed, the room argued with him, talked in that mute tongue with which inanimate but familiar things may converse with a man.

"You can't go," said the room. "You can't go off and leave me."

And Webster argued back, half pleading, half explaining, "I have to go. Can't you understand? It's a friend, an old friend. I will be coming back."

Packing done, Webster returned to the study, slumped into his chair.

He must go and yet he couldn't go. But when the ship arrived, when the time had come, he knew that he would walk out of the house and toward the waiting ship.

He steeled his mind to that, tried to set it in a rigid pattern, tried to blank out everything but the thought that he was leaving.

Things in the room intruded on his brain, as if they were part of a conspiracy to keep him there. Things that he saw as if he were seeing them for the first time. Old, remembered things that suddenly were new. The chronometer that showed both Earthian and Martian time, the days of the month, the phases of the moon. The picture of his dead wife on the desk. The trophy he had won at prep school. The framed short snorter bill that had cost him ten bucks on his trip to Mars.

He stared at them, half unwilling at first, then eagerly, storing up the memory of them in his brain. Seeing them as separate components of a room he had accepted all these years as a finished whole, never realizing what a multitude of things went to make it up.

Dusk was falling, the dusk of early spring, a dusk that smelled of early pussy willows.

The ship should have arrived long ago. He caught himself listening for it, even as he realized that he would not hear it. A ship, driven by atomic motors, was silent except when it gathered speed. Landing and taking off, it floated like thistledown, with not a murmur in it.

It would be here soon. It would have to be here soon or he

could never go. Much longer to wait, he knew, and his high-keyed resolution would crumble like a mound of dust in beating rain. Not much longer could he hold his purpose against the pleading of the room, against the flicker of the fire, against the murmur of the land where five generations of Websters had lived their lives and died.

He shut his eyes and fought down the chill that crept across his body. He couldn't let it get him now, he told himself. He had to stick it out. When the ship arrived he still must be able to get up and walk out the door to the waiting port.

A tap came on the door.

"Come in," Webster called.

It was Jenkins, the light from the fireplace flickering on his shining metal hide.

"Had you called earlier, sir?" he asked.

Webster shook his head.

"I was afraid you might have," Jenkins explained, "and wondered why I didn't come. There was a most extraordinary occurrence, sir. Two men came with a ship and said they wanted you to go to Mars."

"They are here," said Webster. "Why didn't you call me?"

He struggled to his feet.

"I didn't think, sir," said Jenkins, "that you would want to be bothered. It was so preposterous. I finally made them understand you could not possibly want to go to Mars."

Webster stiffened, felt chill fear gripping at his heart. Hands groping for the edge of the desk, he sat down in the chair, sensed the walls of the room closing in about him, a trap that would never let him go.

KINDNESS

Astounding,

October

by Lester Del Rey (1915-   )

*Lester Del Rey has appeared frequently in this
series, and justifiably so, because the first half of the
1940's were productive years for him, years that
saw him bring a quiet strength and emotionality to
science fiction. It is probable that this story was influenced by the events of World War II and the na-
tionalism that often produces conflict. "Kindness"
raises important questions about what it means to
be "normal" (and different), an issue that would be
later addressed frequently in science fiction, most
notably by writers as different from Del Rey as
Robert Sheckley and Philip K. Dick.*

*(I think it's time to tell my favorite Lester Del
Rey story because it deals with the one time when I
clearly got the last word in a verbal exchange with
him. A couple of years ago, I was describing one of
my father's teachings. My father would say to me,
"Don't think, Isaac, that if you associate with bums,
you will make those bums into good people. No!
Those bums will make you into a bum." Upon
which Lester said, "So why do you still associate
with bums, Isaac?" To which I answered instantly,
"Because I love you, Lester." Everyone laughed and
even Lester was so busy laughing he had not time
to think of a riposte.—I.A.)*

The wind eddied idly around the corner and past the se-
cluded park bench. It caught fitfully at the paper on the

ground, turning the pages, then picked up a section and blew away with it, leaving gaudy-colored comics uppermost. Danny moved forward into the sunlight, his eyes dropping to the children's page exposed.

But it was no use; he made no effort to pick up the paper. In a world where even the children's comics needed explaining, there could be nothing of interest to the last living *homo sapiens*—the last normal man in the world. His foot kicked the paper away, under the bench where it would no longer remind him of his deficiencies. There had been a time when he had tried to reason slowly over the omitted steps of logic and find the points behind such things, sometimes successfully, more often not; but now he left it to the quick, intuitive thinking of those about him. Nothing fell flatter than a joke that had to be reasoned out slowly.

Homo sapiens! The type of man who had come out of the caves and built a world of atomic power, electronics and other old-time wonders—thinking man, as it translated from the Latin. In the dim past, when his ancestors had owned the world, they had made a joke of it, shortening it to homo sap, and laughing, because there had been no other species to rival them. Now it was no longer a joke.

Normal man had been only a "sap" to *homo intelligens*—intelligent man—who was now the master of the world. Danny was only a left-over, the last normal man in a world of supermen, hating the fact that he had been born, and that his mother had died at his birth to leave him only loneliness as his heritage.

He drew farther back on the bench as the steps of a young couple reached his ears, pulling his hat down to avoid recognition. But they went by, preoccupied with their own affairs, leaving only a scattered bit of conversation in his ears. He turned it over in his mind, trying senselessly to decode it.

Impossible! Even the casual talk contained too many steps of logic left out. Homo intelligens had a new way of thinking, above reason, where all the long, painful steps of logic could be jumped instantly. They could arrive at a correct picture of the whole from little scattered bits of information. Just as man had once invented logic to replace the trial-and-error thinking that most animals have, so homo intelligens had learned to use intuition. They could look at the first page of an old-time book and immediately know the whole of it, since the little tricks of the author would connect in their intuitive minds and at once build up all the missing links. They didn't even have to try—they just looked, and knew. It was like Newton looking at an apple falling and immediately seeing why the planets circled the sun, and realizing the laws of gravitation; but these new men did it all the time, not just at those rare intervals as it had worked for homo sapiens once.

Man was gone, except for Danny, and he too had to leave this world of supermen. Somehow, soon, those escape plans must be completed, before the last of his little courage was gone! He stirred restlessly, and the little coins in his pocket set up a faint jingling sound. More charity, or occupational therapy! For six hours a day, five days a week, he worked in a little office, painfully doing routine work that could probably have been done better by machinery. Oh, they assured him that his manual skill was as great as theirs and that it was needed, but he could never be sure. In their unfailing kindness, they had probably decided it was better for him to live as normally as they could let him, and then had created the job to fit what he could do.

Other footsteps came down the little path, but he did not look up, until they stopped. "Hi, Danny! You weren't at the library, and Miss Larsen said, pay day, weather, and all, I'd find you here. How's everything?"

Outwardly, Jack Thorpe's body might have been the twin of Danny's own well-muscled one, and the smiling face above it bore no distinguishing characteristics. The mutation that changed man to superman had been within, a quicker, more complex relation of brain cell to brain cell that had no outward signs. Danny nodded at Jack, drawing over reluctantly to make room on the bench for this man who had been his playmate when they were both too young for the difference to matter much.

He did not ask the reason behind the librarian's knowledge of his whereabouts; so far as he knew, there was no particular pattern to his coming here, but to the others there must be one. He found he could even smile at their ability to foretell his plans.

"Hi, Jack! Fine. I thought you were on Mars."

Thorpe frowned, as if an effort were needed to remember that the boy beside him was different, and his words bore the careful phrasing of all those who spoke to Danny. "I finished that, for the time being; I'm supposed to report to Venus next. They're having trouble getting an even balance of boys and girls there, you know. Thought you might want to come along. You've never been Outside, and you were always bugs about those old space stories, I remember."

"I still am, Jack. But—" He knew what it meant, of course. Those who looked after him behind the scenes had detected his growing discontent, and were hoping to distract him with this chance to see the places his father had conquered in the heyday of his race. But he had no wish to see them as they now were, filled with the busy work of the new men; it was better to imagine them as they had once been, rather than see reality. And the ship was *here;* there could be no chance for escape from those other worlds.

Jack nodded quickly, with the almost telepathic understanding of his race. "Of course. Suit yourself, fellow. Going up to the Heights? Miss Larsen says she has something for you."

"Not yet, Jack. I thought I might look at—drop by the old museum."

"Oh." Thorpe got up slowly, brushing his suit with idle fingers. "Danny!"

"Uh?"

"I probably know you better than anyone else, fellow, so—" He hesitated, shrugged, and went on. "Don't mind if I jump to conclusions; I won't talk out of turn. But best of luck—and good-bye, Danny."

He was gone, almost instantly, leaving Danny's heart stuck in his throat. A few words, a facial expression, probably some childhood memories, and Danny might as well have revealed his most cherished secret hope in shouted words! How many others knew of his interest in the old ship in the museum and his carefully made plot to escape this kindly, charity-filled torture world?

He crushed a cigarette under his heel, trying to forget the thought. Jack had played with him as a child, and the others hadn't. He'd have to base his hopes on that and be even more careful never to think of the idea around others. In the meantime he'd stay away from the ship! Perhaps in that way Thorpe's subtle warning might work in his favor—provided the man had meant his promise of silence.

Danny forced his doubts away, grimly conscious that he
dared not lose hope in this last desperate scheme for independence and self-respect; the other way offered only despair and
listless hopelessness, the same empty death from an acute inferiority complex that had claimed the diminishing numbers
of his own kind and left him as the last, lonely specimen.
Somehow, he'd succeed, and in the meantime, he would go to
the library and leave the museum strictly alone.

There was a throng of people leaving the library as Danny
came up the escalator, but either they did not recognize him
with his hat pulled low or sensed his desire for anonymity
and pretended not to know him. He slipped into one of the
less used hallways and made his way toward the historic
documents section, where Miss Larsen was putting away the
reading tapes and preparing to leave.

But she tossed them aside quickly as he came in and
smiled up at him, the rich, warm smile of her people. "Hello,
Danny! Did your friend find you all right?"

"Mm-hmm. He said you had something for me."

"I have." There was pleasure in her face as she turned
back toward the desk behind her to come up with a small
wrapped parcel. For the thousandth time, he caught himself
wishing she were of his race and quenching the feeling as he
realized what her attitude must really be. To her, the small
talk from his race's past was a subject of historic interest, no
more. And he was just a dull-witted hangover from ancient
days. "Guess what?"

But in spite of himself, his face lighted up, both at the
game and the package. "The magazines! The lost issues of
Space Trails?" There had been only the first installment of a
story extant, and yet that single part had set his pulses throbbing as few of the other ancient stories of his ancestors' conquest of space had done. Now, with the missing sections, life
would be filled with zest for a few more hours as he followed
the fictional exploits of a conqueror who had known no fear
of keener minds.

"Not quite, Danny, but almost. We couldn't locate even a
trace of them, but I gave the first installment to Bryant Kenning last week, and he finished it for you." Her voice was
apologetic. "Of course the words won't be quite identical, but
Kenning swears that the story is undoubtedly exactly the

same in structure as it would have been, and the style is duplicated almost perfectly!"

Like that! Kenning had taken the first pages of a novel that had meant weeks and months of thought to some ancient writer and had found in them the whole plot, clearly revealed, instantly his! A night's labor had been needed to duplicate it, probably—a disagreeable and boring piece of work, but not a difficult one! Danny did not question the accuracy of the duplication, since Kenning was their greatest historical novelist. But the pleasure went out of the game.

He took the package, noting that some illustrator had even copied the old artist's style, and that it was set up to match the original format. "Thank you, Miss Larsen. I'm sorry to put all of you to so much trouble. And it was nice of Mr. Kenning!"

Her face had fallen with his, but she pretended not to notice. "He wanted to do it—volunteered when he heard we were searching for the missing copies. And if there are any others with pieces missing, Danny, he wants you to let him know. You two are about the only ones who use this division now; why don't you drop by and see him? If you'd like to go tonight—"

"Thanks. But I'll read this tonight, instead. Tell him I'm very grateful, though, will you?" But he paused, wondering again whether he dared ask for tapes on the history of the asteroids; no, there would be too much risk of her guessing, either now or later. He dared not trust any of them with a hint of his plan.

Miss Larsen smiled again, half winking at him. "Okay, Danny, I'll tell him. 'Night!"

Outside, with the cool of evening beginning to fall, Danny found his way into the untraveled quarters and let his feet guide him. Once, as a group came toward him, he crossed the street without thinking and went on. The package under his arm grew heavy and he shifted it, torn between a desire to find what had happened to the hero and a disgust at his own *sapiens* brain for not knowing. Probably, in the long run, he'd end up by going home and reading it, but for the moment he was content to let his feet carry him along idly, holding most of his thoughts in abeyance.

Another small park was in his path, and he crossed it slowly, the babble of small children's voices only partly heard until he came up to them, two boys and a girl. The supervisor, who should have had them back at the Center, was a dim shape in the far shadows, with another, dimmer shape beside her, leaving the five-year-olds happily engaged in the ancient pastime of getting dirty and impressing each other.

Danny stopped, a slow smile creeping over his lips. At that age, their intuitive ability was just beginning to develop, and their little games and pretenses made sense, acting on him like a tonic. Vaguely, he remembered his own friends of that age beginning uncertainly to acquire the trick of seeming to know everything, and his worries at being left behind. For a time, the occasional flashes of intuition that had always blessed even *homo sapiens* gave him hope, but eventually the supervisor had been forced to tell him that he was different, and why. Now he thrust those painful memories aside and slipped quietly forward into the game.

They accepted him with the easy nonchalance of children who have no repressions, feverishly trying to build their sand castles higher than his; but in that, his experience was greater than theirs, and his judgment of the damp stuff was surer. A perverse glow of accomplishment grew inside him as he added still another story to the towering structure and built a bridge, propped up with sticks and leaves, leading to it.

Then the lights came on, illuminating the sandbox and those inside it and dispelling the shadows of dusk. The smaller of the two boys glanced up, really seeing him for the first time. "Oh, you're Danny Black, ain't you? I seen your pi'ture. Judy, Bobby, look! It's that man—"

But their voices faded out as he ran off through the park and into the deserted byways again, clutching the package to him. Fool! To delight in beating children at a useless game, or to be surprised that they should know him! He slowed to a walk, twitching his lips at the thought that by now the supervisor would be reprimanding them for their thoughtlessness. And still his feet went on, unguided.

It was inevitable, of course, that they should lead him to the museum, where all his secret hopes centered, but he was surprised to look up and see it before him. And then he was glad. Surely they could read nothing into his visit, unpremeditated, just before the place closed. He caught his breath, forced his face into lines of mere casual interest, and went inside, down the long corridors, and to the hall of the ship.

She rested there, pointed slightly skyward, sleek and immense even in a room designed to appear like the distant reaches of space. For six hundred feet, gleaming metal formed a smooth frictionless surface that slid gracefully from the blunt bow back toward the narrow stern with its blackened ion jets.

This, Danny knew, was the last and greatest of the space liners his people had built at the height of their glory. And even before her, the mutation that made the new race of men had been caused by the radiations of deep space, and the results were spreading. For a time, as the log book indicated this ship had sailed out to Mars, to Venus, and to the other points of man's empire, while the tension slowly mounted at home. There had never been another wholly *sapient*-designed ship, for the new race was spreading, making its greater intelligence felt, with the invert-matter rocket replacing this older, less efficient ion rocket which the ship carried. Eventually, unable to compete with the new models, she had been retired from service and junked, while the war between the new and old race passed by her and buried her under tons of rubble, leaving no memory of her existence.

And now, carefully excavated from the old ruins of the drydock where she had lain so long, she had been enthroned in state for the last year, here in the Museum of Sapient History, while all Danny's hopes and prayers had centered around her. There was still a feeling of awe in him as he started slowly across the carpeted floor toward the open lock and the lighted interior.

"Danny!" The sudden word interrupted him, bringing him about with a guilty start, but it was only Professor Kirk, and he relaxed again. The old archaeologist came toward him, his smile barely visible in the half-light of the immense dome. "I'd about given you up, boy, and started out. But I happened to look back and see you. Thought you might be interested in some information I just came onto today."

"Information about the ship?"

"What else? Here, come on inside her and into the lounge—I have a few privileges here, and we might as well be comfortable. You know, as I grow older, I find myself appreciating your ancestors' ideas of comfort, Danny. Sort of a pity our own culture is too new for much luxuriousness yet." Of all the new race, Kirk seemed the most completely at ease before Danny, partly because of his age, and partly because they had shared the same enthusiasm for the great ship when it had first arrived.

Now he settled back into one of the old divans, using his immunity to ordinary rules to light a cigarette and pass one to the younger man. "You know all the supplies and things in the ship have puzzled us both, and we couldn't find any record of them? The log ends when they put the old ship up for junking, you remember; and we couldn't figure out why all this had been restored and restocked, ready for some long voyage to somewhere. Well, it came to light in some further excavations they've completed. Danny, your people did that, during the war; or really, after they'd lost the war to us!"

Danny's back straightened. The war was a period of history he'd avoided thinking about, though he knew the outlines of it. With *homo intelligens* increasing and pressing the older race aside by the laws of survival, his people had made a final desperate bid for supremacy. And while the new race had not wanted the war, they had been forced finally to fight back with as little mercy as had been shown them; and since they had the tremendous advantage of the new intuitive thinking, there had been only thousands left of the original billions of the old race when its brief course was finished. It had been inevitable probably, from the first mutation, but it was not something Danny cared to think of. Now he nodded, and let the other continue.

"Your ancestors, Danny, were beaten then, but they weren't completely crushed, and they put about the last bit of energy they had into rebuilding this ship—the only navigable one left them—and restocking it. They were going to go out somewhere, they didn't know quite where, even to another solar system, and take some of the old race for a new start, away from us. It was their last bid for survival, and it failed when my people learned of it and blasted the docks down over the ship, but it was a glorious failure, boy! I thought you'd want to know."

Danny's thoughts focused slowly. "You mean everything on the ship is of my people? But surely the provisions wouldn't have remained usable after all this time?"

"They did, though; the tests we made proved that conclusively. Your people knew how to preserve things as well as we do, and they expected to be drifting in the ship for half a century, maybe. They'll be usable a thousand years from now." He chucked his cigarette across the room and chuckled in pleased surprise when it fell accurately into a snuffer. "I stuck around, really, to tell you, and I've kept the papers over at the school for you to see. Why not come over with me now?"

"Not tonight, sir. I'd rather stay here a little longer."

Professor Kirk nodded, pulling himself up reluctantly. "As you wish . . . I know how you feel, and I'm sorry about their moving the ship, too. We'll miss her, Danny!"

"Moving the ship?"

"Hadn't you heard? I thought that's why you came around at this hour. They want her over in London, and they're bringing one of the old Lunar ships here to replace her. Too bad!" He touched the walls thoughtfully, drawing his hands down and across the rich nap of the seat. "Well, don't stay too long, and turn her lights out before you leave. Place'll be closed in half an hour. 'Night, Danny."

" 'Night, Professor." Danny sat frozen on the soft seat, listening to the slow tread of the old man and the beating of his own heart. They were moving the ship, ripping his plans to shreds, leaving him stranded in this world of a new race, where even the children were sorry for him.

It had meant so much, even to feel that somehow he would escape, some day! Impatiently, he snapped off the lights, feeling closer to the ship in the privacy of the dark, where no watchman could see his emotion. For a year now he had built his life around the idea of taking this ship out and away, to leave the new race far behind. Long, carefully casual months of work had been spent in learning her structure, finding all her stores, assuring himself bit by bit from a hundred old books that he could operate her.

She had been almost designed for the job, built to be operated by one man, even a cripple, in an emergency, and nearly everything was automatic. Only the problem of a destination had remained, since the planets were all swarming with the others, but the ship's log had suggested the answer even to that.

Once there had been rich men among his people who sought novelty and seclusion, and found them among the larger asteroids; money and science had built them artificial gravities and given them atmospheres, powered by atomic-energy plants that should last forever. Now the rich men were undoubtedly dead, and the new race had abandoned such useless things. Surely, somewhere among the asteroids, there should have been a haven for him, made safe by the very numbers of the little worlds that could discourage almost any search.

Danny heard a guard go by, and slowly got to his feet, to go out again into a world that would no longer hold even that hope. It had been a lovely plan to dream on, a necessary dream. Then the sound of the great doors came to his ears, closing! The Professor had forgotten to tell them of his presence! And—!

All right, so he didn't know the history of all those little worlds; perhaps he would have to hunt through them, one by one, to find a suitable home. Did it matter? In every other way, he could never be more ready. For a moment only, he hesitated; then his hands fumbled with the great lock's control switch, and it swung shut quietly in the dark, shutting the sound of his running feet from outside ears.

The lights came on silently as he found the navigation chair and sank into it. Little lights that spelled out the readiness of the ship. "Ship sealed . . . Air Okay . . . Power, Automatic . . . Engine, Automatic. . . ." Half a hundred little lights and dials that told the story of a ship waiting for his hand. He moved the course plotter slowly along the tiny atmospheric map until it reached the top of the stratosphere; the big star map moved slowly out, with the pointer in his fingers tracing an irregular, jagged line that would lead him somewhere toward the asteroids, well away from the present position of Mars, and yet could offer no clue. Later, he could set the analyzers to finding the present location of some chosen asteroid and determine his course more accurately, but all that mattered now was to get away, beyond all tracing, before his loss could be reported.

Seconds later his fingers pressed down savagely on the main power switch, and there was a lurch of starting, followed by another slight one as the walls of the museum crumpled before the savage force of the great ion rockets. On the map, a tiny spot of light appeared, marking the ship's changing position. The world was behind him now, and there was no one to look at his efforts in kindly pity or remind him of his weakness. Only blind fate was against him, and his ancestors had met and conquered that long before.

A bell rang, indicating the end of the atmosphere, and the big automatic pilot began clucking contentedly, emitting a louder cluck now and then as it found the irregularities in the unorthodox course he had charted and swung the ship to follow. Danny watched it, satisfied that it was working. His ancestors may have been capable of reason only, but they had built machines that were almost intuitive, as the ship about him testified. His head was higher as he turned back to the kitchen, and there was a bit of a swagger to his walk.

The food was still good. He wolfed it down, remembering that supper had been forgotten, and leafing slowly through the big log book which recorded the long voyages made by the ship, searching through it for each casual reference to the asteroids, Ceres, Palas, Vesta, some of the ones referred to by nicknames or numbers? Which ones?

But he had decided by the time he stood once again in the navigation room, watching the aloof immensity of space; out here it was relieved only by the tiny hot pinpoints that must be stars, colored, small and intense as no stars could be through an atmosphere. It would be one of the numbered planetoids, referred to also as "The Dane's" in the log. The word was meaningless, but it seemed to have been one of the newer and more completely terranized, though not the very newest where any search would surely start.

He set the automatic analyzer to running from the key number in the manual and watched it for a time, but it ground on slowly, tracing through all the years that had passed. For a time, he fiddled with the radio, before he remembered that it operated on a wave form no longer used. It was just as well; his severance from the new race would be all the more final.

Still the analyzer ground on. Space lost its novelty, and the operation of the pilot ceased to interest him. He wandered back through the ship toward the lounge, to spy the parcel where he had dropped and forgotten it. There was nothing else to do.

And once begun, he forgot his doubts at the fact that it was Kenning's story, not the original; there was the same sweep to the tale, the same warm and human characters, the same drive of a race that had felt the mastership of destiny so long ago. Small wonder the readers of that time had named it the greatest epic of space to be written!

Once he stopped, as the analyzer reached its conclusions and bonged softly, to set the controls on the automatic for the little world that might be his home, with luck. And then the ship moved on, no longer veering, but making the slightly curved path its selectors found most suitable, while Danny read further, huddled over the story in the navigator's chair, feeling a new and greater kinship with the characters of the story. He was no longer a poor Earthbound charity case, but a man and an adventurer with them!

His nerves were tingling when the tale came to its end, and he let it drop onto the floor from tired fingers. Under his hand, a light had sprung up, but he was oblivious to it, until a crashing gong sounded over him, jerking him from the chair. There had been such a gong described in the story. . . .

And the meaning was the same. His eyes made out the red letters that glared accusingly from the control panel: RADIATION AT TEN O'CLOCK HORIZ—SHIP INDICATED!

Danny's fingers were on the master switch and cutting off all life except pseudogravity from the ship as the thought penetrated. The other ship was not hard to find from the observation window; the great streak of an invert-matter rocket glowed hotly out there, pointed apparently back to Earth— probably the *Callisto!*

For a second he was sure they had spotted him, but the flicker must have been only a minor correction to adjust for the trail continued. He had no knowledge of the new ships and whether they carried warning signals or not, but apparently they must have dispensed with such things. The streak vanished into the distance, and the letters on the panel that had marked it changing position went dead. Danny waited until the fullest amplification showed no response before throwing power on again. The small glow of the ion rocket would be invisible at the distance, surely.

Nothing further seemed to occur; there was a contented purr from the pilot and the faint sleepy hum of raw power from the rear, but no bells or sudden sounds. Slowly, his head fell forward over the navigator's table, and his heavy breathing mixed with the low sounds of the room. The ship went on about its business as it had been designed to do. Its course was charted, even to the old landing sweep, and it needed no further attention.

That was proved when the slow ringing of a bell woke Danny, while the board blinked in time to it: Destination! Destination! Destination Reached!

He shut off everything, rubbing the sleep from his eyes, and looked out. Above, there was weak but warm sunlight streaming down from a bluish sky that held a few small clouds suspended close to the ground. Beyond the ship, where it lay on a neglected sandy landing field, was the green of grass and the wild profusion of a forest. The horizon dropped off sharply, reminding him that it was only a tiny world, but otherwise it might have been Earth. He spotted an unkempt hangar ahead and applied weak power to the underjets, testing until they moved the ship slowly forward and inside, out of the view of any above.

Then he was at the lock, fumbling with the switch. As it opened, he could smell the clean fragrance of growing things, and there was the sound of birds nearby. A rabbit hopped leisurely out from underfoot as he stumbled eagerly out to the sunlight, and weeds and underbrush had already spread to cover the buildings about him. For a moment, he sighed; it had been too easy, this discovery of a heaven on the first wild try.

But the sight of the buildings drove back the doubt. Once, surrounded by a pretentious formal garden, this had been a great stone mansion, now falling into ruins. Beside it and farther from him, a smaller house had been built, seemingly from the wreckage. That was still whole, though ivy had grown over it and half covered the door that came open at the touch of his fingers.

There was still a faint glow to the heaters that drew power from the great atomic plant that gave this little world a perpetual semblance of Earthliness, but a coating of dust was everywhere. The furnishings, though, were in good condition. He scanned them, recognizing some as similar to the pieces in the museum, and the products of his race. One by one he studied them—his fortune, and now his home!

On the table, a book was dropped casually, and there was a sheet of paper propped against it, with what looked like a girl's rough handwriting on it. Curiosity carried him closer, until he could make it out, through the dust that clung even after he shook it.

> Dad:
>   Charley Summers found a wrecked ship of those things, and came for me. We'll be living high on 13. Come on over, if your jets will make it, and meet your son-in-law.

There was no date, nothing to indicate whether "Dad" had returned, or what had happened to them. But Danny dropped it reverently back on the table, looking out across the landing strip as if to see a worn old ship crawl in through the brief twilight that was falling over the tiny world. "Those things" could only be the new race, after the war; and that meant that here was the final outpost of his people. The note might be ten years or half a dozen centuries old—but his people had been here, fighting on and managing to live, after Earth had been lost to them. If they could, so could he!

And unlikely though it seemed, there might possibly be more of them out there somewhere. Perhaps the race was still surviving in spite of time and trouble and even *homo intelligens*.

Danny's eyes were moist as he stepped back from the door and the darkness outside to begin cleaning his new home. If any were there, he'd find them. And if not—

Well, he was still a member of a great and daring race that could never know defeat so long as a single man might live. He would never forget that.

Back on Earth, Bryant Kenning nodded slowly to the small group as he put the communicator back, and his eyes were a bit sad in spite of the smile that lighted his face. "The Director's scout is back, and he did choose 'The Dane's.' Poor kid. I'd begun to think we waited too long, and that he never would make it. Another six months—and he'd have died like a flower out of the sun! Yet I was sure it would work when Miss Larsen showed me that story, with its mythical planetoid-paradises. A rather clever story, if you like pseudohistory. I hope the one I prepared was its equal."

"For historical inaccuracy, fully its equal." But the amusement in old Professor Kirk's voice did not reach his lips.

"Well, he swallowed our lies and ran off with the ship we built him. I hope he's happy, for a while at least."

Miss Larsen folded her things together and prepared to leave. "Poor kid! He was sweet, in a pathetic sort of way. I wish that girl we were working on had turned out better; maybe this wouldn't have been necessary then. See me home, Jack?"

The two older men watched Larsen and Thorpe leave, and silence and tobacco smoke filled the room. Finally Kenning shrugged and turned to face the professor.

"By now he's found the note. I wonder if it was a good idea, after all? When I first came across it in that old story, I was thinking of Jack's preliminary report on Number 67, but now I don't know; she's an unknown quantity, at best. Anyhow, I meant it for kindness."

"Kindness! Kindness to repay with a few million credits and a few thousands of hours of work—plus a lie here and there—for all that we owe the boy's race!" The professor's voice was tired, as he dumped the contents of his pipe into a snuffer, and strode over slowly toward the great window that looked out on the night sky. "I wonder sometimes, Bryant, what kindness Neanderthaler found when the last one came to die. Or whether the race that will follow us when the darkness falls on us will have something better than such kindness."

The novelist shook his head doubtfully, and there was silence again as they looked out across the world and toward the stars.

DESERTION

Astounding, November

by Clifford D. Simak

The fourth of the City series ("Census" appeared in Astounding in September), "Desertion" is the best of a wonderful group, written in direct response to the news of what was happening in the Nazi-run death camps in Europe.

This is one of the great stories about the difficulty of making choices in all of literature, and contains one of the great last lines in the history of science fiction.

(Clearly, 1944 was Simak's big year. This is the third time I've had to talk about him in this volume, after his total absence in the first five of the series. I suppose it's time to own up to a small sin of mine. Since my association with him has been almost entirely by way of correspondence (I met him in person only three times in forty-two years of friendship and then only for a few hours each time), I never had occasion to use or hear his last name expressed in sound. (Even when we did meet I called him Cliff.) The result is that, for some reason, I assumed the "i" in his last name was long and thought of him always as SIGH-mak. Actually, the "i" is short and it is SIM-ak. It may seem a small thing but I am always irritated when anyone mispronounces my name and I should be equally careful of others' names. Fortunately, Cliff is so sweet-tempered a fellow, I can't conceive of him being annoyed at me for so venial a crim—I mean, crime.—I.A.)

Four men, two by two, had gone into the howling maelstrom that was Jupiter and had not returned. They had walked into the keening gale—or rather, they had loped, bellies low against the ground, wet sides gleaming in the rain.

For they did not go in the shape of men.

Now the fifth man stood before the desk of Kent Fowler, head of Dome No. 3, Jovian Survey Commission.

Under Fowler's desk, old Towser scratched a flea, then settled down to sleep again.

Harold Allen, Fowler saw with a sudden pang, was young—too young. He had the easy confidence of youth, the straight back and straight eyes, the face of one who never had known fear. And that was strange. For men in the domes of Jupiter did know fear—fear and humility. It was hard for man to reconcile his puny self with the mighty forces of the monstrous planet.

"You understand," said Fowler, "that you need not do this. You understand that you need not go."

It was formula, of course. The other four had been told the same thing, but they had gone. This fifth one, Fowler knew, would go too. But suddenly he felt a dull hope stir within him that Allen wouldn't go.

"When do I start?" asked Allen.

There was a time when Fowler might have taken quiet pride in that answer, but not now. He frowned briefly.

"Within the hour," he said.

Allen stood waiting, quietly.

"Four other men have gone out and have not returned," said Fowler. "You know that, of course. We want you to return. We don't want you going off on any heroic rescue expedition. The main thing, the only thing, is that you come back, that you prove man can live in a Jovian form. Go to the first survey stake, no farther, then come back. Don't take any chances. Don't investigate anything. Just come back."

Allen nodded. "I understand all that."

"Miss Stanley will operate the converter," Fowler went on. "You need have no fear on that particular point. The other men were converted without mishap. They left the converter in apparently perfect condition. You will be in thoroughly competent hands. Miss Stanley is the best qualified conversion operator in the Solar System. She has had experience on most of the other planets. That is why she's here."

Allen grinned at the woman and Fowler saw something flicker across Miss Stanley's face—something that might have been pity, or rage—or just plain fear. But it was gone again and she was smiling back at the youth who stood before the desk. Smiling in that prim, schoolteacherish way she had of smiling, almost as if she hated herself for doing it.

"I shall be looking forward," said Allen, "to my conversion."

And the way he said it, he made it all a joke, a vast, ironic joke.

But it was no joke.

It was serious business, deadly serious. Upon these tests, Fowler knew, depended the fate of men on Jupiter. If the tests succeeded, the resources of the giant planet would be thrown open. Man would take over Jupiter as he already had taken over the smaller planets. And if they failed—

If they failed, man would continue to be chained and hampered by the terrific pressure, the greater force of gravity, the weird chemistry of the planet. He would continue to be shut within the domes, unable to set actual foot upon the planet, unable to see it with direct, unaided vision, forced to rely upon the awkward tractors and the televisor, forced to work with clumsy tools and mechanisms or through the medium of robots that themselves were clumsy.

For man, unprotected and in his natural form, would be blotted out by Jupiter's terrific pressure of fifteen thousand pounds per square inch, pressure that made Terrestrial sea bottoms seem a vacuum by comparison.

Even the strongest metal Earthmen could devise couldn't exist under pressure such as that, under the pressure and the alkaline rains that forever swept the planet. It grew brittle and flaky, crumbling like clay, or it ran away in little streams and puddles of ammonia salts. Only by stepping up the toughness and strength of that metal, by increasing its electronic tension, could it be made to withstand the weight of thousands of miles of swirling, choking gases that made up the atmosphere. And even when that was done, everything

had to be coated with tough quartz to keep away the rain—
the bitter rain that was liquid ammonia.

Fowler sat listening to the engines in the sub-floor of the
dome. Engines that ran on endlessly, the dome never quiet of
them. They had to run and keep on running. For if they
stopped, the power flowing into the metal walls of the dome
would stop, the electronic tension would ease up and that
would be the end of everything.

Towser roused himself under Fowler's desk and scratched
another flea, his leg thumping hard against the floor.

"Is there anything else?" asked Allen.

Fowler shook his head. "Perhaps there's something you
want to do," he said. "Perhaps you—"

He had meant to say write a letter and he was glad he
caught himself quick enough so he didn't say it.

Allen looked at his watch. "I'll be there on time," he said.
He swung around and headed for the door.

Fowler knew Miss Stanley was watching him and he didn't
want to turn and meet her eyes. He fumbled with a sheaf of
papers on the desk before him.

"How long are you going to keep this up?" asked Miss
Stanley and she bit off each word with a vicious snap.

He swung around in his chair and faced her then. Her lips
were drawn into a straight, thin line, her hair seemed skinned
back from her forehead tighter than ever, giving her face that
queer, almost startling death-mask quality.

He tried to make his voice cool and level. "As long as
there's any need of it," he said. "As long as there's any
hope."

"You're going to keep on sentencing them to death," she
said. "You're going to keep marching them out face to face
with Jupiter. You're going to sit in here safe and comfortable
and send them out to die."

"There is no room for sentimentality, Miss Stanley," Fowler said, trying to keep the note of anger from his voice.
"You know as well as I do why we're doing this. You realize
that man in his own form simply cannot cope with Jupiter.
The only answer is to turn men into the sort of things that
can cope with it. We've done it on the other planets.

"If a few men die, but we finally succeed, the price is
small. Through the ages men have thrown away their lives on

foolish things, for foolish reasons. Why should we hesitate, then, at a little death in a thing as great as this?"

Miss Stanley sat stiff and straight, hands folded in her lap, the lights shining on her graying hair and Fowler, watching her, tried to imagine what she might feel, what she might be thinking. He wasn't exactly afraid of her, but he didn't feel quite comfortable when she was around. Those sharp blue eyes saw too much, her hands looked far too competent. She should be somebody's Aunt sitting in a rocking chair with her knitting needles. But she wasn't. She was the top-notch conversion unit operator in the Solar System and she didn't like the way he was doing things.

"There is something wrong, Mr. Fowler," she declared.

"Precisely," agreed Fowler. "That's why I'm sending young Allen out alone. He may find out what it is."

"And if he doesn't?"

"I'll send someone else."

She rose slowly from her chair, started toward the door, then stopped before his desk.

"Some day," she said, "you will be a great man. You never let a chance go by. This is your chance. You knew it was when this dome was picked for the tests. If you put it through, you'll go up a notch or two. No matter how many men may die, you'll go up a notch or two."

"Miss Stanley," he said and his voice was curt, "young Allen is going out soon. Please be sure that your machine—"

"My machine," she told him, icily, "is not to blame. It operates along the coordinates the biologists set up."

He sat hunched at his desk, listening to her footsteps go down the corridor.

What she said was true, of course. The biologists had set up the coordinates. But the biologists could be wrong. Just a hairbreadth of difference, one iota of digression and the converter would be sending out something that wasn't the thing they meant to send. A mutant that might crack up, go haywire, come unstuck under some condition or stress of circumstance wholly unsuspected.

For man didn't know much about what was going on outside. Only what his instruments told him was going on. And the samplings of those happenings furnished by those instruments and mechanisms had been no more than samplings, for Jupiter was unbelievably large and the domes were very few.

Even the work of the biologists in getting the data on the Lopers, apparently the highest form of Jovian life, had involved more than three years of intensive study and after that two years of checking to make sure. Work that could have been done on Earth in a week or two. But work that, in this case, couldn't be done on Earth at all, for one couldn't take a Jovian life form to Earth. The pressure here on Jupiter couldn't be duplicated outside of Jupiter and at Earth pressure and temperature the Lopers would simply have disappeared in a puff of gas.

Yet it was work that had to be done if man ever hoped to go about Jupiter in the life form of the Lopers. For before the converter could change a man to another life form, every detailed physical characteristic of that life form must be known—surely and positively, with no chance of mistake.

Allen did not come back.

The tractors, combing the nearby terrain, found no trace of him, unless the skulking thing reported by one of the drivers had been the missing Earthman in Loper form.

The biologists sneered their most accomplished academic sneers when Fowler suggested the coordinates might be wrong. Carefully they pointed out that the coordinates worked. When a man was put into the converter and the switch was thrown, the man became a Loper. He left the machine and moved away, out of sight, into the soupy atmosphere.

Some quirk, Fowler had suggested; some tiny deviation from the thing a Loper should be, some minor defect. If there were, the biologists said, it would take years to find it.

And Fowler knew that they were right.

So there were five men now instead of four and Harold Allen had walked out into Jupiter for nothing at all. It was as if he'd never gone so far as knowledge was concerned.

Fowler reached across his desk and picked up the personal file, a thin sheaf of papers neatly clipped together. It was a thing he dreaded but a thing he had to do. Somehow the reason for these strange disappearances must be found. And there was no other way than to send out more men.

He sat for a moment listening to the howling of the wind above the dome, the everlasting thundering gale that swept across the planet in boiling, twisting wrath.

Was there some threat out there, he asked himself? Some danger they did not know about? Something that lay in wait and gobbled up the Lopers, making no distinction between Lopers that were *bona fide* and Lopers that were men? To the gobblers, of course, it would make no difference.

Or had there been a basic fault in selecting the Lopers as the type of life best fitted for existence on the surface of the planet? The evident intelligence of the Lopers, he knew, had been one factor in that determination. For if the thing man became did not have capacity for intelligence, man could not for long retain his own intelligence in such a guise.

Had the biologists let that one factor weigh too heavily, using it to offset some other factor that might be unsatisfactory, even disastrous? It didn't seem likely. Stiffnecked as they might be, the biologists knew their business.

Or was the whole thing impossible, doomed from the very start? Conversion to other life forms had worked on other planets, but that did not necessarily mean it would work on Jupiter. Perhaps man's intelligence could not function correctly through the sensory apparatus provided Jovian life. Perhaps the Lopers were so alien there was no common ground for human knowledge and the Jovian conception of existence to meet and work together.

Or the fault might lie with man, be inherent with the race. Some mental aberration which, coupled with what they found outside, wouldn't let them come back. Although it might not be an aberration, not in the human sense. Perhaps just one ordinary human mental trait, accepted as commonplace on Earth, would be so violently at odds with Jovian existence that it would blast all human intelligence and sanity.

Claws rattled and clicked down the corridor. Listening to them, Fowler smiled wanly. It was Towser coming back from the kitchen, where he had gone to see his friend, the cook.

Towser came into the room, carrying a bone. He wagged his tail at Fowler and flopped down beside the desk, bone between his paws. For a long moment his rheumy old eyes regarded his master and Fowler reached down a hand to ruffle a ragged ear.

"You still like me, Towser?" Fowler asked and Towser thumped his tail.

"You're the only one," said Fowler. "All through the dome they're cussing me. Calling me a murderer, more than likely."

He straightened and swung back to the desk. His hand reached out and picked up the file.

Bennett? Bennett had a girl waiting for him back on Earth.

Andrews? Andrews was planning on going back to Mars Tech just as soon as he earned enough to see him through a year.

Olson? Olson was nearing pension age. All the time telling the boys how he was going to settle down and grow roses.

Carefully, Fowler laid the file back on the desk.

Sentencing men to death. Miss Stanley had said that, her pale lips scarcely moving in her parchment face. Marching men out to die while he, Fowler, sat here safe and comfortable.

They were saying it all through the dome, no doubt, especially since Allen had failed to return. They wouldn't say it to his face, of course. Even the man or men he called before this desk and told they were the next to go, wouldn't say it to him.

They would only say: "When do we start?" For that was formula.

But he would see it in their eyes.

He picked up the file again. Bennett, Andrews, Olson. There were others, but there was no use in going on.

Kent Fowler knew that he couldn't do it, couldn't face them, couldn't send more men out to die.

He leaned forward and flipped up the toggle on the intercommunicator.

"Yes, Mr. Fowler."

"Miss Stanley, please."

He waited for Miss Stanley, listening to Towser chewing half-heartedly on the bone. Towser's teeth were getting bad.

"Miss Stanley," said Miss Stanley's voice.

"Just wanted to tell you, Miss Stanley, to get ready for two more."

"Aren't you afraid," asked Miss Stanley, "that you'll run out of them? Sending out one at a time, they'd last longer, give you twice the satisfaction."

"One of them," said Fowler, "will be a dog."

"A dog!"

"Yes, Towser."

He heard the quick, cold rage that iced her voice. "Your own dog! He's been with you all these years—"

"That's the point," said Fowler. "Towser would be unhappy if I left him behind."

It was not the Jupiter he had known through the televisor. He had expected it to be different, but not like this. He had expected a hell of ammonia rain and stinking fumes and the deafening, thundering tumult of the storm. He had expected swirling clouds and fog and the snarling flicker of monstrous thunderbolts.

He had not expected the lashing downpour would be reduced to drifting purple mist that moved like fleeing shadows over a red and purple sward. He had not even guessed the snaking bolts of lightning would be flares of pure ecstasy across a painted sky.

Waiting for Towser, Fowler flexed the muscles of his body, amazed at the smooth, sleek strength he found. Not a bad body, he decided, and grimaced at remembering how he had pitied the Lopers when he glimpsed them through the television screen.

For it had been hard to imagine a living organism based upon ammonia and hydrogen rather than upon water and oxygen, hard to believe that such a form of life could know the same quick thrill of life that humankind could know. Hard to conceive of life out in the soupy maelstrom that was Jupiter, not knowing, of course, that through Jovian eyes it was no soupy maelstrom at all.

The wind brushed against him with what seemed gentle fingers and he remembered with a start that by Earth standards the wind was a roaring gale, a two-hundred-mile an hour howler laden with deadly gases.

Pleasant scents seeped into his body. And yet scarcely scents, for it was not the sense of smell as he remembered it. It was as if his whole being were soaking up the sensation of lavender—and yet not lavender. It was something, he knew, for which he had no word, undoubtedly the first of many enigmas in terminology. For the words he knew, the thought symbols that served him as an Earthman would not serve him as a Jovian.

The lock in the side of the dome opened and Towser came tumbling out—at least he thought it must be Towser.

He started to call to the dog, his mind shaping the words he meant to say. But he couldn't say them. There was no way to say them. He had nothing to say them with.

For a moment his mind swirled in muddy terror, a blind fear that eddied in little puffs of panic through his brain.

How did Jovians talk? How—

Suddenly he was aware of Towser, intensely aware of the bumbling, eager friendliness of the shaggy animal that had followed him from Earth to many planets. As if the thing that was Towser had reached out and for a moment sat within his brain.

And out of the bubbling welcome that he sensed, came words.

"Hiya, pal."

Not words really, better than words. Thought symbols in his brain, communicated thought symbols that had shades of meaning words could never have.

"Hiya, Towser," he said.

"I feel good," said Towser. "Like I was a pup. Lately I've been feeling pretty punk. Legs stiffening up on me and teeth wearing down to almost nothing. Hard to mumble a bone with teeth like that. Besides, the fleas give me hell. Used to be I never paid much attention to them. A couple of fleas more or less never meant much in my early days."

"But . . . but—" Fowler's thoughts tumbled awkwardly. "You're talking to me!"

"Sure thing," said Towser. "I always talked to you, but you couldn't hear me. I tried to say things to you, but I couldn't make the grade."

"I understood you sometimes," Fowler said.

"Not very well," said Towser. "You knew when I wanted food and when I wanted a drink and when I wanted out, but that's about all you ever managed."

"I'm sorry," Fowler said.

"Forget it," Towser told him. "I'll race you to the cliff."

For the first time, Fowler saw the cliff, apparently many miles away, but with a strange crystalline beauty that sparkled in the shadow of the many-colored clouds.

Fowler hesitated. "It's a long way—"

"Ah, come on," said Towser and even as he said it he started for the cliff.

Fowler followed, testing his legs, testing the strength in that new body of his, a bit doubtful at first, amazed a moment later, then running with a sheer joyousness that was one with the red and purple sward, with the drifting smoke of the rain across the land.

As he ran the consciousness of music came to him, a music that beat into his body, that surged throughout his being, that lifted him on wings of silver speed. Music like bells might make from some steeple on a sunny, springtime hill.

As the cliff drew nearer the music deepened and filled the universe with a spray of magic sound. And he knew the music came from the tumbling waterfall that feathered down the face of the shining cliff.

Only, he knew, it was no waterfall, but an ammonia-fall and the cliff was white because it was oxygen, solidified.

He skidded to a stop beside Towser where the waterfall broke into a glittering rainbow of many hundred colors. Literally many hundred, for here, he saw, was no shading of one primary to another as human beings saw, but a clear-cut selectivity that broke the prism down to its last ultimate classification.

"The music," said Towser.

"Yes, what about it?"

"The music," said Towser, "is vibrations. Vibrations of water falling."

"But, Towser, you don't know about vibrations."

"Yes, I do," contended Towser. "It just popped into my head."

Fowler gulped mentally. "Just popped!"

And suddenly, within his own head, he held a formula—the formula for a process that would make metal to withstand the pressure of Jupiter.

He stared, astounded, at the waterfall and swiftly his mind took the many colors and placed them in their exact sequence in the spectrum. Just like that. Just out of blue sky. Out of nothing, for he knew nothing either of metals or of colors.

"Towser," he cried. "Towser, something's happening to us!"

"Yeah, I know," said Towser.

"It's our brains," said Fowler. "We're using them, all of them, down to the last hidden corner. Using them to figure out things we should have known all the time. Maybe the brains of Earth things naturally are slow and foggy. Maybe we are the morons of the universe. Maybe we are fixed so we have to do things the hard way."

And, in the new sharp clarity of thought that seemed to grip him, he knew that it would not only be the matter of colors in a waterfall or metals that would resist the pressure of Jupiter, he sensed other things, things not yet quite clear. A vague whispering that hinted of greater things, of mysteries beyond the pale of human thought, beyond even the pale of human imagination. Mysteries, fact, logic built on reasoning. Things that any brain should know if it used all its reasoning power.

"We're still mostly Earth," he said. "We're just beginning to learn a few of the things we are to know—a few of the things that were kept from us as human beings, perhaps because we were human beings. Because our human bodies were poor bodies. Poorly equipped for thinking, poorly equipped in certain senses that one has to have to know. Perhaps even lacking in certain senses that are necessary to true knowledge."

He stared back at the dome, a tiny black thing dwarfed by the distance.

Back there were men who couldn't see the beauty that was Jupiter. Men who thought that swirling clouds and lashing rain obscured the face of the planet. Unseeing human eyes. Poor eyes. Eyes that could not see the beauty in the clouds, that could not see through the storms. Bodies that could not feel the thrill of trilling music stemming from the rush of broken water.

Men who walked alone, in terrible loneliness, talking with their tongue like Boy Scouts wigwagging out their messages, unable to reach out and touch one another's mind as he could reach out and touch Towser's mind. Shut off forever from that personal, intimate contact with other living things.

He, Fowler, had expected terror inspired by alien things out here on the surface, had expected to cower before the threat of unknown things, had steeled himself against disgust of a situation that was not of Earth.

But instead he had found something greater than man had ever known. A swifter, surer body. A sense of exhilaration, a deeper sense of life. A sharper mind. A world of beauty that even the dreamers of the Earth had not yet imagined.

"Let's get going," Towser urged.

"Where do you want to go?"

"Anywhere," said Towser. "Just start going and see where we end up. I have a feeling . . . well, a feeling—"

"Yes, I know," said Fowler.

For he had the feeling, too. The feeling of high destiny. A certain sense of greatness. A knowledge that somewhere off beyond the horizons lay adventure and things greater than adventure.

Those other five had felt it, too. Had felt the urge to go and see, the compelling sense that here lay a life of fullness and of knowledge.

That, he knew, was why they had not returned.

"I won't go back," said Towser.

"We can't let them down," said Fowler.

Fowler took a step or two, back toward the dome, then stopped.

Back to the dome. Back to that aching, poison-laden body that he left. It hadn't seemed aching before, but now he knew it was.

Back to the fuzzy brain. Back to muddled thinking. Back to the flapping mouths that formed signals others understood. Back to eyes that now would be worse than no sight at all. Back to squalor, back to crawling, back to ignorance.

"Perhaps some day," he said, muttering to himself.

"We got a lot to do and a lot to see," said Towser. "We got a lot to learn. We'll find things—"

Yes, they could find things. Civilizations, perhaps. Civilizations that would make the civilization of man seem puny by comparison. Beauty and more important—an understanding of that beauty. And a comradeship no one had ever known before—that no man, no dog had ever known before.

And life. The quickness of life after what seemed a drugged existence.

"I can't go back," said Towser.

"Nor I," said Fowler.

"They would turn me back into a dog," said Towser.

"And me," said Fowler, "back into a man."

WHEN THE BOUGH BREAKS

Astounding,

November

by "Lewis Padgett" (Henry Kuttner, 1914-1958, and C. L. Moore, 1911-   )

Henry Kuttner and C. L. Moore continued the brilliant streak of productivity and quality they had started earlier in the 1940's (see Volumes 4 and 5 of this series) in 1944, with stories like "Housing Problem" (Charm, October), "Trophy" (Thrilling Wonder Stories, Winter), and "The Children's Hour" (Astounding, March), But their great collaborative effort of the year was "When the Bough Breaks," a powerful story somewhat similar to their "Mimsy Were the Borogoves" of the previous year. It is frequently argued that great fiction captures the tragic nature of life—if so, this story has greatness written all over it.

(I am frequently asked whether a scientific education is an essential for writing science fiction. One might think it was but clearly it isn't since excellent science fiction is written by writers who lack such an education. As examples I have cited Fredric Brown among the earlier generation and Harlan Ellison (whose stories will start appearing in due course as we proceed with these volumes) in the newer generation. It occurs to me that Henry Kuttner and C. L. Moore are additional examples. Mind you, this doesn't mean they are scientifically ignorant; that would indeed disqualify them. It does mean, however, that what science they needed, they picked up for themselves and that they knew very well how to keep their needs to a minimum and yet do marvelously well.—I.A.)

They were surprised at getting the apartment, what with high rents and written-in clauses in the lease, and Joe Calderon felt himself lucky to be only ten minutes' subway ride from the University. His wife, Myra, fluffed up her red hair in a distracted fashion and said that landlords presumably expected parthenogenesis in their tenants, if that was what she meant. Anyhow, it was where an organism split in two and the result was two mature specimens. Calderon grinned, said, "Binary fission, chump," and watched young Alexander, aged eighteen months, backing up on all fours across the carpet, preparatory to assuming a standing position on his fat bowlegs.

It was a pleasant apartment, at that. The sun came into it at times, and there were more rooms than they had any right to expect, for the price. The next-door neighbor, a billowy blonde who talked of little except her migraine, said that it was hard to keep tenants in 4-D. It wasn't exactly haunted, but it had the queerest visitors. The last lessee, an insurance man who drank heavily, moved out one day talking about little men who came ringing the bell at all hours asking for a Mr. Pott, or somebody like that. Not until some time later did Joe identify Pott with Cauldron—or Calderon.

They were sitting on the couch in a pleased manner, looking at Alexander. He was quite a baby. Like all infants, he had a collar of fat at the back of his neck, and his legs, Calderon said, were like two vast and trunkless limbs of stone—at least they gave that effect. The eyes stopped at their incredible bulging pinkness, fascinated. Alexander laughed like a fool, rose to his feet, and staggered drunkenly toward his parents, muttering unintelligible gibberish. "Madman," Myra said fondly, and tossed the child a floppy velvet pig of whom he was enamored.

"So we're all set for the winter," Calderon said. He was a tall, thin, harassed-looking man, a fine research physicist, and very much interested in his work at the University. Myra was a rather fragile red head, with a tilted nose and sardonic red-brown eyes. She made deprecatory noises.

"If we can get a maid. Otherwise I'll char."

"You sound like a lost soul," Calderon said. "What do you mean, you'll char?"

"Like a charwoman. Sweep, cook, clean. Babies are a great trial. Still, they're worth it."

"Not in front of Alexander. He'll get above himself."

The doorbell rang. Calderon uncoiled himself, wandered vaguely across the room, and opened the door. He blinked at nothing. Then he lowered his gaze somewhat, and what he saw was sufficient to make him stare a little.

Four tiny men were standing in the hall. That is, they were tiny below the brows. Their craniums were immense, watermelon large and watermelon shaped, or else they were wearing abnormally huge helmets of glistening metal. Their faces were wizened, peaked tiny masks that were nests of lines and wrinkles. Their clothes were garish, unpleasantly colored, and seemed to be made of paper.

"Oh?" Calderon said blankly.

Swift looks were exchanged among the four. One of them said, "Are you Joseph Calderon?"

"Yeah."

"We," said the most wrinkled of the quartet, "are your son's descendants. He's a super child. We're here to educate him."

"Yes," Calderon said. "Yes, of course. I . . . *listen!*"

"To what?"

"Super—"

"There he is," another dwarf cried. "It's Alexander! We've hit the right time at last!" He scuttled past Calderon's legs and into the room. Calderon made a few futile snatches, but the small men easily evaded him. When he turned, they were gathered around Alexander. Myra had drawn up her legs under her and was watching with an amazed expression.

"Look at that," a dwarf said. "See his potential tefeetzie?" It sounded like tefeetzie.

"But his skull, Bordent," another put in. "That's the important part. The vyrings are almost perfectly coblastably."

"Beautiful," Bordent acknowledged. He leaned forward. Alexander reached forward into the nest of wrinkles, seized Bordent's nose, and twisted painfully. Bordent bore it stoically until the grip relaxed.

"Undeveloped," he said tolerantly. "We'll develop him."

Myra sprang from the couch, picked up her child, and

stood at bay, facing the little men. "Joe," she said, "are you going to stand for this? Who are these bad-mannered goblins?"

"Lord knows," Calderon said. He moistened his lips. "What kind of a gag is that? Who sent you?"

"Alexander," Bordent said. "From the year . . . ah . . . about 2450, reckoning roughly. He's practically immortal. Only violence can kill one of the Supers, and there's none of that in 2450."

Calderon sighed. "No, I mean it. A gag's a gag. But—"

"Time and again we've tried. In 1940, 1944, 1947—all around this era. We were either too early or too late. But now we've hit on the right time sector. It's our job to educate Alexander. You should feel proud of being his parents. We worship you, you know. Father and mother of the new race."

"Tuh!" Calderon said. "Come off it!"

"They need proof, Dobish," someone said. "Remember, this is their first inkling that Alexander is homo superior."

"Homo nuts," Myra said. "Alexander's a perfectly normal baby."

"He's perfectly supernormal," Dobish said. "We're his descendants."

"That makes you a superman," Calderon said skeptically, eyeing the small man.

"Not in toto. There aren't many of the X Free type. The biological norm is specialization. Only a few are straight-line super. Some specialize in logic, others in vervainity, others—like us—are guides. If we were X Free supers, you couldn't stand there and talk to us. Or look at us. We're only parts. Those like Alexander are the glorious whole."

"Oh, send them away," Myra said, getting tired of it. "I feel like a Thurber woman."

Calderon nodded. "O.K. Blow, gentlemen. Take a powder, I mean it."

"Yes," Dobish said, "they need proof. What'll we do? Skyskinate?"

"Too twisty," Bordent objected. "Object lesson, eh? The stiller."

"Stiller?" Myra asked.

Bordent took an object from his paper clothes and spun it in his hands. His fingers were all double-jointed. Calderon felt a tiny electric shock go through him.

"Joe," Myra said, white-faced. "I can't move."

"Neither can I. Take it easy. This is . . . it's—" He slowed and stopped.

"Sit down," Bordent said, still twirling the object. Calderon and Myra backed up to the couch and sat down. Their tongues froze with the rest of them.

Dobish came over, clambered up, and pried Alexander out of his mother's grip. Horror moved in her eyes.

"We won't hurt him," Dobish said. "We just want to give him his first lesson. Have you got the basics, Finn?"

"In the bag." Finn extracted a foot-long bag from his garments. Things came out of that bag. They came out incredibly. Soon the carpet was littered with stuff—problematical in design, nature, and use. Calderon recognized a tesseract.

The fourth dwarf, whose name, it turned out, was Quat, smiled consolingly at the distressed parents. "You watch. You can't learn; you've not got the potential. You're homo saps. But Alexander, now—"

Alexander was in one of his moods. He was diabolically gay. With the devil-possession of all babies, he refused to collaborate. He crept rapidly backwards. He burst into loud, squalling sobs. He regarded his feet with amazed joy. He stuffed his fist into his mouth and cried bitterly at the result. He talked about invisible things in a soft, cryptic monotone. He punched Dobish in the eye.

The little men had inexhaustible patience. Two hours later they were through. Calderon couldn't see that Alexander had learned much.

Bordent twirled the object again. He nodded affably, and led the retreat. The four little men went out of the apartment, and a moment later Calderon and Myra could move.

She jumped up, staggering on numbed legs, seized Alexander, and collapsed on the couch. Calderon rushed to the door and flung it open. The hall was empty.

"Joe—" Myra said, her voice small and afraid. Calderon came back and smoothed her hair. He looked down at the bright fuzzy head of Alexander.

"Joe. We've got to do—do something."

"I don't know," he said. "If it happened—"

"It happened. They took those things with them. Alexander. Oh!"

"They didn't try to hurt him," Calderon said hesitatingly.

"Our *baby*! He's no superchild."

"Well," Calderon said, "I'll get out my revolver. What else can I do?"

"I'll do something," Myra promised. "Nasty little goblins! I'll do something, just wait."

And yet there wasn't a great deal they could do.

Tacitly they ignored the subject the next day. But at 4 P.M., the same time as the original visitation, they were with Alexander in a theater, watching the latest technicolor film. The four little men could scarcely find them here—

Calderon felt Myra stiffen, and even as he turned, he suspected the worst. Myra sprang up, her breath catching. Her fingers tightened on his arm.

"He's gone!"

"G-gone?"

"He just vanished. I was holding him . . . let's get out of here."

"Maybe you dropped him," Calderon said inanely, and lit a match. There were cries from behind. Myra was already pushing her way toward the aisle. There were no babies under the seat, and Calderon caught up with his wife in the lobby.

"He disappeared," Myra was babbling. "Like that. Maybe he's in the future, Joe, what'll we do?"

Calderon, through some miracle, got a taxi. "We'll go home. That's the most likely place. I hope."

"Yes. Of course it is. Give me a cigarette."

"He'll be in the apartment—"

He was, squatting on his haunches, taking a decided interest in the gadget Quat was demonstrating. The gadget was a gayly-colored egg beater with four-dimensional attachments, and it talked in a thin, high voice. Not in English.

Bordent flipped out the stiller and began to twirl it as the couple came in. Calderon got hold of Myra's arms and held her back. "Hold on," he said urgently. "That isn't necessary. We won't try anything."

"Joe!" Myra tried to wriggle free. "Are you going to let them—"

"Quiet!" he said. "Bordent, put that thing down. We want to talk to you."

"Well—if you promise not to interrupt—"

"We promise." Calderon forcibly led Myra to the couch and held her there. "Look, darling. Alexander's all right. They're not hurting him."

"Hurt him, indeed!" Finn said. "He'd skin us alive in the future if we hurt him in the past."

"Be quiet," Bordent commanded. He seemed to be the leader of the four. "I'm glad you're cooperating, Joseph Calderon. It goes against my grain to use force on a demigod. After all, you're *Alexander's* father."

Alexander put out a fat paw and tried to touch the whirling rainbow egg beater. He seemed to be fascinated. Quat said, "The kivelish is sparkling. Shall I vastinate?"

"Not too fast," Bordent said. "He'll be rational in a week, and then we can speed up the process. Now, Calderon, please relax. Anything you want?"

"A drink."

"They mean alcohol," Finn said. "The Rubaiyat mentions it, remember?"

"Rubaiyat?"

"The singing red gem in Twelve Library."

"Oh, yes," Bordent said. "That one. I was thinking of the Yahveh slab, the one with the thunder effects. Do you want to make some alcohol, Finn?"

Calderon swallowed. "Don't bother. I have some in that sideboard. May I—"

"You're not *prisoners*." Bordent's voice was shocked. "It's just that we've got to make you listen to a few explanations, and after that—well, it'll be different."

Myra shook her head when Calderon handed her a drink, but he scowled at her meaningly. "You won't feel it. Go ahead."

She hadn't once taken her gaze from Alexander. The baby was imitating the thin noise of the egg beater now. It was subtly unpleasant.

"The ray is working," Quat said. "The viewer shows some slight cortical resistance, though."

"Angle the power," Bordent told him.

Alexander said, "Modjewabba?"

"What's that?" Myra asked in a strained voice. "Super language?"

Bordent smiled at her. "No, just baby talk."

Alexander burst into sobs. Myra said, "Super baby or not,

when he cries like that, there's a good reason. Does your tutoring extend to that point?"

"Certainly," Quat said calmly. He and Finn carried Alexander out. Bordent smiled again.

"You're beginning to believe," he said. "That helps."

Calderon drank, feeling the hot fumes of whisky along the backs of his cheeks. His stomach was crawling with cold uneasiness.

"If you were human——" he said doubtfully.

"If we were, we wouldn't be here. The old order changeth. It had to start sometime. Alexander is the first homo superior."

"But why us?" Myra asked.

"Genetics. You've both worked with radioactivity and certain short-wave radiations that effected the germ plasm. The mutation just happened. It'll happen again from now on. But you happen to be the first. You'll die, but Alexander will live on. Perhaps a thousand years."

Calderon said, "This business of coming from the future . . . you say Alexander sent you?"

"The adult Alexander. The mature superman. It's a different culture, of course—beyond your comprehension. Alexander is one of the X Frees. He said to me, through the interpreting-machine, of course, 'Bordent, I wasn't recognized as a super till I was thirty years old. I had only ordinary homo sap development till then. I didn't know my potential myself. And that's bad.' It *is* bad, you know." Bordent digressed. "The full capabilities of an organism can't emerge unless it's given the fullest chance of expansion from birth on. Or at least from infancy. Alexander said to me, 'It's about five hundred years ago that I was born. Take a few guides and go into the past. Locate me as an infant. Give me specialized training, from the beginning. I think it'll expand me.'"

"The past," Calderon said. "You mean it's plastic?"

"Well, it affects the future. You can't alter the past without altering the future, too. But things tend to drift back. There's a temporal norm, a general level. In the original time sector, Alexander wasn't visited by us. Now that's changed. So the future will be changed. But not tremendously. No crucial temporal apexes are involved, no keystones. The only result will be that the mature Alexander will have his potential more fully realized."

Alexander was carried back into the room, beaming. Quat resumed his lesson with the egg beater.

"There isn't a great deal you can do about it," Bordent said. "I think you realize that now."

Myra said, "Is Alexander going to look like you?" Her face was strained.

"Oh, no. He's a perfect physical specimen. I've never seen him, of course, but—"

Calderon said, "Heir to all the ages. Myra, are you beginning to get the idea?"

"Yes. A superman. But he's our baby."

"He'll remain so," Bordent put in anxiously. "We don't want to remove him from the beneficial home and parental influence. An infant needs that. In fact, tolerance for the young is an evolutionary trait aimed at providing for the superman's appearance, just as the vanishing appendix is such a preparation. At certain eras of history mankind is receptive to the preparation of the new race. It's never been quite successful before—there were anthropological miscarriages, so to speak. My squeevers, it's *important!* Infants are awfully irritating. They're helpless for a very long time, a great trial to the patience of the parents—the lower the order of the animal, the faster the infant develops. With mankind, it takes years for the young to reach an independent state. So the parental tolerance increases in proportion. The superchild won't mature, actually, till he's about twenty."

Myra said, "Alexander will still be a baby then?"

"He'll have the physical standards of an eight-year-old specimen of homo sap. Mentally . . . well, call it irrationality. He won't be leveled out to an intellectual or emotional norm. He won't be sane, any more than any baby is. Selectivity takes quite a while to develop. But his peaks will be far, far above the peaks of, say, *you* as a child."

"Thanks," Calderon said.

"His horizons will be broader. His mind is capable of grasping and assimilating far more than yours. The world is really his oyster. He won't be limited. But it'll take a while for his mind, his personality, to shake down."

"I want another drink," Myra said.

Calderon got it. Alexander inserted his thumb in Quat's eye and tried to gouge it out. Quat submitted passively.

"Alexander!" Myra said.

"Sit still," Bordent said. "Quat's tolerance in this regard is naturally more highly developed than yours."

"If he puts Quat's eye out," Calderon said, "it'll be just too bad."

"Quat isn't important, compared to Alexander. He knows it, too."

Luckily for Quat's binocular vision, Alexander suddenly tired of his new toy and fell to staring at the egg beater again. Dobish and Finn leaned over the baby and looked at him. But there was more to it than that, Calderon felt.

"Induced telepathy," Bordent said. "It takes a long time to develop, but we're starting now. I tell you, it was a relief to hit the right time at last. I've rung this doorbell at least a hundred times. But never till now——"

"Move," Alexander said clearly. "Real. Move."

Bordent nodded. "Enough for today. We'll be here again tomorrow. You'll be ready?"

"As ready," Myra said, "as we'll ever be, I suppose." She finished her drink.

They got fairly high that night and talked it over. Their arguments were biased by their realization of the four little men's obvious resources. Neither doubted any more. They knew that Bordent and his companions had come from five hundred years in the future, at the command of a future Alexander who had matured into a fine specimen of superman.

"Amazing, isn't it?" Myra said. "That fat little blob in the bedroom turning into a twelfth-power Quiz Kid."

"Well, it's got to start somewhere. As Bordent pointed out."

"And as long as he isn't going to look like those goblins—ugh!"

"He'll be super. Deucalion and what's-her-name—that's us. Parents of a new race."

"I feel funny," Myra said. "As though I'd given birth to a moose."

"That could never happen," Calderon said consolingly. "Have another slug."

"It might as well have happened. Alexander is a swoose."

"Swoose?"

"I can use that goblin's doubletalk, too. Vopishly woggle in the grand foyer. So there."

"It's a language to them," Calderon said.

"Alexander's going to talk English. I've got my rights."

"Well, Bordent doesn't seem anxious to infringe on them. He said Alexander needed a home environment."

"That's the only reason I haven't gone crazy," Myra said. "As long as he . . . they . . . don't take our baby away from us—"

A week later it was thoroughly clear that Bordent had no intention of encroaching on parental rights—at least, any more than was necessary, for two hours a day. During that period the four little men fulfilled their orders by cramming Alexander with all the knowledge his infantile but super brain could hold. They did not depend on blocks or nursery rhymes or the abacus. Their weapons in the battle were cryptic, futuristic, but effective. And they taught Alexander, there was no doubt of that. As B_1 poured on a plant's roots forces growth, so the vitamin teaching of the dwarfs soaked into Alexander, and his potentially superhuman brain responded, expanding with brilliant, erratic speed.

He had talked intelligibly on the fourth day. On the seventh day he was easily able to hold conversations, though his baby muscles, lingually undeveloped, tired easily. His cheeks were still sucking-disks; he was not yet fully human, except in sporadic flashes. Yet those flashes came oftener now, and closer together.

The carpet was a mess. The little men no longer took their equipment back with them; they left it for Alexander to use. The infant crept—he no longer bothered to walk much, for he could crawl with more efficiency—among the Objects, selected some of them, and put them together. Myra had gone out to shop. The little men wouldn't show up for half an hour. Calderon, tired from his day's work at the University, fingered a highball and looked at his offspring.

"Alexander," he said.

Alexander didn't answer. He fitted a gadget to a Thing, inserted it peculiarly in a Something Else, and sat back with an air of satisfaction. Then—"Yes?" he said. It wasn't perfect pronunciation, but it was unmistakable. Alexander talked somewhat like a toothless old man.

"What are you doing?" Calderon said.

"No."

"What's that?"

"No."

"No?"

"I understand it," Alexander said. "That's enough."

"I see." Calderon regarded the prodigy with faint apprehension. "You don't want to tell me."

"No."

"Well, all right."

"Get me a drink," Alexander said. For a moment Calderon had a mad idea that the infant was demanding a highball. Then he sighed, rose, and returned with a bottle.

"Milk," Alexander said, refusing the potation.

"You said a drink. Water's a drink, isn't it?" My God, Calderon thought, I'm arguing with the kid. I'm treating him like . . . like an adult. But he isn't. He's a fat little baby squatting on his behind on the carpet, playing with a tinkertoy.

The tinkertoy said something in a thin voice. Alexander murmured, "Repeat." The tinkertoy did.

Calderon said, "What was that?"

"No."

"Nuts." Calderon went out to the kitchen and got milk. He poured himself another shot. This was like having relatives drop in suddenly—relatives you hadn't seen for ten years. How the devil did you *act* with a superchild?

He stayed in the kitchen, after supplying Alexander with his milk. Presently Myra's key turned in the outer door. Her cry brought Calderon hurrying.

Alexander was vomiting, with the air of a research man absorbed in a fascinating phenomenon.

"Alexander!" Myra cried. "Darling, are you sick?"

"No," Alexander said. "I'm testing my regurgitative process. I must learn to control my digestive organs."

Calderon leaned against the door, grinning crookedly. "Yeah. You'd better start now, too."

"I'm finished," Alexander said. "Clean it up."

Three days later the infant decided that his lungs needed developing. He cried. He cried at all hours, with interesting variations—whoops, squalls, wails, and high-pitched bellows. Nor would he stop till he was satisfied. The neighbors complained. Myra said, "Darling, is there a pin sticking you? Let me look—"

"Go away," Alexander said. "You're too warm. Open the window. I want fresh air."

"Yes, d-darling. Of course." She came back to bed and Calderon put his arm around her. He knew there would be shadows under her eyes in the morning. In his crib Alexander cried on.

So it went. The four little men came daily and gave Alexander his lessons. They were pleased with the infant's progress. They did not complain when Alexander indulged in his idiosyncrasies, such as batting them heavily on the nose or ripping their paper garments to shreds. Bordent tapped his metal helmet and smiled triumphantly at Calderon.

"He's coming along. He's developing."

"I'm wondering. What about discipline?"

Alexander looked up from his rapport with Quat. "Homo sap discipline doesn't apply to me, Joseph Calderon."

"Don't call me Joseph Calderon. I'm your father, after all."

"A primitive biological necessity. You are not sufficiently well developed to provide the discipline I require. Your purpose is to give me parental care."

"Which makes me an incubator," Calderon said.

"But a deified one," Bordent soothed him. "Practically a logos. The father of the new race."

"I feel more like Prometheus," the father of the new race said dourly. "He was helpful, too. And he ended up with a vulture eating his liver."

"You will learn a great deal from Alexander."

"He says I'm incapable of understanding it."

"Well, aren't you?"

"Sure. I'm just the papa bird," Calderon said, and subsided into a sad silence, watching Alexander, under Quat's tutelary eye, put together a gadget of shimmering glass and twisted metal. Bordent said suddenly, "Quat! Be careful of the egg!" And Finn seized a bluish ovoid just before Alexander's chubby hand could grasp it.

"It isn't dangerous," Quat said. "It isn't connected."

"He might have connected it."

"I want that," Alexander said. "Give it to me."

"Not yet, Alexander," Bordent refused. "You must learn the correct way of connecting it first. Otherwise it might harm you."

"I could do it."

"You are not logical enough to balance your capabilities and lacks as yet. Later it will be safe. I think now, perhaps, a little philosophy, Dobish——eh?"

Dobish squatted and went en rapport with Alexander. Myra came out of the kitchen, took a quick look at the tableau, and retreated. Calderon followed her out.

"I will never get used to it if I live a thousand years," she said with slow emphasis, hacking at the doughy rim of a pie. "He's my baby only when he's asleep."

"We won't live a thousand years," Calderon told her. "Alexander will, though. I wish we could get a maid."

"I tried again today," Myra said wearily. "No use. They're all in war plants. I mention a baby—"

"You can't do all this alone."

"You help," she said, "when you can. But you're working hard too, fella. It won't be forever."

"I wonder if we had another baby . . . if—"

Her sober gaze met his. "I've wondered that, too. But I should think mutations aren't as cheap as that. Once in a lifetime. Still, we don't know."

"Well, it doesn't matter now, anyway. One infant's enough for the moment."

Myra glanced toward the door. "Everything all right in there? Take a look. I worry."

"It's all right."

"I know, but the blue egg—Bordent said it was dangerous, you know. I heard him."

Calderon peeped through the door-crack. The four dwarfs were sitting facing Alexander, whose eyes were closed. Now they opened. The infant scowled at Calderon.

"Stay out," he requested. "You're breaking the rapport."

"I'm so sorry," Calderon said, retreating. "He's O.K., Myra. His own dictatorial little self."

"Well, he *is* a superman," she said doubtfully.

"No. He's a super-baby. There's all the difference."

"His latest trick," Myra said, busy with the oven, "is

riddles. Or something like riddles. I feel so small when he catches me up. But he says it's good for his ego. It compensates for his physical frailness."

"Riddles, eh? I know a few too."

"They won't work on Alexander," Myra said, with grim assurance.

Nor did they. "What goes up a chimney up?" was treated with the contempt it deserved; Alexander examined his father's riddles, turned them over in his logical mind, analyzed them for flaws in semantics and logic, and rejected them. Or else he answered them, with such fine accuracy that Calderon was too embarrassed to give the correct answers. He was reduced to asking why a raven was like a writing desk, and since not even the Mad Hatter had been able to answer his own riddle, was slightly terrified to find himself listening to a dissertation on comparative ornithology. After that, he let Alexander needle him with infantile gags about the relations of gamma rays to photons, and tried to be philosophical. There are few things as irritating as a child's riddles. His mocking triumph pulverizes itself into the dust in which you grovel.

"Oh, leave your father alone," Myra said, coming in with her hair disarranged. "He's trying to read the paper."

"That news is unimportant."

"I'm reading the comics," Calderon said. "I want to see if the Katzenjammers get even with the Captain for hanging them under a waterfall."

"The formula for the humor of an incongruity predicament," Alexander began learnedly, but Calderon disgustedly went into the bedroom, where Myra joined him. "He's asking me riddles again," she said. "Let's see what the Katzenjammers did."

"You look rather miserable. Got a cold?"

"I'm not wearing make-up. Alexander says the smell makes him ill."

"So what? He's no petunia."

"Well," Myra said, "he does get ill. But of course he does it on purpose."

"Listen. There he goes again. What now?"

But Alexander merely wanted an audience. He had found a new way of making imbecilic noises with his fingers and lips. At times the child's normal phases were more trying than his super periods. After a month had passed, however, Calderon felt that the worst was yet to come. Alexander had progressed into fields of knowledge hitherto untouched by homo sap, and he had developed a leechlike habit of sucking his father's brains dry of every scrap of knowledge the wretched man possessed.

It was the same with Myra. The world was indeed Alexander's oyster. He had an insatiable curiosity about everything, and there was no longer any privacy in the apartment. Calderon took to locking the bedroom door against his son at night—Alexander's crib was now in another room—but furious squalls might waken him at any hour.

In the midst of preparing dinner, Myra would be forced to stop and explain the caloric mysteries of the oven to Alexander. He learned all she knew, took a jump into more abstruse aspects of the matter, and sneered at her ignorance. He found out Calderon was a physicist, a fact which the man had hitherto kept carefully concealed, and thereafter pumped his father dry. He asked questions about geodetics and geopolitics. He inquired about monotremes and monorails. He was curious about biremes and biology. And he was skeptical, doubting the depth of his father's knowledge. "But," he said, "you and Myra Calderon are my closest contacts with homo sap as yet, and it's a beginning. Put out that cigarette. It isn't good for my lungs."

"All right," Calderon said. He rose wearily, with his usual feeling these days of being driven from room to room of the apartment, and went in search of Myra. "Bordent's about due. We can go out somewhere, O.K.?"

"Swell." She was at the mirror, fixing her hair, in a trice. "I need a permanent. If I only had the time—!"

"I'll take off tomorrow and stay here. You need a rest."

"Darling, no. The exams are coming up. You simply can't do it."

Alexander yelled. It developed that he wanted his mother to sing for him. He was curious about the tonal range of homo sap and the probable emotional and soporific effect of lullabies. Calderon mixed himself a drink, sat in the kitchen and smoked, and thought about the glorious destiny of his son. When Myra stopped singing, he listened for Alexander's wails, but there was no sound till a slightly hysterical Myra burst in on him, dithering and wide-eyed.

"Joe!" She fell into Calderon's arms. "Quick, give me a drink or . . . or hold me tight or something."

"What is it?" He thrust the bottle into her hands, went to the door, and looked out. "Alexander? He's quiet. Eating candy."

Myra didn't bother with a glass. The bottle's neck clicked against her teeth. "Look at me. Just look at me. I'm a mess."

"What happened?"

"Oh, nothing. Nothing at all. Alexander's turned into a black magician, that's all." She dropped into a chair and passed a palm across her forehead. "Do you know what that genius son of ours just did?"

"Bit you," Calderon hazarded, not doubting it for a minute.

"Worse, far worse. He started asking me for candy. I said there wasn't any in the house. He told me to go down to the grocery for some. I said I'd have to get dressed first, and I was too tired."

"Why didn't you ask me to go?"

"I didn't have the chance. Before I could say boo that infantile Merlin waved a magic wand or something. I . . . I was down at the grocery. Behind the candy counter."

Calderon blinked. "Induced amnesia?"

"There wasn't any time-lapse. It was just *phweet*—and there I was. In this rag of a dress, without a speck of make-up on, and my hair coming down in tassels. Mrs. Busherman was there, too, buying a chicken—that cat across the hall. She was kind enough to tell me I ought to take more care of myself. Meow," Myra ended furiously.

"Good Lord."

"Teleportation. That's what Alexander says it is. Something new he's picked up. I'm not going to stand for it, Joe. I'm not a rag doll, after all." She was half hysterical.

Calderon went into the next room and stood regarding his child. There was chocolate smeared around Alexander's mouth.

"Listen, wise guy," he said. "You leave your mother alone, hear me?"

"I didn't hurt her," the prodigy pointed out, in a blobby voice. "I was simply being efficient."

"Well, don't be so efficient. Where did you learn that trick, anyhow?"

"Teleportation? Quat showed me last night. He can't do it himself, but I'm X Free super, so I can. The power isn't disciplined yet. If I'd tried to teleport Myra Calderon over to Jersey, say, I might have dropped her in the Hudson by mistake."

Calderon muttered something uncomplimentary. Alexander said, "Is that an Anglo-Saxon derivative?"

"Never mind about that. You shouldn't have all that chocolate, anyway. You'll make yourself sick. You've already made your mother sick. And you nauseate me."

"Go away," Alexander said. "I want to concentrate on the taste."

"No. I said you'd make yourself sick. Chocolate's too rich for you. Give it here. You've had enough." Calderon reached for the paper sack. Alexander disappeared. In the kitchen Myra shrieked.

Calderon moaned despondently, and turned. As he had expected, Alexander was in the kitchen, on top of the stove, hoggishly stuffing candy into his mouth. Myra was concentrating on the bottle.

"What a household," Calderon said. "The baby teleporting himself all over the apartment, you getting stewed in the kitchen, and me heading for a nervous breakdown." He started to laugh. "O.K., Alexander. You can keep the candy. I know when to shorten my defensive lines strategically."

"Myra Calderon," Alexander said. "I want to go back into the other room."

"Fly in," Calderon suggested. "Here, I'll carry you."

"Not you. Her. She has a better rhythm when she walks."

"Staggers, you mean," Myra said, but she obediently put aside the bottle, got up, and laid hold of Alexander. She went out. Calderon was not much surprised to hear her scream a moment later. When he joined the happy family, Myra was sitting on the floor, rubbing her arms and biting her lips. Alexander was laughing.

"What now?"

"He-he sh-shocked me," Myra said in a child's voice. "He's

like an electric eel. He d-did it on purpose, too. Oh, Alexander, will you *stop* laughing!"

"You fell down," the infant crowed in triumph. "You yelled and fell down."

Calderon looked at Myra, and his mouth tightened. "Did you do that on purpose?" he asked.

"Yes. She fell down. She looked funny."

"You're going to look a lot funnier in a minute. X Free super or not, what you need is a good paddling."

"Joe—" Myra said.

"Never mind. He's got to learn to be considerate of the rights of others."

"I'm homo superior," Alexander said, with the air of one clinching on argument.

"It's homo posterior I'm going to deal with," Calderon announced, and attempted to capture his son. There was a stinging blaze of jolting nervous energy that blasted up through his synapses; he went backwards ignominiously, and slammed into the wall, cracking his head hard against it. Alexander laughed like an idiot.

"You fell down too," he crowed. "You look funny."

"Joe," Myra said. "Joe. Are you hurt?"

Calderone said sourly that he supposed he'd survive. Though, he added, it would probably be wise to lay in a few splints and a supply of blood plasma. "In case he gets interested in vivisection."

Myra regarded Alexander with troubled speculation. "You're kidding, I hope."

"I hope so, too."

"Well—here's Bordent. Let's talk to him."

Calderon answered the door. The four little men came in solemnly. They wasted no time. They gathered about Alexander, unfolded fresh apparatus from the recesses of their paper clothes, and set to work. The infant said, "I teleported *her* about eight thousand feet."

"That far, eh?" Quat said. "Were you fatigued at all?"

"Not a bit."

Calderon dragged Bordent aside. "I want to talk to you. I think Alexander needs a spanking."

"By voraster!" the dwarf said, shocked. "But he's *Alexander*! He's X Free type super!"

"Not yet. He's still a baby."

"But a superbaby. No, no, Joseph Calderon. I must tell you again that disciplinary measures can be applied only by sufficiently intelligent authorities."

"You?"

"Oh, not yet," Bordent said. "We don't want to overwork him. There's a limit even to super brain power, especially in the very formative period. He's got enough to do, and his attitudes for social contacts won't need forming for a while yet."

Myra joined them. "I don't agree with you there. Like all babies, he's antisocial. He may have superhuman powers but he's subhuman as far as mental and emotional balance go."

"Yeah," Calderon agreed. "This business of giving us electric shocks—"

"He's only playing," Bordent said.

"And teleportation. Suppose he teleports me to Times Square when I'm taking a shower?"

"It's only his play. He's a baby still."

"But what about us?"

"You have the hereditary characteristic of parental tolerance," Bordent explained. "As I told you before, Alexander and his race are the reason why tolerance was created in the first place. There's no great need for it with homo sap. I mean there's a wide space between normal tolerance and normal provocation. An ordinary baby may try his parents severely for a few moments at a time, but that's about all. The provocation is far too small to require the tremendous store of tolerance the parents have. But with the X Free type, it's a different matter."

"There a limit even to tolerance," Calderon said. "I'm wondering about a crèche."

Bordent shook his shiny metallic-sheathed head. "He needs you."

"But," Myra said, "but! Can't you give him just a little discipline?"

"Oh, it isn't necessary. His mind's still immature, and he must concentrate on more important things. You'll tolerate him."

"It's not as though he's our baby any more," she murmured. "He's not Alexander."

"But he is. That's just it. *He's Alexander!*"

"Look, it's normal for a mother to want to hug her baby.

But how can she do that if she expects him to throw her half-way across the room?"

Calderon was brooding. "Will he pick up more . . . more super powers as he goes along?"

"Why, yes. Naturally."

"He's a menace to life and limb. I still say he needs discipline. Next time I'll wear rubber gloves."

"That won't help," Bordent said, frowning. "Besides, I must insist . . . no, Joseph Calderon, it won't do. You mustn't interfere. You're not capable of giving him the right sort of discipline—which he doesn't need yet anyway."

"Just one spanking," Calderon said wistfully. "Not for revenge. Only to show him he's got to consider the rights of others."

"He'll learn to consider the rights of other X Free supers. You must not attempt anything of the sort. A spanking— even if you succeeded, which is far from probable—might warp him psychologically. We are his tutors, his mentors. We must *protect* him. You understand?"

"I think so," Calderon said slowly. "That's a threat."

"You are Alexander's parents, but it's Alexander who is important. If I must apply disciplinary measures to you, I must."

"Oh, forget it," Myra sighed. "Joe, let's go out and walk in the park while Bordent's here."

"Be back in two hours," the little man said. "Good-bye."

As time went past, Calderon could not decide whether Alexander's moronic phrases or his periods of keen intelligence were more irritating. The prodigy had learned new powers; the worst of that was that Calderon never knew what to expect, or when some astounding gag would be sprung on him. Such as the time when a mess of sticky taffy had materialized in his bed, filched from the grocery by deft teleportation. Alexander thought it was very funny. He laughed.

And, when Calderon refused to go to the store to buy candy because he said he had no money—"Now don't try to teleport me. I'm broke."—Alexander had utilized mental energy, warping gravity lines shockingly. Calderon found himself hanging upside-down in midair, being shaken, while loose coins cascaded out of his pocket. He went after the candy.

Humor is a developed sense, stemming basically from cruelty. The more primitive a mind, the less selectivity exists. A cannibal would probably be profoundly amused by the squirmings of his victim in the seething kettle. A man slips on a banana peel and breaks his back. The adult stops laughing at that point, the child does not. And a civilized ego finds embarrassment as acutely distressing as physical pain. A baby, a child, a moron, is incapable of practicing empathy. He cannot identify himself with another individual. He is regrettably autistic; his own rules are arbitrary, and garbage strewn around the bedroom was funny to neither Myra nor Calderon.

There was a little stranger in the house. Nobody rejoiced. Except Alexander. He had a lot of fun.

"No privacy," Calderon said. "He materializes everywhere, at all hours. Darling, I wish you'd see a doctor."

"What would he advise?" Myra asked. "Rest, that's all. Do you realize it's been two months since Bordent took over?"

"And we've made marvelous progress," Bordent said, coming over to them. Quat was en rapport with Alexander on the carpet, while the other two dwarfs prepared the makings of a new gadget. "Or, rather, Alexander has made remarkable progress."

"We need a rest," Calderon growled. "If I lose my job, who'll support that genius of yours?" Myra looked at her husband quickly, noting the possessive pronoun he had used.

Bordent was concerned. "You are in difficulty?"

"The Dean's spoken to me once or twice. I can't control my classes any more. I'm too irritable."

"You don't need to expend tolerance on your students. As for money, we can keep you supplied. I'll arrange to get some negotiable currency for you."

"But I want to work. I like my job."

"Alexander is your job."

"I need a maid," Myra said, looking hopeless. "Can't you make me a robot or something? Alexander scares every maid I've managed to hire. They won't stay a day in this madhouse."

"A mechanical intelligence would have a bad effect on Alexander," Bordent said. "No."

"I wish we could have guests in once in a while. Or go out visiting. Or just be alone," Myra sighed.

"Some day Alexander will be mature, and you'll reap your

reward. The parents of Alexander. Did I ever tell you that we have images of you two in the Great Fogy Hall?"

"They must look terrible," Calderon said. "I know we do now."

"Be patient. Consider the destiny of your son."

"I do. Often. But he gets a little wearing sometimes. That's quite an understatement."

"Which is where tolerance comes in," Bordent said. "Nature planned well for the new race."

"Mm-m-m."

"He is working on sixth-dimensional abstractions now. Everything is progressing beautifully."

"Yeah," Calderon said. And he went away, muttering, to join Myra in the kitchen.

Alexander worked with facility at his gadgets, his pudgy fingers already stronger and surer. He still had an illicit passion for the blue ovoid, but under Bordent's watchful eye he could use it only along the restricted lines laid out by his mentors. When the lesson was finished, Quat selected a few of the objects and locked them in a cupboard, as was his custom. The rest he left on the carpet to provide exercise for Alexander's ingenuity.

"He develops," Bordent said. "Today we've made a great step."

Myra and Calderon came in time to hear this. "What goes?" he asked.

"A psychic bloc-removal. Alexander will no longer need to sleep."

"What?" Myra said.

"He won't require sleep. It's an artificial habit anyway. The super race has no need of it."

"He won't sleep any more, eh?" Calderon said. He had grown a little pale.

"Correct. He'll develop faster now, twice as fast."

At 3:30 A.M. Calderon and Myra lay in bed, wide awake, looking through the open door into the full blaze of light where Alexander played. Seen there clearly, as if upon a lighted stage, he did not look quite like himself any more. The difference was subtle, but it was there. Under the golden down his head had changed shape slightly, and there was a look of intelligence and purpose upon the blobby features. It was not an attractive look. It didn't belong there. It made Alexander look less like a super-baby than a debased oldster. All a child's normal cruelty and selfishness—perfectly healthy, natural traits in the developing infant—flickered across Alexander's face as he played absorbedly with solid crystal blocks which he was fitting into one another like a Chinese puzzle. It was quite a shocking face to watch.

Calderon heard Myra sigh beside him.

"He isn't our Alexander any more," she said. "Not a bit."

Alexander glanced up and his face suddenly suffused. The look of paradoxical age and degeneracy upon it vanished as he opened his mouth and bawled with rage, tossing the blocks in all directions. Calderon watched one roll through the bedroom door and come to rest upon the carpet, spilling out of its solidity a cascade of smaller and smaller solid blocks that tumbled winking toward him. Alexander's cries filled the apartment. After a moment windows began to slam across the court, and presently the phone rang. Calderon reached for it, sighing.

When he hung up he looked across at Myra and grimaced. Above the steady roars he said, "Well, we have notice to move."

Myra said, "Oh. Oh, well."

"That about covers it."

They were silent for a moment. Then Calderon said, "Nineteen years more of it. I thing we can expect about that. They did say he'd mature at twenty, didn't they?"

"He'll be an orphan long before then," Myra groaned. "Oh, my head! I think I caught cold when he teleported us up to the roof just before dinner. Joe, do you suppose we're the first parents who ever got . . . got caught like this?"

"What do you mean?"

"I mean, was there ever another super-baby before Alexander? It does seem like a waste of a lot of tolerance if we're the first to need it."

"We could use a lot more. We'll need a lot." He said nothing more for awhile, but he lay there thinking and trying not to hear his super-child's rhythmic howling. Tolerance. Every parent needed a great deal of it. Every child was intolerable from time to time. The race had certainly needed parental love in vast quantities to permit its infants to survive. But no parents before had ever been tried consistently up to the very last degree of tolerance. No parents before had ever had to face twenty years of it, day and night, strained to the final notch. Parental love is a great and all-encompassing emotion, but—

"I wonder," he said thoughtfully. "I wonder if we *are* the first."

Myra's speculations had been veering. "I suppose it's like tonsils and appendix," she murmured. "They've outlived their use, but they still hang on. This tolerance is vestigial in reverse. It's been hanging on all these millenniums, waiting for Alexander."

"Maybe. I wonder— Still, if there ever had been an Alexander before now, we'd have heard of him. So—"

Myra rose on one elbow and looked at her husband. "You think so?" she said softly. "I'm not so sure. I think it might have happened before."

Alexander suddenly quieted. The apartment rang with silence for a moment. Then a familiar voice, without words, spoke in both their brains simultaneously.

"Get me some more milk. And I want it just warm, not hot."

Joe and Myra looked at one another again, speechless. Myra sighed and pushed the covers back. "I'll go this time," she said. "Something new, eh? I—"

"Don't dawdle," said the wordless voice, and Myra jumped and gave a little shriek. Electricity crackled audibly through the room, and Alexander's bawling laughter was heard through the doorway.

"He's about as civilized now as a well-trained monkey, I suppose," Joe remarked, getting out of bed. "I'll go. You crawl back in. And in another year he may reach the elevation of a bushman. After that, if we're still alive, we'll have the pleasure of living with a super-powered cannibal. Eventually he may work up to the level of practical joker. That ought to be interesting." He went out, muttering to himself.

Ten minutes later, returning to bed, Joe found Myra clasping her knees and looking into space.

"We aren't the first, Joe," she said, not glancing at him. "I've been thinking. I'm pretty sure we aren't."

"But we've never heard of any supermen developing—"

She turned her head and gave him a long, thoughtful look. "No," she said.

They were silent. Then, "Yes, I see what you mean," he nodded.

Something crashed in the living room. Alexander chuckled and the sound of splintering wood was loud in the silence of the night. Another window banged somewhere outside.

"There's a breaking point," Myra said quietly. "There's got to be."

"Saturation," Joe murmured. "Tolerance saturation—or something. It could have happened."

Alexander trundled into sight, clutching something blue. He sat down and began to fiddle with bright wires. Myra rose suddenly.

"Joe, he's got that blue egg! He must have broken into the cupboard."

Calderon said, "But Quat told him—"

"It's dangerous!"

Alexander looked at them, grinned, and bent the wires into a cradle-shape the size of the egg.

Calderon found himself out of bed and halfway to the door. He stopped before he reached it. "You know," he said slowly, "he might hurt himself with that thing."

"We'll have to get it away from him," Myra agreed, heaving herself up with tired reluctance.

"Look at him," Calderon urged. "Just look."

Alexander was dealing competently with the wires, his hands flickering into sight and out again as he balanced a tesseract beneath the cradle. That curious veil of knowledge gave his chubby face the debased look of senility which they had come to know so well.

"This will go on and on, you know," Calderon murmured. "Tomorrow he'll look a little less like himself than today. Next week—next month—what will he be like in a year?"

"I know." Myra's voice was an echo. "Still, I suppose we'll have to—" Her voice trailed to a halt. She stood barefoot beside her husband, watching.

"I suppose the gadget will be finished," she said, "once he connects up that last wire. We ought to take it away from him."

"Think we could?"

"We ought to try."

They looked at each other. Calderon said, "It looks like an Easter egg. I never heard of an Easter egg hurting anybody."

"I suppose we're doing him a favor, really," Myra said in a low voice. "A burnt child dreads the fire. Once a kid burns himself on a match, he stays away from matches."

They stood in silence, watching.

It took Alexander about three more minutes to succeed in his design, whatever it was. The results were phenomenally effective. There was a flash of white light, a crackle of split air, and Alexander vanished in the dazzle, leaving only a faint burnt smell behind him.

When the two could see again, they blinked distrustfully at the empty place. "Teleportation?" Myra whispered dazedly.

"I'll make sure." Calderon crossed the floor and stood looking down at a damp spot on the carpet, with Alexander's shoes in it. He said, "No. Not teleportation." Then he took a long breath. "He's gone, all right. So he never grew up and sent Bordent back in time to move in on us. It never happened."

"We weren't the first," Myra said in an unsteady, bemused voice. "There's a breaking point, that's all. How sorry I feel for the first parents who don't reach it!"

She turned away suddenly, but not so suddenly that he could not see she was crying. He hesitated, watching the door. He thought he had better not follow her just yet.

KILLDOZER!

Astounding,
November

by Theodore Sturgeon (1918-   )

Ted Sturgeon returned to the pages of Astounding *after an absence of several years with this thrilling masterpiece. "Possession" stories are usually the province of fantasy, but since the possessor in this case is an alien intelligence, "Killdozer!" qualifies as science fiction. The theme of man vs. machine is an old one in science fiction, but it has rarely been treated with as much skill as it is here. Sturgeon was a heavy machine operator and knew of what he wrote. The story was filmed (a made-for-television production) in 1974 but failed to capture the dramatic tension of the original.*

(World War II meant a fall-off in the output of a number of science fiction's leading authors. The years 1942 to 1945, for instance, saw Robert Heinlein, Sprague de Camp and myself working on the same floor of the same building at the U.S. Navy Yard in Philadelphia. It meant that Bob and Sprague wrote virtually nothing for three years (though I myself managed to find spare time in which to continue my Foundation series and my positronic robot stories). Ted Sturgeon was another one of the fall-offs (and it all drove poor John Campbell half-crazy, as you can well imagine). When Ted came back, however, it was with his best straight science fiction piece, the one you are about to read, so maybe it was all for the best.—I.A.)

Before the race was the deluge, and before the deluge another race, whose nature it is not for mankind to understand. Not unearthly, not alien, for this was their earth and their home.

There was a war between this race, which was a great one, and another. The other was truly alien, a sentient cloudform, an intelligent grouping of tangible electrons. It was spawned in mighty machines by some accident of a science before our aboriginal conception of its complexities. And the machines, servants of the people, became the people's masters, and great were the battles that followed. The electron-beings had the power to warp the delicate balances of atom-structure, and their life-medium was metal, which they permeated and used to their own ends. Each weapon the people developed was possessed and turned against them, until a time when the remnants of that vast civilization found a defense—

An insulator. The terminal product or by-product of all energy research—neutronium.

In its shelter they developed a weapon. What it was we shall never know, and our race will live—or we shall know, and our race will perish as theirs perished. For, to destroy the enemy, it got out of hand and its measureless power destroyed them with it, and their cities, and their possessed machines. The very earth dissolved in flame, the crust writhed and shook and the ocean boiled. Nothing escaped it, nothing that we know as life, and nothing of the pseudolife that had evolved within the mysterious force-fields of their incomprehensible machines, save one hardy mutant.

Mutant it was, and ironically this one alone could have been killed by the first simple measures used against its kind—but it was past time for simple expediences. It was an organized electron-field possessing intelligence and mobility and a will to destroy, and little else. Stunned by the holocaust, it drifted over the grumbling globe, and in a lull in the violence of the forces gone wild on Earth, sank to the steaming ground in its half-conscious exhaustion. There it found shelter—shelter built by and for its dead enemies. An envelope of neutronium. It drifted in, and its consciousness at last fell to its lowest ebb. And there it lay while the neutronium, with its strange constant flux, its interminable striving for perfect balance, extended itself and closed the opening. And thereafter in the turbulent eons that followed, the envelope tossed like a gray bubble on the surface of the roiling sphere, for no substance on Earth would have it or combine with it.

The ages came and went, and chemical action and reaction did their mysterious work, and once again there was life and evolution. And a tribe found the mass of neutronium, which is not a substance but a static force, and were awed by its aura of indescribable chill, and they worshiped it and built a temple around it and made sacrifices to it. And ice and fire and the seas came and went, and the land rose and fell as the years went by, until the ruined temple was on a knoll, and the knoll was an island. Islanders came and went, lived and built and died, and races forgot. So now, somewhere in the Pacific to the west of the archipelago called Islas Revillagigeda, there was an uninhabited island. And one day—

Chub Horton and Tom Jaeger stood watching the *Sprite* and her squat tow of three cargo lighters dwindle over the glassy sea. The big ocean-going towboat and her charges seemed to be moving out of focus rather than traveling away. Chub spat cleanly around the cigar that grew out of the corner of his mouth.

"That's that for three weeks. How's it feel to be a guinea pig?"

"We'll get it done." Tom had little crinkles all around the outer ends of his eyes. He was a head taller than Chub and rangy, and not so tough, and he was a real operator. Choosing him as a foreman for the experiment had been wise, for he was competent and he commanded respect. The theory of airfield construction that they were testing appealed vastly to him, for here were no officers-in-charge, no government inspectors, no timekeeping or reports. The government had allowed the company a temporary land grant, and the idea was to put production-line techniques into the layout and grading of the project. There were six operators and two mechanics and more than a million dollars' worth of the best equipment that money could buy. Government acceptance was to be on a partially completed basis, and contingent on government standards. The theory obviated both gold-bricking and graft, and neatly sidestepped the manpower shortage. "When that blacktopping crew gets here, I reckon we'll be ready for 'em," said Tom.

He turned and scanned the island with an operator's vision and saw it as it was, and in all the stages it would pass through, and as it would look when they had finished, with four thousand feet of clean-draining runway, hard-packed shoulders, four acres of plane-park, the access road and the short taxiway. He saw the lay of each lift that the power shovel would cut as it brought down the marl bluff, and the ruins on top of it that would give them stone to haul down the salt-flat to the little swamp at the other end, there to be walked in by the dozers.

"We got time to walk the shovel up there to the bluff before dark."

They walked down the beach toward the outcropping where the equipment stood surrounded by crates and drums of supplies. The three tractors were ticking over quietly, the two-cycle Diesel chuckling through their mufflers and the big D-7 whacking away its metronomic compression knock on every easy revolution. The Dumptors were lined up and silent, for they would not be ready to work until the shovel was ready to load them. They looked like a mechanical interpretation of Dr. Dolittle's "Pushme-pullyou," the fantastic animal with two front ends. They had two large driving wheels and two small steerable wheels. The motor and the driver's seat were side by side over the front—or smaller—wheels; but the driver faced the dump body between the big rear wheels, exactly the opposite of the way he would sit in a dump truck. Hence, in traveling from shovel to dumping-ground, the operator drove backwards, looking over his shoulder, and in dumping he backed the machine up but he himself traveled forward—quite a trick for fourteen hours a day! The shovel squatted in the midst of all the others, its great hulk looming over them, humped there with its boom low and its iron chin on the ground, like some great tired dinosaur.

Rivera, the Puerto Rican mechanic, looked up grinning as Tom and Chub approached, and stuck a bleeder wrench into the top pocket of his coveralls.

"She says 'Sigalo,'" he said, his white teeth flashlighting out of the smear of grease across his mouth. "She says she wan' to get dirt on dis paint." He kicked the blade of the Seven with his heel.

Tom sent the grin back—always a surprising thing in his grave face.

"That Seven'll do that, and she'll take a good deal off her bitin' edge along with the paint before we're through. Get in the saddle, Goony. Build a ramp off the rocks down to the flat there, and blade us off some humps from here to the bluff yonder. We're walking the dipper up there."

The Puerto Rican was in the seat before Tom had finished, and with a roar the Seven spun in its length and moved back along the outcropping to the inland edge. Rivera dropped his blade and the sandy marl curled and piled up in front of the dozer, loading the blade and running off in two even rolls at the ends. He shoved the load toward the rocky edge, the Seven revving down as it took the load, *blat blat blatting* and pulling like a supercharged ox as it fired slowly enough for them to count the revolutions.

"She's a hunk of machine," said Tom.

"A hunk of operator, too," gruffed Chub, and added, "for a mechanic."

"The boy's all right," said Kelly. He was standing there with them, watching the Puerto Rican operate the dozer, as if he had been there all along, which was the way Kelly always arrived places. He was tall, slim, with green eyes too long and an easy stretch to the way he moved, like an attenuated cat. He said, "Never thought I'd see the day when equipment was shipped set up ready to run like this. Guess no one ever thought of it before."

"There's times when heavy equipment has to be unloaded in a hurry these days," Tom said. "If they can do it with tanks, they can do it with construction equipment. We're doin' it to build something instead, is all. Kelly, crank up the shovel. It's oiled. We're walking it over to the bluff."

Kelly swung up into the cab of the big dipper-stick and, diddling the governor control, pulled up the starting handle. The Murphy Diesel snorted and settled down into a thudding idle. Kelly got into the saddle, set up the throttle a little, and began to boom up.

"I still can't get over it," said Chub. "Not more'n a year ago we'd a had two hundred men on a job like this."

Tom smiled. "Yeah, and the first thing we'd have done

would be to build an office building, and then quarters. Me, I'll take this way. No timekeepers, no equipment-use reports, no progress and yardage summaries, no nothin' but eight men, a million bucks worth of equipment, an' three weeks. A shovel an' a mess of tool crates'll keep the rain off us, an' army field rations'll keep our bellies full. We'll get it done, we'll get out and we'll get paid."

Rivera finished the ramp, turned the Seven around and climbed it, walking the new fill down. At the top he dropped his blade, floated it, and backed down the ramp, smoothing out the rolls. At a wave from Tom he started out across the shore, angling up toward the bluff, beating out the humps and carrying fill into the hollows. As he worked, he sang, feeling the beat of the mighty motor, the micrometric obedience of that vast implacable machine.

"Why doesn't that monkey stick to his grease guns?"

Tom turned and took the chewed end of a match stick out of his mouth. He said nothing, because he had for some time been trying to make a habit of saying nothing to Joe Dennis. Dennis was an ex-accountant, drafted out of an office at the last gasp of a defunct project in the West Indies. He had become an operator because they needed operators badly. He had been released with alacrity from the office because of his propensity for small office politics. It was a game he still played, and completely aside from his boiled-looking red face and his slightly womanish walk, he was out of place in the field; for boot-licking and back-stabbing accomplish even less out on the field than they do in an office. Tom, trying so hard to keep his mind on his work, had to admit to himself that of all Dennis' annoying traits the worst was that he was good a pan operator as could be found anywhere, and no one could deny it.

Dennis certainly didn't.

"I've seen the day when anyone catching one of those goonies so much as sitting on a machine during lunch, would kick his fanny," Dennis groused. "Now they give 'em a man's work and a man's pay."

"*Doin'* a man's work, ain't he?" Tom said.

"He's a Puerto Rican!"

Tom turned and looked at him levelly. "Where was it you said *you* come from," he mused. "Oh yeah. Georgia."

"What do you mean by that?"

Tom was already striding away. "Tell you as soon as I have to," he flung back over his shoulder. Dennis went back to watching the Seven.

Tom glanced at the ramp and then waved Kelly on. Kelly set his house-brake so the shovel could not swing, put her into travel gear, and shoved the swing lever forward. With a crackling of drive chains and a massive scrunching of compacting coral sand, the shovel's great flat pads carried her over and down the ramp. As she tipped over the peak of the ramp the heavy manganese steel bucket-door gaped open and closed, like a hungry mouth, slamming up against the bucket until suddenly it latched shut and was quiet. The big Murphy Diesel crooned hollowly under compression as the machine ran downgrade and then the sensitive governor took hold and it took up its belly-beating thud.

Peebles was standing by one of the door-pan combines, sucking on his pipe and looking out to sea. He was grizzled and heavy, and from under the bushiest gray brows looked the calmest gray eyes Tom had ever seen. Peebles had never gotten angry at a machine—a rare trait in a born mechanic—and in fifty-odd years he had learned it was even less use getting angry at a man. Because no matter what, you could always fix what was wrong with a machine. He said around his pipestem:

"Hope you'll give me back my boy, there."

Tom's lips quirked in a little grin. There had been an understanding between old Peebles and himself ever since they had met. It was one of those things which exists unspoken—they knew little about each other because they had never found it necessary to make small talk to keep their friendship extant. It was enough to know that each could expect the best from the other, without persuasion.

"Rivera?" Tom asked. "I'll chase him back as soon as he finishes that service road for the dipper-stick. Why—got anything on?"

"Not much. Want to get that arc welder drained and flushed and set up a grounded table in case you guys tear anything up." He paused. "Besides, the kid's filling his head up with too many things at once. Mechanicing is one thing; operating is something else."

"Hasn't got in his way much so far, has it?"

"Nope. Don't aim t' let it, either. 'Less you need him."

Tom swung up on the pan tractor. "I don't need him that bad, Peeby. If you want some help in the meantime, get Dennis."

Peebles said nothing. He spat. He didn't say anything at all.

"What's the matter with Dennis?" Tom wanted to know.

"Look yonder," said Peebles, waving his pipestem. Out on the beach Dennis was talking to Chub, in Dennis' indefatigable style, standing beside Chub, one hand on Chub's shoulder. As they watched they saw Dennis call his side-kick, Al Knowles.

"Dennis talks too much," said Peebles. "That most generally don't amount to much, but that Dennis, he sometimes *says* too much. Ain't got what it takes to run a show, and knows it. Makes up for by messin' in between folks."

"He's harmless," said Tom.

Still looking up the beach, Peebles said slowly:

"Is, so far."

Tom started to say something, then shrugged. "I'll send you Rivera," he said, and opened the throttle. Like a huge electric dynamo, the two-cycle motor whined to a crescendo. Tom lifted the dozer with a small lever by his right thigh and raised the pan with the long control sprouting out from behind his shoulder. He moved off, setting the rear gate of the scraper so that anything the blade bit would run off to the side instead of loading into the pan. He slapped the tractor into sixth gear and whined up to and around the crawling shovel, cutting neatly in under the boom and running on ahead with his scraper blade just touching the ground, dragging to a fine grade the service road Rivera had cut.

Dennis was saying, "It's that little Hitler stuff. Why should I take that kind of talk? 'You come from Georgia,' he says. What is he—a Yankee or something?"

"A crackah f'm Macon," chortled Al Knowles, who came from Georgia, too. He was tall and stringy and round-shouldered. All of his skill was in his hands and feet, brains being a commodity he had lived without all his life until he had met Dennis and used him as a reasonable facsimile thereof.

"Tom didn't mean nothing by it," said Chub.

"No, he didn't mean nothin'. Only that we do what he says the way he says it, specially if he finds a way we don't like it.

You wouldn't do like that, Chub. Al, think Chub would carry on thataway?"

"Sure wouldn't," said Al, feeling it expected of him.

"Nuts," said Chub, pleased and uncomfortable, and thinking, what have I got against Tom?—not knowing, not liking Tom as well as he had. "Tom's the man here, Dennis. We got a job to do—let's skit and git. Man can take anything for a lousy six weeks."

"Oh, sho'," said Al.

"Man can take just so much," Dennis said. "What they put a man like that on top for, Chub? What's the matter with you? Don't you know grading and drainage as good as Tom? Can Tom stake out a side hill like you can?"

"Sure, sure, but what's the difference, long as we get a field built? An' anyhow, hell with bein' the boss-man. Who gets the blame if things don't run right, anyway?"

Dennis stepped back, taking his hand off Chub's shoulder, and stuck an elbow in Al's ribs.

"You see that, Al? Now there's a smart man. That's the thing Uncle Tom didn't bargain for. Chub, you can count on Al and me to do just that little thing."

"Do just what little thing?" asked Chub, genuinely puzzled.

"Like you said. If the job goes wrong, the boss gets blamed. So if the boss don't behave, the job goes wrong."

"Uh-huh," agreed Al with the conviction of mental simplicity.

Chub double-took this extraordinary logical process and grasped wildly at anger as the conversation slid out from under him. "I didn't say any such thing! This job is goin' to get done, no matter what! Hitler ain't hangin' no iron cross on me or anybody else around here if I can help it."

"Tha's the ol' fight," feinted Dennis. "We'll show that guy what we think of his kind of sabotage."

"You talk too much," said Chub and escaped with the remnants of coherence. Every time he talked with Dennis he walked away feeling as if he had an unwanted membership card stuck in his pocket that he couldn't throw away with a clear conscience.

Rivera ran his road up under the bluff, swung the Seven around, punched out the master clutch and throttled down, idling. Tom was making his pass with the pan, and as he approached, Rivera slipped out of the seat and behind the tractor, laying a sensitive hand on the final drive casing and sprocket bushings, checking for overheating. Tom pulled alongside and beckoned him up on the pan tractor.

"*Que pase,* Goony? Anything wrong?"

Rivera shook his head and grinned. "Nothing wrong. She is perfect, that '*De Siete.*' She—"

"That what? 'Daisy Etta'?"

"*De siete.* In Spanish, D-7. It means something in English?"

"Got you wrong," smiled Tom. "But Daisy Etta is a girl's name in English, all the same."

He shifted the pan tractor into neutral and engaged the clutch, and jumped off the machine. Rivera followed. They climbed aboard the Seven, Tom at the controls.

Rivera said "Daisy Etta," and grinned so widely that a soft little chuckling noise came from behind his back teeth. He reached out his hand, crooked his little finger around one of the tall steering clutch levers, and pulled it all the way back. Tom laughed outright.

"You got something there," he said. "The easiest runnin' cat ever built. Hydraulic steerin' clutches and brakes that'll bring you to a dead stop if you spit on 'em. Forward an' reverse lever so's you got all your speeds front and backwards. A little different from the old jobs. They had no booster springs, eight-ten years ago; took a sixty-pound pull to get a steerin' clutch back. Cuttin' a side-hill with an angle-dozer really was a job in them days. You try it sometime, dozin' with one hand, holdin' her nose out o' the bank with the other, ten hours a day. And what'd it get you? Eighty cents an hour an' "—Tom took his cigarette and butted the fiery end out against the horny palm of his hand—"these."

"*Santa Maria!*"

"Want to talk to you, Goony. Want to look over the bluff, too, at that stone up there. It'll take Kelly pret' near an hour to get this far and sumped in, anyhow."

They started up the slope, Tom feeling the ground under the four-foot brush, taking her up in a zigzag course like a hairpin road on a mountainside. Though the Seven carried a muffler on the exhaust stack that stuck up out of the hood before them, the blat of four big cylinders hauling fourteen tons of steel upgrade could outshout any man's conversation, so they sat without talking, Tom driving, Rivera watching his hands flick over the controls.

The bluff started in a low ridge running almost the length of the little island, like a lopsided backbone. Toward the center it rose abruptly, sent a wing out toward the rocky outcropping at the beach where their equipment had been unloaded, and then rose again to a small, almost square plateau area, half a mile square. It was humpy and rough until they could see all of it, when they realized how incredibly level it was, under the brush and ruins that covered it. In the center—and exactly in the center they realized suddenly—was a low, overgrown mound. Tom threw out the clutch and revved her down.

"Survey report said there was stone up here," Tom said, vaulting out of the seat. "Let's walk around some."

They walked toward the knoll, Tom's eyes casting about as he went. He stooped down into the heavy, short grass and scooped up a piece of stone, blue-gray, hard and brittle.

"Rivera—look at this. This is what the report was talking about. See—more of it. All in small pieces, though. We need big stuff for the bog if we can get it."

"Good stone?" asked Rivera.

"Yes, boy—but it don't belong here. Th' whole island's sand and marl and sandstone on the outcrop down yonder. This here's a bluestone, like diamond clay. Harder'n blazes. I never saw this stuff on a marl hill before. Or near one. Anyhow, root around and see if there is any big stuff."

They walked on. Rivera suddenly dipped down and pulled grass aside.

"Tom—here's a beeg one."

Tom came over and looked down at the corner of stone sticking up out of the topsoil. "Yeh. Goony, get your girlfriend over here and we'll root it out."

Rivera sprinted back to the idling dozer and climbed aboard. He brought the machine over to where Tom waited, stopped, stood up and peered over the front of the machine to locate the stone, then sat down and shifted gears. Before he could move the machine Tom was on the fender beside him, checking him with a hand on his arm.

"No, boy—no. Not third. First. And half throttle. That's it. Don't try to bash a rock out of the ground. Go on up to it easy; set your blade against it, lift it out, don't boot it out.

Take it with the middle of your blade, not the corner—get the load on both hydraulic cylinders. Who told you to do like that?"

"No one tol' me, Tom. I see a man do it, I do it."

"Yeah? Who was it?"

"Dennis, but—"

"Listen, Goony, if you want to learn anything from Dennis, watch him while he's on a pan. He dozes like he talks. That reminds me—what I wanted to talk to you about. You ever have any trouble with him?"

Rivera spread his hands. "How I have trouble when he never talk to me?"

"Well, that's all right then. You keep it that way. Dennis is O.K., I guess, but you better keep away from him."

He went on to tell the boy then about what Peebles had said concerning being an operator and a mechanic at the same time. Rivera's lean dark face fell, and his hand strayed to the blade control, touching it lightly, feeling the composition grip and the machined locknuts that held it. When Tom had quite finished he said:

"O.K., Tom—if you want, you break 'em, I feex 'em. But if you wan' help some time, I run *Daisy Etta* for you, no?"

"Sure, kid, sure. But don't forget, no man can do everything."

"You can do everything," said the boy.

Tom leaped off the machine and Rivera shifted into first and crept up to the stone, setting the blade gently against it. Taking the load, the mighty engine audibly bunched its muscles; Rivera opened the throttle a little and the machine set solidly against the stone, the tracks slipping, digging into the ground, piling loose earth up behind. Tom raised a fist, thumb up, and the boy began lifting his blade. The Seven lowered her snout like an ox pulling through mud; the front of the tracks buried themselves deeper and the blade slipped upward an inch on the rock, as if it were on a ratchet. The stone shifted, and suddenly heaved itself up out of the earth that covered it, bulging the sod aside like a ship's slow bow wave. And the blade lost its grip and slipped over the stone. Rivera slapped out the master clutch within an ace of letting the mass of it poke through his radiator core. Reversing, he set the blade against it again and rolled it at last into daylight.

Tom stood staring at it, scratching the back of his neck. Rivera got off the machine and stood beside him. For a long time they said nothing.

The stone was roughly rectangular, shaped like a brick with one end cut at about a thirty-degree angle. And on the angled face was a square-cut ridge, like the tongue on a piece of milled lumber. The stone was about $3 \times 2 \times 2$ feet, and must have weighed six or seven hundred pounds.

"Now that," said Tom, bug-eyed, "didn't grow *here,* and if it did it never grew that way."

"*Una piedra de una casa,*" said Rivera softly. "Tom, there was a building here, no?"

Tom turned suddenly to look at the knoll.

"There is a building here—or what's left of it. Lord on'y knows how old—"

They stood there in the slowly dwindling light, staring at the knoll; and there came upon them a feeling of oppression, as if there were no wind and no sound anywhere. And yet there was wind, and behind them *Daisy Etta* whacked away with her muttering idle, and nothing had changed and—was that it? That nothing had changed? That nothing would change, or could, here?

Tom opened his mouth twice to speak, and couldn't, or didn't want to—he didn't know which. Rivera slumped down suddenly on his hunkers, back erect, and his eyes wide.

It grew very cold. "It's cold," Tom said, and his voice sounded harsh to him. And the wind blew warm on them, the earth was warm under Rivera's knees. The cold was not a lack of heat, but a lack of something else—warmth, but the specific warmth of life-force, perhaps. The feeling of oppression grew, as if their recognition of the strangeness of the place had started it, and their increasing sensitivity to it made it grow.

Rivera said something, quietly, in Spanish.

"What are you looking at?" asked Tom.

Rivera started violently, threw up an arm, as if to ward off the crash of Tom's voice.

"I . . . there is nothin' to see, Tom. I feel this way wance before. I dunno—" He shook his head, his eyes wide and blank. "An' after, there was being wan hell of a thunderstorm—" His voice petered out.

Tom took his shoulder and hauled him roughly to his feet. "Goony! You slap-happy?"

The boy smiled, almost gently. The down on his upper lip held little spheres of sweat. "I ain' nothin', Tom. I'm jus' scare like hell."

"You scare yourself right back up there on that cat and git to work," Tom roared. More quietly then he said, "I know there's something—wrong—here, Goony, but that ain't goin' to get us a runway built. Anyhow, I know what to do about a dawg 'at gits gun-shy. Ought to be able to do as much fer you. Git along to th' mound now and see if it ain't a cache o' big stone for us. We got a swamp down there to fill."

Rivera hesitated, started to speak, swallowed and then walked slowly over to the Seven. Tom stood watching him, closing his mind to the impalpable pressure of something, somewhere near, making his guts cold.

The bulldozer nosed over to the mound, grunting, reminding Tom suddenly that the machine's Spanish slang name was *puerco*—pig, boar. Rivera angled into the edge of the mound with the cutting corner of the blade. Dirt and brush curled up, fell away from the mound and loaded from the bank side, out along the moldboard. The boy finished his pass along the mound, carried the load past it and wasted it out on the flat, turned around and started back again.

Ten minutes later Rivera struck stone, the manganese steel screaming along it, a puff of gray dust spouting from the cutting corner. Tom knelt and examined it after the machine had passed. It was the same kind of stone they had found out on the flat—and shaped the same way. But here it was a wall, the angled faces of the block ends obviously tongued and grooved together.

Cold, cold as—

Tom took one deep breath and wiped sweat out of his eyes.

"I don't care," he whispered, "I got to have that stone. I got to fill me a swamp." He stood back and motioned to Rivera to blade into a chipped crevice in the buried wall.

The Seven swung into the wall and stopped while Rivera shifted into first, throttled down and lowered his blade. Tom looked up into his face. The boy's lips were white. He

eased in the master clutch, the blade dipped and the corner
swung neatly into the crevice.

The dozer blatted protestingly and began to crab sideways,
pivoting on the end of the blade. Tom jumped out of the
way, ran around behind the machine, which was almost parallel with the wall now, and stood in the clear, one hand
ready to signal, his eyes on the straining blade. And then
everything happened at once.

With a toothy snap the block started and came free, pivoting outward from its square end, bringing with it its neighbor. The block above them dropped, and the whole mound
seemed to settle. And *something* whooshed out of the black
hole where the rocks had been. Something like a fog, but
not a fog that could be seen, something huge that could not
be measured. With it came a gust of that cold which was
not cold, and the smell of ozone, and the prickling crackle
of a mighty static discharge.

Tom was fifty feet from the wall before he knew he had
moved. He stopped and saw the Seven suddenly buck like a
wild stallion, once, and Rivera turning over twice in the air.
Tom shouted some meaningless syllable and tore over to the
boy, where he sprawled in the rough grass, lifted him in his
arms, and ran. Only then did he realize that he was running
from the machine.

It was like a mad thing. Its moldboard rose and fell. It
curved away from the mound, howling governor gone wild,
controls flailing. The blade dug repeatedly into the earth,
gouging it up in great dips through which the tractor plunged,
clanking and bellowing furiously. It raced away in a great irregular arc, turned and came snorting back to the mound,
where it beat at the buried wall, slewed and scraped and
roared.

Tom reached the edge of the plateau sobbing for breath,
and kneeling, laid the boy gently down on the grass.

"Goony, boy . . . hey—"

The long silken eyelashes fluttered, lifted. Something
wrenched in Tom as he saw the eyes, rolled right back so that
only the whites showed. Rivera drew a long quivering breath
which caught suddenly. He coughed twice, threw his head
from side to side so violently that Tom took it between his
hands and steadied it.

"*Ay . . . Maria madre . . . que ha me pasado*, Tom—w'at has happen to me?"

"Fell off the Seven, stupid. You . . . how you feel?"

Rivera scrabbled at the ground, got his elbows half under him, then sank back weakly. "Feel O.K. Headache like hell. W-w'at happen to my feets?"

"Feet? They hurt?"

"No hurt—" The young face went gray, the lips tightened with effort. "No, nothin', Tom."

"You can't move 'em?"

Rivera shook his head, still trying. Tom stood up. "You take it easy. I'll go get Kelly. Be right back."

He walked away quickly and when Rivera called to him he did not turn around. Tom had seen a man with a broken back before.

At the edge of the little plateau Tom stopped, listening. In the deepening twilight he could see the bulldozer standing by the mound. The motor was running; she had not stalled herself. But what stopped Tom was that she wasn't idling, but revving up and down as if an impatient hand were on the throttle—*hroom hroooom*, running up and up far faster than even a broken governor should permit, then coasting down to near silence, broken by the explosive punctuation of sharp and irregular firing. Then it would run up and up again, almost screaming, sustaining a r.p.m. that threatened every moving part, shaking the great machine like some deadly ague.

Tom walked swiftly toward the Seven, a puzzled and grim frown on his weatherbeaten face. Governors break down occasionally, and once in a while you will have a motor tear itself to pieces, revving up out of control. But it will either do that or it will rev down and quit. If an operator is fool enough to leave his machine with the master clutch engaged, the machine will take off and run the way the Seven had— but it will not turn unless the blade corner catches in something unresisting, and then the chances are very strong that it will stall. But in any case, it was past reason for any machine to act this way, revving up and down, running, turning, lifting and dropping the blade.

The motor slowed as he approached, and at last settled

down into something like a steady and regular idle. Tom had the sudden crazy impression that it was watching him. He shrugged off the feeling, walked up and laid a hand on the fender.

The Seven reacted like a wild stallion. The big Diesel roared, and Tom distinctly saw the master clutch lever snap back over center. He leaped clear, expecting the machine to jolt forward, but apparently it was in a reverse gear, for it shot backward, one track locked, and the near end of the blade swung in a swift vicious arc, breezing a bare fraction of an inch past his hip as he danced back out of the way.

And as if it had bounced off a wall, the tractor had shifted and was bearing down on him, the twelve-foot blade rising, the two big headlights looming over him on their bowlegged supports, looking like the protruding eyes of some mighty toad. Tom had no choice but to leap straight up and grasp the top of the blade in his two hands, leaning back hard to brace his feet against the curved moldboard. The blade dropped and sank into the soft topsoil, digging a deep little swale in the ground. The earth loading on the moldboard rose and churned around Tom's legs; he stepped wildly, keeping them clear of the rolling drag of it. Up came the blade then, leaving a four-foot pile at the edge of the pit; down and up the tractor raced as the tracks went into it; up and up as they climbed the pile of dirt. A quick balance and overbalance as the machine lurched up and over like a motorcycle taking a jump off a ramp, and then a spine-shaking crash as fourteen tons of metal smashed blade-first into the ground.

Part of the leather from Tom's tough palms stayed with the blade as he was flung off. He went head over heels backwards, but had his feet gathered and sprang as they touched the ground; for he knew that no machine could bury its blade like that and get out easily. He leaped to the top of the blade, got one hand on the radiator cap, vaulted. Perversely, the cap broke from its hinge and came away in his hand, in that split instant when only that hand rested on anything. Off balance, he landed on his shoulder with his legs flailing the air, his body sliding off the hood's smooth shoulder toward the track now churning the earth beneath. He made a wild grab at the air intake pipe, barely had it in his fingers when the dozer freed itself and shot backwards up and over the hump. Again that breathless flight pivoting over the top, and the clanking crash as the machine landed, this time almost flat on its tracks.

The jolt tore Tom's hand away, and as he slid back over the hood the crook of his elbow caught the exhaust stack, the dull red metal biting into his flesh. He grunted and clamped the arm around it. His momentum carried him around it, and his feet crashed into the steering clutch levers. Hooking one with his instep, he doubled his legs and whipped himself back, scrabbling at the smooth warm metal, crawling frantically backward until he finally fell heavily into the seat.

"Now," he gritted through a red wall of pain, "you're gonna git operated." And he kicked out the master clutch.

The motor wailed, with the load taken off so suddenly. Tom grasped the throttle, his thumb clamped down on the ratchet release, and he shoved the lever forward to shut off the fuel.

It wouldn't shut off; it went down to a slow idle, but it wouldn't shut off.

"There's one thing you can't do without," he muttered, "compression."

He stood up and leaned around the dash, reaching for the compression-release lever. As he came up out of the seat, the engine revved up again. He turned to the throttle, which had snapped back into the "open" position. As his hand touched it the master clutch lever snapped in and the howling machine lurched forward with a jerk that snapped his head on his shoulders and threw him heavily back into the seat. He snatched at the hydraulic blade control and threw it to "float" position; and then as the falling moldboard touched the ground, into "power down." The cutting edge bit into the ground and the engine began to labor. Holding the blade control, he pushed the throttle forward with his other hand. One of the steering clutch levers whipped back and struck him agonizingly on the kneecap. He involuntarily let go of the blade control and the moldboard began to rise. The engine began to turn faster and he realized that it was not responding to the throttle. Cursing, he leaped to his feet; the suddenly flailing levers struck him three times in the groin before he could get between them.

Blind with pain, Tom clung gasping to the dash. The oil-pressure gauge fell off the dash to his right, with a tinkling of broken glass, and from its broken quarter-inch line scalding oil drenched him. The shock of it snapped back his wavering consciousness. Ignoring the blows of the left steering clutch and the master clutch which had started the same mad punching, he bent over the left end of the dash and grasped the compression lever. The tractor rushed forward and spun sickeningly, and Tom knew he was thrown. But as he felt himself leave the decking his hand punched the compression lever down. The great valves at the cylinder heads opened and locked open; atomized fuel and superheated air chattered out, and as Tom's head and shoulders struck the ground the great wild machine rolled to a stop, stood silently except for the grumble of water boiling in the cooling system.

Minutes later Tom raised his head and groaned. He rolled over and sat up, his chin on his knees, washed by wave after wave of pain. As they gradually subsided, he crawled to the machine and pulled himself to his feet, hand over hand on the track. And groggily he began to cripple the tractor, at least for the night.

He opened the cock under the fuel tank, left the warm yellow fluid gushing out on the ground. He opened the drain on the reservoir by the injection pump. He found a piece of wire in the crank box and with it tied down the compression release lever. He crawled up on the machine, wrenched the hood and ball jar off the air intake precleaner, pulled off his shirt and stuffed it down the pipe. He pushed the throttle all the way forward and locked it with the locking pin. And he shut off the fuel on the main line from the tank to the pump.

Then he climbed heavily to the ground and slogged back to the edge of the plateau where he had left Rivera.

They didn't know Tom was hurt until an hour and a half later—there had been too much to do—rigging a stretcher for the Puerto Rican, building him a shelter, an engine crate with an Army pup tent for a roof. They brought out the first-aid kit and the medical books and did what they could—tied and splinted and dosed with an opiate. Tom was a mass of bruises, and his right arm, where it had hooked the exhaust stack, was a flayed mass. They fixed him up then, old Peebles handling the sulfa powder and bandages like a trained nurse. And only then was there talk.

"I've seen a man thrown off a pan," said Dennis, as they

sat around the coffee urn munching C rations. "Sittin' up on the armrest on a cat, looking backwards. Cat hit a rock and bucked. Threw him off on the track. Stretched him out ten feet long." He in-whistled some coffee to dilute the mouthful of food he had been talking around, and masticated noisily. "Man's a fool to set up there on one side of his butt even on a pan. Can't see why th' goony was doin' it on a dozer."

"He wasn't," said Tom.

Kelly rubbed his pointed jaw. "He set flat on th' seat an' was th'owed?"

"That's right."

After an unbelieving silence Dennis said, "What was he doin'—drivin' over sixty?"

Tom looked around the circle of faces lit up by the over-artificial brilliance of a pressure lantern, and wondered what the reaction would be if he told it all just as it was. He had to say something, and it didn't look as if it could be the truth.

"He was workin'," he said finally. "Bucking stone out of the wall of an old building up on the mesa there. One turned loose an' as it did the governor must've gone haywire. She bucked like a loco hoss and run off."

"Run off?"

Tom opened his mouth and closed it again, and just nodded.

Dennis said, "Well, reckon that's what happens when you put a mechanic to operatin'."

"That had nothin' to do with it," Tom snapped.

Peebles spoke up quickly. "Tom—what about the Seven? Broke up any?"

"Some," said Tom. "Better look at the steering clutches. An' she was hot."

"Head's cracked," said Harris, a burly young man with shoulders like a buffalo and a famous thirst.

"How do you know?"

"Saw it when Al and me went up with the stretcher to get the kid while you all were building the shelter. Hot water runnin' down the side of the block."

"You mean you walked all the way out to the mound to look at that tractor while the kid was lyin' there? I told you where he was!"

"Out to the mound!" Al Knowles's bulging eyes teetered

out of their sockets. "We found that cat stalled twenty feet away from where the kid was!"

"What!"

"That's right, Tom," said Harris. "What's eatin' you? Where'd you leave it?"

"I told you . . . by the mound . . . the ol' building we cut into."

"Leave the startin' motor runnin'?"

"Starting motor?" Tom's mind caught the picture of the small, two-cylinder gasoline engine bolted to the side of the big diesel's crankcase, coupled through a Bendix gear and clutch to the flywheel of the diesel to crank it. He remembered his last glance at the still machine, silent but for the sound of water boiling. "Hell no!"

Al and Harris exchanged a glance. "I guess you were sort of slap-happy at the time, Tom," Harris said, not unkindly. "When we were halfway up the hill we heard it, and you know you can't mistake that racket. Sounded like it was under a load."

Tom beat softly at his temples with his clenched fists. "I left that machine dead," he said quietly. "I got compression off her and tied down the lever. I even stuffed my shirt in the intake. I drained the tank. But—I didn't touch the starting motor."

Peebles wanted to know why he had gone to all that trouble. Tom just looked vaguely at him and shook his head. "I shoulda pulled the wires. I never thought about the starting motor," he whispered. Then, "Harris—you say you found the starting motor running when you got to the top?"

"No—she was stalled. And hot—awmighty hot. I'd say the startin' motor was seized up tight. That must be it, Tom. You left the startin' motor runnin' and somehow engaged the clutch an' Bendix." His voice lost conviction as he said it—it takes seventeen separate motions to start a tractor of this type. "Anyhow, she was in gear an' crawled along on the little motor."

"I done that once," said Chub. "Broke a con rod on an Eight, on a highway job. Walked her about three-quarters of a mile on the startin' motor that way. Only I had to stop every hundred yards and let her cool down some."

Not without sarcasm, Dennis said, "Seems to me like the

Seven was out to get th' goony. Made one pass at him and then went back to finish the job."

Al Knowles haw-hawed extravagantly.

Tom stood up, shaking his head, and went off among the crates to the hospital they had jury-rigged for the kid.

A dim light was burning inside, and Rivera lay very still, with his eyes closed. Tom leaned in the doorway—the open end of the engine crate—and watched him for a moment. Behind him he could hear the murmur of the crew's voices; the night was otherwise windless and still. Rivera's face was the peculiar color that olive skin takes when drained of blood. Tom looked at his chest and for a panicky moment thought he could discern no movement there. He entered and put a hand over the boy's heart. Rivera shivered, his eyes flew open, and he drew a sudden breath which caught raggedly at the back of his throat. "Tom . . . Tom!" he cried weakly.

"O. K., Goony . . . *que pasa?*"

"She comeen back . . . Tom!"

"Who?"

"*El de siete.*"

Daisy Etta—"She ain't comin' back, kiddo. You're off the mesa now. Keep your chin up, fella."

Rivera's dark, doped eyes stared up at him without expression. Tom moved back and the eyes continued to stare. They weren't seeing anything. "Go to sleep," he whispered. The eyes closed instantly.

Kelly was saying that nobody ever got hurt on a construction job unless somebody was dumb. "An' most times you don't realize how dumb what you're doin' is until somebody does get hurt."

"The dumb part was gettin' a kid, an' not even an operator at that, up on a machine," said Dennis in his smuggest voice.

"I heard you try to sing that song before," said old Peebles quietly. "I hate to have to point out anything like this to a man because it don't do any good to make comparisons. But I've worked with that fella Rivera for a long time now, an' I've seen 'em as good but doggone few better. As far as you're concerned, you're O. K. on a pan, but the kid could give you cards and spades and still make you look like a cost accountant on a dozer."

Dennis half rose and mouthed something filthy. He looked

at Al Knowles for backing and got it. He looked around the circle and got none. Peebles lounged back, sucking on his pipe, watching from under those bristling brows. Dennis subsided, running now on another tack.

"So what does that prove? The better you say he is, the less reason he had to fall off a cat and get himself hurt."

"I haven't got the thing straight yet," said Chub, in a voice whose tone indicated "I hate to admit it, but—"

About this time Tom returned, like a sleepwalker, standing with the brilliant pressure lantern between him and Dennis. Dennis rambled right on, not knowing he was anywhere near: "That's something you never will find out. That Puerto Rican is a pretty husky kid. Could be Tom said somethin' he didn't like an' he tried to put a knife in Tom's back. They all do, y'know. Tom didn't get all that bashin' around just stoppin' a machine. They must've went round an' round for a while an' the goony wound up with a busted back. Tom sets the dozer to walk him down while he lies there and comes on down here and tries to tell us—" His voice fluttered to a stop as Tom loomed over him.

Tom grabbed the pan operator up by the slack of his shirt front with his uninjured arm and shook him like an empty burlap bag.

"Skunk," he growled. "I oughta lower th' boom on you." He set Dennis on his feet and backhanded his face with the edge of his forearm. Dennis went down—cowered down, rather than fell. "Aw, Tom, I was just talkin'. Just a joke, Tom, I was just—"

"Yellow, too," snarled Tom, stepping forward, raising a solid Texan boot. Peebles barked "Tom!" and the foot came back to the ground.

"Out o' my sight," rumbled the foreman. "Git!"

Dennis got. Al Knowles said vaguely, "Naow, Tom, y'all cain't—"

"You, y'wall-eyed string bean!" Tom raved, his voice harsh and strained. "Go 'long with yer Siamese twin!"

"O. K., O. K.," said Al, white-faced, and disappeared into the dark after Dennis.

"Nuts to this," said Chub. "I'm turnin' in." He went to a crate and hauled out a mosquito-hooded sleeping bag and went off without another word. Harris and Kelly, who were both on their feet, sat down again. Old Peebles hadn't moved.

Tom stood staring out into the dark, his arms straight at his sides, his fists knotted.

"Sit down," said Peebles gently. Tom turned and stared at him.

"Sit down. I can't change that dressing 'less you do." He pointed at the bandage around Tom's elbow. It was red, a widening stain, the tattered tissues having parted as the big Georgian bunched his infuriated muscles. He sat down.

"Talkin' about dumbness," said Harris calmly, as Peebles went to work, "I was about to say that I got the record. I done the dumbest thing anybody ever did on a machine. You can't top it."

"I could," said Kelly. "Runnin' a crane dragline once. Put her in boom gear and started to boom her up. Had an eighty-five-foot stick on her. Machine was standing on wooden mats in th' middle of a swamp. Heard the motor miss and got out of the saddle to look at the filer-glass. Messed around back there longer than I figured, and the boom went straight up in the air and fell backwards over the cab. Th' jolt tilted my mats an' she slid backwards slowly and stately as you please, butt-first into the mud. Buried up to the eyeballs, she was." He laughed quietly. "Looked like a ditching machine!"

"I still say I done the dumbest thing ever, bar none," said Harris. "It was on a river job, widening a channel. I come back to work from a three-day binge, still rum-dumb. Got up on a dozer an' was workin' around on the edge of a twenty-foot cliff. Down at the foot of the cliff was a big hickory tree, an' growin' right along the edge was a great big limb. I got the dopey idea I should break it off. I put one track on the limb and the other on the cliff edge and run out away from the trunk. I was about halfway out, an' the branch saggin' some, before I thought what would happen if it broke. Just about then it did break. You know hickory—if it breaks at all it breaks altogether. So down we go into thirty feet of water—me an' the cat. I got out from under somehow. When all them bubbles stopped comin' up I swum around lookin' down at it. I was still paddlin' around when the superintendent came rushin' up. He wants to know what's up. I yell at him, 'Look down there, the way that water is movin' an' shiftin', looks like the cat is workin' down there.' He pursed his lips and *tsk tsked*. My, that man said some nasty things to me."

"Where'd you get your next job?" Kelly exploded.

"Oh, he didn't fire me," said Harris soberly. "Said he couldn't afford to fire a man as dumb as that. Said he wanted me around to look at whenever he felt bad."

Tom said, "Thanks, you guys. That's as good a way as any of sayin' that everybody makes mistakes." He stood up, examining the new dressing, turning his arm in front of the lantern. "You all can think what you please, but I don't recollect there was any dumbness went on on that mesa this evenin'. That's finished with, anyway. Do I have to say that Dennis's idea about it is all wet?"

Haris said one foul word that completely disposed of Dennis and anything he might say.

Peebles said, "It'll be all right. Dennis an' his pop-eyed friend'll hang together, but they don't amount to anything. Chub'll do whatever he's argued into."

"So you got 'em all lined up, hey?" Tom shrugged. "In the meantime, are we going to get an airfield built?"

"We'll get it built," Peebles said. "Only—Tom, I got no right to give you any advice, but go easy on the rough stuff after this. It does a lot of harm."

"I will if I can," said Tom gruffly. They broke up and turned in.

Peebles was right. It did do harm. It made Dennis use the word "murder" when they found, in the morning, that Rivera had died during the night.

The work progressed in spite of everything that had happened. With equipment like that, it's hard to slow things down. Kelly bit two cubic yards out of the bluff with every swing of the big shovel, and Dumptors are the fastest short-haul earth movers yet devised. Dennis kept the service road clean for them with his pan, and Tom and Chub spelled each other on the bulldozer they had detached from its pan to make up for the lack of the Seven, spending their alternate periods with transit and stakes. Peebles was rod-man for the surveys, and in between times worked on setting up his field shop, keeping the water cooler and battery chargers running, and lining up his forge and welding tables. The operators fueled and serviced their own equipment, and there was little delay. Rocks and marl came out of the growing cavity in the side of the central mesa—a whole third of it had to come out—were spun down to the edge of the swamp, which lay across the lower end of the projected runway, in the hornet-howling dump-tractors, their big driving wheels churned up vast clouds of dust, and were dumped and spread and walked in by the whining two-cycle dozer. When muck began to pile up in front of the fill, it was blasted out of the way with carefully placed charges of sixty percent dynamite and the craters filled with rocks, stone from the ruins, and surfaced with easily compacting marl, run out of a clean deposit by the pan.

And when he had his shop set up, Peebles went up the hill to get the Seven. When he got to it he just stood there for a moment scratching his head, and then, shaking his head, he ambled back down the hill and went for Tom.

"Been looking at the Seven," he said, when he had flagged the moaning two-cycle and Tom had climbed off.

"What'd you find?"

Peebles held out an arm. "A list as long as that." He shook his head. "Tom, what really happened up there?"

"Governor went haywire and she run away," Tom said promptly, deadpan.

"Yeah, but—" For a long moment he held Tom's gaze. Then he sighed. "O. K., Tom. Anyhow, I can't do a thing up there. We'll have to bring her back and I'll have to have this tractor to tow her down. And first I have to have some help—the track idler adjustment bolt's busted and the right track is off the track rollers."

"Oh-h-h. So that's why she couldn't get to the kid, running on the starting motor. Track would hardly turn, hey?"

"It's a miracle she ran as far as she did. That track is really jammed up. Riding right up on the roller flanges. And that ain't the half of it. The head's gone, like Harris said, and Lord only knows what I'll find when I open her up."

"Why bother?"

"What?"

"We can get along without that dozer," said Tom suddenly. "Leave her where she is. There's lots more for you to do."

"But what for?"

"Well, there's no call to go to all that trouble."

Peebles scratched the side of his nose and said, "I got a new head, track master pins—even a spare starting motor. I

got tools to make what I don't stock." He pointed at the long
row of dumps left by the hurtling dump-tractors while they
had been talking. "You got a pan tied up because you're
using this machine to doze with, and you can't tell me you
can't use another one. You're gonna have to shut down one
or two o' those Dumptors if you go on like this."

"I had all that figured out as soon as I opened my mouth,"
Tom said sullenly. "Let's go."

They climbed on the tractor and took off, stopping for a
moment at the beach outcropping to pick up a cable and
some tools.

Daisy Etta sat at the edge of the mesa, glowering out of
her stilted headlights at the soft sward which still bore the
impression of a young body and the tramplings of the
stretcher-bearers. Her general aspect was woebegone—there
were scratches on her olive-drab paint and the bright metal of
the scratches was already dulled red by the earliest powder-
rust. And though the ground was level, she was not, for her
right track was off its lower rollers, and she stood slightly
canted, like a man who has had a broken hip. And whatever
passed for consciousness within her mulled over that paradox
of the bulldozer that every operator must go through while he
is learning his own machine.

It is the most difficult thing of all for the beginner to understand, that paradox. A bulldozer is a crawling powerhouse,
a behemoth of noise and toughness, the nearest thing to the
famous irresistible force. The beginner, awed and with the
pictures of unconquerable Army tanks printed on his mind
from the newsreels, takes all in his stride and with a sense of
limitless power treats all obstacles alike, not knowing the
fragility of a cast-iron radiator core, the mortality of tem-
pered manganese, the friability of overheated babbitt, and
most of all, the ease with which a tractor can bury itself in
mud. Climbing off to stare at a machine which he has
reduced in twenty seconds to a useless hulk, or which was
running a half-minute before on ground where it now has its
tracks out of sight, he has that sense of guilty disappointment
which overcomes any man on having made an error in judgment.

So, as she stood, *Daisy Etta* was broken and useless. These
soft persistent bipeds had built her, and if they were like any

other race that built machines, they could care for them. The ability to reverse the tension of a spring, or twist a control rod, or reduce to zero the friction in a nut and lock-washer, was not enough to repair the crack in a cylinder head nor bearings welded to a crankshaft in an overheated starting motor. There had been a lesson to learn. It had been learned. *Daisy Etta* would be repaired, and the next time—well, at least she would know her own weaknesses.

Tom swung the two-cycle machine and edged in next to the Seven, with the edge of his blade all but touching *Daisy Etta's* push-beam. They got off and Peebles bent over the drum-tight right track.

"Watch yourself," said Tom.

"Watch what?"

"Oh—nothin', I guess." He circled the machine, trained eyes probing over frame and fittings. He stepped forward suddenly and grasped the fuel-tank drain cock. It was closed. He opened it; golden oil gushed out. He shut it off, climbed up on the machine and opened the fuel cap on top of the tank. He pulled out the bayonet gauge, wiped it in the crook of his knee, dipped and withdrew it.

The tank was more than three quarters full.

"What's the matter?" asked Peebles, staring curiously at Tom's drawn face.

"Peeby, I opened the cock to drain this tank. I left it with oil runnin' out on the ground. She shut herself off."

"Now, Tom, you're lettin' this thing get you down. You just thought you did. I've seen a main-line valve shut itself off when it's worn bad, but only 'cause the fuel pump pulls it shut when the motor's runnin'. But not a gravity drain."

"Main-line valve?" Tom pulled the seat up and looked. One glance was enough to show him that this one was open.

"She opened this one, too."

"O. K.—O. K. Don't look at me like that!" Peebles was as near to exasperation as he could possibly get. "What difference does it make?"

Tom did not answer. He was not the type of man who, when faced with something beyond his understanding, would begin to doubt his own sanity. His was a dogged insistence that what he saw and sensed was what had actually happened. In him was none of the fainting fear of madness that another, more sensitive, man might feel. He doubted neither himself nor his evidence, and so could free his mind for searching out the consuming "why" of a problem. He knew instinctively that to share "unbelievable" happenings with anyone else, even if they had really occurred, was to put even further obstacles in his way. So he kept his clamlike silence and stubbornly, watchfully, investigated.

The slipped track was so tightly drawn up on the roller flanges that there could be no question of pulling the master pin and opening the track up. It would have to be worked back in place—a very delicate operation, for a little force applied in the wrong direction would be enough to run the track off altogether. To complicate things, the blade of the Seven was down on the ground and would have to be lifted before the machine could be maneuvered, and its hydraulic hoist was useless without the motor.

Peebles unhooked twenty feet of half-inch cable from the rear of the smaller dozer, scratched a hole in the ground under the Seven's blade, and pushed the eye of the cable through. Climbing over the moldboard, he slipped the eye on to the big towing hook bolted to the underside of the belly-guard. The other end of the cable he threw out on the ground in front of the machine. Tom mounted the other dozer and swung into place, ready to tow. Peebles hooked the cable onto Tom's drawbar, hopped up on the Seven. He put her in neutral, disengaged the master clutch, and put the blade control over into "float" position, then raised an arm.

Tom perched upon the armrest of his machine, looking backwards, moved slowly, taking up the slack in the cable. It straightened and grew taut, and as it did it forced the Seven's blade upward. Peebles waved for slack and put the blade control into "hold." The cable bellied downward away from the blade.

"Hydraulic system's O. K., anyhow," called Peebles, as Tom throttled down. "Move over and take a strain to the right, sharp as you can without fouling the cable on the track. We'll see if we can walk this track back on."

Tom backed up, cut sharply to the right, and drew the cable out almost at right angles to the other machine. Peebles held the right track of the Seven with the brake and released both steering clutches. The left track now could turn free, the right not at all. Tom was running at a quarter throttle in his lowest gear, so that his machine barely crept along, taking the strain. The Seven shook gently and began to pivot on the taut right track, unbelievable foot-pounds of energy coming to bear on the front of the track where it rode high up on the idler wheel. Peebles released the right brake with his foot and applied it again in a series of skilled, deft jerks. The track would move a few inches and stop again, force being applied forward and sideways alternately, urging the track persuasively back in place. Then, a little jolt and she was in, riding true on the five truck rollers, the two track carrier rollers, the driving sprocket and the idler.

Peebles got off and stuck his head in between the sprocket and the rear carrier, squinting down and sideways to see if there were any broken flanges or roller bushes. Tom came over and pulled him out by the seat of his trousers. "Time enough for that when you get her in the shop," he said, masking his nervousness. "Reckon she'll roll?"

"She'll roll. I never saw a track in that condition come back that easy. By gosh, it's as if she was tryin' to help!"

"They'll do it sometimes," said Tom stiffly. "You better take the tow-tractor, Peeby. I'll stay with this'n."

"Anything you say."

And cautiously they took the steep slope down, Tom barely holding the brakes, giving the other machine a straight pull all the way. And so they brought *Daisy Etta* down to Peebles's outdoor shop, where they pulled her cylinder head off, took off her starting motor, pulled out a burned clutch facing, had her quite helpless—

And put her together again.

"I tell you it was outright, cold-blooded murder," said Dennis hotly. "An' here we are takin' orders from a guy like that. What are we goin' to do about it?" They were standing by the cooler—Dennis had run his machine there to waylay Chub.

Chub Horton's cigar went down and up like a semaphore with a short circuit. "We'll skip it. The blacktopping crew will be here in another two weeks or so, an' we can make a report. Besides, I don't know what happened up there any more than you do. In the meantime we got a runway to build."

"You don't know what happened up there? Chub, you're a smart man. Smart enough to run this job better than Tom

Jaeger even if he wasn't crazy. And you're surely smart enough not to believe all that cock and bull about that tractor runnin' out from under that grease-monkey. Listen—" he leaned forward and tapped Chub's chest. "He said it was the governor. I saw that governor myself an' heard ol' Peebles say there wasn't a thing wrong with it. Th' throttle control rod had slipped off its yoke, yeah—but you know what a tractor will do when the throttle control goes out. It'll idle or stall. It won't run away, whatever."

"Well, maybe so, but—"

"But nothin'! A guy that'll commit murder ain't sane. If he did it once, he can do it again and I ain't fixin' to let that happen to me."

Two things crossed Chub's steady but not too bright mind at this. One was that Dennis, whom he did not like but could not shake, was trying to force him into something that he did not want to do. The other was that under all of his swift talk Dennis was scared spitless.

"What do you want to do—call up the sheriff?"

Dennis ha-ha-ed appreciatively—one of the reasons he was so hard to shake. "I'll tell you what we can do. As long as we have you here, he isn't the only man who knows the work. If we stop takin' orders from him, you can give 'em as good or better. An' there won't be anything he can do about it."

"Doggone it, Dennis," said Chub, with sudden exasperation. "What do you think you're doin'—handin' me over the keys to the kingdom or something? What do you want to see me bossin' around here for?" He stood up. "Suppose we did what you said? Would it get the field built any quicker? Would it get me any more money in my pay envelope? What do you think I want—glory? I passed up a chance to run for councilman once. You think I'd raise a finger to get a bunch of mugs to do what I say—when they do it anyway?"

"Aw, Chub—I wouldn't cause trouble just for the fun of it. That's not what I mean at all. But unless we do something about that guy we ain't safe. Can't you get that through your head?"

"Listen, windy. If a man keeps busy enough he can't get into no trouble. That goes for Tom—you might keep that in mind. But it goes for you, too. Get back up on that rig an' get back to the marl pit." Dennis, completely taken by surprise, turned to his machine.

"It's a pity you can't move earth with your mouth," said Chub, as he walked off. "They could have left you to do this job singlehanded."

Chub walked slowly toward the outcropping, switching at beach pebbles with a grade stake and swearing to himself. He was essentially a simple man and believed in the simplest possible approach to everything. He liked a job where he could do everything required and where nothing turned up to complicate things. He had been in the grading business for a long time as an operator and survey party boss, and he was remarkable for one thing—he had always held aloof from the cliques and internecine politics that are the breath of life to most construction men. He was disturbed and troubled at the back-stabbing that went on around him on various jobs. If it was blunt, he was disgusted, and subtlety simply left him floundering and bewildered. He was stupid enough so that his basic honesty manifested itself in his speech and actions, and he had learned that complete honesty in dealing with men above and below him was almost invariably painful to all concerned, but he had not the wit to act otherwise, and did not try to. If he had a bad tooth, he had it pulled out as soon as he could. If he got a raw deal from a superintendent over him, that superintendent would get told exactly what the trouble was, and if he didn't like it, there were other jobs. And if the pulling and hauling of cliques got in his hair, he had always said so and left. Or he had sounded off and stayed; his completely selfish reaction to things that got in the way of his work had earned him a lot of regard from men he had worked under. And so, in this instance, he had no hesitation about choosing a course of action. Only—how did you go about asking a man if he was a murderer?

He found the foreman with an enormous wrench in his hand, tightening up the new track adjustment bolt they had installed in the Seven.

"Hey, Chub! Glad you turned up. Let's get a piece of pipe over the end of this thing and really bear down." Chub went for the pipe, and they fitted it over the handle of the four-foot wrench and hauled until the sweat ran down their backs, Tom checking the track clearance occasionally with a crow-bar. He finally called it good enough and they stood there in the sun gasping for breath.

"Tom," panted Chub, "did you kill that Puerto Rican?"

Tom's head came up as if someone had burned the back of his neck with a cigarette.

"Because," said Chub, "if you did you can't go on runnin' this job."

Tom said, "That's a lousy thing to kid about."

"You know I ain't kiddin'. Well, did you?"

"No!" Tom sat down on a keg, wiped his face with a bandanna. "What's got into you?"

"I just wanted to know. Some of the boys are worried about it."

Tom's eyes narrowed. "Some of the boys, huh? I think I get it. Listen to me, Chub. Rivera was killed by that thing there." He thumbed over his shoulder at the Seven, which was standing ready now, awaiting only the building of a broken cutting corner on the blade. Peebles was winding up the welding machine as he spoke. "If you mean, did I put him up on the machine before he was thrown, the answer is yes. That much I killed him, and don't think I don't feel it. I had a hunch something was wrong up there, but I couldn't put my finger on it and I certainly didn't think anybody was going to get hurt."

"Well, what was wrong?"

"I still don't know." Tom stood up. "I'm tired of beatin' around the bush, Chub, and I don't much care any more what anybody thinks. There's somethin' wrong with that Seven, something that wasn't built into her. They don't make tractors better'n that one, but whatever it was happened up there on the mesa has queered this one. Now go ahead and think what you like, and dream up any story you want to tell the boys. In the meantime you can pass the word—nobody runs that machine but me, understand? Nobody!"

"Tom—"

Tom's patience broke. "That's all I'm going to say about it! If anybody else gets hurt, it's going to be me, understand? What more do you want?"

He strode off, boiling. Chub stared after him, and after a long moment reached up and took the cigar from his lips. Only then did he realize that he had bitten it in two; half the butt was still inside his mouth. He spat and stood there, shaking his head.

"How's she going, Peeby?"

Peebles looked up from the welding machine. "Hi, Chub, have her ready for you in twenty minutes." He gauged the distance between the welding machine and the big tractor. "I should have forty feet of cable," he said, looking at the festoons of arc and ground cables that hung from the storage hooks in the back of the welder. "Don't want to get a tractor over here to move the thing, and don't feel like cranking up the Seven just to get it close enough." He separated the arc cable and threw it aside, walked to the tractor, paying the ground cable off his arm. He threw out the last of his slack and grasped the ground clamp when he was eight feet from the machine. Taking it in his left hand, he pulled hard, reaching out with his right to grasp the moldboard of the Seven, trying to get it far enough to clamp on to the machine.

Chub stood there watching him, chewing on his cigar, absentmindedly diddling with the controls on the arc-welder. He pressed the starter button, and the six-cylinder motor responded with a purr. He spun the work-selector dials idly, threw the arc generator switch—

A bolt of incredible energy, thin, searing, blue-white, left the rod-holder at his feet, stretched itself *fifty feet* across to Peebles, whose fingers had just touched the moldboard of the tractor. Peebles's head and shoulders were surrounded for a second by a violet nimbus, and then he folded over and dropped. A circuit breaker clacked behind the control board of the welder, but too late. The Seven rolled slowly backward, without firing, on level ground, until it brought up against a road-roller.

Chub's cigar was gone, and he didn't notice it. He had the knuckles of his right hand in his mouth, and his teeth sunk into the pudgy flesh. His eyes protruded; he crouched there and quivered, literally frightened out of his mind. For old Peebles was almost burned in two.

They buried him next to Rivera. There wasn't much talk afterwards; the old man had been a lot closer to all of them than they had realized until now. Harris, for once in his rum-dumb, lighthearted life, was quiet and serious, and Kelly's walk seemed to lose some of its litheness. Hour after hour Dennis's flabby mouth worked, and he bit at his lower lip until it was swollen and tender. Al Knowles seemed more or less unaffected, as was to be expected from a man who had something less than the brains of a chicken. Chub Horton had snapped out of it after a couple of hours and was very nearly himself again. And in Tom Jaeger swirled a black, furious anger at this unknowable curse that had struck the camp.

And they kept working. There was nothing else to do. The shovel kept up its rhythmic swing and dig, swing and dump, and the Dumptors screamed back and forth between it and the little that there was left of the swamp. The upper end of the runway was grassed off; Chub and Tom set grade stakes and Dennis began the long job of cutting and filling the humpy surface with his pan. Harris manned the other and followed him, a cut behind. The shape of the runway emerged from the land, and then that of the paralleling taxiway; and three days went by. The horror of Peebles's death wore off enough so that they could talk about it, and very little of the talk helped anybody. Tom took his spells at everything, changing over with Kelly to give him a rest from the shovel, making a few rounds with a pan, putting in hours on a Dumptor. His arm was healing slowly but clean, and he worked grimly in spite of it, taking a perverse sort of pleasure from the pain of it. Every man on the job watched his machine with the solicitude of a mother with her firstborn; a serious breakdown would have been disastrous without a highly skilled mechanic.

The only concession that Tom allowed himself in regard to Peebles's death was to corner Kelly one afternoon and ask him about the welding machine. Part of Kelly's rather patchy past had been spent in a technical college, where he had studied electrical engineering and women. He had learned a little of the former and enough of the latter to get him thrown out on his ear. So, on the off-chance that he might know something about the freak arc, Tom put it to him.

Kelly pulled off his high-gauntlet gloves and batted sandflies with them. "What sort of an arc was that? Boy, you got me there. Did you ever hear of a welding machine doing like that before?"

"I did not. A welding machine just don't have that sort o' push. I saw a man get a full jolt from a 400-amp welder once, an' although it sat him down it didn't hurt him any."

"It's not amperage that kills people," said Kelly, "it's voltage. Voltage is the pressure behind a current, you know. Take an amount of water, call it amperage. If I throw it in your face, it won't hurt you. If I put it through a small hose you'll feel it. But if I pump it through the tiny holes on a diesel injector nozzle at about twelve hundred pounds, it'll draw blood. But a welding arc generator just is not wound to build up that kind of voltage. I can't see where any short circuit anywhere through the armature or field windings could do such a thing."

"From what Chub said, he had been foolin' around with the work selector. I don't think anyone touched the dials after it happened. The selector dial was run all the way over to the low-current application segment, and the current control was around the halfway mark. That's not enough juice to get you a good bead with a quarter-inch rod, let alone kill somebody—or roll a tractor back thirty feet on level ground."

"Or jump fifty feet," said Kelly. "It would take thousands of volts to generate an arc like that."

"Is it possible that something in the Seven could have pulled that arc? I mean, suppose the arc wasn't driven over, but was drawn over? I tell you, she was hot for four hours after that."

Kelly shook his head. "Never heard of any such thing. Look, just to have something to call them, we call direct current terminals positive and negative, and just because it works in theory we say that current flows from negative to positive. There couldn't be any more positive attraction in one electrode than there is negative drive in the other; see what I mean?"

"There couldn't be some freak condition that would cause a sort of oversize positive field? I mean one that would suck out the negative flow all in a heap, make it smash through under a lot of pressure like the water you were talking about through an injector nozzle?"

"No, Tom. It just don't work that way, far as anyone knows. I dunno, though—there are some things about static electricity that nobody understands. All I can say is that what happened couldn't happen and if it did it couldn't have killed Peebles. And you know the answer to that."

Tom glanced away at the upper end of the runway, where the two graves were. There was bitterness and turbulent anger naked there for a moment, an he turned and walked away without another word. And when he went back to have another look at the welding machine, *Daisy Etta* was gone.

Al Knowles and Harris squatted together near the water cooler.

"Bad," said Harris.

"Nevah saw anythin' like it," said Al. "Ol' Tom come back f'm the shop theah jus' *raisin'* Cain. 'Weah's 'at Seven gone? Weah's 'at Seven?' I never heered sech cah'ins on."

"Dennis did take it, huh?"

"Sho' did."

Harris said, "He came spoutin' around to me a while back, Dennis did. Chub'd told him Tom said for everybody to stay off that machine. Dennis was mad as a wet hen. Said Tom was carryin' that kind o' business too far. Said there was probably somethin' about the Seven Tom didn't want us to find out. Might incriminate him. Dennis is ready to say Tom killed the kid."

"Reckon he did, Harris?"

Harris shook his head. "I've known Tom too long to think that. If he won't tell us what really happened up on the mesa, he has a reason for it. How'd Dennis come to take the dozer?"

"Blew a front tire on his pan. Came back heah to git anothah rig—maybe a Dumptor. Saw th' Seven standin' theah ready to go. Stood theah lookin' at it and cussin' Tom. Said he was tired of bashin' his kindeys t'pieces on them othah rigs an' bedamned if he wouldn't take suthin' that rode good fo' a change. I tol' him ol' Tom'd raise th' roof when he found him on it. He had a couple mo' things t'say 'bout Tom then."

"I didn't think he had the guts to take the rig."

"Aw, he talked hisself blind mad."

They looked up as Chub Horton trotted up, panting. "Hey, you guys, come on. We better get up there to Dennis."

"What's wrong?" asked Harris, climbing to his feet.

"Tom passed me a minute ago lookin' like the wrath o' God and hightallin' it for the swamp fill. I asked him what was the matter and he hollered that Dennis had took the Seven. Said he was always talkin' about murder, and he'd get his fill of it foolin' around that machine." Chub went walleyed, licked his lips beside his cigar.

"Oh-oh," said Harris quietly. "That's the wrong kind o' talk for just now."

"You don't suppose he—"

"Come on!"

They saw Tom before they were halfway there. He was walking slowly, with his head down. Harris shouted. Tom raised his face, stopped, stood there waiting with a peculiarly slumped stance.

"Where's Dennis?" barked Chub.

Tom waited until they were almost up to him and then weakly raised an arm and thumbed over his shoulder. His face was green.

"Tom—is he—"

Tom nodded, and swayed a little. His granite jaw was slack.

"Al, stay with him. He's sick. Harris, let's go."

Tom was sick, then and there. Very. Al stood gaping at him, fascinated.

Chub and Harris found Dennis. All of twelve square feet of him, ground and churned and rolled out into a torn-up patch of earth. *Daisy Etta* was gone.

Back at the outcropping, they sat with Tom while Al Knowles took a Dumptor and roared away to get Kelly.

"You saw him?" he said dully after a time.

Harris said, "Yeh."

The screaming Dumptor and a mountainous cloud of dust arrived, Kelly driving, Al holding on with a death-grip to the dump-bed guards. Kelly flung himself off, ran to Tom. "Tom—what is all this? Dennis dead? And you . . . you—"

Tom's head came up slowly, the slackness going out of his long face, a light suddenly coming into his eyes. Until this moment it had not crossed his mind what these men might think.

"I—what?"

"Al says you killed him."

Tom's eyes flicked at Al Knowles, and Al winced as if the glance had been a quirt.

Harris said, "What about it, Tom?"

"Nothing about it. He was killed by that Seven. You saw that for yourself."

"I stuck with you all along," said Harris slowly. "I took everything you said and believed it."

"This is too strong for you?" Tom asked.

Harris nodded. "Too strong, Tom."

Tom looked at the grim circle of faces and laughed suddenly. He stood up, put his back against a tall crate. "What do you plan to do about it?"

There was a silence. "You think I went up there and knocked that windbag off the machine and ran over him?" More silence. "Listen. I went up there and saw what you saw. He was dead before I got there. That's not good enough either?" He paused and licked his lips. "So after I killed him I got up on the tractor and drove it far enough away so you couldn't see or hear it when you got there. And then I sprouted wings and flew back so's I was halfway here when you met me—*ten minutes* after I spoke to Chub on my way up!"

Kelly said vaguely, "Tractor?"

"Well," said Tom harshly to Harris, "was the tractor there when you and Chub went up and saw Dennis?"

"No—"

Chub smacked his thigh suddenly. "You could've drove it into the swamp, Tom."

Tom said angrily, "I'm wastin' my time. You guys got it all figured out. Why ask me anything at all?"

"Aw, take it easy," said Kelly. "We just want the facts. Just what did happen? You met Chub and told him that Dennis would get all the murderin' he could take if he messed around that machine. That right?"

"That's right."

"Then what?"

"Then the machine murdered him."

Chub, with remarkable patience, asked, "What did you mean the day Peebles was killed when you said that something had queered the Seven up there on the mesa?"

Tom said furiously, "I meant what I said. You guys are set to crucify me for this and I can't stop you. Well, listen. Something's got into that Seven. I don't know what it is and I don't think I ever will know. I thought that after she smashed herself up that it was finished with. I had an idea that when we had her torn down and helpless we should have left her that way. I was dead right but it's too late now. She's killed

Rivera and she's killed Dennis and she sure had something to do with killing Peebles. And my idea is that she won't stop as long as there's a human being alive on this island."

"Whaddaya know!" said Chub.

"Sure, Tom, sure," said Kelly quietly. "That tractor is out to get us. But don't worry; we'll catch it and tear it down. Just don't you worry about it any more; it'll be all right."

"That's right, Tom," said Harris. "You just take it easy around camp for a couple of days till you feel better. Chub and the rest of us will handle things for you. You had too much sun."

"You're a swell bunch of fellows," gritted Tom, with the deepest sarcasm. "You want to live," he shouted, "git out there and throw that maverick bulldozer!"

"That maverick bulldozer is at the bottom of the swamp where you put it," growled Chub. His head lowered and he started to move in. "Sure we want to live. The best way to do that is to put you where you can't kill anybody else. *Get him!*"

He leaped. Tom straightened him with his left and crossed with his right. Chub went down, tripping Harris. Al Knowles scuttled to a toolbox and dipped out a fourteen-inch crescent wrench. He circled around, keeping out of trouble, trying to look useful. Tom loosened a haymaker at Kelly, whose head seemed to withdraw like a turtle's; it whistled over, throwing Tom badly off balance. Harris, still on his knees, tackled Tom's legs; Chub hit him in the small of the back with a meaty shoulder, and Tom went flat on his face. Al Knowles, holding the wrench in both hands, swept it up and back like a baseball bat; at the top of its swing Kelly reached over, snatched it out of his hands and tapped Tom delicately behind the ear with it. Tom went limp.

It was late, but nobody seemed to feel like sleeping. They sat around the pressure lantern, talking idly. Chub and Kelly played an inconsequential game of casino, forgetting to pick up their points; Harris paced up and down like a man in a cell, and Al Knowles was squinched up close to the light, his eyes wide and watching, watching—

"I need a drink," said Harris.

"Tens," said one of the casino players.

Al Knowles said, "We shoulda killed him. We oughta kill him now."

"There's been too much killin' already," said Chub. "Shut up, you." And to Kelly, "With big casino," sweeping up cards.

Kelly caught his wrist and grinned. "Big casino's the ten of diamonds, not the ten of hearts. Remember?"

"Oh."

"How long before the blacktopping crew will be here?" quavered Al Knowles.

"Twelve days," said Harris. "And they better bring some likker."

"Hey, you guys."

They fell silent.

"Hey!"

"It's Tom," said Kelly. "Building sixes, Chub."

"I'm gonna go kick his ribs in," said Knowles, not moving.

"I heard that," said the voice from the darkness. "If I wasn't hogtied—"

"We know what you'd do," said Chub. "How much proof do you think we need?"

"Chub, you don't have to do any more to him!" It was Kelly, flinging his cards down and getting up. "Tom, you want water?"

"Yes."

"Siddown, siddown," said Chub.

"Let him lie there and bleed," Al Knowles said.

"Nuts!" Kelly went and filled a cup and brought it to Tom. The big Georgian was tied thoroughly, wrists together, taut rope between elbows and elbows behind his back, so that his hands were immovable over his solar plexus. His knees and ankles were bound as well, although Knowles' little idea of a short rope between ankles and throat hadn't been used.

"Thanks, Kelly." Tom drank greedily, Kelly holding his head. "Goes good." He drank more. "What hit me?"

"One of the boys. 'Bout the time you said the cat was haunted."

"Oh, yeah." Tom rolled his head and blinked with pain.

"Any sense asking you if you blame us?"

"Kelly, does somebody else have to get killed before you guys wake up?"

"None of us figure there will be any more killin'—now."

The rest of the men drifted up. "He willing to talk sense?" Chub wanted to know.

Al Knowles laughed, "Hyuk! Hyuk! Don't he look dangerous now!"

Harris said suddenly, "Al, I'm gonna hafta tape your mouth with the skin off your neck."

"Am I the kind of guy that makes up ghost stories?"

"Never have that I know of, Tom." Harris kneeled down beside him. "Never killed anyone before, either."

"Oh, get away from me. Get away," said Tom tiredly.

"Get up and make us," jeered Al.

Harris got up and backhanded him across the mouth. Al squeaked, took three steps backward and tripped over a drum of grease. "I told you," said Harris almost plaintively. "I *told* you, Al."

Tom stopped the bumble of comment. "Shut up!" he hissed. "SHUT UP!" he roared.

They shut.

"Chub," said Tom, rapidly, evenly, "what did you say I did with that Seven?"

"Buried it in the swamp."

"Yeh. Listen."

"Listen at what?"

"Be quiet and listen!"

So they listened. It was another still, windless night, with a thin crescent of moon showing nothing true in the black and muffled silver landscape. The smallest whisper of surf drifted up from the beach, and from far off to the right, where the swamp was, a scandalized frog croaked protest at the manhandling of his mudhole. But the sound that crept down, freezing their bones, came from the bluff behind their camp.

It was the unmistakable staccato of a starting engine.

"The Seven!"

" 'At's right, Chub," said Tom.

"Wh-who's crankin' her up?"

"Are we all here?"

"All but Peebles and Dennis and Rivera," said Tom.

"It's Dennis's ghost," moaned Al.

Chub snapped, "Shut up, lamebrain."

"She's shifted to diesel," said Kelly, listening.

"She'll be here in a minute," said Tom. "Y'know, fellas, we

can't all be crazy, but you're about to have a time convincin' yourself of it."

"You like this, doncha?"

"Some ways. Rivera used to call that machine *Daisy Etta*, 'cause she's *de siete* in Spig. *Daisy Etta*, she wants her a man."

"Tom," said Harris, "I wish you'd stop that chatterin'. You make me nervous."

"I got to do somethin'. I can't run," Tom drawled.

"We're going to have a look," said Chub. "If there's nobody on that cat, we'll turn you loose."

"Mighty white of you. Reckon you'll get back before she does?"

"We'll get back. Harris, come with me. We'll get one of the pan tractors. They can outrun a Seven. Kelly, take Al and get the other one."

"Dennis's machine has a flat tire on the pan," said Al's quavering voice.

"Pull the pin and cut the cables, then! Git!" Kelly and Al Knowles ran off.

"Good huntin', Chub."

Chub went to him, bent over. "I think I'm goin' to have to apologize to you, Tom."

"No you ain't. I'd a done the same. Get along now, if you think you got to. But hurry back."

"I got to. An' I'll hurry back."

Harris said, "Don't go 'way, boy." Tom returned the grin, and they were gone. But they didn't hurry back. They didn't come back at all.

It was Kelly who came pounding back, with Al Knowles on his heels, a half hour later. "Al—gimme your knife."

He went to work on the ropes. His face was drawn.

"I could see some of it," whispered Tom. "Chub and Harris?"

Kelly nodded. "There wasn't nobody on the Seven like you said." He said it as if there were nothing else in his mind, as if the most rigid self-control was keeping him from saying it over and over.

"I could see the lights," said Tom. "A tractor angling up the hill. Pretty soon another, crossing it, lighting up the whole slope."

"We heard it idling up there somewhere," Kelly said. "Olive-drab paint—couldn't see it."

"I saw the pan tractor turn over—oh, four, five times down the hill. It stopped, lights still burning. Then something hit it and rolled it again. That sure blacked it out. What turned it over first?"

"The Seven. Hanging up there just at the brow of the bluff. Waited until Chub and Harris were about to pass, sixty, seventy feet below. Tipped over the edge and rolled down on them with her clutches out. Must've been going thirty miles an hour when she hit. Broadside. They never had a chance. Followed the pan as it rolled down the hill and when it stopped booted it again."

"Want me to rub yo' ankles?" asked Al.

"You! Get outa my sight!"

"Aw, Tom—" whimpered Al.

"Skip it, Tom," said Kelly. "There ain't enough of us left to carry on that way. Al, you mind your manners from here on out, hear?"

"Ah jes' wanted to tell y'all. I knew you weren't lyin' 'bout Dennis, Tom, if only I'd stopped to think. I recollect when Dennis said he'd take that tractuh out . . . 'membah, Kelly? . . . He went an' got the crank and walked around to th' side of th' machine and stuck it in th' hole. It was barely in theah befo' the startin' engine kicked off. 'Whadda ya know!' he says t'me. 'She started by here'f! I nevah pulled that handle!' And I said, 'She sho' rarin' t'go!' "

"You pick a fine time to 'recollec'' something," gritted Tom. "C'mon—let's get out of here."

"Where to?"

"What do you know that a Seven can't move or get up on?"

"That's a large order. A big rock, maybe."

"Ain't nothing that big around here," said Tom.

Kelly thought a minute, then snapped his fingers. "Up on the top of my last cut with the shovel," he said. "It's fourteen feet if it's an inch. I was pullin' out small rock an' topsoil, and Chub told me to drop back and dip out marl from a pocket there. I sumped in back of the original cut and took out a whole mess o' marl. That left a big neck of earth sticking thirty feet or so out of the cliff. The narrowest part is only about four feet wide. If *Daisy Etta* tries to get us from the top, she'll straddle the neck and hang herself. If she tries to get us from below, she can't get traction to climb; it's too lose and too steep."

"And what happens if she builds herself a ramp?"

"We'll be gone from there."

"Let's go."

Al agitated for the choice of a Dumptor because of its speed, but was howled down. Tom wanted something that could not get a flat tire and that would need something really powerful to turn it over. They took the two-cycle pan tractor with the bulldozer blade that had been Dennis's machine and crept out into the darkness.

It was nearly six hours later that *Daisy Etta* came and woke them up. Night was receding before a paleness in the east, and a fresh ocean breeze had sprung up. Kelly had taken the first lookout and Al the second, letting Tom rest the night out. And Tom was far too tired to argue the arrangement. Al had immediately fallen asleep on his watch, but fear had such a sure, cold hold on his vitals that the first faint growl of the big diesel engine snapped him erect. He tottered on the edge of the tall neck of earth that they slept on and squeaked as he scrabbled to get his balance.

"What's giving?" asked Kelly, instantly wide awake.

"It's coming," blubbered Al. "Oh my, oh my—"

Kelly stood up and stared into the fresh, dark dawn. The motor boomed hollowly, in a peculiar way heard twice at the same time as it was thrown to them and echoed back by the bluffs under and around them.

"It's coming and what are we goin' to do?" chanted Al. "What is going to happen?"

"My head is going to fall off," said Tom sleepily. He rolled to a sitting position, holding the brutalized member between his hands. "If that egg behind my ear hatches, it'll come out a full-sized jack-hammer." He looked at Kelly. "Where is she?"

"Don't rightly know," said Kelly. "Somewhere down around the camp."

"Probably pickin' up our scent."

"Figure it can do that?"

"I figure it can do anything," said Tom. "Al, stop your moanin'."

The sun slipped its scarlet edge into the thin slot between sea and sky, and rosy light gave each rock and tree a shape and a shadow. Kelly's gaze swept back and forth, back and forth, until, minutes later, he saw movement.

"There she is!"

"Where?"

"Down by the grease rack."

Tom rose and stared. "What's she doin'?"

After an interval Kelly said, "She's workin'. Diggin' a swale in front of the fuel drums."

"You don't say. Don't tell me she's goin' to give herself a grease job."

"She don't need it. She was completely greased and new oil put in the crankcase after we set her up. But she might need fuel."

"Not more'n half a tank."

"Well, maybe she figures she's got a lot of work to do today." As Kelly said this Al began to blubber. They ignored him.

The fuel drums were piled in a pyramid at the edge of the camp, in forty-four-gallon drums piled on their sides. The Seven was moving back and forth in front of them, close up, making pass after pass, gouging earth up and wasting it out past the pile. She soon had a huge pit scooped out, about fourteen feet wide, six feet deep and thirty feet long, right at the very edge of the pile of drums.

"What you reckon she's playin' at?"

"Search me. She seems to want fuel, but I don't . . . look at that! She's stopped in the hole; she's pivoting, smashing the top corner of the moldboard into one of the drums on the bottom!"

Tom scraped the stubble on his jaw with his nails. "An' you wonder how much that critter can do! Why, she's got the whole thing figured out. She knows if she tried to punch a hole in a fuel drum that she'd only kick it around. If she did knock a hole in it, how's she going to lift it? She's not equipped to handle hose, so . . . see? Look at her now! She just gets herself lower than the bottom drum on the pile, and punches a hole. She can do that then, with the whole weight of the pile holding it down. Then she backs her tank under the stream of fuel runnin' out!"

"How'd she get the cap off?"

Tom snorted and told them how the radiator cap had come

off its hinges as he vaulted over the hood the day Rivera was hurt.

"You know," he said after a moment's thought, "if she knew as much then as she does now, I'd be snoozin' beside Rivera and Peebles. She just didn't know her way around then. She run herself like she'd never run before. She's learned plenty since."

"She has," said Kelly, "and here's where she uses it on us. She's headed this way."

She was. Straight out across the roughed-out runway she came, grinding along over the dew-sprinkled earth, yesterday's dust swirling up from under her tracks. Crossing the shoulder line, she took the rougher ground skillfully, angling up over the occasional swags in the earth, by-passing stones, riding free and fast and easily. It was the first time Tom had actually seen her clearly running without an operator, and his flesh crept as he watched. The machine was unnatural, her outline somehow unreal and dreamlike purely through the lack of the small silhouette of a man in the saddle. She looked hulked, compact, dangerous.

"What are we gonna do?" wailed Al Knowles.

"We're gonna sit and wait," said Kelly, "and you're gonna shut your trap. We won't know for five minutes yet whether she's going to go after us from down below or from up here."

"If you want to leave," said Tom gently, "go right ahead." Al sat down.

Kelly looked down at his beloved power shovel, sitting squat and unlovely in the cut below them and away to their right. "How do you reckon she'd stand up against the dipper stick?"

"If it ever came to a rough-and-tumble," said Tom, "I'd say it would be just too bad for *Daisy Etta*. But she wouldn't fight. There's no way you could get the shovel within punchin' range; *Daisy*'d just stand there and laugh at you."

"I can't see her now," whined Al.

Tom looked. "She's taken the bluff. She's going to try it from up here. I move we sit tight and see if she's foolish enough to try to walk out here over that narrow neck. If she does, she'll drop on her belly with one truck on each side. Probably turn herself over trying to dig out."

The wait then was interminable. Back over the hill they could hear the laboring motor; twice they heard the machine stop momentarily to shift gears. Once they looked at each other hopefully as the sound rose to a series of bellowing roars, as if she were backing and filling; then they realized that she was trying to take some particularly steep part of the bank and having trouble getting traction. But she made it; the motor revved up as she made the brow of the hill, and she shifted into fourth gear and came lumbering out into the open. She lurched up to the edge of the cut, stopped, throttled down, dropped her blade on the ground and stood there idling. Al Knowles backed away to the very edge of the tongue of earth they stood on, his eyes practically on stalks.

"O.K.—put up or shut up," Kelly called across harshly.

"She's looking the situation over," said Tom. "That narrow pathway don't fool her a bit."

Daisy Etta's blade began to rise, and stopped just clear of the ground. She shifted without clashing her gears, began to back slowly, still at little more than an idle.

"She's gonna jump!" screamed Al. "I'm gettin' out of here!"

"Stay here, you fool," shouted Kelly. "She can't get us as long as we're up here! If you go down, she'll hunt you down like a rabbit."

The blast of the Seven's motor was the last straw for Al. He squeaked and hopped over the edge, scrambling and sliding down the almost sheer face of the cut. He hit the bottom running.

Daisy Etta lowered her blade and raised her snout and growled forward, the blade loading. Six, seven, seven and a half cubic yards of dirt piled up in front of her as she neared the edge. The loaded blade bit into the narrow pathway that led out to their perch. It was almost all soft, white, crumbly marl, and the great machine sank nose down into it, the monstrous overload of topsoil spilling down on each side.

"She's going to bury herself!" shouted Kelly.

"No—wait." Tom caught his arm. "She's trying to turn— she made it! She made it! She's ramping herself down to the flat!"

"She is—and she's cut us off from the bluff!"

The bulldozer, blade raised as high as it could possibly go, the hydraulic rod gleaming clean in the early light, freed herself of the last of her tremendous load, spun around and headed back upward, sinking her blade again. She made one more pass between them and the bluff, making a cut now far too wide for them to jump, particularly to the cumbly footing at the bluff's edge. Once down again, she turned to face their haven, now an isolated pillar of marl, and revved down, waiting.

"I never thought of this," said Kelly guiltily. "I knew we'd be safe from her ramping up, and I never thought she'd try it the other way!"

"Skip it. In the meantime, here we sit. What happens—do we wait up here until she idles out of fuel, or do we starve to death?"

"Oh, this won't be a siege, Tom. That thing's too much of a killer. Where's Al? I wonder if he's got guts enough to make a pass near here with our tractor and draw her off?"

"He had just guts enough to take our tractor and head out," said Tom. "Didn't you know?"

"He took our—*what?*" Kelly looked out toward where they had left their machine the night before. It was gone. "Why the dirty little yellow rat!"

"No sense cussin'," said Tom steadily, interrupting what he knew was the beginning of some really flowery language. "What else could you expect?"

Daisy Etta decided, apparently, how to go about removing their splendid isolation. She uttered the snort of too-quick throttle, and moved into their peak with a corner of her blade, cutting out a huge swipe, undercutting the material over it so that it fell on her side and track as she passed. Eight inches disappeared from that side of their little plateau.

"Oh-oh. That won't do a-tall," said Tom.

"Fixin' to dig us down," said Kelly grimly. "Take her about twenty minutes. Tom, I say leave."

"It won't be healthy. You just got no idea how fast that thing can move now. Don't forget, she's a good deal more than she was when she had a man runnin' her. She can shift from high to reverse to fifth speed forward like that"—he snapped his fingers—"and she can pivot faster'n you can blink and throw that blade just where she wants it."

The tractor passed under them, bellowing, and their little table was suddenly a foot shorter.

"Awright," said Kelly. "So what do you want to do? Stay here and let her dig the ground out from under our feet?"

"I'm just warning you," said Tom. "Now listen. We'll wait until she's taking a load. It'll take her a second to get rid of it when she knows we're gone. We'll split—she can't get both of us. You head out in the open, try to circle the curve of the bluff and get where you can climb it. Then come back over here to the cut. A man can scramble off a fourteen-foot cut faster'n any tractor ever built. I'll cut in close to the cut, down at the bottom. If she takes after you, I'll get clear all right. If she takes after me, I'll try to make the shovel and at least give her a run for her money. I can play hide an' seek in an' around and under that dipper-stick all day if she wants to play."

"Why me out in the open?"

"Don't you think those long laigs o' yours can outrun her in that distance?"

"Reckon they got to," grinned Kelly. "O.K., Tom."

They waited tensely. *Daisy Etta* backed close by, started another pass. As the motor blatted under the load, Tom said, "Now!" and they jumped. Kelly, catlike as always, landed on his feet. Tom, whose knees and ankles were black and blue with rope bruises, took two staggering steps and fell. Kelly scooped him to his feet as the dozer's steel prow came around the bank. Instantly she was in fifth gear and howling down at them. Kelly flung himself to the left and Tom to the right, and they pounded away, Kelly out toward the runway, Tom straight for the shovel. *Daisy Etta* let them diverge for a moment, keeping her course, trying to pursue both; then she evidently sized Tom up as the slower, for she swung toward him. The instant's hesitation was all Tom needed to get the little lead necessary. He tore up to the shovel, his legs going like pistons, and dived down between the shovel's tracks.

As he hit the ground, the big manganese-steel moldboard hit the right track of the shovel, and the impact set all forty-seven tons of the great machine quivering. But Tom did not stop. He scrabbled his way under the rig, stood up behind it, leaped and caught the sill of the rear window, clapped his other hand on it, drew himself up and tumbled inside. Here he was safe for the moment; the huge tracks themselves were higher than the Seven's blade could rise, and the floor of the cab was a good sixteen inches higher than the top of the track. Tom went to the cab door and peeped outside. The tractor had drawn off and was idling.

"Study away," gritted Tom, and went to the big Murphy diesel. He unhurriedly checked the oil with the bayonet gauge, replaced it, took the governor cut-out rod from its rack and inserted it in the governor casing. He set the master throttle at the halfway mark, pulled up the starter-handle, twitched the cut-out. The motor spat a wad of blue smoke out of its hooded exhaust and caught. Tom put the rod back, studied the fuel-flow glass and pressure gauges, and then went to the door and looked out again. The Seven had not moved, but it was revving up and down in that uneven fashion it had shown up on the mesa. Tom had the extraordinary idea that it was gathering itself to spring. He slipped into the saddle, threw the master clutch. The big gears that half-filled the cab obediently began to turn. He kicked the brake locks loose with his heels, let his feet rest lightly on the pedals as they rose.

Then he reached over his head and snapped back the throttle. As the Murphy picked up he grasped both hoist and swing levers and pulled them back. The engine howled; the two-yard bucket came up off the ground with a sudden jolt as the cold friction grabbed it. The big machine swung hard to the right; Tom snapped his hoist lever forward and checked the bucket's rise with his foot on the brake. He shoved the crowd lever forward; the bucket ran out to the end of its reach, and the heel of the bucket wiped across the Seven's hood, taking with it the exhaust stack, muffler and all, and the pre-cleaner on the air intake. Tom cursed. He had figured on the machine's leaping backward. If it had, he would have smashed the cast-iron radiator core. But she had stood still, making a split-second decision.

Now she moved, though, and quickly. With that incredibly fast shifting, she leaped backwards and pivoted out of range before Tom could check the shovel's mad swing. The heavy swing-friction blocks smoked acridly as the machine slowed, stopped and swung back. Tom checked her as he was facing the Seven, hoisted his bucket a few feet, and rehauled, bringing it about halfway back, ready for anything. The four great dipper-teeth gleamed in the sun. Tom ran a practiced eye over cables, boom and dipper-stick, liking the black polish of crater compound on the sliding parts, the easy tension of well-greased cables and links. The huge machine stood strong, ready and profoundly subservient for all its brute power.

Tom looked searchingly at the Seven's ruined engine hood. The gaping end of the broken air-intake pipe stared back at him. "Aha!" he said. "A few cupfuls of nice dry marl down there'll give you something to chew on."

Keeping a wary eye on the tractor, he swung into the bank, dropped his bucket and plunged it into the marl. He crowded it deep, and the Murphy yelled for help but kept on pushing. At the peak of the load a terrific jar rocked him in the saddle. He looked back over his shoulder through the door and saw the Seven backing off again. She had run up and delivered a terrific punch to the counterweight at the back of the cab. Tom grinned tightly. She'd have to do better than that. There was nothing back there but eight or ten tons of solid steel. And he didn't much care at the moment whether or not she scratched his paint.

He swung back again, white marl running away on both sides of the heaped bucket. The shovel rode perfectly now, for a shovel is counterweighted to balance true when standing level with the bucket loaded. The hoist and swing frictions and the brake linings had heated and dried themselves of the night's condensation moisture, and she answered the controls in a way that delighted the operator in him. He handled the swing lever lightly, back to swing to the right, forward to swing to the left, following the slow dance the Seven had started to do, stepping warily back and forth like a fighter looking for an opening. Tom kept the bucket between himself and the tractor, knowing that she could not hurl a tool that was built to smash hard rock for twenty hours a day and like it.

Daisy Etta bellowed and rushed in. Tom snapped the hoist lever back hard, and the bucket rose, letting the tractor run underneath. Tom punched the bucket trip, and the great steel jaw opened, cascading marl down on the broken hood. The tractor's fan blew it back in a huge billowing cloud. The instant that it took Tom to check and dump was enough, however, for the tractor to dance back out of the way, for when he tried to drop it on the machine to smash the coiled injector tubes on top of the engine block, she was gone.

The dust cleared away, and the tractor moved in again, feinted to the left, then swung her blade at the bucket, which was just clear of the ground. Tom swung to meet her, her feint having gotten her in a little closer than he liked, and bucket met blade with a shower of sparks and a clank that could be heard for half a mile. She had come in with her blade high, and Tom let out a wordless shout as he saw the A-frame brace behind the blade had caught between two of his dipper-teeth. He snatched at his hoist lever and the bucket came up, lifting with it the whole front end of the bulldozer.

Daisy Etta plunged up and down and her tracks dug violently into the earth as she raised and lowered her blade, trying to shake herself free. Tom rehauled, trying to bring the tractor in closer, for the boom was set too low to attempt to lift such a dead weight. As it was, the shovel's off track was trying its best to get off the ground. But the crowd and rehaul frictions could not handle her alone; they began to heat and slip.

Tom hoisted a little; the shovel's off track came up a foot off the ground. Tom cursed and let the bucket drop, and in an instant the dozer was free and running clear. Tom swung wildly at her, missed. The dozer came in on a long curve; Tom swung to meet her again, took a vicious swipe at her which she took on her blade. But this time she did not withdraw after being hit, but bored right in, carrying the bucket before her. Before Tom realized what she was doing, his bucket was around in front of the tracks and between them, on the ground. It was as swift and skillful a maneuver as could be imagined, and it left the shovel without the ability to swing as long as *Daisy Etta* could hold the bucket trapped between the tracks.

Tom crowded furiously, but that succeeded only in lifting the boom higher in the air, since there is nothing to hold a boom down but its own weight. Hoisting did nothing but make his frictions smoke and rev the engine down dangerously close to the stalling point.

Tom swore again and reached down to the cluster of small levers at his left. These were the gears. On this type of shovel, the swing lever controls everything except crowd and hoist. With the swing lever, the operator, having selected his gear, controls the travel—that is, power to the tracks—in forward and reverse; booming up and booming down; and swinging. The machine can do only one of these things at a time. If she is in travel gear, she cannot swing. If she is in swing gear, she cannot boom up or down. Not once in years of operating would this inability bother an operator; now, however, nothing was normal.

Tom pushed the swing gear control down and pulled up on the travel. The clutches involved were jaw clutches, not frictions, so that he had to throttle down to an idle before he could make the castellations mesh. As the Murphy revved down, *Daisy Etta* took it as a signal that something could be done about it, and she shoved furiously into the bucket. But Tom had all controls in neutral and all she succeeded in doing was to dig herself in, her sharp new cleats spinning deep into the dirt.

Tom set his throttle up again and shoved the swing lever forward. There was a vast crackling of drive chains; and the big tracks started to turn.

Daisy Etta had sharp cleats; her pads were twenty inches wide and her tracks were fourteen feet long, and there were fourteen tons of steel on them. The shovel's big flat pads were three feet wide and twenty feet long, and forty-seven tons aboard. There was simply no comparison. The Murphy bellowed the fact that the work was hard, but gave no indications of stalling. *Daisy Etta* performed the incredible feat of shifting into a forward gear while she was moving backwards, but it did her no good. Round and round her tracks went, trying to drive her forward, gouging deep; and slowly and surely she was forced backward toward the cut wall by the shovel.

Tom heard a sound that was not part of a straining machine; he looked out and saw Kelly up on top of the cut, smoking, swinging his feet over the edge, making punching motions with his hands as if he had a ringside seat at a big fight—which he certainly had.

Tom now offered the dozer little choice. If she did not turn aside before him, she would be borne back against the bank and her fuel tank crushed. There was every possibility that, having her pinned there, Tom would have time to raise his bucket over her and smash her to pieces. And if she turned before she was forced against the bank, she would have to free Tom's bucket. This she had to do.

The Murphy gave him warning, but not enough. It crooned as the load came off, and Tom knew then that the dozer was shifting into a reverse gear. He whipped the hoist lever back, and the bucket rose as the dozer backed away from him. He crowded it out and let it come smashing down—and missed. For the tractor danced aside—and while he was in travel gear he could not swing to follow it. *Daisy Etta* charged then, put one track on the bank and went over almost on her beam-ends, throwing one end of her blade high in the air. So totally unexpected was it that Tom was quite unprepared. The tractor flung itself on the bucket, and the cutting edge of the blade dropped between the dipper teeth. This time there was the whole weight of the tractor to hold it there. There would be no way for her to free herself—but at the same time she had trapped the bucket so far out from the center pin of the shovel that Tom couldn't hoist without overbalancing and turning the monster over.

Daisy Etta ground away in reverse, dragging the bucket out until it was checked by the bumper-blocks. Then she began to crab sideways, up against the bank and when Tom tried tentatively to rehaul, she shifted and came right with him, burying one whole end of her blade deep into the bank.

Stalemate. She had hung herself up on the bucket, and she had immobilized it. Tom tried to rehaul, but the tractor's anchorage in the bank was too solid. He tried to swing, to hoist. All the overworked frictions could possibly give out was smoke. Tom grunted and throttled to an idle, leaned out the window. *Daisy Etta* was idling too, loudly without her muffler, the stackless exhaust giving out an ugly flat sound. But after the roar of the two great motors the partial silence was deafening.

Kelly called down, "Double knockout, hey?"

"Looks like it. What say we see if we can't get close enough to her to quiet her down some?"

Kelly shrugged. "I dunno. If she's really stopped herself, it's the first time. I respect that rig, Tom. She wouldn't have got herself into that spot if she didn't have an ace up her sleeve."

"Look at her, man! Suppose she was a civilized bulldozer and you had to get her out of there. She can't raise her blade high enough to free it from those dipper-teeth, y'know. Think you'd be able to do it?"

"It might take several seconds," Kelly drawled. "She's sure high and dry."

"O.K., let's spike her guns."

"Like what?"

"Like taking a bar and prying out her tubing." He referred to the coiled brass tubing that carried the fuel, under pressure, from the pump to the injectors. There were many feet of it, running from the pump reservoir, stacked in expansion coils over the cylinder head.

As he spoke *Daisy Etta*'s idle burst into that maniac revving up and down characteristic of her.

"What do you know!" Tom called above the racket. "Eavesdropping!"

Kelly slid down the cut, stood up on the track of the shovel and poked his head in the window. "Well, you want to get a bar and try?"

"Let's go!"

Tom went to the toolbox and pulled out the pinch bar that Kelly used to replace cables on his machine, and swung to the ground. They approached the tractor warily. She revved up as they came near, began to shudder. The front end rose and dropped and the tracks began to turn as she tried to twist out of the vise her blade had dropped into.

"Take it easy, sister," said Tom. "You'll just bury yourself. Set still and take it, now, like a good girl. You got it comin'."

"Be careful," said Kelly. Tom hefted the bar and laid a hand on the fender.

The tractor literally shivered, and from the rubber hose connection at the top of the radiator, a blinding stream of hot water shot out. It fanned and caught them both full in the face. They staggered back, cursing.

"You O.K. Tom?" Kelly gasped a moment later. He had got most of it across the mouth and cheek. Tom was on his knees, his shirt tail out, blotting at his face.

"My eyes . . . oh, my eyes—"

"Let's see!" Kelly dropped down beside him and took him by the wrists, gently removing Tom's hands from his face. He whistled. "Come on," he gritted. He helped Tom up and led him away a few feet. "Stay here," he said hoarsely. He turned, walked back toward the dozer, picking up the pinch-bar. "You dirty——!" he yelled, and flung it like a javelin at the tube coils. It was a little high. It struck the ruined hood, made a deep dent in the metal. The dent promptly inverted with a loud *thung-g-g!* and flung the bar back at him. He ducked; it whistled over his head and caught Tom in the calves of his legs. He went down like a poled ox, but staggered to his feet again.

"Come on!" Kelly snarled, and taking Tom's arm, hustled him around the turn of the cut. "Sit down! I'll be right back."

"Where you going? Kelly—be careful!"

"Careful and how!"

Kelly's long legs ate up the distance back to the shovel. He swung into the cab, reached back over the motor and set up the master throttle all the way. Stepping up behind the saddle, he opened the running throttle and the Murphy howled. Then he hauled back on the hoist lever until it knuckled in, turned and leaped off the machine in one supple motion.

The hoist drum turned and took up slack; the cable straightened as it took the strain. The bucket stirred under the dead weight of the bulldozer that rested on it; and slowly, then, the great flat tracks began to lift their rear ends off the ground. The great obedient mass of machinery teetered forward on the tips of her tracks, the Murphy revved down and under the incredible load, but it kept the strain. A strand of the two-part hoist cable broke and whipped around, singing; and then she was balanced—over-balanced—

And the shovel had hauled herself right over and had fallen with an earth-shaking crash. The boom, eight tons of solid steel, clanged down onto the blade of the bulldozer, and lay there, crushing it down tightly onto the imprisoning row of dipper-teeth.

Daisy Etta sat there, not trying to move now, racing her motor impotently. Kelly strutted past her, thumbing his nose, and went back to Tom.

"Kelly! I thought you were never coming back! What happened?"

"Shovel pulled herself over on her nose."

"Good boy! Fall on the tractor?"

"Nup. But the boom's laying across the top of her blade. Caught like a rat in a trap."

"Better watch out the rat don't chew its leg off to get out," said Tom, drily. "Still runnin', is she?"

"Yep. But we'll fix that in a hurry."

"Sure. Sure. How?"

"How? I dunno. Dynamite, maybe. How's the optics?"

Tom opened one a trifle and grunted. "Rough. I can see a

little, though. My eyelids are parboiled, mostly. Dynamite, you say? Well—"

Tom sat back against the bank and stretched out his legs. "I tell you, Kelly, I been too blessed busy these last few hours to think much, but there's one thing that keeps comin' back to me—somethin' I was mullin' over long before the rest of you guys knew anything was up at all, except that Rivera had got hurt in some way I wouldn't tell you all about. But I don't reckon you'll call me crazy if I open my mouth now and let it all run out?"

"From now on," Kelly said fervently, "nobody's crazy. After this I'll believe anything."

"O.K. Well, about that tractor. What do you suppose has got into her?"

"Search me. I dunno."

"No—don't say that. I just got an idea we can't stop at 'I dunno.' We got to figure all the angles on this thing before we know just what to do about it. Let's just get this thing lined up. When did it start? On the mesa. How? Rivera was opening an old building with the Seven. This thing came out of there. Now here's what I'm getting at. We can dope these things out about it: It's intelligent. It can only get into a machine and not into a man. It—"

"What about that? How do you know it can't?"

"Because it had the chance to and didn't. I was standing right by the opening when it kited out. Rivera was upon the machine at the time. It didn't directly harm either of us. It got into the tractor, and the tractor did. By the same token, it can't hurt a man when it's out of a machine, but that's all it wants to do when it's in one. O.K.?"

"To get on: once it's in one machine it can't get out again. We know that because it had plenty of chances and didn't take them. That scuffle with the dipper-stick, f'r instance. My face woulda been plenty red if it had taken over the shovel—and you can bet it would have if it could."

"I got you so far. But what are we going to do about it?"

"That's the thing. You see, I don't think it's enough to wreck the tractor. We might burn it, blast it, take whatever it was that got into it up on the mesa."

"That makes sense. But I don't see what else we can do than just break up the dozer. We haven't got a line on actually what the thing is."

"I think we have. Remember I asked you all those screwy questions about the arc that killed Peebles. Well, when that happened, I recollected a flock of other things. One—when it got out of that hole up there, I smelled that smell that you notice when you're welding; sometimes when lightning strikes real close."

"Ozone," said Kelly.

"Yeah—ozone. Then, it likes metal, not flesh. But most of all, there was that arc. Now, that was absolutely screwy. You know as well as I do—better—that an arc generator simply don't have the push to do a thing like that. It can't kill a man, and it can't throw an arc no fifty feet. But it did. An' that's why I asked you if there could be something—a field, or some such—that could *suck* current out of a generator, all at once, faster than it could flow. Because this thing's electrical; it fits all around."

"Electronic," said Kelly doubtfully, thoughtfully.

"I wouldn't know. Now then. When Peebles was killed, a funny thing happened. Remember what Chub said? The Seven moved back—straight back, about thirty feet, until it bumped into a roadroller that was standing behind it. It did that with no fuel in the starting engine—without even using the starting engine, for that matter—and with the compression valves locked open!

"Kelly, that thing in the dozer can't do much, when you come right down to it. It couldn't fix itself up after the joyride on the mesa. It can't make the machine do too much more than the machine can do ordinarily. What it actually can do, seems to me, is to make a spring push instead of pull, like the control levers, and make a fitting slip when it's supposed to hold, like the ratchet on the throttle lever. It can turn a shaft, like the way it cranks its own starting motor. But if it was so all-fired high-powered, it wouldn't have to use the starting motor! The absolute biggest job it's done so far, seems to me, was when it walked back from that welding machine when Peebles got his. Now, why did it do that just then?"

"Reckon it didn't like the brimstone smell, like it says in the Good Book," said Kelly sourly.

"That's pretty close, seems to me. Look, Kelly—this thing *feels* things. I mean, it can get sore. If it couldn't it never woulda kept driving in at the shovel like that. It can think. But if it can do all those things, then it can be *scared!*"

"Scared? Why should it be scared?"

"Listen. Something went on in that thing when the arc hit it. What's that I read in a magazine once about heat—something about molecules runnin' around with their heads cut off when they got hot?"

"Molecules do. They go into rapid motion when heat is applied. But—"

"But nothin'. That machine was hot for four hours after that. But she was hot in a funny way. Not just around the place where the arc hit, like as if it was a welding arc. But hot all over—from the moldboard to the fuel-tank cap. Hot everywhere. And just as hot behind the final drive housings as she was at the top of the blade where the poor guy put his hand.

"And look at this." Tom was getting excited, as his words crystallized his ideas. "She was scared—scared enough to back off from that welder, putting everything she could into it, to get back from that welding machine. And after that, she was sick. I say that because in the whole time she's had that whatever-ya-call-it in her, she's never been near men without trying to kill them, except for those two days after the arc hit her. She had juice enough to start herself when Dennis came around with the crank, but she still needed someone to run her till she got her strength back."

"But why didn't she turn and smash up the welder when Dennis took her?"

"One of two things. She didn't have the strength, or she didn't have the guts. She was scared, maybe, and wanted out of there, away from that thing."

"But she had all night to go back for it!"

"Still scared. Or . . . oh, *that's* it! She had other things to do first. Her main idea is to kill men—there's no other way you can figure it. It's what she was built to do. Not the tractor—they don't build 'em sweeter'n that machine; but the thing that's runnin' it."

"What *is* that thing?" Kelly mused. "Coming out of that old building—temple—what have you—how old is it? How long was it there? What kept it in there?"

"What kept it in there was some funny gray stuff that lined the inside of the buildin'," said Tom. "It was like rock, an' it was like smoke.

"It was a color that scared you to look at it, and it gave

Rivera and me the creeps when we got near it. Don't ask me
what it was. I went up there to look at it, and it's gone. Gone
from the building, anyhow. There was a little lump of it on
the ground. I don't know whether that was a hunk of it, or
all of it rolled up into a ball. I get the creeps again thinkin'
about it."

Kelly stood up. "Well, the heck with it. We been beatin'
our gums up here too long anyhow. There's just enough sense
in what you say to make me want to try something nonsensi-
cal, if you see what I mean. If that welder can sweat the Ol'
Nick out of that tractor, I'm on. Especially from fifty feet
away. There should be a Dumptor around here somewhere;
let's move from here. Can you navigate now?"

"Reckon so, a little." Tom rose and together they followed
the cut until they came on the Dumptor. They climbed on,
cranked it up and headed toward camp.

About halfway there Kelly looked back, gasped, and putting his mouth close to Tom's ear, bellowed against the
scream of the motor, "Tom! 'Member what you said about
the rat in the trap biting off a leg?"

Tom nodded.

"Well, *Daisy* did too! She's left her blade an' pushbeams
an' she's followin' us in!"

They howled into the camp, gasping against the dust that
followed when they pulled up by the welder.

Kelly said, "You cast around and see if you can find a
drawpin to hook that rig up to the Dumptor with. I'm goin'
after some water an' chow!"

Tom grinned. Imagine old Kelly forgetting that a Dumptor
had no drawbar! He groped around to a toolbox, peering out
of the narrow slit beneath swollen lids, felt behind it and lo-
cated a shackle. He climbed up on the Dumptor, turned it
around and backed up to the welding machine. He passed the
shackle through the ring at the end of the steering tongue of
the welder, screwed in the pin and dropped the shackle over
the front towing hook of the Dumptor. A dumptor being
what it is, having no real front and no real rear, and direct
reversing gears in all speeds, it was no trouble to drive it
"backwards" for a change.

Kelly came pounding back, out of breath. "Fix it? Good.
Shackle? No drawbar! *Daisy's* closin' up fast; I say let's take

the beach. We'll be concealed until we have a good lead out o' this pocket, and the going's pretty fair, long as we don't bury this jalopy in the sand."

"Good," said Tom as they climbed on and he accepted an open tin of K. "Only go easy; bump around too much and the welder'll slip off the hook. An' I somehow don't want to lose it just now."

They took off, zooming up the beach. A quarter of a mile up, they sighted the Seven across the flat. It immediately turned and took a course that would intercept them.

"Here she comes," shouted Kelly, and stepped down hard on the accelerator. Tom leaned over the back of the seat, keeping his eye on their tow. "Hey! Take it easy! Watch it! *Hey!*"

But it was too late. The tongue of the welding machine responded to that one bump too many. The shackle jumped up off the hook, the welder lurched wildly, slewed hard to the left. The tongue dropped to the sand and dug in; the machine rolled up on it and snapped it off, finally stopped, leaning crazily askew. By a miracle it did not quite turn over.

Kelly tramped on the brakes and both their heads did their utmost to snap off their shoulders. They leaped off and ran back to the welder. It was intact, but towing it was now out of the question.

"If there's going to be a showdown, it's gotta be here."

The beach here was about thirty yards wide, the sand almost level, and undercut banks of sawgrass forming the landward edge in a series of little hummocks and headlands. While Tom stayed with the machine, testing starter and generator contacts, Kelly walked up one of the little mounds, stood up on it and scanned the beach back the way he had come. Suddenly he began to shout and wave his arms.

"What's got into you?"

"It's Al!" Kelly called back. "With the pan tractor!"

Tom dropped what he was doing, and came to stand beside Kelly. "Where's the Seven? I can't see."

"Turned on the beach and followin' our track. Al! Al! You little skunk, c'mere!"

Tom could now dimly make out the pan tractor cutting across directly toward them and the beach.

"He don't see *Daisy Etta*," remarked Kelly disgustedly, "or he'd sure be headin' the other way."

Fifty yards away Al pulled up and throttled down. Kelly shouted and waved to him. Al stood up on the machine, cupped his hands around his mouth. "Where's the Seven?"

"Never mind that! Come here with that tractor!"

Al stayed where he was. Kelly cursed and started out after him.

"You stay away from me," he said when Kelly was closer.

"I ain't got time for you now," said Kelly. "Bring that tractor down to the beach."

"Where's that *Daisy Etta?*" Al's voice was oddly strained.

"Right behind us." Kelly thumbed over his shoulder. "On the beach."

Al's bulging eyes clicked wide almost audibly. He turned on his heel and jumped off the machine and started to run. Kelly uttered a wordless syllable that was somehow more obscene than anything else he had ever uttered, and vaulted into the seat of the machine. "Hey!" he bellowed after Al's rapidly diminishing figure. "You're runnin' right into her." Al appeared not to hear, but went pelting down the beach.

Kelly put her into fifth gear and poured on the throttle. As the tractor began to move he whacked out the master clutch, snatched the overdrive lever back to put her into sixth, rammed the clutch in again, all so fast that she did not have time to stop rolling. Bucking and jumping over the rough ground, the fast machine whined for the beach.

Tom was fumbling back to the welder, his ears telling him better than his eyes how close the Seven was—for she was certainly no nightingale, particularly without her exhaust stack. Kelly reached the machine as he did.

"Get behind it," snapped Tom. "I'll jam the tierod with the shackle, and you see if you can't bunt her up into that pocket between these two hummocks. Only take it easy—you don't want to tear up that generator. Where's Al?"

"Don't ask me. He run down the beach to meet *Daisy.*"

"He *what?*"

The whine of the two-cycle drowned out Kelly's answer, if any. He got behind the welder and set his blade against it. Then in a low gear, slipping his clutch in a little, he slowly nudged the machine toward the place Tom had indicated. It was a little hollow in between two projecting banks. The surf and the high-tide mark dipped inland here to match it; the water was only a few feet away.

Tom raised his arm and Kelly stopped. From the other side of the projecting shelf, out of their sight now, came the flat roar of the Seven's exhaust. Kelly sprang off the tractor and went to help Tom, who was furiously throwing out coils of cable from the rack back of the welder. "What's the game?"

"We got to ground that Seven some way," panted Tom. He threw the last bit of cable out to clear it of kinks and turned to the panel. "How was it—about sixty volts and the amperage on 'special application'?" He spun the dials, pressed the starter button. The motor responded instantly. Kelly scooped up ground clamp and rod holder and tapped them together. The solenoid governor picked up the load and the motor hummed as a good live spark took the jump.

"Good," said Tom, switching off the generator. "Come on, Lieutenant General Electric, figure me out a way to ground that maverick."

Kelly tightened his lips, shook his head. "I dunno—unless somebody actually clamps this thing on her."

"No, boy, can't do that. If one of us gets killed—"

Kelly tossed the ground clamp idly, his lithe body taut. "Don't give me that, Tom. You know I'm elected because you can't see good enough yet to handle it. You know you'd do it if you could. You—"

He stopped short, for the steadily increasing roar of the approaching Seven had stopped, was blatting away now in that extraordinary irregular throttling that *Daisy Etta* affected.

"Now, what's got into her?"

Kelly broke away and scrambled up the bank. "Tom!" he gasped. "Tom—come up here!"

Tom followed, and they lay side by side, peering out over the top of the escarpment at the remarkable tableau.

Daisy Etta was standing on the beach, near the water, not moving. Before her, twenty or thirty feet away, stood Al Knowles, his arms out in front of him, talking a blue streak. *Daisy* made far too much racket for them to hear what he was saying.

"Do you reckon he's got guts enough to stall her off for us?" said Tom.

"If he has, it's the queerest thing that's happened yet on his old island," Kelly breathed, "an' that's saying something."

The Seven revved up till she shook, and then throttled back. She ran down so low then that they thought she had shut herself down, but she caught on the last two revolutions and began to idle quietly. And then they could hear.

Al's voice was high, hysterical. "—I come t' he'p you, I come t' he'p you, don' kill me, I'll he'p you—" He took a step forward; the dozer snorted and he fell to his knees. "I'll wash you an' grease you and change yo' ile," he said in a high singsong.

"The guy's not human," said Kelly wonderingly.

"He ain't housebroke either," Tom chuckled.

"—lemme he'p you. I'll fix you when you break down. I'll he'p you kill those other guys—"

"She don't need any help!" said Tom.

"The louse," growled Kelly. "The rotten little double-crossing polecat!" He stood up. "Hey, you Al! Come out o' that. I mean now! If she don't get you I will, if you don't move."

Al was crying now. "Shut up!" he screamed. "I know who's bawss hereabouts, an' so do you!" He pointed at the tractor. "She'll kill us all off'n we don't do what she wants!" He turned back to the machine. "I'll k-kill 'em fo' you. I'll wash you and shine you up and f-fix yo' hood. I'll put yo' blade back on. . . ."

Tom reached out and caught Kelly's leg as the tall man started out, blind mad. "Git back here," he barked. "What you want to do—get killed for the privilege of pinnin' his ears back?"

Kelly subsided and came back, threw himself down beside Tom, put his face in his hands. He was quivering with rage.

"Don't take on so," Tom said. "The man's plumb loco. You can't argue with him any more'n you can with *Daisy*, there. If he's got to get his, *Daisy*'ll give it to him."

"Aw, Tom, it ain't that. I know he ain't worth it, but I can't sit up here and watch him get himself killed. I can't, Tom."

Tom thumped him on the shoulder, because there were simply no words to be said. Suddenly he stiffened, snapped his fingers.

"There's our ground," he said urgently, pointing seaward. "The water—the wet beach where the surf runs. If we can get our ground clamp out there and her somewhere near it—"

"Ground the pan tractor. Run it out into the water. It ought to reach—partway, anyhow."

"That's it—c'mon."

They slid down the bank, snatched up the ground clamp, attached it to the frame of the pan tractor.

"I'll take it," said Tom, and as Kelly opened his mouth, Tom shoved him back against the welding machine. "No time to argue," he snapped, swung on to the machine, slapped her in gear and was off. Kelly took a step toward the tractor, and then his quick eye saw a bight of the ground cable about to foul a wheel of the welder. He stooped and threw it off, spread out the rest of it so it would pay off clear. Tom, with the incredible single-mindedness of the trained operator, watched only the black line of the trailing cable on the sand behind him. When it straightened, he stopped. The front of the tracks were sloshing in the gentle surf. He climbed off the side away from the Seven and tried to see. There was movement, and the growl of her motor now running at a bit more than idle, but he could not distinguish much.

Kelly picked up the rod-holder and went to peer around the head of the protruding bank. Al was on his feet, still crooning hysterically, sidling over toward *Daisy Etta.* Kelly ducked back, threw the switch on the arc generator, climbed the bank and crawled along through the sawgrass paralleling the beach until the holder in his hand tugged and he knew he had reached the end of the cable. He looked out at the beach; measured carefully with his eye the arc he would travel if he left his position and, keeping the cable taut, went out on the beach. At no point would he come within seventy feet of the possessed machine, let alone fifty. She had to be drawn in closer. And she had to be maneuvered out to the wet sand, or in the water—

Al Knowles, encouraged by the machine's apparent decision not to move, approached, though warily, and still running off at the mouth. "—we'll kill'em off an' then we'll keep it a secret and th' bahges'll come an' take us offen th' island and we'll go to anothah job an' kill us lots mo' . . . an' when yo' tracks git dry an' squeak we'll wet 'em up with blood, and you'll be rightly king o' th' hill . . . look yondah, look yondah, *Daisy Etta,* see them theah, by the otheh tractuh, theah they are, kill 'em, *Daisy,* kill 'em, *Daisy,* an' lemme he'p . . . heah me. *Daisy,* heah me, say you heah me—" and the motor roared in response. Al laid a timid hand on the radiator guard, leaning far over to do it, and the tractor still stood there grumbling but not moving. Al stepped back, motioned with his arm, began to walk off slowly toward the pan tractor, looking backwards as he did so like a man training a dog. "C'mon, c'mon, theah's one theah, le's *kill'm, kill'm, kill'm. . . .*"

And with a snort the tractor revved up and followed.

Kelly licked his lips without effect because his tongue was dry, too. The madman passed him, walking straight up the center of the beach, and the tractor, now no longer a bulldozer, followed him; and there the sand was bone dry, sundried, dried to powder. As the tractor passed him, Kelly got up on all fours, went over the edge of the bank onto the beach, crouched there.

Al crooned, "I love ya, honey, I love ya, 'deed I do——"

Kelly ran crouching, like a man under machine-gun fire, making himself as small as possible and feeling as big as a barn door. The torn-up sand where the tractor had passed was under his feet now; he stopped, afraid to get much closer, afraid that a weakened, badly grounded arc might leap from the holder in his hand and serve only to alarm and infuriate the thing in the tractor. And just then Al saw him.

"There!" he screamed; and the tractor pulled up short. "Behind you! Get'm, *Daisy! Kill'm, kill'm, kill'm.*"

Kelly stood up almost wearily, fury and frustration too much to be borne. "In the water," he yelled, because it was what his whole being wanted. "Get'er in the water! Wet her tracks, Al!"

"*Kill'm, kill'm——*"

As the tractor started to turn, there was a commotion over by the pan tractor. It was Tom, jumping, shouting, waving his arms, swearing. He ran out from behind his machine, straight at the Seven. *Daisy Etta's* motor roared and she swung to meet him, Al barely dancing back out of the way. Tom cut sharply, sand spouting under his pumping feet, and ran straight into the water. He went out to about waist deep, suddenly disappeared. He surfaced, spluttering, still trying to shout. Kelly took a better grip on his rod holder and rushed.

Daisy Etta, in following Tom's crazy rush, had swung in beside the pan tractor, not fifteen feet away; and she, too, was now in the surf. Kelly closed up the distance as fast as his long legs would let him; and as he approached to within that crucial fifty feet, Al Knowles hit him.

Al was frothing at the mouth, gibbering. The two men hit full tilt; Al's head caught Kelly in the midriff as he missed a straightarm, and the breath went out of him in one great *whoosh!* Kelly went down like tall timber, the whole world turned to one swirling red-gray haze. Al flung himself on the bigger man, clawing, smacking, too berserk to ball his fists.

"Ah'm go' to kill you," he gurgled. "She'll git one, I'll git t'other, an' then she'll know——"

Kelly covered his face with his arms, and as some wind was sucked at last into his laboring lungs, he flung them upward and sat up in one mighty surge. Al was hurled upward and to one side, and as he hit the ground Kelly reached out a long arm, and twisted his fingers into the man's coarse hair, raised him up, and came across with his other fist in a punch that would have killed him had it landed square. But Al managed to jerk to one side enough so that it only amputated a cheek. He fell and lay still. Kelly scrambled madly around in the sand for his welding-rod holder, found it and began to run again. He couldn't see Tom at all now, and the Seven was standing in the surf, moving slowly from side to side, backing out, ravening. Kelly held the rod-clamp and its trailing cable blindly before him and ran straight at the machine. And then it came—that thin, soundless bolt of energy. But this time it had its full force, for poor old Peebles's body had not been the ground that this swirling water offered. *Daisy Etta* literally leaped backwards toward him, and the water around her tracks spouted upward in hot steam. The sound of her engine ran up and up, broke, took on the rhythmic, uneven beat of a swing drummer. She threw herself from side to side like a cat with a bag over its head. Kelly stepped a little closer, hoping for another bolt to come from the clamp in his hand, but there was none, for—

"The circuit breaker!" cried Kelly.

He threw the holder up on the deck plate of the Seven in front of the seat, and ran across the little beach to the welder. He reached behind the switchboard, got his thumb on the contact hinge and jammed it down.

Daisy Etta leaped again, and then again, and suddenly her motor stopped. Heat in turbulent waves blurred the air over her. The little gas tank for the starting motor went out with a cannon's roar, and the big fuel tank, still holding thirty-odd gallons of diesel oil followed. It puffed itself open rather than exploded, and threw a great curtain of flame over the ground behind the machine. Motor or no motor, then, Kelly distinctly saw the tractor shudder convulsively. There was a crawling movement of the whole frame, a slight wave of motion away from the fuel tank, approaching the front of the machine, and moving upward from the tracks. It culminated in the crown of the radiator core, just in front of the radiator cap; and suddenly an area of six or seven square inches literally *blurred* around the edges. For a second, then, it was normal, and finally it slumped molten, and liquid metal ran down the sides, throwing out little sparks as it encountered what was left of the charred paint. And only then was Kelly conscious of agony in his left hand. He looked down. The welding machine's generator had stopped, though the motor was still turning, having smashed the friable coupling on its drive shaft. Smoke poured from the generator, which had become little more than a heap of slag. Kelly did not scream, though, until he looked and saw what had happened to his hand—

When he could see straight again, he called for Tom, and there was no answer. At last he saw something out in the water, and plunged in after it. The splash of cold salt water on his left hand he hardly felt, for the numbness of shock had set in. He grabbed at Tom's shirt with his good hand, and then the ground seemed to pull itself out from under his feet. That was it, then—a deep hole right off the beach. The Seven had run right to the edge of it, had kept Tom there out of his depth and—

He flailed wildly, struck out for the beach, so near and so hard to get to. He gulped a stinging lungful of brine, and only the lovely shock of his knee striking solid beach kept him from giving up to the luxury of choking to death. Sobbing with effort, he dragged Tom's dead weight inshore and clear of the surf. It was then that he became conscious of a child's shrill weeping; for a mad moment he thought it was himself, and then he looked and saw that it was Al Knowles. He left Tom and went over to the broken creature.

"Get up, you," he snarled. The weeping only got louder. Kelly rolled him over on his back—he was quite unresisting—and belted him back and forth across the mouth until Al began to choke. Then he hauled him to his feet and led him over to Tom.

"Kneel down, scum. Put one of your knees between his knees." Al stood still. Kelly hit him again and he did as he was told.

"Put your hands on his lower ribs. There. O.K. Lean, you rat. Now sit back." He sat down, holding his left wrist in his right hand, letting the blood drop from the ruined hand. "Lean. Hold it—sit back. Lean. Sit. Lean. Sit."

Soon Tom sighed and began to vomit weakly, and after that he was all right.

This is the story of *Daisy Etta*, the bulldozer that went mad and had a life of its own, and not the story of the flat-top *Marokuru* of the Imperial Japanese Navy, which has been told elsewhere. But there is a connection. You will remember how the *Marokuru* was cut off from its base by the concentrated attack on Truk, how it slipped far to the south and east and was sunk nearer to our shores than any other Jap warship in the whole course of the war. And you will remember how a squadron of five planes, having been separated by three vertical miles of water from their flight deck, turned east with their bombloads and droned away for a suicide mission. You read that they bombed a minor airfield in the outside of Panama's far-flung defenses, and all hands crashed in the best sacrificial fashion.

Well, that was no airfield, no matter what it might have looked like from the air. It was simply a roughly graded runway, white marl against brown scrub-grass.

The planes came two days after the death of *Daisy Etta*, as Tom and Kelly sat in the shadow of the pile of fuel drums, down in the coolness of the swag that *Daisy* had dug there to fuel herself. They were poring over paper and pencil, trying to complete the impossible task of making a written statement of what had happened on the island, and why they and their company had failed to complete their contract. They had found Chub and Harris, and had buried them next to the other three. Al Knowles was tied up in the camp, because they had heard him raving in his sleep, and it seemed he could not believe that *Daisy* was dead and he still wanted to go around killing operators for her. They knew that there must be an investigation, and they knew just how far their story would go; and having escaped a monster like *Daisy Etta,* life was far too sweet for them to want to be shot for sabotage. And murder.

The first stick of bombs struck three hundred yards behind them at the edge of the camp, and at the same instant a plane whistled low over their heads, and that was the first they knew about it. They ran to Al Knowles and untied his feet and the three of them headed for the bush. They found refuge, strangely enough, inside the mound where *Daisy Etta* had first met her possessor.

"Bless their black little hearts," said Kelly as he and Tom stood on the bluff and looked at the flaming wreckage of a camp and five medium bombers below them. And he took the statement they had been sweating out and tore it across.

"But what about him?" said Tom, pointing at Al Knowles, who was sitting on the ground, playing with his fingers. "He'll still spill the whole thing, no matter if we do try to blame it all on the bombing."

"What's the matter with that?" said Kelly.

Tom thought a minute, then grinned. "Why, nothing! That's just the sort of thing they'll expect from him!"

NO WOMAN BORN

Astounding,
December

by C. L. Moore

The mid-1940's were truly great years in the writing career of Catherine L. Moore, both individually and in collaboration with her husband, Henry Kuttner. This story was (we think) hers alone, and it is certainly her finest solo effort. The concept of the "cyborg," part-machine and part-human, had existed in science fiction before this story was published, but no one had explored the potential of the idea until "No Woman Born." It was also one of the first to examine the future of the arts in science fiction, and a classic story of anguish and rebirth.

(A couple of years ago, I attended a science fiction convention at which Catherine Moore was scheduled to speak. I was eager to see her for I had met her only once and that was thirty-five years before. She looked amazingly youthful still, and gave a good talk. It was delightful to see how lightly the years rested upon her. It helped, I am sure, that she was married again, and happily. Why not? Poor Hank had been dead for twenty years. —And yet, no one dating back to the older days of science fiction could think of Moore without Kuttner or Kuttner without Moore and I sat there feeling dissociated. How could they have been separated— I.A.)

She had been the loveliest creature whose image ever moved along the airways. John Harris, who was once her manager, remembered doggedly how beautiful she had been as he rose in the silent elevator toward the room where Deirdre sat waiting for him.

Since the theater fire that had destroyed her a year ago, he had never been quite able to let himself remember her beauty clearly, except when some old poster, half in tatters, flaunted her face at him, or a maudlin memorial program flashed her image unexpectedly across the television screen. But now he had to remember.

The elevator came to a sighing stop and the door slid open. John Harris hesitated. He knew in his mind that he had to go on, but his reluctant muscles almost refused him. He was thinking helplessly, as he had not allowed himself to think until this moment, of the fabulous grace that had poured through her wonderful dancer's body, remembering her soft and husky voice with the little burr in it that had fascinated the audiences of the whole world.

There had never been anyone so beautiful.

In times before her, other actresses had been lovely and adulated, but never before Deirdre's day had the entire world been able to take one woman so wholly to its heart. So few outside the capitals had ever seen Bernhardt or the fabulous Jersey Lily. And the beauties of the movie screen had had to limit their audiences to those who could reach the theaters. But Deirdre's image had once moved glowingly across the television screens of every home in the civilized world. And in many outside the bounds of civilization. Her soft, husky songs had sounded in the depths of jungles, her lovely, languorous body had woven its patterns of rhythm in desert tents and polar huts. The whole world knew every smooth motion of her body and every cadence of her voice, and the way a subtle radiance had seemed to go on behind her features when she smiled.

And the whole world had mourned her when she died in the theater fire.

Harris could not quite think of her as other than dead, though he knew what sat waiting him in the room ahead. He kept remembering the old words James Stephens wrote long ago for another Deirdre, also lovely and beloved and unforgotten after two thousand years.

The time comes when our hearts sink utterly,
When we remember Deirdre and her tale,
And that her lips are dust. . . .
There has been again no woman born
Who was so beautiful; not one so beautiful
Of all the women born—

That wasn't quite true, of course—there had been one. Or maybe, after all, this Deirdre who died only a year ago had not been beautiful in the sense of perfection. He thought the other one might not have been either, for there are always women with perfection of feature in the world, and they are not the ones that legend remembers. It was the light within, shining through her charming, imperfect features, that had made this Deirdre's face so lovely. No one else he had ever seen had anything like the magic of the lost Deirdre.

Let all men go apart and mourn together—
No man can ever love her. Not a man
Can dream to be her lover. . . . No man say—
What could one say to her? There are no words
That one could say to her.

No, no words at all. And it was going to be impossible to go through with this. Harris knew it overwhelmingly just as his finger touched the buzzer. But the door opened almost instantly, and then it was too late.

Maltzer stood just inside, peering out through his heavy spectacles. You could see how tensely he had been waiting. Harris was a little shocked to see that the man was trembling. It was hard to think of the confident and imperturbable Maltzer, whom he had known briefly a year ago, as shaken like this. He wondered if Deirdre herself were as tremulous with sheer nerves—but it was not time yet to let himself think of that.

"Come in, come in," Maltzer said irritably. There was no reason for irritation. The year's work, so much of it in secrecy and solitude, must have tried him physically and mentally to the very breaking point.

"She all right?" Harris asked inanely, stepping inside.

"Oh yes . . . yes, *she's* all right." Maltzer bit his thumbnail and glanced over his shoulder at an inner door, where Harris guessed she would be waiting.

"No," Maltzer said, as he took an involuntary step toward it. "We'd better have a talk first. Come over and sit down. Drink?"

Harris nodded, and watched Maltzer's hands tremble as he tilted the decanter. The man was clearly on the very verge of collapse, and Harris felt a sudden cold uncertainty open up in him in the one place where until now he had been oddly confident.

"She *is* all right?" he demanded, taking the glass.

"Oh yes, she's perfect. She's so confident it scares me." Maltzer gulped his drink and poured another before he sat down.

"What's wrong, then?"

"Nothing, I guess. Or . . . well, I don't know. I'm not sure anymore. I've worked toward this meeting for nearly a year, but now—well, I'm not sure it's time yet. I'm just not sure."

He stared at Harris, his eyes large and blurred behind the lenses. He was a thin, wire-taut man with all the bone and sinew showing plainly beneath the dark skin of his face. Thinner now than he had been a year ago when Harris saw him last.

"I've been too close to her," he said now. "I have no perspective anymore. All I can see is my own work. And I'm just not sure that's ready yet for you or anyone to see."

"She thinks so?"

"I never saw a woman so confident." Maltzer drank, the glass clicking on his teeth. He looked up suddenly through the distorting lenses. "Of course a failure now would mean— well, absolute collapse," he said.

Harris nodded. He was thinking of the year of incredibly painstaking work that lay behind this meeting, the immense fund of knowledge, of infinite patience, the secret collaboration of artists, sculptors, designers, scientists, and the genius of Maltzer governing them all as an orchestra conductor governs his players.

He was thinking too, with a certain unreasoning jealousy, of the strange, cold, passionless intimacy between Maltzer and Deirdre in that year, a closer intimacy than any two humans can ever have shared before. In a sense the Deirdre whom he saw in a few minutes would *be* Maltzer, just as he thought he detected in Maltzer now and then small mannerisms of inflection and motion that had been Deirdre's own. There had been between them a sort of unimaginable marriage stranger than anything that could ever have taken place before.

"—so many complications," Maltzer was saying in his worried voice with its faintest possible echo of Deirdre's lovely, cadenced rhythm. (The sweet, soft huskiness he would never hear again.) "There was shock, of course. Terrible shock. And a great fear of fire. We had to conquer that before we could take the first steps. But we did it. When you go in you'll probably find her sitting before the fire." He caught the startled question in Harris' eyes and smiled. "No, she can't feel the warmth now, of course. But she likes to watch the flames. She's mastered any abnormal fear of them quite beautifully."

"She can—" Harris hesitated. "Her eyesight's normal now?"

"Perfect," Maltzer said. "Perfect vision was fairly simple to provide. After all, that sort of thing has already been worked out, in other connections. I might even say her vision's a little better than perfect, from our own standpoint." He shook his head irritably. "I'm not worried about the mechanics of the thing. Luckily they got to her before the brain was touched at all. Shock was the only danger to her sensory centers, and we took care of all that first of all, as soon as communication could be established. Even so, it needed great courage on her part. Great courage." He was silent for a moment, staring into his empty glass.

"Harris," he said suddenly, without looking up, "have I made a mistake? Should we have let her die?"

Harris shook his head helplessly. It was an unanswerable question. It had tormented the whole world for a year now. There had been hundreds of answers and thousands of words written on the subject. Has anyone the right to preserve a brain alive when its body is destroyed? Even if a new body can be provided, necessarily so very unlike the old?

"It's not that she's—ugly—now," Maltzer went on hurriedly, as if afraid of an answer. "Metal isn't ugly. And Deirdre . . . well, you'll see. I tell you, I can't see myself. I know the whole mechanism so well—it's just mechanics to me. Maybe she's—grotesque. I don't know. Often I've wished I hadn't been on the spot, with all my ideas, just when the

fire broke out. Or that it could have been anyone but
Deirdre. She was so beautiful— Still, if it had been someone
else I think the whole thing might have failed completely. It
takes more than just an uninjured brain. It takes strength and
courage beyond common, and—well, something more. Something—unquenchable. Deirdre has it. She's still Deirdre. In a
way she's still beautiful. But I'm not sure anybody but myself
could see that. And you know what she plans?"

"No—what?"

"She's going back on the air-screen."

Harris looked at him in stunned disbelief.

"She *is* still beautiful," Maltzer told him fiercely. "She's got
courage, and a serenity that amazes me. And she isn't in the
least worried or resentful about what's happened. Or afraid
what the verdict of the public will be. But I am, Harris. I'm
terrified."

They looked at each other for a moment more, neither
speaking. Then Maltzer shrugged and stood up.

"She's in there," he said, gesturing with his glass.

Harris turned without a word, not giving himself time to
hesitate. He crossed toward the inner door.

The room was full of a soft, clear, indirect light that cli-
maxed in the fire crackling on a white tiled hearth. Harris
paused inside the door, his heart beating thickly. He did not
see her for a moment. It was a perfectly commonplace room,
bright, light, with pleasant furniture, and flowers on the
tables. Their perfume was sweet on the clear air. He did not
see Deirdre.

Then a chair by the fire creaked as she shifted her weight
in it. The high back hid her, but she spoke. And for one
dreadful moment it was the voice of an automaton that
sounded in the room, metallic, without inflection.

"Hel-lo—" said the voice. Then she laughed and tried
again. And it was the old, familiar, sweet huskiness he had
not hoped to hear again as long as he lived.

In spite of himself he said, "Deirdre!" and her image rose
before him as if she herself had risen unchanged from the
chair, tall, golden, swaying a little with her wonderful
dancer's poise, the lovely, imperfect features lighted by the
glow that made them beautiful. It was the cruelest thing his
memory could have done to him. And yet the voice—after
that one lapse, the voice was perfect.

"Come and look at me, John," she said.

He crossed the floor slowly, forcing himself to move. That instant's flash of vivid recollection had nearly wrecked his hard-won composure. He tried to keep his mind perfectly blank as he came at last to the verge of seeing what no one but Maltzer had so far seen or known about in its entirety. No one at all had known what shape would be forged to clothe the most beautiful woman on Earth, now that her beauty was gone.

He had envisioned many shapes. Great, lurching robot forms, cylindrical, with hinged arms and legs. A glass case with the brain floating in it and appendages to serve its needs. Grotesque visions, like nightmares come nearly true. And each more inadequate than the last, for what metal shape could possibly do more than house ungraciously the mind and brain that had once enchanted a whole world?

Then he came around the wing of the chair, and saw her.

The human brain is often too complicated a mechanism to function perfectly. Harris's brain was called upon now to perform a very elaborate series of shifting impressions. First, incongruously, he remembered a curious inhuman figure he had once glimpsed leaning over the fence rail outside a farmhouse. For an instant the shape had stood up, integrated, ungainly, impossibly human, before the glancing eye resolved it into an arrangement of brooms and buckets. What the eye had found only roughly humanoid, the suggestible brain had accepted fully formed. It was thus now, with Deirdre.

The first impression that his eyes and mind took from sight of her was shocked and incredulous, for his brain said to him unbelievingly, *"This is Deirdre! She hasn't changed at all!"*

Then the shift of perspective took over, and even more shockingly, eye and brain said, "No, not Deirdre—not human. Nothing but metal coils. Not Deirdre at all—" And that was the worst. It was like waking from a dream of someone beloved and lost, and facing anew, after that heartbreaking reassurance of sleep, the inflexible fact that nothing can bring the lost to life again. Deirdre was gone, and this was only machinery heaped in a flowered chair.

Then the machinery moved, exquisitely, smoothly, with a grace as familiar as the swaying form he remembered. The sweet, husky voice of Deirdre said,

"It's me, John darling. It really is, you know."

And it was.

That was the third metamorphosis, and the final one. Illusion steadied and became factual, real. It was Deirdre.

He sat down bonelessly. He had no muscles. He looked at her speechless and unthinking, letting his senses take in the sight of her without trying to rationalize what he saw.

She was golden still. They had kept that much of her, the first impression of warmth and color which had once belonged to her sleek hair and the apricot tints of her skin. But they had had the good sense to go no further. They had not tried to make a wax image of the lost Deirdre. (*No woman born who was so beautiful—Not one so beautiful, of all the women born—*)

And so she had no face. She had only a smooth, delicately modeled ovoid for her head, with a . . . a sort of crescent-shaped mask across the frontal area where her eyes would have been if she had needed eyes. A narrow, curved quarter-moon, with the horns turned upward. It was filled in with something translucent, like cloudy crystal, and tinted the aquamarine of the eyes Deirdre used to have. Through that, then, she saw the world. Through that she looked without eyes, and behind it, as behind the eyes of a human—she was.

Except for that, she had no features. And it had been wise of those who designed her, he realized now. Subconsciously he had been dreading some clumsy attempt at human features that might creak like a marionette's in parodies of animation. The eyes, perhaps, had had to open in the same place upon her head, and at the same distance apart, to make easy for her an adjustment to the stereoscopic vision she used to have. But he was glad they had not given her two eye-shaped openings with glass marbles inside them. The mask was better.

(Oddly enough, he did not once think of the naked brain that must lie inside the metal. The mask was symbol enough for the woman within. It was enigmatic; you did not know if her gaze was on you searchingly, or wholly withdrawn. And it had no variations of brilliance such as once had played across the incomparable mobility of Deirdre's face. But eyes, even human eyes, are as a matter of fact enigmatic enough. They have no expression except what the lids impart; they take all animation from the features. We automatically watch the eyes of the friend we speak with, but if he happens to be lying down so that he speaks across his shoulder and his face is upside-down to us, quite as automatically we watch the mouth. The gaze keeps shifting nervously between mouth and eyes in their reversed order, for it is the position in the face, not the feature itself, which we are accustomed to accept as the seat of the soul. Deirdre's mask was in that proper place; it was easy to accept it as a mask over eyes.)

She had, Harris realized as the first shock quieted, a very beautifully shaped head—a bare, golden skull. She turned it a little, gracefully upon her neck of metal, and he saw that the artist who shaped it had given her the most delicate suggestion of cheekbones, narrowing in the blankness below the mask to the hint of a human face. Not too much. Just enough so that when the head turned you saw by its modeling that it had moved, lending perspective and foreshortening to the expressionless golden helmet. Light did not slip uninterrupted as if over the surface of a golden egg. Brancusi himself had never made anything more simple or more subtle than the modeling of Deirdre's head.

But all expression, of course, was gone. All expression had gone up in the smoke of the theater fire, with the lovely, mobile, radiant features which had meant Deirdre.

As for her body, he could not see its shape. A garment hid her. But they had made no incongruous attempt to give her back the clothing that once had made her famous. Even the softness of cloth would have called the mind too sharply to the remembrance that no human body lay beneath the folds, nor does metal need the incongruity of cloth for its protection. Yet without garments, he realized, she would have looked oddly naked, since her new body was humanoid, not angular machinery.

The designer had solved his paradox by giving her a robe of very fine metal mesh. It hung from the gentle slope of her shoulders in straight, pliant folds like a longer Grecian chlamys, flexible, yet with weight enough of its own not to cling too revealingly to whatever metal shape lay beneath.

The arms they had given her were left bare, and the feet and ankles. And Maltzer had performed his greatest miracle in the limbs of the new Deirdre. It was a mechanical miracle basically, but the eye appreciated first that he had also showed supreme artistry and understanding.

Her arms were pale shining gold, tapered smoothly, without modeling, and flexible their whole length in diminishing metal bracelets fitting one inside the other clear down to the slim, round wrists. The hands were more nearly human than any other feature about her, though they, too, were fitted together in delicate, small sections that slid upon one another with the flexibility almost of flesh. The fingers' bases were solider than human, and the fingers themselves tapered to longer tips.

Her feet, too, beneath the tapering broader rings of the metal ankles, had been constructed upon the model of human feet. Their finely tooled sliding segments gave her an arch and a heel and a flexible forward section formed almost like the *sollerets* of medieval armor.

She looked, indeed, very much like a creature in armor, with her delicately plated limbs and her featureless head like a helmet with a visor of glass, and her robe of chain-mail. But no knight in armor ever moved as Deirdre moved, or wore his armor upon a body of such inhumanly fine proportions. Only a knight from another world, or a knight of Oberon's court, might have shared that delicate likeness.

Briefly he had been surprised at the smallness and exquisite proportions of her. He had been expecting the ponderous mass of such robots as he had seen, wholly automatons. And then he realized that for them, much of the space had to be devoted to the inadequate mechanical brains that guided them about their duties. Deirdre's brain still preserved and proved the craftsmanship of an artisan far defter than man. Only the body was of metal, and it did not seem complex, though he had not yet been told how it was motivated.

Harris had no idea how long he sat staring at the figure in the cushioned chair. She was still lovely—indeed, she was still Deirdre—and as he looked he let the careful schooling of his face relax. There was no need to hide his thoughts from her.

She stirred upon the cushions, the long, flexible arms moving with a litheness that was not quite human. The motion disturbed him as the body itself had not, and in spite of himself his face froze a little. He had the feeling that from behind the crescent mask she was watching him very closely.

Slowly she rose.

The motion was very smooth. Also it was serpentine, as if the body beneath the coat of mail were made in the same interlocking sections as her limbs. He had expected and feared mechanical rigidity; nothing had prepared him for this more than human suppleness.

She stood quietly, letting the heavy mailed folds of her garment settle about her. They fell together with a faint ringing sound, like small bells far off, and hung beautifully in pale golden, sculptured folds. He had risen automatically as she did. Now he faced her, staring. He had never seen her stand perfectly still, and she was not doing it now. She swayed just a bit, vitality burning inextinguishably in her brain as once it had burned in her body, and stolid immobility was as impossible for her as it had always been. The golden garment caught points of light from the fire and glimmered at him with tiny reflections as she moved.

Then she put her featureless helmeted head a little to one side, and he heard her laughter as familiar in its small, throaty, intimate sound as he had ever heard it from her living throat. And every gesture, every attitude, every flowing of motion into motion was so utterly Deirdre that the overwhelming illusion swept his mind again and this was the flesh-and-blood woman as clearly as if he saw her standing there whole once more, like Phoenix from the fire.

"Well, John," she said in the soft, husky, amused voice he remembered perfectly. "Well, John, is it I?" She knew it was. Perfect assurance sounded in the voice. "The shock will wear off, you know. It'll be easier and easier as time goes on. I'm quite used to myself now. See?"

She turned away from him and crossed the room smoothly, with the old, poised, dancer's glide, to the mirror that paneled one side of the room. And before it, as he had so often seen her preen before, he watched her preening now, running flexible metallic hands down the folds of her metal garment, turning to admire herself over one metal shoulder, making the mailed folds tinkle and sway as she struck an arabesque position before the glass.

His knees let him down into the chair she had vacated. Mingled shock and relief loosened all his muscles in him, and she was more poised and confident than he.

"It's a miracle," he said with conviction. "It's *you*. But I don't see how—" He had meant, "—how, without face or body—" but clearly he could not finish that sentence.

She finished it for him in her own mind, and answered without self-consciousness. "It's motion, mostly," she said,

still admiring her own suppleness in the mirror. "See?" And
very lightly on her springy, armored feet she flashed through
an enchaînement of brilliant steps, swinging round with a
pirouette to face him. "That was what Maltzer and I worked
out between us, after I began to get myself under control
again." Her voice was somber for a moment, remembering a
dark time in the past. Then she went on, "It wasn't easy, of
course, but it was fascinating. You'll never guess how fascinating, John! We knew we couldn't work out anything like a
facsimile of the way I used to look, so we had to find some
other basis to build on. And motion is the other basis of
recognition, after actual physical likeness."

She moved lightly across the carpet toward the window
and stood looking down, her featureless face averted a little
and the light shining across the delicately hinted curves of the
cheekbones.

"Luckily," she said, her voice amused, "I never was beautiful. It was all—well, vivacity, I suppose, and muscular co-or-
dination. Years and years of training, and all of it engraved
here"—she struck her golden helmet a light, ringing blow
with golden knuckles—"in the habit patterns grooved into my
brain. So this body . . . did he tell you? . . . works entirely
through the brain. Electromagnetic currents flowing along
from ring to ring, like this." She rippled a boneless arm at
him with a motion like flowing water. "Nothing holds me together—nothing!—except muscles of magnetic currents. And
if I'd been somebody else—somebody who moved differently,
why the flexible rings would have moved differently too,
guided by the impulse from another brain. I'm not conscious
of doing anything I haven't always done. The same impulses
that used to go out to my muscles go out now to—this." And
she made a shuddering, serpentine motion of both arms at
him, like a Cambodian dancer, and then laughed wholeheart-
edly, the sound of it ringing through the room with such
full-throated merriment that he could not help seeing again
the familiar face crinkled with pleasure, the white teeth shining. "It's all perfectly subconscious now," she told him. "It
took lots of practice at first, of course, but now even my
signature looks just as it always did—the coordination is
duplicated that delicately." She rippled her arms at him
again and chuckled.

"But the voice, too," Harris protested inadequately. "It's *your* voice, Deirdre."

"The voice isn't only a matter of throat construction and breath control, my darling Johnnie! At least, so Professor Maltzer assured me a year ago, and I certainly haven't any reason to doubt him!" She laughed again. She was laughing a little too much, with a touch of the bright, hysteric overexcitement he remembered so well. But if any woman ever had reason for mild hysteria, surely Deirdre had it now.

The laughter rippled and ended, and she went on, her voice eager. "He says voice control is almost wholly a matter of hearing what you produce, once you've got adequate mechanism, of course. That's why deaf people, with the same vocal chords as ever, let their voices change completely and lose all inflection when they've been deaf long enough. And luckily, you see, I'm not deaf!"

She swung around to him, the folds of her robe twinkling and ringing, and rippled up and up a clear, true scale to a lovely high note, and then cascaded down again like water over a falls. But she left him no time for applause. "Perfectly simple, you see. All it took was a little matter of genius from the professor to get it worked out for me! He started with a new variation of the old Vodor you must remember hearing about, years ago. Originally, of course, the thing was ponderous. You know how it worked—speech broken down to a few basic sounds and built up again in combinations produced from a keyboard. I think originally the sounds were a sort of *ktch* and a *shooshing* noise, but we've got it all worked to a flexibility and range quite as good as human now. All I do is—well, mentally play on the keyboard of my . . . my sound-unit, I suppose it's called. It's much more complicated than that, of course, but I've learned to do it unconsciously. And I regulate it by ear, quite automatically now. If you were—*here*—instead of me, and you'd had the same practice, your own voice would be coming out of the same keyboard and diaphragm instead of mine. It's all a matter of the brain patterns that operated the body and now operate the machinery. They send out very strong impulses that are stepped up as much as necessary somewhere or other in here—" Her hands waved vaguely over the mesh-robed body.

She was silent a moment, looking out the window. Then she turned away and crossed the floor to the fire, sinking again into the flowered chair. Her helmet-skull turned its mask to face him and he could feel a quiet scrutiny behind the aquamarine of its gaze.

"It's—odd," she said, "being here in this . . . this . . . instead of a body. But not as odd or as alien as you might think. I've thought about it a lot—I've had plenty of time to think—and I've begun to realize what a tremendous force the human ego really is. I'm not sure I want to suggest it has any mystical power it can impress on mechanical things, but it does seem to have a power of some sort. It does instill its own force into inanimate objects, and they take on a personality of their own. People do impress their personalities on the houses they live in, you know. I've noticed that often. Even empty rooms. And it happens with other things too, especially, I think, with inanimate things that men depend on for their lives. Ships, for instance—they always have personalities of their own.

"And planes—in wars you always hear of planes crippled too badly to fly, but struggling back anyhow with their crews. Even guns acquire a sort of ego. Ships and guns and planes are 'she' to the men who operate them and depend on them for their lives. It's as if machinery with complicated moving parts almost simulates life, and does acquire from the men who used it—well, not exactly life, of course—but a personality. I don't know what. Maybe it absorbs some of the actual electrical impulses their brains throw off, especially in times of stress.

"Well, after awhile I began to accept the idea that this new body of mine could behave at least as responsively as a ship or a plane. Quite apart from the fact that my own brain controls its 'muscles.' I believe there's an affinity between men and the machines they make. They make them out of their own brains, really, a sort of mental conception and gestation, and the result responds to the minds that created them, and to all human minds that understand and manipulate them."

She stirred uneasily and smoothed a flexible hand along her mesh-robed metal thigh. "So this is myself," she said. "Metal—but me. And it grows more and more myself the longer I live in it. It's my house and the machine my life depends on, but much more intimately in each case than any real house or machine ever was before to any other human. And you know, I wonder if in time I'll forget what flesh felt like—my own flesh, when I touched it like this—and the metal against the metal will be so much the same I'll never even notice?"

Harris did not try to answer her. He sat without moving, watching her expressionless face. In a moment she went on.

"I'll tell you the best thing, John," she said, her voice softening to the old intimacy he remembered so well that he could see superimposed upon the blank skull the warm, intent look that belonged with the voice. "I'm not going to live forever. It may not sound like a—best thing—but it is, John. You know, for a while that was the worst of all, after I knew I was—after I woke up again. The thought of living on and on in a body that wasn't mine, seeing everyone I knew grow old and die, and not being able to stop—

"But Maltzer says my brain will probably wear out quite normally—except, of course, that I won't have to worry about looking old!—and when it gets tired and stops, the body I'm in won't be any longer. The magnetic muscles that hold it into my own shape and motions will let go when the brain lets go, and there'll be nothing but a . . . a pile of disconnected rings. If they ever assemble it again, it won't be me." She hesitated. "I like that, John," she said, and he felt from behind the mask a searching of his face.

He knew and understood that somber satisfaction. He could not put it into words; neither of them wanted to do that. But he understood. It was the conviction of mortality, in spite of her immortal body. She was not cut off from the rest of her race in the essence of their humanity, for though she wore a body of steel and they perishable flesh, yet she must perish too, and the same fears and faiths still united her to mortals and humans, though she wore the body of Oberon's inhuman knight. Even in her death she must be unique—dissolution in a shower of tinkling and clashing rings, he thought, and almost envied her the finality and beauty of that particular death—but afterward, oneness with humanity in however much or little awaited them all. So she could feel that this exile in metal was only temporary, in spite of everything.

(And providing, of course, that the mind inside the metal did not veer from its inherited humanity as the years went by. A dweller in a house may impress his personality upon the walls, but subtly the walls too, may impress their own shape upon the ego of the man. Neither of them thought of that, at the time.)

Deirdre sat a moment longer in silence. Then the mood vanished and she rose again, spinning so that the robe belled out ringing about her ankles. She rippled another scale up and down, faultlessly and with the same familiar sweetness of tone that had made her famous.

"So I'm going right back on the stage, John," she said serenely. "I can still sing. I can still dance. I'm still myself in everything that matters, and I can't imagine doing anything else for the rest of my life."

He could not answer without stammering a little. "Do you think . . . will they accept you, Deirdre? After all—"

"They'll accept me," she said in that confident voice. "Oh, they'll come to see a freak at first, of course, but they'll stay to watch—Deirdre. And come back again and again just as they always did. You'll see, my dear."

But hearing her sureness, suddenly Harris himself was unsure. Maltzer had not been, either. She was so regally confident, and disappointment would be so deadly a blow at all that remained of her—

She was so delicate a being now, really. Nothing but a glowing and radiant mind poised in metal, dominating it, bending the steel to the illusion of her lost loveliness with a sheer self-confidence that gleamed through the metal body. But the brain sat delicately on its base of reason. She had been through intolerable stresses already, perhaps more terrible depths of despair and self-knowledge than any human brain had yet endured before her, for—since Lazarus himself—who had come back from the dead?

But if the world did not accept her as beautiful, what then? If they laughed, or pitied her, or came only to watch a jointed freak performing as if on strings where the loveliness of Deirdre had once enchanted them, what then? And he could not be perfectly sure they would not. He had known her too well in the flesh to see her objectively even now, in metal. Every inflection of her voice called up the vivid memory of the face that had flashed its evanescent beauty in some look to match the tone. She was Deirdre to Harris simply because she had been so intimately familiar in every pose and attitude, through so many years. But people who knew her only slightly, or saw her for the first time in metal—what would they see?

A marionette? Or the real grace and loveliness shining through?

He had no possible way of knowing. He saw her too clearly as she had been to see her now at all, except so linked with the past that she was not wholly metal. And he knew what Maltzer feared, for Maltzer's psychic blindness toward her lay at the other extreme. He had never known Deirdre except as a machine, and he could not see her objectively any more than Harris could. To Maltzer she was pure metal, a robot his own hands and brain had devised, mysteriously animated by the mind of Deirdre, to be sure, but to all outward seeming a thing of metal solely. He had worked so long over each intricate part of her body, he knew so well how every jointure in it was put together, that he could not see the whole. He had studied many film records of her, of course, as she used to be, in order to gauge the accuracy of his facsimile, but this thing he had made was a copy only. He was too close to Deirdre to see her. And Harris, in a way, was too far. The indomitable Deirdre herself shone so vividly through the metal that his mind kept superimposing one upon the other.

How would an audience react to her? Where in the scale between these two extremes would their verdict fall?

For Deirdre, there was only one possible answer.

"I'm not worried," Deirdre said serenely, and spread her golden hands to the fire to watch lights dancing in reflection upon their shining surfaces. "I'm still myself. I've always had . . . well, power over my audiences. Any good performer knows when he's got it. Mine isn't gone. I can still give them what I always gave, only now with greater variations and more depths than I ever have done before. Why, look—" She gave a little wriggle of excitement.

"You know the arabesque principle—getting the longest possible distance from fingertip to toetip with a long, slow curve through the whole length? And the brace of the other leg and arm giving contrast? Well, look at me. I don't work on hinges now. I can make every motion a long curve if I want to. My body's different enough now to work out a whole new school of dancing. Of course there'll be things I used to do that I won't attempt now—no more dancing *sur*

les pointes, for instance—but the new things will more than
balance the loss. I've been practicing. Do you know I can
turn a hundred *fouettés* now without a flaw? And I think I
could go right on and turn a thousand, if I wanted."

She made the firelight flash on her hands, and her robe
rang musically as she moved her shoulders a little. "I've
already worked out one new dance for myself," she said.
"God knows I'm no choreographer, but I did want to experiment first. Later, you know, really creative men like Massan-
chine or Fokhileff may want to do something entirely new for
me—a whole new sequence of movements based on a new
technique. And music—that could be quite different, too. Oh,
there's no end to the possibilities! Even my voice has more
range and power. Luckily I'm not an actress—it would be
silly to try to play Camille or Juliet with a cast of ordinary
people. Not that I couldn't, you know." She turned her head
to stare at Harris through the mask of glass. "I honestly think
I could. But it isn't necessary. There's too much else. Oh, I'm
not worried!"

"Maltzer's worried," Harris reminded her.

She swung away from the fire, her metal robe ringing, and
into her voice came the old note of distress that went with a
furrowing of her forehead and a sideways tilt of the head.
The head went sideways as it had always done, and he could
see the furrowed brow almost as clearly as if flesh still
clothed her.

"I know. And I'm worried about him, John. He's worked
so awfully hard over me. This is the doldrums now, the let-
down period, I suppose. I know what's on his mind. He's
afraid I'll look just the same to the world as I look to him.
Tooled metal. He's in a position no one ever quite achieved
before, isn't he? Rather like God." Her voice rippled a little
with amusement. "I suppose to God we must look like a collection of cells and corpuscles ourselves. But Maltzer lacks a
god's detached viewpoint."

"He can't see you as I do, anyhow." Harris was choosing
his words with difficulty. "I wonder, though—would it help
him any if you postponed your debut awhile? You've been
with him too closely, I think. You don't quite realize how
near a breakdown he is. I was shocked when I saw him just
now."

The golden head shook. "No. He's close to a breaking

point, maybe, but I think the only cure's action. He wants me to retire and stay out of sight, John. Always. He's afraid for anyone to see me except a few old friends who remember me as I was. People he can trust to be—kind." She laughed. It was very strange to hear that ripple of mirth from the blank, unfeatured skull. Harris was seized with sudden panic at the thought of what reaction it might evoke in an audience of strangers. As if he had spoken the fear aloud, her voice denied it. "I don't need kindness. And it's no kindness to Maltzer to hide me under a bushel. He *has* worked too hard, I know. He's driven himself to a breaking point. But it'll be a complete negation of all he's worked for if I hide myself now. You don't know what a tremendous lot of geniuses and artistry went into me, John. The whole idea from the start was to recreate what I'd lost so that it could be proved that beauty and talent need not be sacrificed by the destruction of parts or all the body.

"It wasn't only for me that we meant to prove that. There'll be others who suffer injuries that once might have ruined them. This was to end all suffering like that forever. It was Maltzer's gift to the whole race as well as to me. He's really a humanitarian, John, like most great men. He'd never have given up a year of his life to this work if it had been for any one individual alone. He was seeing thousands of others beyond me as he worked. And I won't let him ruin all he's achieved because he's afraid to prove it now he's got it. The whole wonderful achievement will be worthless if I don't take the final step. I think his breakdown, in the end, would be worse and more final if I never tried than if I tried and failed."

Harris sat in silence. There was no answer he could make to that. He hoped the little twinge of shamefaced jealousy he suddenly felt did not show, as he was reminded anew of the intimacy closer than marriage which had of necessity bound these two together. And he knew that any reaction of his would in its way be almost as prejudiced as Maltzer's, for a reason at once the same and entirely opposite. Except that he himself came fresh to the problem, while Maltzer's viewpoint was colored by a year of overwork and physical and mental exhaustion.

"What are you going to do?" he asked.

She was standing before the fire when he spoke, swaying

just a little so that highlights danced all along her golden body. Now she turned with a serpentine grace and sank into the cushioned chair beside her. It came to him suddenly that she was much more than humanly graceful—quite as much as he had once feared she would be less than human.

"I've already arranged for a performance," she told him, her voice a little shaken with a familiar mixture of excitement and defiance.

Harris sat up with a start. "How? Where? There hasn't been any publicity at all yet, has there? I didn't know—"

"Now, now, Johnnie," her amused voice soothed him. "You'll be handling everything just as usual once I get started back to work—that is, if you still want to. But this I've arranged for myself. It's going to be a surprise. I . . . I felt it had to be a surprise." She wriggled a little among the cushions. "Audience psychology is something I've always felt rather than known, and I do feel this is the way it ought to be done. There's no precedent. Nothing like this ever happened before. I'll have to go by my own intuition."

"You mean it's to be a complete surprise?"

"I think it must be. I don't want the audience coming in with preconceived ideas. I want them to see me exactly as I am now *first*, before they know who or what they're seeing. They must realize I can still give as good a performance as ever before they remember and compare it with my past performances. I don't want them to come ready to pity my handicaps—I haven't got any!—or full of morbid curiosity. So I'm going on the air after the regular eight-o'clock telecast of the feature from Teleo City. I'm just going to do one specialty in the usual vaude program. It's all been arranged. They'll build up to it, of course, as the highlight of the evening, but they aren't to say who I am until the end of the performance—if the audience hasn't recognized me already, by then."

"Audience?"

"Of course. Surely you haven't forgotten they still play to a theater audience at Teleo City? That's why I want to make my debut there. I've always played better when there were people in the studio, so I could gauge reactions. I think most performers do. Anyhow, it's all arranged."

"'Does Maltzer know?"

She wriggled uncomfortably. "Not yet."

"But he'll have to give his permission too, won't he? I mean—"

"Now look, John! That's another idea you and Maltzer will have to get out of your minds. I don't belong to him. In a way he's just been my doctor through a long illness, but I'm free to discharge him whenever I choose. If there were ever any legal disagreement, I suppose he'd be entitled to quite a lot of money for the work he's done on my new body—for the body itself, really, since it's his own machine, in one sense. But he doesn't own it, or me. I'm not sure just how the question would be decided by the courts—there again, we've got a problem without precedent. The body may be his work, but the brain that makes it something more than a collection of metal rings is *me,* and he couldn't restrain me against my will even if he wanted to. Not legally, and not—" She hesitated oddly and looked away. For the first time Harris was aware of something beneath the surface of her mind which was quite strange to him.

"Well, anyhow," she went on, "that question won't come up. Maltzer and I have been much too close in the past year to clash over anything as essential as this. He knows in his heart that I'm right, and he won't try to restrain me. His work won't be completed until I do what I was built to do. And I intend to do it."

That strange little quiver of something—something un-Deirdre—which had so briefly trembled beneath the surface of familiarity stuck in Harris's mind as something he must recall and examine later. Now he said only, "All right. I suppose I agree with you. How soon are you going to do it?"

She turned her head so that even the glass mask through which she looked out at the world was foreshortened away from him, and the golden helmet with its hint of sculptured cheekbone was entirely enigmatic.

"Tonight," she said.

Maltzer's thin hand shook so badly that he could not turn the dial. He tried twice and then laughed nervously and shrugged at Harris.

"You get her," he said.

Harris glanced at his watch. "It isn't time yet. She won't be on for half an hour."

Maltzer made a gesture of violent impatience. "Get it, get it!"

Harris shrugged a little in turn and twisted the dial. On the tilted screen above them shadows and sound blurred together and then clarified into a somber medieval hall, vast, vaulted, people in bright costumes moving like pygmies through its dimness. Since the play concerned Mary of Scotland, the actors were dressed in something approximating Elizabethan garb, but as every era tends to translate costume into terms of the current fashions, the women's hair was dressed in a style that would have startled Elizabeth, and their footgear was entirely anachronistic.

The hall dissolved and a face swam up into soft focus upon the screen. The dark, lush beauty of the actress who was playing the Stuart queen glowed at them in velvety perfection from the clouds of her pearl-strewn hair. Maltzer groaned.

"She's competing with *that*," he said hollowly.

"You think she can't?"

Maltzer slapped the chair arms with angry palms. Then the quivering of his fingers seemed suddenly to strike him, and he muttered to himself, "Look at 'em! I'm not even fit to handle a hammer and saw." But the mutter was an aside. "Of course she can't compete," he cried irritably. "She hasn't any sex. She isn't female any more. She doesn't know that yet, but she'll learn."

Harris stared at him, feeling a little stunned. Somehow the thought had not occurred to him before at all, so vividly had the illusion of the old Deirdre hung about the new one.

"She's an abstraction now," Maltzer went on, drumming his palms upon the chair in quick, nervous rhythms. "I don't know what it'll do to her, but there'll be change. Remember Abelard? She's lost everything that made her essentially what the public wanted, and she's going to find it out the hard way. After that——" He grimaced savagely and was silent.

"She hasn't lost everything," Harris defended. "She can dance and sing as well as ever, maybe better. She still has grace and charm and——"

"Yes, but where did the grace and charm come from? Not out of the habit patterns in her brain. No, out of human contacts, out of all the things that stimulate sensitive minds to creativeness. And she's lost three of her five senses. Everything she can't see and hear is gone. One of the strongest stimuli to a woman of her type was the knowledge of sex competition. You know how she sparkled when a man came into the room? All that's gone, and it was an essential. You know how liquor stimulated her? She's lost that. She couldn't taste food or drink even if she needed it. Perfume, flowers, all the odors we respond to mean nothing to her now. She can't feel anything with tactual delicacy any more. She used to surround herself with luxuries—she drew her stimuli from them—and that's all gone too. She's withdrawn from all physical contacts."

He squinted at the screen, not seeing it, his face drawn into lines like the lines of a skull. All flesh seemed to have dissolved off his bones in the past year, and Harris thought almost jealously that even in that way he seemed to be drawing nearer Deirdre in her fleshlessness with every passing week.

"Sight," Maltzer said, "is the most highly civilized of the senses. It was the last to come. The other senses tie us in closely with the very roots of life; I think we perceive with them more keenly than we know. The things we realize through taste and smell and feeling stimulate directly, without a detour through the centers of conscious thought. You know how often a taste or odor will recall a memory to you so subtly you don't know exactly what caused it? We need those primitive senses to tie us in with nature and the race. Through those ties Deirdre drew her vitality without realizing it. Sight is a cold, intellectual thing compared with the other senses. But it's all she has to draw on now. She isn't a human being any more, and I think what humanity is left in her will drain out little by little and never be replaced. Abelard, in a way, was a prototype. But Deirdre's loss is complete."

"She isn't human," Harris agreed slowly. "But she isn't pure robot either. She's something somewhere between the two, and I think it's a mistake to try to guess just where, or what the outcome will be."

"I don't have to guess," Maltzer said in a grim voice. "I know. I wish I'd let her die. I've done something to her a thousand times worse than the fire ever could. I should have let her die in it."

"Wait," said Harris. "Wait and see. I think you're wrong."

On the television screen Mary of Scotland climbed the

scaffold to her doom, the gown of traditional scarlet clinging
warmly to supple young curves as anachronistic in their way
as the slippers beneath the gown, for—as everyone but play-
wrights knows—Mary was well into middle age before she
died. Gracefully this latter-day Mary bent her head, sweeping
the long hair aside, kneeling to the block.

Maltzer watched stonily, seeing another woman entirely.

"I shouldn't have let her," he was muttering. "I shouldn't
have let her do it."

"Do you really think you'd have stopped her if you
could?" Harris asked quietly. And the other man after a moment's pause shook his head jerkily.

"No, I suppose not. I keep thinking if I worked and waited
a little longer maybe I could make it easier for her, but—no,
I suppose not. She's got to face them sooner or later, being
herself." He stood up abruptly, shoving back his chair. "If
she only weren't so . . . so frail. She doesn't realize how delicately poised her very sanity is. We gave her what we
could—the artists and the designers and I, all gave our very
best—but she's so pitifully handicapped even with all we
could do. She'll always be an abstraction and a . . . a freak,
cut off from the world by handicaps worse in their way than
anything any human being ever suffered before. Sooner or
later she'll realize it. And then—" He began to pace up and
down with quick, uneven steps, striking his hands together.
His face was twitching with a little *tic* that drew up one eye
to a squint and released it again at irregular intervals. Harris
could see how very near collapse the man was.

"Can you imagine what it's like?" Maltzer demanded
fiercely. "Penned into a mechanical body like that, shut out
from all human contacts except what leaks in by way of sight
and sound? To know you aren't human any longer? She's
been through shocks enough already. When that shock fully
hits her—"

"Shut up," said Harris roughly. "You won't do her any
good if you break down yourself. Look—the vaude's starting."

Great golden curtains had swept together over the unhappy
Queen of Scotland and were parting again now, all sorrow
and frustration wiped away once more as cleanly as the passing centuries had already expunged them. Now a line of tiny
dancers under the tremendous arch of the stage kicked and
pranced with the precision of little mechanical dolls too small

and perfect to be real. Vision rushed down upon them and swept along the row, face after stiffly smiling face racketing by like fence pickets. Then the sight rose into the rafters and looked down upon them from a great height, the grotesquely foreshortened figures still prancing in perfect rhythm even from this inhuman angle.

There was applause from an invisible audience. Then someone came out and did a dance with lighted torches that streamed long, weaving ribbons of fire among clouds of what looked like cotton wool but was most probably asbestos. Then a company in gorgeous pseudo-period costumes postured its way through the new singing ballet form of dance, roughly following a plot which had been announced as *Les Sylphides,* but had little in common with it. Afterward the precision dancers came on again, solemn and charming as performing dolls.

Maltzer began to show signs of dangerous tension as act succeeded act. Deirdre's was to be the last, of course. It seemed very long indeed before a face in close-up blotted out the stage, and a master of ceremonies with features like an amiable marionette's announced a very special number as the finale. His voice was almost cracking with excitement—perhaps he, too, had not been told until a moment before what lay in store for the audience.

Neither of the listening men heard what it was he said, but both were conscious of a certain indefinable excitement rising among the audience, murmurs and rustlings and a mounting anticipation as if time had run backward here and knowledge of the great surprise had already broken upon them.

Then the golden curtains appeared again. They quivered and swept apart on long upward arcs, and between them the stage was full of a shimmering golden haze. It was, Harris realized in a moment, simply a series of gauze curtains, but the effect was one of strange and wonderful anticipation, as if something very splendid must be hidden in the haze. The world might have looked like this on the first morning of creation, before heaven and earth took form in the mind of God. It was a singularly fortunate choice of stage set in its symbolism, though Harris wondered how much necessity had figured in its selection, for there could not have been much time to prepare an elaborate set.

The audience sat perfectly silent, and the air was tense.

This was no ordinary pause before an act. No one had been told, surely, and yet they seemed to guess—

The shimmering haze trembled and began to thin, veil by veil. Beyond was darkness, and what looked like a row of shining pillars set in a balustrade that began gradually to take shape as the haze drew back in shining folds. Now they could see that the balustrade curved up from left and right to the hand of a sweep of stairs. Stage and stairs were carpeted in black velvet; black velvet draperies hung just ajar behind the balcony, with a glimpse of dark sky beyond them trembling with dim synthetic stars.

The last curtain of golden gauze withdrew. The stage was empty. Or it seemed empty. But even through the aerial distances between this screen and the place it mirrored, Harris thought that the audience was not waiting for the performer to come on from the wings. There was no rustling, no coughing, no sense of impatience. A presence upon the stage was in command from the first drawing of the curtains; it filled the theater with its calm domination. It gauged its timing, holding the audience as a conductor with lifted baton gathers and holds the eyes of his orchestra.

For a moment everything was motionless upon the stage. Then, at the head of the stairs, where the two curves of the pillared balustrade swept together, a figure stirred.

Until that moment she had seemed another shining column in the row. Now she swayed deliberately, light catching and winking and running molten along her limbs and her robe of metal mesh. She swayed just enough to show that she was there. Then, with every eye upon her, she stood quietly to let them look their fill. The screen did not swoop to a close-up upon her. Her enigma remained inviolate and the television watchers saw her no more clearly than the audience in the theater.

Many must have thought her at first some wonderfully animate robot, hung perhaps from wires invisible against the velvet, for certainly she was no woman dressed in metal—her proportions were too thin and fine for that. And perhaps the impression of robotism was what she meant to convey at first. She stood quiet, swaying just a little, a masked and inscrutable figure, faceless, very slender in her robe that hung in folds as pure as a Grecian chlamys, though she did not look Grecian at all. In the visored golden helmet and the robe of mail that odd likeness to knighthood was there again, with its implications of medieval richness behind the simple lines. Except that in her exquisite slimness she called to mind no human figure in armor, not even the comparative delicacy of a St. Joan. It was the chivalry and delicacy of some other world implicit in her outlines.

A breath of surprise had rippled over the audience when she moved. Now they were tensely silent again, waiting. And the tension, the anticipation, was far deeper than any mood the scene itself could ever have evoked. Even those who thought her a manikin seemed to feel the forerunning of greater revelations.

Now she swayed and came slowly down the steps, moving with a suppleness just a little better than human. The swaying strengthened. By the time she reached the stage floor she was dancing. But it was no dance that any human creature could ever have performed. The long, slow, languorous rhythms of her body would have been impossible to a figure hinged at its joints as human figures hinge. (Harris remembered incredulously that he had feared once to find her jointed like a mechanical robot. But it was humanity that seemed, by contrast, jointed and mechanical now.)

The languor and the rhythm of her patterns looked impromptu, as all good dances should, but Harris knew what hours of composition and rehearsal must lie behind it, what laborious graving into her brain of strange new pathways, the first to replace the old ones and govern the mastery of metal limbs.

To and fro over the velvet carpet, against the velvet background, she wove the intricacies of her serpentine dance, leisurely and yet with such hypnotic effect that the air seemed full of looping rhythms, as if her long, tapering limbs had left their own replicas hanging upon the air and fading only slowly as she moved away. In her mind, Harris knew, the stage was a whole, a background to be filled in completely with the measured patterns of her dance, and she seemed almost to project that completed pattern to her audience so that they saw her everywhere at once, her golden rhythms fading upon the air long after she had gone.

Now there was music, looping and hanging in echoes after her like the shining festoons she wove with her body. But it was no orchestral music. She was humming, deep and sweet and wordlessly, as she glided her easy, intricate path about the stage. And the volume of the music was amazing. It seemed to fill the theater, and it was not amplified by hidden loudspeakers. You could tell that. Somehow, until you heard the music she made, you had never realized before the subtle distortions that amplification puts into music. This was utterly pure and true as perhaps no ear in all her audience had ever heard music before.

While she danced the audience did not seem to breathe. Perhaps they were beginning already to suspect who and what it was that moved before them without any fanfare of the publicity they had been half-expecting for weeks now. And yet, without the publicity, it was not easy to believe the dancer they watched was not some cunningly motivated manikin swinging on unseen wires about the stage.

Nothing she had done yet had been human. The dance was no dance a human being could have performed. The music she hummed came from a throat without vocal chords. But now the long, slow rhythms were drawing to their close, the pattern tightening in to a finale. And she ended as inhumanly as she had danced, willing them not to interrupt her with applause, dominating them now as she had always done. For her implication here was that a machine might have performed the dance, and a machine expects no applause. If they thought unseen operators had put her through those wonderful paces, they would wait for the operators to appear for their bows. But the audience was obedient. It sat silently, waiting for what came next. But its silence was tense and breathless.

The dance ended as it had begun. Slowly, almost carelessly, she swung up the velvet stairs, moving with rhythms as perfect as her music. But when she reached the head of the stairs she turned to face her audience, and for a moment stood motionless, like a creature of metal, without volition, the hands of the operator slack upon its strings.

Then, startlingly, she laughed.

It was lovely laughter, low and sweet and full-throated. She threw her head back and let her body sway and her shoulders shake, and the laughter, like the music, filled the theater, gaining volume from the great hollow of the roof and sounding in the ears of every listener, not loud, but as intimately as if each sat alone with the woman who laughed.

And she was a woman now. Humanity had dropped over her like a tangible garment. No one who had ever heard that laughter before could mistake it here. But before the reality of who she was had quite time to dawn upon her listeners she let the laughter deepen into music, as no human voice could have done. She was humming a familiar refrain close in the ear of every hearer. And the humming in turn swung into words. She sang in her clear, light, lovely voice:

"The yellow rose of Eden, is blooming in my heart—"

It was Deirdre's song. She had sung it first upon the airways a month before the theater fire that had consumed her. It was a commonplace little melody, simple enough to take first place in the fancy of a nation that had always liked its songs simple. But it had a certain sincerity too, and no taint of the vulgarity of tune and rhythm that foredooms so many popular songs to oblivion after their novelty fades.

No one else was ever able to sing it quite as Deirdre did. It had been identified with her so closely that though for awhile after her accident singers tried to make it a memorial for her, they failed so conspicuously to give it her unmistakable flair that the song died from their sheer inability to sing it. No one ever hummed the tune without thinking of her and the pleasant, nostalgic sadness of something lovely and lost.

But it was not a sad song now. If anyone had doubted whose brain and ego motivated this shining metal suppleness, they could doubt no longer. For the voice was Deirdre, and the song. And the lovely, poised grace of her mannerisms that made up recognition as certainly as sight of a familiar face.

She had not finished the first line of her song before the audience knew her.

And they did not let her finish. The accolade of their interruption was a tribute more eloquent than polite waiting could ever have been. First a breath of incredulity rippled over the theater, and a long, sighing gasp that reminded Harris irrelevantly as he listened of the gasp which still goes up from matinee audiences at the first glimpse of the fabulous Valentino, so many generations dead. But this gasp did not sigh itself away and vanish. Tremendous tension lay behind it, and the rising tide of excitement rippled up in little murmurs and spatterings of applause that ran together into one overwhelming roar. It shook the theater. The television screen trembled and blurred a little to the volume of that transmitted applause.

Silenced before it, Deirdre stood gesturing on the stage, bowing and bowing as the noise rolled up about her, shaking perceptibly with the triumph of her own emotion.

Harris had an intolerable feeling that she was smiling radiantly and that the tears were pouring down her cheeks. He even thought, just as Maltzer leaned forward to switch off the screen, that she was blowing kisses over the audience in the time-honored gesture of the grateful actress, her golden arms shining as she scattered kisses abroad from the featureless helmet, the face that had no mouth.

"Well?" Harris said, not without triumph.

Maltzer shook his head jerkily, the glasses unsteady on his nose so that the blurred eyes behind them seemed to shift.

"Of course they applauded, you fool," he said in a savage voice. "I might have known they would under this setup. It doesn't prove anything. Oh she was smart to surprise them—I admit that. But they were applauding themselves as much as her. Excitement, gratitude for letting them in on a historic performance, mass hysteria—*you* know. It's from now on the test will come, and this hasn't helped any to prepare her for it. Morbid curiosity when the news gets out—people laughing when she forgets she isn't human. And they will, you know. There are always those who will. And the novelty wearing off. The slow draining away of humanity for lack of contact with any human stimuli any more—"

Harris remembered suddenly and reluctantly the moment that afternoon which he had shunted aside mentally, to consider later. The sense of something unfamiliar beneath the surface of Deirdre's speech. Was Maltzer right? Was the drainage already at work? Or was there something deeper than this obvious answer to the question? Certainly she had been through experiences too terrible for ordinary people to comprehend. Scars might still remain. Or, with her body, had she put on a strange, metallic something of the mind, that spoke to no sense which human minds could answer?

For a few minutes neither of them spoke. Then Maltzer rose abruptly and stood looking down at Harris with an abstract scowl.

"I wish you'd go now," he said.

Harris glanced up at him, startled. Maltzer began to pace again, his steps quick and uneven. Over his shoulder he said, "I've made up my mind, Harris. I've got to put a stop to this."

Harris rose. "Listen," he said. "Tell me one thing. What makes you so certain you're right? Can you deny that most of it's speculation—hearsay evidence? Remember, I talked to Deirdre, and she was just as sure as you are in the opposite direction. Have you any real reason for what you think?"

Maltzer took his glasses off and rubbed his nose carefully, taking a long time about it. He seemed reluctant to answer. But when he did, at last, there was a confidence in his voice Harris had not expected.

"I have a reason," he said. "But you won't believe it. Nobody would."

"Try me."

Maltzer shook his head. "Nobody *could* believe it. No two people were ever in quite the same relationship before as Deirdre and I have been. I helped her come back out of complete—oblivion. I knew her before she had voice or hearing. She was only a frantic mind when I first made contact with her, half insane with all that had happened and fear of what would happen next. In a very literal sense she was reborn out of that condition, and I had to guide her through every step of the way. I came to know her thoughts before she thought them. And once you've been that close to another mind, you don't lose the contact easily." He put the glasses back on and looked blurrily at Harris through the heavy lenses. "Deirdre is worried," he said. "I know it. You won't believe me, but I can—well, sense it. I tell you, I've been too close to her very mind itself to make any mistake. You don't see it, maybe. Maybe even she doesn't know it yet. But the worry's there. When I'm with her, I feel it. And I don't want it to come any nearer the surface of her mind than it's come already. I'm going to put a stop to this before it's too late."

Harris had no comment for that. It was too entirely outside his own experience. He said nothing for a moment. Then he asked simply, "How?"

"I'm not sure yet. I've got to decide before she comes back. And I want to see her alone."

"I think you're wrong," Harris told him quietly. "I think you're imagining things. I don't think you *can* stop her."

Maltzer gave him a slanted glance. "I can stop her," he said, in a curious voice. He went on quickly, "She has enough already—she's nearly human. She can live normally as other people live, without going back on the screen. Maybe this taste of it will be enough. I've got to convince her it is. If she retires now, she'll never guess how cruel her own audiences could be, and maybe that deep sense of—distress, uneasiness, whatever it is—won't come to the surface. It mustn't. She's too fragile to stand that." He slapped his hands together sharply. "I've got to stop her. For her own sake I've got to do it!" He swung round again to face Harris. "Will you go now?"

Never in his life had Harris wanted less to leave a place. Briefly he thought of saying simply, "No I won't." But he had to admit in his own mind that Maltzer was at least partly right. This was a matter between Deirdre and her creator, the culmination, perhaps, of that year's long intimacy so like marriage that this final trial for supremacy was a need he recognized.

He would not, he thought, forbid the showdown if he could. Perhaps the whole year had been building up to this one moment between them in which one or the other must prove himself victor. Neither was very well stable just now, after the long strain of the year past. It might very well be that the mental salvation of one or both hinged upon the outcome of the clash. But because each was so strongly motivated not by selfish concern but by solicitude for the other in this strange combat, Harris knew he must leave them to settle the thing alone.

He was in the street and hailing a taxi before the full significance of something Maltzer had said came to him. *"I can stop her,"* he had declared, with an odd inflection in his voice.

Suddenly Harris felt cold. Maltzer had made her—of course he could stop her if he chose. Was there some key in that supple golden body that could immobilize it at its maker's will? Could she be imprisoned in that cage of her own body? No body before in all history, he thought, could have been designed more truly to be a prison for its mind than Deirdre's, if Maltzer chose to turn the key that locked her in. There must be many ways to do it. He could simply withhold whatever source of nourishment kept her brain alive, if that were the way he chose.

But Harris could not believe he would do it. The man wasn't insane. He would not defeat his own purpose. His determination rose from his solicitude for Deirdre; he would not even in the last extremity try to save her by imprisoning her in the jail of her own skull.

For a moment Harris hesitated on the curb, almost turning back. But what could he do? Even granting that Maltzer would resort to such tactics, self-defeating in their very nature, how could any man on earth prevent him if he did it subtly enough? But he never would. Harris knew he never would. He got into his cab slowly, frowning. He would see them both tomorrow.

He did not. Harris was swamped with excited calls about yesterday's performance, but the message he was awaiting did not come. The day went by very slowly. Toward evening he surrendered and called Maltzer's apartment.

It was Deirdre's face that answered, and for once he saw no remembered features superimposed upon the blankness of her helmet. Masked and faceless, she looked at him inscrutably.

"Is everything all right?" he asked, a little uncomfortable.

"Yes, of course," she said, and her voice was a bit metallic for the first time, as if she were thinking so deeply of some other matter that she did not trouble to pitch it properly. "I had a long talk with Maltzer last night, if that's what you mean. You know what he wants. But nothing's been decided yet."

Harris felt oddly rebuffed by the sudden realization of the metal of her. It was impossible to read anything from face or voice. Each had its mask.

"What are you going to do?" he asked.

"Exactly as I'd planned," she told him, without inflection.

Harris floundered a little. Then, with an effort at practicality, he said, "Do you want me to go to work on bookings, then?"

She shook the delicately modeled skull. "Not yet. You saw

the reviews today, of course. They—*did* like me." It was an understatement, and for the first time a note of warmth sounded in her voice. But the preoccupation was still there, too. "I'd already planned to make them wait awhile after my first performance," she went on. "A couple of weeks, anyhow. You remember that little farm of mine in Jersey, John? I'm going over today. I won't see anyone except the servants there. Not even Maltzer. Not even you. I've got a lot to think about. Maltzer has agreed to let everything go until we've both thought things over. He's taking a rest, too. I'll see you the moment I get back, John. Is that all right?"

She blanked out almost before he had time to nod and while the beginning of a stammered argument was still on his lips. He sat there staring at the screen.

The two weeks that went by before Maltzer called him again were the longest Harris had ever spent. He thought of many things in the interval. He believed he could sense in that last talk with Deirdre something of the inner unrest that Maltzer had spoken of—more an abstraction than a distress, but some thought had occupied her mind which she would not—or was it that she could not?—share even with her closest confidants. He even wondered whether, if her mind was as delicately poised as Maltzer feared, one would ever know whether or not it had slipped. There was so little evidence one way or the other in the unchanging outward form of her.

Most of all he wondered what two weeks in a new environment would do to her untried body and newly patterned brain. If Maltzer were right, then there might be some perceptible—drainage—by the time they met again. He tried not to think of that.

Maltzer televised him on the morning set for her return. He looked very bad. The rest must have been no rest at all. His face was almost a skull now, and the blurred eyes behind their lenses burned. But he seemed curiously at peace, in spite of his appearance. Harris thought he had reached some decision, but whatever it was had not stopped his hands from shaking or the nervous *tic* that drew his face sideways into a grimace at intervals.

"Come over," he said briefly, without preamble. "She'll be here in half an hour." And he blanked out without waiting for an answer.

When Harris arrived, he was standing by the window looking down and steadying his trembling hands on the sill.

"I can't stop her," he said in a monotone, and again without preamble. Harris had the impression that for the two weeks his thoughts must have run over and over the same track, until any spoken word was simply a vocal interlude in the circling of his mind. "I couldn't do it. I even tried threats, but she knew I didn't mean them. There's only one way out Harris." He glanced up briefly, hollow-eyed behind the lenses. "Never mind. I'll tell you later."

"Did you explain everything to her that you did to me?"

"Nearly all. I even taxed her with that . . . that sense of distress I *know* she feels. She denied it. She was lying. We both knew. It was worse after the performance than before. When I saw her that night, I tell you I *knew*—she senses something wrong, but she won't admit it." He shrugged. "Well—"

Faintly in the silence they heard the humming of the elevator descending from the helicopter platform on the roof. Both men turned to the door.

She had not changed at all. Foolishly, Harris was a little surprised. Then he caught himself and remembered that she would never change—never, until she died. He himself might grow white-haired and senile; she would move before him then as she moved now, supple, golden, enigmatic.

Still, he thought she caught her breath a little when she saw Maltzer and the depths of his swift degeneration. She had no breath to catch, but her voice was shaken as she greeted them.

"I'm glad you're both here," she said, a slight hesitation in her speech. "It's a wonderful day outside. Jersey was glorious. I'd forgotten how lovely it is in summer. Was the sanitarium any good, Maltzer?"

He jerked his head irritably and did not answer. She went on talking in a light voice, skimming the surface, saying nothing important.

This time Harris saw her as he supposed her audiences would, eventually, when the surprise had worn off and the image of the living Deirdre faded from memory. She was all metal now, the Deirdre they would know from today on. And she was not less lovely. She was not even less human—yet.

Her motion was a miracle of flexible grace, a pouring of suppleness along every limb. (From now on, Harris realized suddenly, it was her body and not her face that would have mobility to express emotion; she must act with her limbs and her lithe, robed torso.)

But there was something wrong. Harris sensed it almost tangibly in her inflections, her elusiveness, the way she fenced with words. This was what Maltzer had meant, this was what Harris himself had felt just before she left for the country. Only now it was strong—certain. Between them and the old Deirdre whose voice still spoke to them a veil of—detachment—had been drawn. Behind it she was in distress. Somehow, somewhere, she had made some discovery that affected her profoundly. And Harris was terribly afraid that he knew what the discovery must be. Maltzer was right.

He was still leaning against the window, staring out unseeingly over the vast panorama of New York, webbed with traffic bridges, winking with sunlit glass, its vertinginous distances plunging downward into the blue shadows of Earth-level. He said now, breaking into the light-voiced chatter, "Are you all right, Deirdre?"

She laughed. It was lovely laughter. She moved lithely across the room, sunlight glinting on her musical mailed robe, and stooped to a cigarette box on a table. Her fingers were deft.

"Have one?" she said, and carried the box to Maltzer. He let her put the brown cylinder between his lips and hold a light to it, but he did not seem to be noticing what he did. She replaced the box and then crossed to a mirror on the far wall and began experimenting with a series of gliding ripples that wove patterns of pale gold in the glass. "Of course I'm all right," she said.

"You're lying."

Deirdre did not turn. She was watching him in the mirror, but the ripple of her motion went on slowly, languorously, undisturbed.

"No," she told them both.

Maltzer drew deeply on his cigarette. Then with a hard pull he unsealed the window and tossed the smoking stub far out over the gulfs below. He said, "You can't deceive me, Deirdre." His voice was suddenly, quite calm. "I created you, my dear. I know. I've sensed that uneasiness in you growing and growing for a long while now. It's much stronger today than it was two weeks ago. Something happened to you in the country. I don't know what it was, but you've changed. Will you admit to yourself what it is, Deirdre? Have you realized yet that you must not go back on the screen?"

"Why, no," said Deirdre, still not looking at him except obliquely, in the glass. Her gestures were slower now, weaving lazy patterns in the air. "No, I haven't changed my mind."

She was all metal—outwardly. She was taking unfair advantage of her own metal-hood. She had withdrawn far within, behind the mask of her voice and her facelessness. Even her body, whose involuntary motions might have betrayed what she was feeling, in the only way she could be subject to betrayal now, she was putting through ritual motions that disguised it completely. As long as these looping, weaving patterns occupied her, no one had any way of guessing even from her motion what went on in the hidden brain inside her helmet.

Harris was struck suddenly and for the first time with the completeness of her withdrawal. When he had seen her last in this apartment she had been wholly Deirdre, not masked at all, overflowing the metal with the warmth and ardor of the woman he had known so well. Since then—since the performance on the stage—he had not seen the familiar Deirdre again. Passionately he wondered why. Had she begun to suspect even in her moment of triumph what a fickle master an audience could be? Had she caught, perhaps, the sound of whispers and laughter among some small portion of her watchers, though the great majority praised her?

Or was Maltzer right? Perhaps Harris's first interview with her had been the last bright burning of the lost Deirdre, animated by excitement and the pleasure of meeting after so long a time, animation summoned up in a last strong effort to convince him. Now she was gone, but whether in self-protection against the possible cruelties of human beings, or to withdraw to metal-hood, he could not guess. Humanity might be draining out of her fast, and the brassy taint of metal permeating the brain it housed.

Maltzer laid his trembling hand on the edge of the opened

window and looked out. He said in a deepened voice, the querulous note gone for the first time: "I've made a terrible mistake, Deirdre. I've done you irreparable harm." He paused a moment, but Deirdre said nothing. Harris dared not speak. In a moment Maltzer went on. "I've made you vulnerable, and given you no weapons to fight your enemies with. And the human race is your enemy, my dear, whether you admit it now or later. I think you know that. I think it's why you're so silent. I think you must have suspected it on the stage two weeks ago, and verified it in Jersey while you were gone. They're going to hate you, after a while, because you are still beautiful, and they're going to persecute you because you are different—and helpless. Once the novelty wears off, my dear, your audience will be simply a mob."

He was not looking at her. He has bent forward a little, looking out the window and down. His hair stirred in the wind that blew very strongly up this high, and whined thinly around the open edge of the glass.

"I meant what I did for you," he said, "to be for everyone who meets with accidents that might have ruined them. I should have known my gift would mean worse ruin than any mutilation could be. I know now that there's only one legitimate way a human being can create life. When he tries another way, as I did, he has a lesson to learn. Remember the lesson of the student Frankenstein? He learned, too. In a way, he was lucky—the way he learned. He didn't have to watch what happened afterward. Maybe he wouldn't have had the courage—I know I haven't."

Harris found himself standing without remembering that he rose. He knew suddenly what was about to happen. He understood Maltzer's air of resolution, his new, unnatural calm. He knew, even, why Maltzer had asked him here today, so that Deirdre might not be left alone. For he remembered that Frankenstein, too, had paid with his life for the unlawful creation of life.

Maltzer was leaning head and shoulders from the window now, looking down with almost hypnotized fascination. His voice came back to them remotely in the breeze, as if a barrier already lay between them.

Deirdre had not moved. Her expressionless mask, in the mirror, watched him calmly. She *must* have understood. Yet she gave no sign, except that the weaving of her arms had almost stopped now, she moved so slowly. Like a dance seen in a nightmare, under water.

It was impossible, of course, for her to express any emotion. The fact that her face showed none now should not, in fairness, be held against her. But she watched so wholly without feeling— Neither of them moved toward the window. A false step, now, might send him over. They were quiet, listening to his voice.

"We who bring life into the world unlawfully," said Maltzer, almost thoughtfully, "must make room for it by withdrawing our own. That seems to be an inflexible rule. It works automatically. The thing we create makes living unbearable. No, it's nothing you can help, my dear. I've asked you to do something I created you incapable of doing. I made you to perform a function, and I've been asking you to forgo the one thing you were made to do. I believe that if you do it, it will destroy you, but the whole guilt is mine, not yours. I'm not even asking you to give up the screen, anymore. I know you can't, and live. But I can't live and watch you. I put all my skill and all my love in one final masterpiece, and I can't bear to watch it destroyed. I can't live and watch you do only what I made you to do, and ruin yourself because you must do it.

"But before I go, I have to make sure you understand." He leaned a little farther, looking down, and his voice grew more remote as the glass came between them. He was saying almost unbearable things now, but very distantly, in a cool, passionless tone filtered through wind and glass and with the distant humming of the city mingled with it, so that the words were curiously robbed of poignancy. "I can be a coward," he said, "and escape the consequences of what I've done, but I can't go and leave you—not understanding. It would be even worse than the thought of your failure, to think of you bewildered and confused when the mob turns on you. What I'm telling you, my dear, won't be any real news—I think you sense it already, though you may not admit it to yourself. We've been too close to lie to each other, Deirdre—I know when you aren't telling the truth. I know the distress that's been growing in your mind. You are not wholly human, my dear. I think you know that. In so many

ways, in spite of all I could do, you must always be less than
human. You've lost the senses of perception that kept you in
touch with humanity. Sight and hearing are all that remain,
and sight, as I've said before, was the last and coldest of the
senses to develop. And you're so delicately poised on a sort
of thin edge of reason. You're only a clear, glowing mind an-
imating a metal body, like a candle flame in a glass. And as
precariously vulnerable to the wind."

He paused. "Try not to let them ruin you completely," he
said after a while. "When they turn against you, when they
find out you're more helpless than they—I wish I could have
made you stronger, Deirdre. But I couldn't. I had too much
skill for your good and mine, but not quite enough skill for
that."

He was silent again, briefly, looking down. He was balanced precariously now, more than halfway over the sill and
supported only by one hand on the glass. Harris watched
with an agonized uncertainty, not sure whether a sudden leap
might catch him in time or send him over. Deirdre was still
weaving her golden patterns, slowly and unchangingly,
watching the mirror and its reflection, her face and masked
eyes enigmatic.

"I wish one thing, though," Maltzer said in his remote
voice. "I wish—before I finish—that you'd tell me the truth,
Deirdre. I'd be happier if I were sure I'd—reached you. Do
you understand what I've said? Do you believe me? Because
if you don't, then I know you're lost beyond all hope. If
you'll admit your own doubt—and I know you do doubt—I
can think there may be a chance for you after all. Were you
lying to me, Deirdre? Do you know how . . . how wrong I've
made you?"

There was silence. Then very softly, a breath of sound,
Deirdre answered. The voice seemed to hang in midair, because she had no lips to move and localize it for the imagination.

"Will you listen, Maltzer?" she asked.

"I'll wait," he said. "Go on. Yes or no?"

Slowly she let her arms drop to her sides. Very smoothly
and quietly she turned from the mirror and faced him. She
swayed a little, making her metal robe ring.

"I'll answer you," she said. "But I don't think I'll answer

that. Not with yes or no, anyhow. I'm going to walk a little, Maltzer. I have something to tell you, and I can't talk standing still. Will you let me move about without—going over?"

He nodded distantly. "You can't interfere from that distance," he said. "But keep the distance. What do you want to say?"

She began to pace a little way up and down her end of the room, moving with liquid ease. The table with the cigarette box was in her way, and she pushed it aside carefully, watching Maltzer and making no swift motions to startle him.

"I'm not—well, sub-human," she said, a faint note of indignation in her voice. "I'll prove it in a minute, but I want to say something else first. You must promise to wait and listen. There's a flaw in your argument, and I resent it. I'm not a Frankenstein monster made out of dead flesh. I'm myself—alive. You didn't create my life, you only preserved it. I'm not a robot, with compulsions built into me that I have to obey. I'm free-willed and independent, and Maltzer—I'm human."

Harris had relaxed a little. She knew what she was doing. He had no idea what she planned, but he was willing to wait now. She was not the indifferent automaton he had thought. He watched her come to the table again in a lap of her pacing, and stoop over it, her eyeless mask turned to Maltzer to make sure a variation of her movement did not startle him.

"I'm human," she repeated, her voice humming faintly and very sweetly. "Do you think I'm not?" she asked, straightening and facing them both. And then suddenly, almost overwhelmingly, the warmth and the old ardent charm were radiant all around her. She was robot no longer, enigmatic no longer. Harris could see as clearly as in their first meeting the remembered flesh still gracious and beautiful as her voice evoked his memory. She stood swaying a little, as she had always swayed, her head on one side, and she was chuckling at them both. It was such a soft and lovely sound, so warmly familiar.

"Of course I'm myself," she told them, and as the words sounded in their ears neither of them could doubt it. There was hypnosis in her voice. She turned away and began to pace again, and so powerful was the human personality which she had called up about her that it beat out at them in deep pulses, as if her body were a furnace to send out those comforting waves of warmth. "I have handicaps, I know," she said. "But my audiences will never know. I won't let them know. I think you'll believe me, both of you, when I say I could play Juliet just as I am now, with a cast of ordinary people, and make the world accept it. Do you think I could, John? Maltzer, don't you believe I could?"

She paused at the far end of her pacing path and turned to face them, and they both stared at her without speaking. To Harris she was the Deirdre he had always known, pale gold, exquisitely graceful in remembered postures, the inner radiance of her shining through metal as brilliantly as it had ever shone through flesh. He did not wonder, now, if it were real. Later he would think again that it might be only a disguise, something like a garment she had put off with her lost body, to wear again only when she chose. Now the spell of her compelling charm was too strong for wonder. He watched, convinced for the moment that she was all she seemed to be. She could play Juliet if she said she could. She could sway a whole audience as easily as she swayed himself. Indeed, there was something about her just now more convincingly human than anything he had noticed before. He realized that in a split second of awareness before he saw what it was.

She was looking at Maltzer. He, too, watched, spellbound in spite of himself, not dissenting. She glanced from one to the other. Then she put back her head and laughter came welling and choking from her in a great, full-throated tide. She shook in the strength of it. Harris could almost see her round throat pulsing with the sweet low-pitched waves of laughter that were shaking her—honest mirth, with a little derision in it.

Then she lifted one arm and tossed her cigarette into the empty fireplace.

Harris choked, and his mind went blank for one moment of blind denial. He had not sat here watching a robot smoke and accepting it as normal. He could not! And yet he had. That had been the final touch of conviction which swayed his hypnotized mind into accepting her humanity. And she had done it so deftly, so naturally, wearing her radiant humanity with such rightness, that his watching mind had not even questioned what she did.

He glanced at Maltzer. The man was still halfway over the window ledge, but through the opening of the window he, too, was staring in stupefied disbelief and Harris knew they had shared the same delusion.

Deirdre was still shaking a little with laughter. "Well," she demanded, the rich chuckling making her voice quiver, "am I all robot, after all?"

Harris opened his mouth to speak, but he did not utter a word. This was not his show. The byplay lay wholly between Deirdre and Maltzer; he must not interfere. He turned his head to the window and waited.

And Maltzer for a moment seemed shaken in his conviction.

"You . . . you *are* an actress," he admitted slowly. "But I . . . I'm not convinced I'm wrong. I think—" He paused. The querulous note was in his voice again, and he seemed racked once more by the old doubts and dismay. Then Harris saw him stiffen. He saw the resolution come back, and understood why it had come. Maltzer had gone too far already upon the cold and lonely path he had chosen to turn back, even for stronger evidence than this. He had reached his conclusions only after mental turmoil too terrible to face again. Safety and peace lay in the course he had steeled himself to follow. He was too tired, too exhausted by months of conflict, to retrace his path and begin all over. Harris could see him groping for a way out, and in a moment he saw him find it.

"That was a trick," he said hollowly. "Maybe you could play it on a larger audience, too. Maybe you have more tricks to use. I might be wrong. But Deirdre"—his voice grew urgent—"you haven't answered the one thing I've got to know. You can't answer it. You *do* feel—dismay. You've learned your own inadequacy, however well you can hide it from us—even from us. I *know*. Can you deny that, Deirdre?"

She was not laughing now. She let her arms fall, and the flexible golden body seemed to droop a little all over, as if the brain that a moment before had been sending out strong, sure waves of confidence had slackened its power, and the intangible muscles of her limbs slackened with it. Some of the glowing humanity began to fade. It receded within her and

was gone, as if the fire in the furnace of her body were sinking and cooling.

"Maltzer," she said uncertainly, "I can't answer that—yet.
I can't—"

And then, while they waited in anxiety for her to finish the
sentence, she *blazed*. She ceased to be a figure in stasis—she
blazed.

It was something no eyes could watch and translate into
terms the brain could follow; her motion was too swift. Maltzer in the window was a whole long room-length away. He
had thought himself safe at such a distance, knowing no normal human being could reach him before he moved. But
Deirdre was neither normal nor human.

In the same instant she stood drooping by the mirror she
was simultaneously at Maltzer's side. Her motion negated
time and destroyed space. And as a glowing cigarette tip in
the dark describes closed circles before the eye when the
holder moves it swiftly, so Deirdre blazed in one continuous
flash of golden motion across the room.

But curiously, she was not blurred. Harris, watching, felt
his mind go blank again, but less in surprise than because no
normal eyes and brain could perceive what it was he looked
at.

(In that moment of intolerable suspense his complex human brain paused suddenly, annihilating time in its own way,
and withdrew to a cool corner of its own to analyze in a
flashing second what it was he had just seen. The brain could
do it timelessly; words are slow. But he knew he had watched
a sort of tesseract of human motion, a parable of fourth-dimensional activity. A one-dimensional point, moved through
space, creates a two-dimensional line, which in motion creates
a three-dimensional cube. Theoretically the cube, in motion,
would produce a fourth-dimensional figure. No human creature had ever seen a figure of three dimensions moved
through space and time before—until this moment. She had
not blurred; every motion she made was distinct, but not like
moving figures on a strip of film. Not like anything that those
who use our language had ever seen before, or created words
to express. The mind saw, but without perceiving. Neither
words nor thoughts could resolve what happened into terms
for human brains. And perhaps she had not actually and

literally moved through the fourth dimension. Perhaps—since Harris was able to see her—it had been almost and not quite that unimaginable thing. But it was close enough.)

While to the slow mind's eye she was still standing at the far end of the room, she was already at Maltzer's side, her long, flexible fingers gentle but very firm upon his arms. She waited—

The room shimmered. There was sudden violent heat beating upon Harris's face. Then the air steadied again and Deirdre was saying softly, in a mournful whisper: "I'm sorry—I had to do it. I'm sorry—I didn't mean you to know—"

Time caught up with Harris. He saw it overtake Maltzer too, saw the man jerk convulsively away from the grasping hands, in a ludicrously futile effort to forestall what had already happened. Even thought was slow, compared with Deirdre's swiftness.

The sharp outward jerk was strong. It was strong enough to break the grasp of human hands and catapult Maltzer out and down into the swimming gulfs of New York. The mind leaped ahead to a logical conclusion and saw him twisting and turning and diminishing with dreadful rapidity to a tiny point of darkness that dropped away through sunlight toward the shadows near the earth. The mind even conjured up a shrill, thin cry that plummeted away with the falling body and hung behind it in the shaken air.

But the mind was reckoning on human factors.

Very gently and smoothly Deirdre lifted Maltzer from the window sill and with effortless ease carried him well back into the safety of the room. She set him down before a sofa and her golden fingers unwrapped themselves from his arms slowly, so that he could regain control of his own body before she released him.

He sank to the sofa without a word. Nobody spoke for an unmeasurable length of time. Harris could not. Deirdre waited patiently. It was Maltzer who regained speech first, and it came back on the old track, as if his mind had not yet relinquished the rut it had worn so deep.

"All right," he said breathlessly. "All right, you can stop me this time. But I know, you see. I know! You can't hide your feeling from me, Deirdre. I know the trouble you feel. And next time—next time I won't wait to talk!"

Deirdre made the sound of a sigh. She had no lungs to expel the breath she was imitating, but it was hard to realize that. It was hard to understand why she was not panting heavily from the terrible exertion of the past minutes; the mind knew why, but could not accept the reason. She was still too human.

"You still don't see," she said. "Think, Maltzer, think!"

There was a hassock beside the sofa. She sank upon it gracefully, clasping her robed knees, her head tilted back to watch Maltzer's face. She saw only stunned stupidity on it now; he had passed through too much emotional storm to think at all.

"All right," she told him. "Listen—I'll admit it. You're right. I *am* unhappy. I do know what you said was true—but not for the reason you think. Humanity and I are far apart, and drawing farther. The gap will be hard to bridge. Do you hear me, Maltzer?"

Harris saw the tremendous effort that went into Maltzer's wakening. He saw the man pull his mind back into focus and sit up on the sofa with weary stiffness.

"You . . . you do admit it, then?" he asked in a bewildered voice.

Deirdre shook her head sharply.

"Do you still think of me as delicate?" she demanded. "Do you know I carried you here at arm's length halfway across the room? Do you realize you weigh *nothing* to me? I could"—she glanced around the room and gestured with sudden, rather appalling violence—"tear this building down," she said quietly. "I could tear my way through these walls, I think. I've found no limit yet to the strength I can put forth if I try." She held up her golden hands and looked at them. "The metal would break, perhaps," she said reflectively, "but then, I have no feeling—"

Maltzer gasped, *"Deirdre—"*

She looked up with what must have been a smile. It sounded clearly in her voice. "Oh, I won't. I wouldn't have to do it with my hands, if I wanted. Look—listen!"

She put her head back and a deep, vibrating hum gathered and grew in what one still thought of as her throat. It deepened swiftly and the ears began to ring. It was deeper, and the furniture vibrated. The walls began almost imperceptibly to shake. The room was full and bursting with a sound that shook every atom upon its neighbor with a terrible, disrupting force.

The sound ceased. The humming died. Then Deirdre laughed and made another and quite differently pitched sound. It seemed to reach out like an arm in one straight direction—toward the window. The opened panel shook. Deirdre intensified her hum, and slowly, within-perceptible jolts that merged into smoothness, the window jarred itself shut.

"You see?" Deirdre said. "You see?"

But still Maltzer could only stare. Harris was staring too, his mind beginning slowly to accept what she implied. Both were too stunned to leap ahead to any conclusions yet.

Deirdre rose impatiently and began to pace again, in a ringing of metal robe and a twinkling of reflected lights. She was pantherlike in her suppleness. They could see the power behind that lithe motion now; they no longer thought of her as helpless, but they were far still from grasping the truth.

"You were wrong about me, Maltzer," she said with an effort at patience in her voice. "But you were right too, in a way you didn't guess. I'm not afraid of humanity. I haven't anything to fear from them. Why"—her voice took on a tinge of contempt—"already I've set a fashion in women's clothing. By next week you won't see a woman on the street without a mask like mine, and every dress that isn't cut like a chlamys will be out of style. I'm not afraid of humanity! I won't lose touch with them unless I want to. I've learned a lot—I've learned too much already."

Her voice faded for a moment, and Harris had a quick and appalling vision of her experimenting in the solitude of her farm, testing the range of her voice, testing her eyesight—could she see microscopically and telescopically?—and was her hearing as abnormally flexible as her voice?

"You were afraid I had lost feeling and scent and taste," she went on, still pacing with that powerful, tigerish tread. "Hearing and sight would not be enough, you think? But why do you think sight is the last of the senses? It may be the latest, Maltzer—Harris—*but why do you think it's the last?*"

She may not have whispered that. Perhaps it was only their hearing that made it seem thin and distant, as the brain contracted and would not let the thought come through in its stunning entirety.

"No," Deirdre said, "I haven't lost contact with the human race. I never will, unless I want to. It's too easy . . . too easy."

She was watching her shining feet as she paced, and her masked face was averted. Sorrow sounded in her soft voice now.

"I didn't mean to let you know," she said. "I never would have, if this hadn't happened. But I couldn't let you go believing you'd failed. You made a perfect machine, Maltzer. More perfect than you knew."

"But Deirdre—" breathed Maltzer, his eyes fascinated and still incredulous upon her, "but Deirdre, if we did succeed—what's wrong? I can feel it now—I've felt it all along. You're so unhappy—you still are. Why, Deirdre?"

She lifted her head and looked at him, eyelessly, but with a piercing stare.

"Why are you so sure of that?" she asked gently.

"You think I could be mistaken, knowing you as I do? But I'm not Frankenstein . . . you say my creation's flawless. Then what—"

"Could you ever duplicate this body?" she asked.

Maltzer glanced down at his shaking hands. "I don't know. I doubt it. I—"

"Could anyone else?"

He was silent. Deirdre answered for him. "I don't believe anyone could. I think I was an accident. A sort of mutation halfway between flesh and metal. Something accidental and . . . and unnatural, turning off on a wrong course of evolution that never reaches a dead end. Another brain in a body like this might die or go mad, as you thought I would. The synapses are too delicate. You were—call it lucky—with me. From what I know now, I don't think a . . . a baroque like me could happen again." She paused a moment. "What you did was kindle the fire for the Phoenix, in a way. And the Phoenix rises perfect and renewed from its own ashes. Do you remember why it had to reproduce itself that way?"

Maltzer shook his head.

"I'll tell you," she said. "It was because there was only one Phoenix. Only one in the whole world."

They looked at each other in silence. Then Deirdre shrugged a little.

"He always came out of the fire perfect, of course. I'm not weak, Maltzer. You needn't let that thought bother you any more. I'm not vulnerable and helpless. I'm not sub-human." She laughed dryly. "I suppose," she said, "that I'm—super-human."

"But—not happy."

"I'm afraid. It isn't unhappiness, Maltzer—it's fear. I don't want to draw so far away from the human race. I wish I needn't. That's why I'm going back on the stage—to keep in touch with them while I can. But I wish there could be others like me. I'm . . . I'm lonely, Maltzer."

Silence again. Then Maltzer said, in a voice as distant as when he had spoken to them through glass, over gulfs as deep as oblivion: "Then I am Frankenstein, after all."

"Perhaps you are," Deirdre said very softly. "I don't know. Perhaps you are."

She turned away and moved smoothly, powerfully, down the room to the window. Now that Harris knew, he could almost hear the sheer power purring along her limbs as she walked. She leaned the golden forehead against the glass—it clinked faintly, with a musical sound—and looked down into the depths Maltzer had hung above. Her voice was reflective as she looked into those dizzy spaces which had offered oblivion to her creator.

"There's one limit I can think of," she said, almost inaudibly. "Only one. My brain will wear out in another forty years or so. Between now and then I'll learn . . . I'll change . . . I'll know more than I can guess today. I'll change— That's frightening. I don't like to think about that." She laid a curved golden hand on the latch and pushed the window open a little, very easily. Wind whined around its edge. "I could put a stop to it now, if I wanted," she said. "If I wanted. But I can't, really. There's so much still untried. My brain's human, and no human brain could leave such possibilities untested. I wonder, though . . . I do wonder—"

Her voice was soft and familiar in Harris's ears, the voice Deirdre had spoken and sung with, sweetly enough to enchant a world. But as preoccupation came over her a certain flatness crept into the sound. When she was not listening to her own voice, it did not keep quite to the pitch of trueness. It sounded as if she spoke in a room of brass, and echoes from the walls resounded in the tones that spoke there.

"I wonder," she repeated, the distant taint of metal already in her voice.